WITHDRAWN

NICK TAUSSIG is the author of three critically acclaimed novels: *Love and Mayhem*, *Don Don* and *Gorilla Guerrilla*. *The Distinguished Assassin* is his fourth book. He read literature and philosophy at Durham University, where he obtained a First, then went on to acquire a Master's in Russian literature from University College London's School of Slavonic and East European Studies.

He also works as a film producer, his recent productions including the crime thriller *Offender*, Plan B aka Ben Drew's highly praised BIFA-nominated debut feature *iLL Manors* and the BAFTA-nominated documentary film *Taking Liberties*. His second novel, *Don Don*, is currently being adapted for the screen by the team behind Nicholas Winding Refn's *Bronson*.

Taussig is also co-founder of Mtaala Foundation, which creates and supports educational communities in Uganda for vulnerable children and at-risk youth, including those affected by poverty, war and HIV/AIDS.

THE DISTINGUISHED ASSASSIN

NICK TAUSSIG

dissident

X000 000 0479748

DISSIDENT

Dissident Ltd
1 Glyn House, 43 Burgh Heath Road
Epsom, Surrey KT17 4LY
England, UK

www.dissidentgroup.com

First published in Great Britain in 2013 by Dissident

ISBN: 978-1-905978-18-2

Cover design by Ash Stevenson
Cover images © Dissident Ltd

A CIP Catalogue record for this book is available from the British Library

Text design and typesetting by Dexter Haven Associates Ltd, London
Printed and bound by TJ International

For my wife, Klara Cecmanova

CONTENTS

THE USSR

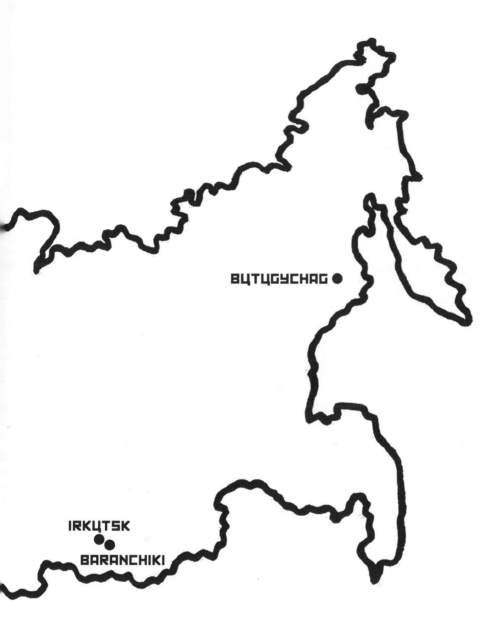

BYTYGYCHAG ●

IRKUTSK ●
●
BARANCHIKI

400   800   1200   KILOMETRES

        400   800 MILES

PROLOGUE

'If only there were evil people somewhere insidiously committing evil deeds, and it were necessary only to separate them from the rest of us and destroy them. But the line dividing good and evil cuts through the heart of every human being. And who is willing to destroy a piece of his own heart? During the life of any heart this line keeps changing place; sometimes it is squeezed one way by exuberant evil and sometimes it shifts to allow enough space for good to flourish. One and the same human being is, at various stages, under various circumstances, a totally different human being. At times he is close to being a devil, at times to sainthood. But his name doesn't change, and to that name we ascribe the whole lot, good and evil.'

Aleksandr Solzhenitsyn

17TH DECEMBER 1952
MOSCOW

The city...hard, cold and grey. Aleksei longed for sun, for light, but no. Moscow felt bleaker to him and Koba could be felt everywhere, his grave dark presence. This monster, he had been the country's leader the greater part of Aleksei's life and had even succeeded in making the city in his own image – bolshy, monotone and sombre.

Drunks filled the metro, their breath bad, clothes dirty, hair and skin filthy. The inside of the train, the carriage, it was brown, a characterless brown. Off the train at the newly opened Taganskaya Aleksei was confronted by the metro art, its innumerable bas-reliefs and mosaics – this charade of the great Soviet life, he brooded, as he reached the end of the central hall where there stood a large sculptural group of Comrade Stalin and youth.

As Aleksei headed towards his old apartment he looked up at some of Koba's creations, his architecture so recognisable, full of machismo and solemnity. How it needed to be feminine, humble, playful. Like the man who inspired these butch and ugly creations, they held no subtlety, no humility, Aleksei thought. They were defiantly Stalinist, Soviet, possessing none of the splendour of what preceded them, the buildings of the Tsars, which were opulent, bourgeois, excessive but beautiful.

Crossing the river he spied a gaggle of old women bathing in the dirty water. What were they doing, bathing here? he wondered.

Aleksei stood in a doorway opposite and waited. How he longed to see Natasha. How he hoped that Ivan Ivanovich and Boris Andreyevich were not right about her betrayal. He did not know what day it was, a workday he presumed. Was she still teaching at the Institution? Was she still painting and drawing? How would she look? Would Katya be with her? Was Katya still dancing? So many unanswered questions.

The wait would be long, he sensed. Aleksei kneeled down, leaned against the side of the building.

Morning turned to afternoon, another few hours passed.

Then the tap of heels on the pavement, a woman's walk he was sure. Aleksei looked across the street…and yes, he was right. The woman was tall and slender, light-brown hair brushed back over her face. Her walk captivated him, the sway of her hips and legs. It was Natasha.

Aleksei stood up. Though he could not distinguish her face yet, he knew it was her. As she got nearer he saw her better. She looked pale, skinny. He found himself longing for her to smile. How he loved that smile! He always hated seeing her unhappy. He felt the urge to run up to her, throw his arms around her. If he did, he would never let go, he thought. For he could not bear to lose her again. And now she smiled, yes, Natasha was happy. She had seen someone. Was it Katya? Aleksei turned his head sharply at this instant, looking back at the entrance to the apartment, searching for her, but instead *he*, the bastard, stood there, Vladimir Vladimirovich. He held the heavy front door open, his cruel handsome face lit up by the whitish Moscow sky, and next she had reached him and he kissed her, and Aleksei could not bear to look. A few moments later he heard Katya's voice calling, 'Momma…Momma.'

Ivan Ivanovich and Boris Andreyevich were right. His wife *was* betraying him.

Saliva rushed up his throat and into his mouth and before Aleksei knew it he was dry retching, nothing but white spit coming from his mouth, and he was unable to stop. He heaved loudly, violently, and out of the corner of his eye caught Vladimir Vladimirovich looking over at him. He seemed to stare right through Aleksei as if he was not there – he surely could not make him out from this distance – before closing the door behind him. Aleksei felt dizzy and his legs wobbled, next gave way, and he clasped at the wall behind him, his fingertips sliding down it, knees buckling to the concrete. Then he was bent over on his knees, forehead pressed against the stone of the wall, and he no longer retched but gasped for air, sucking it in like a fish out of water.

Time passed, Aleksei did not know how long, and he was on his way again, staggering towards he did not know where, anywhere, as far away from here as possible. He did not stop until he was exhausted, until he could see a church, St Vasily's. He thought of Nikolai. Aleksei had promised him that he would say a prayer. Not for his sins – he had very few, the man had been near perfect, to Aleksei – but rather for the suffering of everyone swept up in the violence of revolution and war. Nikolai should not have died. Why? It should have been me! he chastised himself. The sun shone, Moscow had light, and he marvelled at the cathedral's spew of confused colour, exploding red, yellow, green and blue, which at this moment seemed to capture perfectly the dichotomy of the Russian soul, torn between chaos and calm, extremity and moderation. And after this he was drawn to the tallest chapel, and his eyes followed its tent-roof up to its gold dome pinnacle, which shone and sparkled like a gigantic gem in the sky, disorienting him, mystifying him, enthralling him. The sun beamed hard and Aleksei flinched, forced to look away, through fear that he might be blinded like its architect. For rumour had it that this was the only way Ivan the Terrible could ensure he would not try and reproduce his magnificent creation elsewhere.

What was he going to do? Aleksei wondered as he walked away from the cathedral. He knew he should just get himself to Boris Andreyevich but something was holding him back. He suspected it was the intuitive sense that once he went and saw him there was no turning back, that this meeting would mark the end of any ordinary life he might have still had, even though it was doubtful that such a life was possible for him any more. He had to eat something. Aleksei found a bread and soup kitchen. The food here was basic, much like camp food, served in old metal pots. The man beside him reeked of vodka, this great elixir of the Union, the opiate of the Soviet masses. He slurped his soup, it dribbled from his mouth, got caught in his thick brown beard. He mopped up the base of the pot with the bread, wiping it clean of soup, his fingers thick with crumbs and goo. At the back of the canteen a few men gathered round a television set and stared blankly at it, occasionally muttering obscenities. The programme appeared to be about the people of the Caucasus, and one of the men showed himself to be particularly contemptuous, shouting, 'These darkies…fucking monkeys!' Aleksei would need to find work soon if he was to try and get by on his own, otherwise he would run out of money. He found a quiet and secluded place to put his head down for the night, in a disused coal cellar behind a restaurant.

Morning. He watched a woman in her forties wearing a yellow dress wheel a pram down the road. He noticed it did not contain a child but rather apples, hundreds of them, piled high, red and rosy. As she strolled past she threw Aleksei one, which he just about managed to catch. This would sustain him, he mused, though not for long. He got up and spent the morning walking, to where he did not know. He stopped at a kiosk and dropped his remaining kopecks on the counter. He asked for a loaf of bread. The shopkeeper urged him to buy cigarettes as well, tapping the counter's glass with one of the coins Aleksei had put down, but he had to be disciplined, spend the remaining money he had on the bare essentials only – camp life had taught him this – and so bought a pack of lard instead. That was it; he'd no money left. This and the bread would keep him going for a few more days only, he realised.

Aleksei ambled aimlessly the rest of the day, and settled down at dusk at the foot of the State Library. The wind was bitterly cold: it ripped through him. He felt fraught, wondered what he was going to do. An old homeless man sat not far from him. Aleksei looked closely at the man's hands in an attempt to discern his history. He carried the name of a camp on his right hand: 'Vorkuta'. Another survivor! He wore a thick-padded jacket and felt boots, his old tatty clothes resembling those he must have worn when he was a prisoner. Perhaps they were the very same and he was simply unable to part with them. For they had become him. He turned to look at Aleksei, seeming to peer over his wild, overgrown beard and dirty cheeks. 'I have a hot tea here, my friend,' he said. 'The lady in the library canteen, she brings me a cup at this time. Please have it. You look colder than me, you need it more.'

'That's very kind, but how about we share it?' Aleksei replied. 'I think we both need it.'

His name was Fyodor. Aleksei offered him something in return, some of his bread and lard, which he graciously accepted. They sat and talked for about an hour, after which Fyodor took his leave, insisting he must go, otherwise he would lose his nighttime sanctuary. 'She lets me in every night,' he explained, pointing once more to the library. 'I sleep in a cupboard just outside the back of the canteen's kitchen.'

'Aha,' Aleksei replied.

'I'm sorry, my friend, I would invite you in but she doesn't allow me any visitors. Just me, that's the deal.'

'I understand, Fyodor,' Aleksei said. 'I'll see you in the morning.'

Fyodor patted him warmly on the shoulder, smiled sweetly, then got to his feet and shuffled off.

It was cold tonight. Aleksei did not think he could bear another night out here in the Moscow winter. He pulled out the knife Ivan Ivanovich had given him and read from its handle, 'Bolshaya Nikitskaya.' That's in Barrikadnaya, Aleksei recalled. He must live in one of the old mansion blocks there. Aleksei finally made his way to Boris Andreyevich.

He rang on the bell and was met by two men, blue-eyed crew-cut Slavs, tall and heavy set, with forearms and biceps that resembled giant slabs of meat. Both men carried scars on their faces, marks of their criminal history, Aleksei presumed. They said nothing at first, just stared at him. One chomped on a toothpick, the other tapped his foot. 'What d'you want?' the one with the toothpick eventually asked.

'I'm here to see Boris Andreyevich,' he answered.

'And who are you?'

'My name is Aleksei Nikolayevich Klebnikov. I was sent by Ivan Ivanovich.'

'By Ivan Ivanovich?'

'Yes.'

He paused, before saying, 'Come in,' gesturing for Aleksei to enter.

He closed the front door and escorted Aleksei down a long dark corridor towards a door at the very end. He walked in front, the other big Slav behind. When they reached the end, he turned round and said, 'Wait here.'

Opening the door only partially, he entered the room and immediately closed the door behind him. Meanwhile Aleksei stood in the corridor with the other man, the foot-tapper, breathing down his neck. Minutes passed and he heard nothing, either from inside the room or from the man behind him, until the door was reopened and the tooth-picker stood before him again, nodding for Aleksei to come in.

A man sat in a large black leather armchair at the back of the dimly lit room. He wore a black shirt, black trousers and shoes that were obviously the mark of his status, black, slender and elegant. His clothes conveyed that he was someone gracious and meticulous, yet his face and body betrayed this impression, in fact expressed the very opposite. He had thick cauliflower ears, a lopsided nose and cheeks that were hard and threatening, and though he was sitting down it was clear he was short, squat and muscular. His hair was black, as were his eyes, which possessed a violent glint. On the side table next to him rested a briefcase, also black. This colour, it seemed to Aleksei, was his defining characteristic, a reflection of his soul. He looked like he did not need the two big Slavs. This was Boris Andreyevich.

'Please, sit down, Aleksei Nikolayevich,' he grumbled through a low, coarse voice, gesturing to the small chair in front of him.

'Thank you,' Aleksei answered, and sat down opposite him.

'I'm sorry about your wife.'

'Yes, so am I.'

'Women can never be trusted.'

Aleksei did not respond to this remark.

'Bitches, all of them!' Boris Andreyevich went on, smiling at him.

Aleksei looked at him, but did not return his smile.

'So, why are you here?' Boris Andreyevich continued.

'I...'

'Don't be shy, Aleksei. Spit it out!'

'I need to get on my feet.'

'Yes, I can see that. You look like shit.'

'Yep, and I feel it too.'

'I'll get you to meet Yakov. He needs someone.'

'Right…'

'There's a place nearby you can stay in for the time being. It has everything you need… a bed, small kitchen, bathroom,' and he threw Aleksei a set of keys.

'Thank you.'

'It's Ivan Ivanovich you should thank.'

'Yes.'

'I'll get hold of some new papers for you, which Yakov will also provide,' he concluded. 'You're lucky to have got this far without them. Internal travel controls are tight, as ever.'

'Yes, I know,' Aleksei replied, staring down at the dark wood floor.

'I'll have them for you in several weeks, by which point Aleksei Nikolayevich Klebnikov will be dead, an escaped convict executed by the authorities.'

'Right,' Aleksei muttered, now preoccupied with the thought that he was about to assume a completely new identity, become someone else.

1ST APRIL 1949
MOSCOW

First, they frisked him down, then they started to go through the apartment, this shoddy home of Aleksei and Natasha Klebnikov, with its plaster cracks which crisscrossed the walls; its peeling wallpaper, which drooped from the ceiling; its old pipes, which coughed and spluttered; its rickety wood furniture, which barely held together; its plethora of paintings, which hung from the walls breathing precious colour and life; and its many books, these vital sources of knowledge and analysis, interpretation and imagination, piled high like great pillars from floor to ceiling. Watching them, these NKVD officers, these State Security operatives – though they had been renamed MVD a few years ago they were the very same, no less vicious – it was clear to Aleksei they were determined to know every last bit about him, their eyes and ears everywhere, full of hate, mistrust, even madness. It made him furious, this level of intrusion. Should he fight not to be treated like this, a common criminal? he asked. And yet no Russian citizen fought, but rather was acquiescent. For this was the Soviet way. Normalno. This was life. We breathe, he concluded.

They wanted to know why he had a map of America on the wall. Had Aleksei been contaminated by the West? Was he a traitor? Should he be charged with VAD, Praise of American

Democracy, or PZ, Toadyism Towards the West? His heart had to reside solely with Mother Russia. Was this a sign of his allegiance to a foreign power? His copies of *Kommunist* were long gone. He needed to be purified, re-educated. Would he die for this now, this map? he wondered. Suspicion and fear governed everything, and the people, devoid of choice, were made compliant, hopeless. Thirty-six years old, Aleksei was tired of being constantly watched, monitored. He'd had this his whole adult life! The radio still played in the background. A session of the Supreme Soviet Council was being broadcast. This appeared to have been on for days. Perhaps this particular session would never end, he speculated.

One of the officers, Aleksei's age, short and handsome but a little overweight, went into the bedroom. Aleksei listened to the harsh, officious tap of his jackboots on the wood floor. This was Vladimir Vladimirovich Primakov; he knew Aleksei well, had been following him for some time. It was Aleksei's turn to follow him now, however. His wife's knickers lay on the unmade bed. Vladimir Vladimirovich picked them up, brought them to his face, sniffed them greedily, and smiled. 'Natasha...she smells good, huh.' He took another deep breath, held it, then exhaled, 'Aaaggghhh...' as if he felt perfectly satisfied at this moment. He did not then return them to the bed but held onto them, clenching them in his fist like a prize token, something valuable he had gained and won, a dog with his bone. 'How I'd love to fuck her!' he concluded.

Aleksei wanted to hit him, could not bear that he referred to her, his beautiful and graceful wife, in this way. A big man, not that tall but with a broad chest and shoulders, and powerful arms, Aleksei could have dispensed with Vladimir Vladimirovich quite easily. 'Where is she?' he continued.

'At work,' Aleksei answered.

'And why aren't you at work?'

'You know I was forced out, and that's why you're here, at this time of day.'

'Yes,' Vladimir Vladimirovich replied.

'You used to only do this at night… drag people from their homes!'

'With you, we can be more flexible.'

How Aleksei wished he were still at the university, at Moscow State, with his beloved books, his beloved history, instead of here, forced to languish at home while Natasha worked. It seemed the state had even managed to rid him of his masculinity. Like other Russian men, he had too much pride. 'Mother Russia, we might refer to her as feminine,' Aleksei had remarked to Natasha, 'yet under Koba she has become unreservedly masculine. In fact, she and her citizens have a propensity for violence that only men are capable of. Freud has had little impact in Russia, and this is not solely because his work is dismissed as the product of a bourgeois Jewish mind, but also because the Russian man simply possesses too much machismo and bravado to lose himself in endless self-reflection,' he had concluded.

The country was full of *apparatchik* like these two men before Aleksei, millions in its service, unable to resist the lure of power. Once more, it seemed, he was suspected of anti-Soviet activity, of working with a small group of dissident academics, artists and poets. Would they find his writings? He should not have kept any of them here! Aleksei rebuked himself.

Katya began to cry, and he hurried to his daughter's room. 'Where are you off to?' Vladimir Vladimirovich called after him, stuffing Natasha's knickers in his trouser pocket.

'You heard her!' Aleksei shouted back.

The other officer, tall, skinny and rather gawky, stood over Katya as she squatted on the floor, looking petrified, half way through a painting. His beloved Katya, she loved to paint like her mother, though dance was her forte. How she could dance!

'What are you doing in here?' Vladimir Vladimirovich asked his colleague.

'Seeing what's in the girl's room,' he replied.

'Why isn't she at school?'

'She has a day off,' Aleksei answered.

'So, a parasite just like her father,' Vladimir Vladimirovich replied.

Katya, she painted Pokrovsky Cathedral, St Vasily's. They probably supposed that Aleksei was pushing on his daughter not only anti-Soviet ideology but also religion. It was unclear which they considered the greater evil. The former, Aleksei suspected. For though they would not admit it, they had a penchant for the latter: Soviet ideology was their religion now. Katya's mind, just thirteen years old, was young enough not to be weighed down with the burden of dogma, ideology – for there was too much of it in Russia, it seemed to dominate everything. How Aleksei hoped that her mind remained free: clear, light and lucid. And yet such a mind was very rare. People here were either fervently committed to the realisation of a Socialist utopia or wholly ambivalent about it. 'You come with us,' the tall and skinny officer said to Katya, taking her arm and lifting her, forcibly, to her feet.

Aleksei lunged at him, shouting, 'Let go of her! Let go!'

He was grabbed from behind by Vladimir Vladimirovich, who wrestled him to the floor, pulled his big arms behind his back and handcuffed him. Next, he grabbed the back of Aleksei's head, clutched a fistful of hair – this thick light brown wild and unwieldy mop which Natasha called 'the professor in him' defying his burly body that made him look more like a prize fighter than an academic – and slammed his forehead on the old wooden floor until it was bloody and throbbing. After this, he pulled Aleksei onto his knees.

And so here he knelt, as if genuflecting before Vladimir Vladimirovich, his head feeling heavy like his neck could no longer support its weight. His vision was blurred, everything hazy – if only this was because of drink, he thought.

'You are under arrest,' Vladimir Vladimirovich said contemptuously, relishing these words.

Katya wept at this moment; Aleksei heard her soft and frightened whimpers. He tried to reach his handcuffed hands sideways towards her, to comfort her, but was pulled away, towards the door. Vladimir Vladimirovich would not allow him anything, not even a change of underwear or bar of soap. He needed to look at her, his daughter; he had to, as this might be the last time.

Though Vladimir Vladimirovich still clutched a fistful of his hair, Aleksei forced his head round and blinked repeatedly, hoping that he might just see clearly, if only for an instant, her light brown hair, the hair of her mother, and her soft pale skin, her mother's also.

He made her out... yes, he could see her... but then she was gone, and Aleksei wondered whether he saw her at all. Perhaps he had simply imagined her.

THE FIRST KILL
26ᵀᴴ JANUARY 1953
MOSCOW

Aleksei stepped out of Boris Andreyevich's nineteenth-century mansion block and strolled down the road, in the direction of the river. He was now Georgi Petrovich Solonik, according to his new papers, and even if he did now arouse suspicion with this new identity, of the criminal rather than the political kind, the former State Security would likely not care, he thought. For just as in the camps, it was far worse to be a political than a criminal disruption. It was the middle of the night. Aleksei felt the cold Moscow air, beneath his jacket, jumper and shirt, on his skin. He could not hear anything except his own footsteps.

Ivan Ivanovich had offered him a mission: to kill six leading Communists, *nomenklatura*, in one year. 'He wants these men dead, Aleksei Nikolayevich,' Boris Andreyevich had said. 'They have all wronged him. He has chosen them with your character and principles firmly in mind. All of them have abused their position and power absolutely. All of them have committed terrible abuses against the decent and innocent.' The thief-in-law was offering him a lot of money, more than he could hope to earn doing anything else. However, it was not this that made him now seriously consider this mission, rather his desire to get at those who continued to prop up, sustain this system – this awful system – and those who continued to destroy so many good and honest lives.

Was it possible? Aleksei asked himself. That meant one assassination every two months. Each would require at least four weeks of careful reconnaissance work, Boris Andreyevich estimated, and then there was the small matter of actually killing each man, seizing the most opportune moment, in which one always had to allow for the unforeseen, Aleksei pondered. He'd also have to travel the length and breadth of the Union to get to each man, thousands of kilometres from one to the next, and his travel time would inevitably be longer as, in spite of the false papers he'd be carrying, he would have to use more discretion in his choice of transport, which bus and train he took, and when he took it. And then beyond all this there was his own reconnaissance work, the work he'd have to do himself to ensure that each man he was about to kill was utterly deserving of his fate. For Aleksei could only kill the unrepentant and irredeemable. Boris Andreyevich had also made clear that Ivan Ivanovich, in spite of the unique relationship he had with Aleksei, who was not a career criminal or fellow thief-in-law, did expect him to complete the mission in the time allocated, just one year.

Would he agree to it, therefore, in spite of all these obstacles? he asked himself again as he reached the river and looked at the dark shadow which the Kremlin cast on its surface. Yes, he would, he decided, turning to look at the Kremlin itself, this home of cruelty and injustice, the monster's lair. He would kill them all, these men who did the monster's dirty work!

Ivan Ivanovich had also wanted to know whether he'd got his revenge and killed Vladimir Vladimirovich. Aleksei would tell Boris Andreyevich to let the thief-in-law know he hadn't, but that he would, though only after he'd completed the mission. He knew that Vladimir Vladimirovich's murder would drive him further underground – the bastard had become even more senior in State Security – however he no longer cared. He struggled even to think of Natasha any more, now that he knew Vladimir Vladimirovich had been inside her. How could she have betrayed him like this? How!? Aleksei agonised, pressing his lips together and clenching his teeth, as he turned off the street and entered his grim apartment block. He slowly climbed the stairs. Was he killing him, this *apparatchik*, to satisfy his male pride? Maybe. And yet the only way he could eradicate this terrible image from his mind, this bastard fucking his wife, was to dispense with him.

He was desperate to see Katya, though he knew he could not. Knowing Poppa was back would only put her at risk. But even if it were safe for him to see her he was not sure that he wanted to. For then she would see what he, her father, was becoming. What the hell had happened to him to make him agree to this assignment? Aleksei asked himself this even though he knew full well what had, and it was this – this hell he had been subjected to and forced to live through – which drove him now, which provided him with the justification to do what he was about to do, kill all these men.

Ivan Ivanovich acknowledged, it seemed to Aleksei, that if he, Aleksei Nikolayevich Klebnikov, were to be his assassin, he would only kill those men he was sure were guilty. Boris Andreyevich had assured him that all the men Ivan Ivanovich wanted him to kill, the men on the list, deserved their fate – their crimes were not solely against the thief-in-law – and that none of them warranted forgiveness. For Ivan Ivanovich knew that Aleksei would only kill those men who had abused their Communist power absolutely, the utterly repugnant and shameless, and would struggle to kill any man who possessed even a whiff of goodness or remorse.

Aleksei closed the door to his small and shabby apartment, walked into the living room, hung his jacket on the back of the chair and sat at the little bureau there. He removed a brown envelope from his jacket pocket, which he placed carefully in front of him. He opened it slowly. This was the list which Boris Andreyevich had given him before he left his apartment. Ivan Ivanovich was obviously confident he'd agree to the mission, Aleksei thought. He read the names a number of times, from top to bottom: Lavrenti Romanovich Anichkov, Yevsei Pavlovich Ivankov, Grigory Stepanovich Zhdanok, Andrei Edmundovich Smidovich, Pavel Maximilianovich Kalegaev and Sergei Ilyich Valuev. Then he added one more...Vladimir Vladimirovich Primakov, his nemesis, the man who had hounded him, imprisoned him and stolen his wife. And with this final act, he sat back and closed his eyes.

The first man, Lavrenti Romanovich Anichkov, was known to the thief-in-law and his circle as 'Beria'. According to the file that Boris Andreyevich gave him the following morning after Aleksei had confirmed he would carry out the mission, with detailed biography and old and current photographs, he was, like his namesake, a sexual sadist with a penchant for raping young women. He resembled Beria physically too, short and chubby, and wore glasses with little round lenses. However, unlike his *doppelgänger*, he was not completely bald but rather had a high, arched receding brow. What Anichkov did not know, however, was that one of his first victims had been a former lover of Ivan Ivanovich, when the thief-in-law had been a young man in Moscow. Immediately after the rape, Anna Dementieva had started drinking heavily, her only way of coping with the trauma of Anichkov's brutal assault, and three months later the thief-in-law had discovered her frozen body in a Moscow alleyway: she had drunk herself to death. Kneeling over Anna's dead body, he'd promised her that Anichkov would get his comeuppance one day. Over the past few years Lavrenti Romanovich's sexual appetite had increased, turning even more rapacious and violent. The last young woman Anichkov had had sex with in the back of his government car he'd left half-dead.

Just like with the Azerbaijani, Aleksei knew he needed to be thorough in his preparation – he had to follow Anichkov obsessively, learn his every movement, before striking – and in order to do this he would need Yakov to loan him his van, which he did. Over the following days and weeks, he started making notes and sketches of the assassination, pinning these, along with the biographical pages of Anichkov's file and the accompanying photographs, on the wall above his little bureau.

It soon became clear that the best place to strike was outside Anichkov's place, which overlooked Gorky Park. He normally returned there, to his wife and children, in the middle of the night after he had finished carousing the dimly lit Moscow streets with his driver, procuring vulnerable young women to have his way with. He was always careful to cover his tracks, never returning home in the government car but rather transferring to his own, which carried none of his sordid and shameful exploits, his driver left to wipe away all traces of his transgressions – the sweat, sperm, vaginal discharge, pubic hair and blood. How he, the driver, was able do this night after night Aleksei did not know. He could not look a man in the eye after cleaning up after him in such a manner. Yet the driver also transported him to his victims, and then turned a blind eye while Anichkov did what he did with them in the back, everything for him, it seemed, in the service of his master's dark desires.

Standing in the kitchen, sipping hot tea, gazing out of the small window at a grey and overcast early-morning sky, Aleksei decided he must strike tonight. He spent the day in his apartment getting ready. In the morning he prepped the gun he intended to use, a Second World War-issue Tokarev pistol that Boris Andreyevich had got for him. Seated at the small kitchen table, the handgun lying on an old tablecloth, he scrubbed the inside of the frame and cylinder with a toothbrush which he had dipped in cleaning solvent, then used a rag to wipe away all the dirt and grease. After this he took the cleaning rod, fixed a cloth patch dipped in solvent onto the end and ran it gently into the barrel, the patch coming out the other end. He repeated this process, then attached another patch, dry this time, and ran it through with the rod. Lastly, he oiled the moving parts.

For the remainder of the morning he made a silencer, fashioning one out of a length of pipe with several rubber baffles inside. The construction, though fairly crude, would be sufficient: he intended to shoot Anichkov just once, in the middle of the forehead.

In the afternoon he lay in the bath, in the silence – his one luxury after the frozen filth of Kolyma – watching the steam rise and evaporate, and listening to his breath. Later on, standing naked before the small bathroom mirror, he shaved, then stared at his reflection. Could he really do this? Aleksei asked himself. He had killed the Azerbaijani in order to protect his dear friend – Nikolai would have been killed otherwise. However, what he was about to do now was execute someone. There suddenly seemed to be nothing right or defensible in this act he was about to perform, in spite of the repugnant character of his intended victim, in spite of the terrible abuses he, Aleksei, had suffered at the hands of men like Anichkov. And yet he could hardly turn back, having agreed to the mission, could he? he thought.

As evening fell Aleksei ambled into the bedroom, where he had laid out the clothes he would wear – a grey cotton shirt, black trousers and dark-brown leather boots. He did not dress right away but sat naked on the bed staring through to the living room, at the wall above the bureau, this his mentor, his guide, almost the whole wall covered now, detailing exactly who he was going to kill and how he was going to kill them. He studied its contents thoroughly one last time, his eyes perusing the typed pages, handwritten notes, sketches and photographs over and over. Lastly he dressed, then reached for the three-quarter-length dark-brown leather coat he had recently bought, which hung from the single hook on the back of the bedroom door.

Aleksei was ready, and reluctantly left his apartment, his mind still riddled with doubt.

Evening settled in and he started tailing Anichkov – this had now become almost routine for him – the government car taking the same back streets, the ones frequented by society's detritus, where he was most likely to find the vulnerable. Tonight Anichkov was particularly cruel and foul, having sex with a skinny blonde girl who could not have been more than sixteen.

When he had finished with her, Aleksei watched him push her out of the car, and she fell like a rag doll onto the curb. Anichkov then proceeded to get out himself, stand over her and urinate on her face, before declaring, full of self-satisfaction, 'I'm done!' And with these few words he calmly buttoned up his trouser fly, looked up at the night sky and brushed back his small mop of receding hair with the palm of his right hand, this gesture almost camp.

Aleksei grimaced with anger. But then Anichkov extended his contempt further, kicking the girl in the stomach as she lay there on the ground. What should he do? Aleksei wondered. He could not just sit here, across the street, and let this poor girl continue to be abused. He had to intervene. But no, he could not – Anichkov was still accompanied by his driver. Aleksei had to wait until the sadist was on his own. But then, what about the girl? The mission – his assassination not only of Anichkov but the others – was surely more important than the fate of a single girl. Yet Anichkov might kill her, and Aleksei watched as he kicked her again, with more force this time. He had to help her, Aleksei decided, and so got out of Yakov's van and started running towards Anichkov. Hand in his pocket, he prepared to draw his gun and fire – he was within range – yet at this moment the driver unexpectedly got out of the car and Anichkov stepped away from the girl. It seemed that for once even the driver was concerned by his master's brutality. He looked first to Anichkov, then over his shoulder at the unknown figure rushing towards them. Anichkov turned at this moment also, until both men faced Aleksei. He had to abort, before they got a clear view of him and before they realised what he was up to. Aleksei veered to the left and disappeared down a narrow alley, giving the impression that he was perhaps in pursuit of someone, or something, else.

As he ran he prayed they had not seen his face, the van. How could he have been so bloody foolish!? he scolded himself. What on earth was he thinking? His mission was to kill Anichkov. The driver had been there, ultimately, to intervene and save the girl. All he'd had to do was wait another half an hour for Anichkov to be dropped off at his car, then follow him home and kill him as he parked. He was an amateur. How could he expect to fulfill this mission successfully and kill all the men on the list if he acted in this manner? Perhaps he had to abandon it absolutely. Ivan Ivanovich would understand, of course he would. But then, he might not? Aleksei fretted. And anyway, men such as Anichkov deserved to die. Look at what he had done, the misery he'd brought. Aleksei had to fight back against this wicked system, make his mark on it. He could not simply hide in the shadows. He finally stopped running and walked for a number of hours, thoughts whirling like an endless carousel, until he eventually returned to the van and got in. He would kill him tomorrow, that was that.

The following evening and night came soon enough, though Anichkov was curiously gentle with the girl he coaxed into the back, talking to her for over an hour before he even attempted to kiss her, and when he did, deciding not to go any further and have sex with her, instead just holding her, running his fingers through her long auburn hair. Perhaps he sensed his fate and so was looking to make amends, to be gentle and kind to at least one young woman before he died.

Anichkov did not leave her until the early hours, his customary clap of the hands signalling his readiness to depart. From there, Aleksei followed him back to Gorky Park, as usual transferring to his own car en route.

He knew that when Anichkov parked and turned his engine off, he would not get out right away but rather would move a few items from the glove box to his briefcase. And so Aleksei parked up on the street and proceeded swiftly, approaching his car not directly from behind – Anichkov might have looked in his rear-view mirror and caught him in the darkness – but instead from a slight angle.

Aleksei paused when he was right beside his car – heart racing, mind full of dread – next waited for Anichkov to get out. As he did Aleksei stepped out in front of him, put the gun to his forehead, stared at him uneasily and, voice wavering, said, 'Ivan Ivanovich sent me. Look at me.'

Anichkov glanced at him with the innocence and frailty of a young child, next turned away terrified. Was the man remorseful? Might he cease his abuse? Could he really do this, kill a man in this manner, in cold blood? Aleksei enquired with desperation, as he continued to look at the quivering, petrified figure in front of him.

'Into my eyes,' Aleksei insisted, needing answers to these questions.

Anichkov hesitated, then faced him once more.

Aleksei held his stare, looking deeply, searchingly, into Anichkov's eyes. He had to know.

When Anichkov went to look away once more, however, as if he could no longer bear such intense scrutiny, Aleksei pulled the trigger, shooting him straight between the eyes.

The silencer successfully muffled the shot, and Anichkov fell to the floor, dropping his briefcase.

He died instantly.

Aleksei stared at the dead man sprawled in front of him, unable to breathe and gasping for air, horrified by what he had just done. He stood like this for a number of minutes, fighting to steady his breath and regain some composure.

Then he kneeled down, removed Anichkov's keys from his jacket pocket, opened the boot of his car and laid his body inside it, walked back to the van and got in.

Glancing to his right Aleksei suddenly saw Katya. There she was, his daughter, sitting right beside him. 'Where have you been, Poppa?' she asked. 'What have you done?'

'I don't know, Katya, I don't know...' he replied, his voice breaking, even though he knew, in truth, that she was not really there.

THREE YEARS, ELEVEN MONTHS, TWO WEEKS EARLIER

1ST APRIL 1949 CONTINUED
MOSCOW

In the back of the car, seated next to Vladimir Vladimirovich, who held the scruff of his neck as if he were a poorly behaved dog, Aleksei saw the Lubyanka come into view. They obviously judged him to be a serious threat, he realised. The building's front might have been grand and stately, but its rear, with its grisly black iron gates, was certainly not. Dragged out of the car, he was immediately hauled inside this home of State Security, its interior also far from majestic, ragged and run-down, and led down a long grimy corridor. He sensed what his fate was: he was to be exiled. And for what? His frustration with Communism, his desire for something better than this. He should not be punished, rather commended, Aleksei thought.

He had imagined that after the war things would be different. For the Russian people had suffered terribly and needed time to heal. They had fought against Fascism, a cruel and malign system. He had battled hard with his brothers, endured the hell of Stalingrad. And yet for what? The defence of a tyranny with another name – Soviet Communism. They had a new enemy already – democratic capitalism. It was now even illegal to marry a foreigner! Natasha would be distraught when she returned home and found that he was not there, Aleksei realised, as he was bundled into what appeared to be a reception area populated by a number of moody, truculent guards. She'd know right away what had happened to him, that he'd been arrested, taken by the authorities. Staring at the dirty walls he recalled what she'd said to him when her father had died, just one year after her mother. 'Now they've both gone, Aleksei, you must promise that you'll never go…never leave me…ever!'

He was registered, photographed and fingerprinted.

'Take off your clothes…all of them!' a young ginger-haired officer with a face thick with freckles barked indifferently.

Aleksei followed his instructions, his mind now turning to Katya. Where was she? he panicked. When they returned her to her mother, assuming they returned her, she'd wonder where Poppa had gone. 'Please let her not think that I've abandoned her,' Aleksei muttered.

'What are you talking about!?' the young ginger-haired officer demanded.

'Nothing,' Aleksei mumbled.

His trouser belt and bootlaces were confiscated, as were his underpants (they contained elastic) and the buttons on his shirt: they were obviously concerned that he might take his own life, and had to control all of him, had to dictate even how he died.

Naked, Aleksei stood before them.

The search began. It was not enough that they went through his clothes. No, they also went through his body. They inspected every part of it. They started with his head and upper body – his mouth, nostrils, eyes, ears, armpits. And after this they moved to his feet and lower body – his toes, foreskin, penis, buttocks, anus. They prodded, they pulled, they poked, they squeezed. Pulling his finger sharply out of Aleksei's anus, the young ginger-haired officer looked at him with a conceited smirk and asked, 'How was that, Professor?'

It was the ultimate humiliation, abasement, and he, this young State Security operative, relished it.

Aleksei was dragged down the dank corridor and thrown into a holding cell. It was very small, about one-and-a-half by two-and-a-half metres. It contained a small wooden bench and a slop bucket. It was little more than a kennel. Now he had to wait… to be questioned, or rather interrogated. He stood at the back, leaning against the wall, and stared up at the cement ceiling. He tried to contain his thoughts, his emotions, yet was unable to. He recalled his father; he'd had to endure this as well.

Poppa, a professor of literature, had been judged not to be enthusiastic enough about Koba, our 'Great Leader', in his lectures, and so in '37 was arrested in the middle of the night, pulled from his bed, as so many were, by the NKVD. Aleksei's mother was sure that she'd never see him again: one of the arresting officers had insisted that her husband would 'not need his coat as he will be back soon', and this meant only one thing. But under heavy and intense interrogation – eighteen hours of it in fact – he suffered a stroke. They had dealt with Poppa brutally, sitting him on a chair, tying him to it, then beating him on his feet, back and face with wooden mallets. They subsequently hospitalised him. The stroke came at the right time. For it seemed certain that he would have been exiled to Siberia otherwise, or died under interrogation.

When did I become an enemy of the state? Aleksei asked. It was a year ago, he thought, when he made reference to *The Wizard of Oz* in a lecture. Yes, another lecture! Like father like son. He had described how in awe he was of the film's Technicolor, and had cited its success as 'a good illustration of American idealism and progress in the twentieth century.' If only he had not been so impressed by a musical fantasy! He was accused by his more conservative academic colleagues of not being sufficiently critical of American democratic capitalism, and thus in turn stirring up anti-Soviet feeling. Absurd, but then, he should have expected nothing less from Koba's Russia, which had persecuted his mother's friend, the violinist, for stringing his instruments with Austrian rather than Russian strings. For was this gesture not a deliberate attack on the Soviet system!? This was when Vladimir Vladimirovich had first entered his life. He had come to the university, to Lomonosov, barged into Aleksei's office, flashed his maroon-coloured identity card, thrown his weight around. He'd demanded to see his identification, and Aleksei had felt terribly nervous, like a schoolboy awaiting his master's punishment even though he'd done nothing wrong, blood rushing to his head. What was it about his damn uniform!? It symbolised perfectly the power he had over me, Aleksei had reflected, which like the state was ruthless, intolerant, impersonal, and he'd suddenly found it very difficult to breathe – his chest tightening like a rope had been wrapped around it and a man was tugging at either end. Aleksei had needed to calm his mind, but perspective, then, had been almost impossible, as it was now. An accused man, he felt utterly alone.

Why the suspicion, the fear, the anger? Must we, the Russians, really live like this? Aleksei wondered. He wished they would force him to emigrate. However, he sensed they would rather keep him here, on home soil. For at least then they could send him to war again, if need be, despite his injury; he had been shot in the leg by a German sniper. Who would he be made to fight next? He suspected the Americans. They had been his allies just four years ago. Or maybe they'd throw him on a train, on a cattle wagon, and pack him off to Siberia. It seemed to Aleksei that such repressive measures were back in vogue. Yes, perhaps he was destined to join the many innocents who had already perished there, many of them no more than fictional counter-revolutionaries. He prayed that his fate would not be *katorga*, exile with forced labour. Perhaps they'd take him all the way to the Far East, to Magadan, this city on the edge of the

Union built by prisoners. Those who had survived this labour, of constructing a city at the foot of the Kolymsky Mountains on the Sea of Okhotsk, had then been forced to build the road inland to the mines, and along the way they had perished. And those few who'd made it miraculously to the end had then had to construct their own camps before finally dying in a mountain of gold and ice deep in Kolyma's heart. 'Aleksei…you must stop this, must calm down,' he appealed to himself.

It was not clear to him how long they'd held him here in this cell. Though it felt like days, it might have been just hours. His mind had lost touch with the outer world, consumed with panic, the dialogue of catastrophe.

They fed him, a small bowl of soup. It tasted foul, resembling pig slop, consisting of rotten beet tops, grain and animal entrails, which species it was not clear.

They started to deprive him of sleep, bashing the iron door to his cell at frequent intervals. This lasted for days. 'You're on the conveyor now, huh!' the ginger-haired young officer quipped, shouting at Aleksei through the Judas hole. Not allowed to lie down, he tried to sleep standing up. He could not.

He was held like this for about a week, it transpired, before at last being questioned. His mind was exhausted, felt empty, like all his memories had vanished. It was unable to function on so little sleep.

The door opened and a guard he had not seen before stood in front of him. He looked at Aleksei as if he was not a man but rather an animal, or less than that, a mere object. He was quintessentially Soviet Russian, this guard in his thirties – big and fair, ambivalent and solemn – and without saying a word he took Aleksei's cuffed hands and led him down the corridor towards, Aleksei presumed, an interrogation room.

They were met by Vladimir Vladimirovich, in gruff spirits today, who ushered Aleksei into a large grey room. The walls were bare, there were no windows, there was a large desk and a few metal chairs. The heavy door was slammed shut.

The guard stepped forward and slapped Aleksei hard across the face. He stayed on his feet. The guard then pushed him to the ground, into the dark corner of the room, and hit him in quick succession with his rubber truncheon. 'Get up, undress, and go and sit on one of those chairs,' he said, pointing at them.

Aleksei did as he said.

Naked, he sat there, staring at the room's barren walls, then at the large desk in front of him. His eyes finally settled on a portrait of Koba. The monster was ubiquitous, he thought. A file was thrown into his lap. 'Your file!' Vladimir Vladimirovich shouted.

Aleksei did not respond. For the best thing he could do, he sensed, was act like him, an NKVD man – evasive, moody, monosyllabic.

'Anything more to tell us?' Vladimir Vladimirovich asked.

Aleksei was silent, struck by his voice, which, like the state he served, possessed no humanity.

'No?'

He continued to stare blankly at Stalin's portrait.

'You sure?' Vladimir Vladimirovich went on, clearly frustrated by Aleksei's reticence as his bottom lip curled.

Still, he said nothing.

'Says here that you've been saying anti-Soviet things again, talking of democracy and all that crap. Another fucking diversionist, another fucking counter-revolutionary, eh?'

'If that's what you say,' Aleksei replied, eventually breaking his silence. 'You should know. It's all your work in there, your allegations. And anyway, shouldn't an interrogator be doing this? This isn't part of your job remit.'

Vladimir Vladimirovich smiled at him, and Aleksei waited for him to speak again.

'It's my bit of extracurricular fun, and anyhow, I made sure you were part of that remit. You're off to Sybir this time, off to hell, you know that!' he bellowed.

Siberia still preceded hell, well…just about. Aleksei had imagined the worst, and it seemed they intended to deliver it.

This would mark his ultimate alienation from the state, Aleksei considered, as he looked at Vladimir Vladimirovich, his nemesis. He had been pushed further and further to the margins of life, Soviet life, out of the university, from one job to the next, judged to be a security risk, and furthermore an unfit citizen. He might have been a good soldier yet he was not a good citizen. Perhaps he had always been destined to end up in Siberia.

'Don't you have anything to say, now I've told you where you're going? Don't you want to try and defend yourself, stop me sending you there!?' Vladimir Vladimirovich asked smugly, a living embodiment of the state he served, then lit a cigarette, inhaled deeply and blew the smoke in Aleksei's face.

'Well, it seems you've decided my fate already.'

'Yes.'

'Is my arrest helping you meet your quota?' Aleksei asked.

'I've met my quota this month already. With you, I'm exceeding it. Perhaps I'll get a bonus. Who knows, maybe I'll even get to fuck Natasha once you're out of the way? She'll denounce you soon enough, they all do. Bitches, the lot of them!'

'You…'

'You…what?'

Aleksei was silent again.

'You deserve to be punished.'

'For what?'

'For who you are.'

'And who's that?'

'An agitator, a traitor, an enemy of the people,' Vladimir Vladimirovich answered. 'Would you like to confess?' he asked, taking his burning cigarette from his mouth and holding it over Aleksei's hand.

'No,' Aleksei replied.

'Throw him back in the fucking kennel then!' Vladimir Vladimirovich said contemptuously, extinguishing his cigarette on Aleksei's skin.

The interrogation was all of a sudden over, almost as soon as it had started, and Aleksei, reeling from the pain of the burning flesh on his hand, realised that even if he expressed a desire for something different, different from the way things currently were, that this was enough to be guilty.

It was at last clear to him what had broken his father, why he was never quite the same after his time here, but frailer, weaker. Like Aleksei, he too had had a slight limp, his feet never fully recovering from the beating they'd given him. The fire in Poppa, which had driven him to write not only some wonderful papers on Dostoevsky and Tolstoy but also his own poetry, had been extinguished.

Aleksei was returned to his cell, hurled inside it, and subjected to one final indignity: the guard emptied the contents of his slop bucket over his head.

He spent the next three days crawling in his own shit. Thoughts of his beautiful Natasha sustained him: her blue-grey eyes, her high cheekbones, her long slender legs, her small yet exquisite lips. When he fell in love with her, this woman born the very same year as him, these physical attributes assumed an even greater beauty, if this were possible. For they complemented her spirit, which he discovered, the more time he spent with her, was so warm, alive, full of life and love.

On the fourth day, he was at last hosed down.

This went on for weeks, this pattern of interrogation and forced confession. Aleksei thought about his wife and daughter constantly, dreamt about them day and night. Natasha's soft gentle voice, he heard it in his ear, the way she bade him farewell whenever she left him, 'Bye, bye, bye,' uttering these words like a bird about to commence flight. Would he hear these words from her lips again? he wondered.

Aleksei was tormented in other ways as well. They made him stand for days at a time; they beat him. Koba's minions obviously did not receive sufficient satisfaction from seeing him squirm under questioning, and so employed physical violence to ensure he suffered more. They were yet to use the lash on him, however. He waited for this particular instrument of torture with dread. Some days he heard the screams of others as they were whipped to the point of death. Such brutality was meant to have been outlawed in '39, after the monster's great purges. Clearly not! Aleksei concluded.

He had a dream tonight, though not about Natasha and Katya, rather Momma. It was a memory of the two of them at the *dacha* in Oryol one afternoon when Aleksei was twelve – the year his mother had taken her sabbatical from teaching in order to write a book on Tchaikovsky – lying in the long brown grass for many hours. It had rained that morning, rained constantly, though with noon had come a rainbow, the grey sky turning white, then blue as the sun pushed through and lit up everything, drying all that it touched – bark, branches, leaves, flowers, grass – and as they walked down to the meadow the dispersing clouds had cast shadows over the long grass, the dark outlines shimmering in the gentle breeze. They listened to a cuckoo, next lay down together in the long grass, side by side, holding hands and heads touching, staring up at the sky. He loved the feel of Momma's head against his, her soft hair on his cheek, and her smell, always a gentle lavender. Mother and son had lain like this until sunset, saying nothing.

It was not enough that political prisoners were locked up for twenty-four hours a day. No, they were also forbidden to talk or shout, make any noise at all, and this enforced silence was hard, extremely hard. Aleksei began to dread certain sounds: the thud of a guard's boot on the floor, the jangle of his keys, the sobs of the prisoner he beat. He feared he was starting to lose his mind too.

In one interrogation, after Aleksei had been punched repeatedly in the face then had the back of his head banged on the concrete floor, he was reminded that 'No one is arrested who is not guilty.'

'Then why even question me?' he asked, and was hit again.

'What did you expect in here…a right to a fair trial, a hearing? Why would you get that if you are guilty?' Vladimir Vladimirovich asked, and Aleksei saw that he was certain of this, his guilt, that the system he worked for was never wrong, and that his interrogation was not about establishing the facts, the truth, but was merely a display of the state's absolute power over the individual. He was a member of an 'Enemy Social Structure', 'He was not a proud Soviet citizen.' There was a blind, misplaced patriotism at work in the country, especially since the war, and any deviation from the Soviet norm was not tolerated. Aleksei was a bloody nuisance, a fucking intellectual, a pain in the arse, a worthless piece of shit. The sooner they got rid of him the better. However, they had to have their fun with him first.

Back in his cell he did not examine his wounds, his cuts and bruises. Vanity had left Aleksei long ago. His skin had assumed a grey-blue tone due to the absence of light and clean air.

He started to try and keep his mind by counting, and got as far as 21,612 on one occasion, this taking him more than twelve hours without a break. He also recalled key episodes in

Russian history. And when he was tired of both these mental exercises, he simply studied the bumps, scratches and stains on the walls, this cell's grisly history.

Today, Aleksei sensed, would be his last day in here. Vladimir Vladimirovich seemed determined finally to get him charged and on a train. 'Your confession is inevitable,' he said, holding a searchlight to Aleksei's face, its beam extremely bright. 'If you do not give it to us, we'll simply make it up.'

'I've always known this,' Aleksei said, squinting, his eyes hurting.

'Then why not just tell us what we want to hear, you stubborn prick?'

'Because you've already decided my fate.'

'Yes, we have.'

'Well, there we are.'

'Yes, there we are.'

Vladimir Vladimirovich put the searchlight down, opened his desk drawer, pulled out a single sheet of paper, and read from it. 'After me then, "I, Aleksei Nikolayevich Klebnikov, confess to anti-Soviet agitation and to being a member of a pro-democratic, anti-Stalinist political circle." Okay, after me…'

Aleksei did not say anything.

'And then…' Vladimir Vladimirovich said, becoming impatient, 'you go on to say, "I am an enemy of the Soviet people, and of Stalin." Come on. Say it!' he demanded.

'No,' Aleksei replied. 'Read the Code to me, Article 10, what does it say? I want to hear it.'

'Fuck the Code!' Vladimir Vladimirovich replied. He sniffed hard, spat in his face, then pushed the typewritten confession in front of Aleksei and forced a fountain pen into his hand. 'Sign it!' he shouted.

'No.'

Vladimir Vladimirovich jumped up from his seat, rushed round behind Aleksei, put his gun to his head and forced his hand to the paper, 'Sign it!'

Aleksei did not move his hand, so Vladimir Vladimirovich moved it for him, his name appearing illegibly at the bottom of the sheet.

'A signed confession!' Vladimir Vladimirovich shouted. 'Aleksei Nikolayevich, he confesses at last.'

Aleksei began to cry at this moment, could not help himself, and Vladimir Vladimirovich turned away. It seemed he was uncomfortable looking at Aleksei in tears. For he had not seen him cry before.

His tears eventually subsided and Aleksei managed to speak. 'This system that we live under is wrong, you must see that. It's cruel, indifferent and unjust...we're not happy...we're not free...we...' and he was suddenly shouting, but then was hit hard, from behind, on the back of the head.

'Shut up, just shut up!' Vladimir Vladimirovich screamed.

'Let me at least see my wife and child!' Aleksei cried.

'No,' Vladimir Vladimirovich said flatly, trying to gather himself, 'and thank you for finally confessing, giving us what we want,' and he said this like he meant it, as if he was genuinely grateful to Aleksei. 'You'll get twenty-five for this, I'll make sure of that. Shit, if only they still executed subversives and diversionists!'

Aleksei's confession, if that was what you could call it, had given Vladimir Vladimirovich legitimacy. There had been purpose behind his weeks and months of abuse and cruelty after all – he was acting in the interests of the state, rooting out a potential enemy.

'Can you at least pass on a message to my wife that I love her?'

'Sure, I'll tell her when I next see her, while she's got my cock in her mouth,' Vladimir Vladimirovich said, winking at Aleksei, and after this motioned to the guard to take him away, just get rid of him.

'Vermin!' the guard hissed into Aleksei's ear, dragging him away.

THE SECOND KILL
3ʳᴰ APRIL 1953
SVERDLOVSK
(1416ₖₘ SOUTHEAST OF MOSCOW)

Щ hen he arrived in Sverdlovsk, this factory-fort built by Peter the Great, Aleksei was relieved at last to be off the train. The journey had been awful. Aleksei had not wanted to get on a train east again, but if he was to kill the second man on Ivan Ivanovich's list after Anichkov he'd had no choice. He continued to doubt the first assassination – his conscience had plagued him ever since he'd pulled the trigger – yet here he was, about to carry out the second. He knew full well his anger and need for vengeance outweighed his uncertainty, his capacity to accept what had happened to him, and his ability to forgive.

The train he had boarded had broken down about one hundred kilometres short of its final destination, and he'd been dumped unceremoniously, along with all the other passengers, at a local station – he did not know its name – and had little inclination to ask. It was small, dilapidated and desolate, and had reminded him of the transit camp in Vladivostok. He and the other passengers had been herded like cattle through a small gate; he could not see what was on the other side. Did an abattoir await them? Aleksei had wondered. Koba might at last be dead, though still the people could not escape his legacy, the country continuing to treat its people like animals, remaining authoritarian, he'd thought. Aleksei had struggled to breathe at that moment, convinced that he was headed for Kolyma once more. He could no longer tolerate such cramped, constrictive conditions, which wreaked havoc with his imagination, encouraging him to catastrophise. Next into a waiting room, the walls painted an off-white, not quite grey, rows of chairs laid out, and he and the others had been made to sit in these rows in silence and wait for eleven hours, after which they'd eventually been deposited back on the train.

Walking out of the main station now, Aleksei recalled the Romanovs – here they were murdered, Tsar Nicholas II and his family, by the Bolsheviks in July 1918. The men here, in this industrial heartland of the Urals, wore a uniform of grey jacket and grey felt boots. All of them smoked, it seemed constantly, and at least half of them were drunk. It was ten o'clock in the morning. One man stared at Aleksei, his eyes heavy with alcohol, dazed and piercing. He hacked up phlegm, almost violently, spitting it onto the pavement, then swigged from a bottle of vodka, after which he wiped his mouth with the back of his fat grubby hand.

The second man on the list was Yevsei Pavlovich Ivankov, a real Party lackey, according to the file Boris Andreyevich had given him before he left Moscow, and member of the Central Committee, who, as an ambitious young man fresh out of university with big political aspirations, had earned his Party ribbons working diligently behind the scenes between '29 and '33 helping Stalin Russify, or rather de-Ukrainianise, Ukraine – a euphemism, of course, for genocide. He had been one of the key bureaucrats behind the carefully orchestrated famine there, ensuring that all grain was exported rather than ending up in the mouths of the increasingly hungry indigenous peasant population. Born in then Yekaterinburg, now Sverdlovsk, Ivankov had returned to his home city after the war. Ivan Ivanovich, as a desperate young orphan in Moscow, had been helped by the Ukrainian missionary Maria Akhmatova, who ran a children's shelter. Throughout his childhood and adolescence she'd always ensured he was fed when he could not find food and had a roof over his head when he needed it. She had returned to her homeland when the famines had first started, and on discovering her family had been reduced to cannibalism like so many others, had killed herself, unable to accept what her loved ones had become. Ivan Ivanovich had been devastated on hearing the news of her suicide, and as with Anichkov, had vowed then that he'd seek justice for her.

Ivankov had a ten o'clock meeting every Wednesday morning in the same room at the Sverdlovsk Hotel, room 505. Aleksei watched this meeting for a number of weeks, discreetly from the end of the corridor, out of view of the chambermaid, and every afternoon returned to his own hotel, shoddy and shabby by comparison, and added yet more information to the wall above the small desk in his room. Yes, he was following the same method as before, but also had to guarantee his mission's secrecy this time round in light of the fact that he was staying in a hotel and not a private residence, and so asked the chambermaid to refrain from cleaning his room, rewarding her generously for her discretion. He took a further precaution also, inserting a small toothpick in between the door and the frame whenever he went out. Should it not be in the very same place when he returned, then he'd know his mission was no longer covert.

It became clear that Ivankov's Wednesday morning meeting followed an identical format each week. Room service delivered fresh coffee at two minutes to ten, two men arrived dead on the hour, then left exactly one hour later. At two minutes past eleven, room service returned to clear the room. If Aleksei was able temporarily to block the lift at this point, thus delaying room service, this would give him time to enter the room, posing as a hotel employee, and kill Ivankov.

That evening, he decided to see Olga, a prostitute who lived and worked in the city: Aleksei needed female company and Boris Andreyevich had suggested he look her up whilst here. 'She'll help you forget about that traitor wife of yours!' he'd quipped.

Olga lived in a newly constructed tower block, which though only just completed already looked to be in a state of disrepair. Aleksei stood in the tiny lift, big enough for just two, as it crept its way reluctantly to the seventeenth floor, then knocked on Olga's door.

'It's open,' she called out, and he pushed the door to see a woman of about thirty standing at the end of a closet-size hallway wearing just a pink silk negligée against a foreground of patched wood panelling, grey walls, a grubby brown carpet and a single light bulb that hung precariously from the ceiling.

She swung one of her arms in a circular motion, gesturing to the front room like a cheap cabaret artist, and Aleksei accepted her invitation and sat down on a well-worn brown leather sofa, its springs creaking and whining as he made himself comfortable. Beside him, on the arm of the sofa, was a tray of meat pies.

Olga poured him a vodka, then herself one, which she knocked back without hesitation. She was drunk.

She straddled Aleksei first, then kissed him. He felt uncomfortable. He had not been with a woman since Natasha, four years ago.

After this, Olga clumsily clambered off him, removed her negligee and knelt on the floor, on a bright red rug, the one vivid colour amidst an ocean of drab Soviet brown and grey.

She pushed her arse out and wiggled her buttocks, turning over her shoulder to look at Aleksei, smiling and giggling. He looked at her bent over naked on the floor, and after this stared at the small bust of Lenin, which from this angle looked as if it sat on top of her buttocks. Vladimir Ilyich Ulyanov would have found more truth in human nature here than in Marx's *Das Kapital*, Aleksei concluded.

He stood up, took off his trousers and knelt down, waiting to be sufficiently aroused to enter her. How his Communist brothers would disapprove of what he was doing here! Aleksei thought. Soviet society was a prudish one. They were as threatened by sexuality as the old Orthodox Church had been. What the Church had dismissed as unholy, the Communist Party dismissed as bourgeois decadence. Both were moral judgements, however, and Communism, judgmental and prescriptive about human behaviour, was little more than another organised religion, Aleksei felt.

'Come on, come on,' Olga said impatiently, grabbing his flaccid penis and trying to bring some life to it.

Aleksei became frustrated. She craned her neck to look at him, and smiled kindly. The empathy of a woman. He could not go on.

'I'm sorry, I'm sorry,' he muttered, standing and pulling up his trousers.

'Another woman?' Olga asked.

'Yes,' Aleksei replied, and left.

The next Wednesday finally came around and he was anxious to get the job done: he had had enough of Sverdlovsk. Aleksei followed the same ritual as before as he readied himself for the kill, preparing his gun, bathing and studying the wall one last time, and at ten minutes to eleven strolling into the hotel's brown and grey lobby, this the default colour scheme of a Soviet building, he mused, past a surly security guard, this the default expression of a Soviet citizen. He got into the lift and took it to the fifth floor. He was as nervous as he'd been the first time, not about his proficiency to carry out the hit successfully, but rather his ability to live with himself afterwards. He'd felt a growing darkness in his soul since the killing of Anichkov, though at the same time a compulsion to carry out the mission in full, to kill all the men on the list. Yet was it right to carry on now the monster was dead? he wondered. And would not things be different now?

He remembered watching the funeral procession last month. He'd stood underneath a small stone porch as the coffin passed him. Koba, his victims were innumerable, Aleksei had reflected then, this thought accompanied by a heavy sigh, an old woman in front turning round and scowling at him, as if this weary and disheartened utterance were sacrilegious. How dare he make such a sound at the funeral of Comrade Stalin!? the old woman had seemed to protest. Many howled, some with sorrow, others delight, as he, Koba, had been paraded through the streets in his red coffin. Did this mean the whole system might suddenly collapse now its 'Great Leader' had gone? Aleksei had asked. No, as history had shown us, for the most part, that this would not happen, because though the absolute ruler was dead, his chief collaborators were not, and should the system collapse they would be implicated and punished. Thus the system had to go on, he had concluded, watching the coffin disappear out of sight then walking off down the road, in the opposite direction to the procession.

He stood in his usual place, at the end of the hotel corridor, and waited for the two men to exit the room and take the lift downstairs. They were on time, as usual, and Aleksei watched them make their descent before calling the lift back up and obstructing the doors, thus rendering it briefly out of service. He headed straight for the room and checked his watch. Two minutes past. He knocked, just as room service always did, and waited for Ivankov to summon him inside. He breathed heavily, battling to compose himself. 'Come in!' Ivankov eventually called out.

Aleksei entered slowly, closed the door behind him, and walked the short corridor towards the bedroom. As he turned the corner into it, he saw Ivankov sitting by the bureau. He looked up, realised Aleksei was not a hotel employee and called out, 'Who the fuck are you!?'

Ivankov reached clumsily for his gun, appearing even less physically adept than Anichkov, a bureaucrat through and through. He might have been able to plan and orchestrate the murder of millions from behind a desk, Aleksei considered, yet Ivankov seemed incapable of killing one man by his own hand.

Still as anxious as he was the first time, Aleksei urged himself to be calm, to hold his nerve. He responded decisively, 'Put the gun down,' which Ivankov did, after which he marched towards him and put the gun to his forehead.

He went on, 'Ivan Ivanovich sent me. Look at me.'

Aleksei stared at this rather pathetic figure before him, this slender man with fair hair combed militantly with a parting and the face of a weasel with small, distrustful eyes. Just like Anichkov, he, Ivankov, could not look at him.

'Into my eyes,' Aleksei insisted, needing to be sure of the man's guilt, as if this certainty would somehow make the action of killing him more appropriate, more justifiable.

Again, like his predecessor, Ivankov hesitated before facing Aleksei once more.

He held his stare, as he did Anichkov's, looking deeply, searchingly, into Ivankov's eyes. Was he sure now? Aleksei asked himself.

When Ivankov went to look away, similarly unable to tolerate further scrutiny, Aleksei pulled the trigger, shooting him straight between the eyes.

He looked down at Ivankov's dead body, realising he'd just killed the second man on the list, and was therefore one month ahead of schedule, having killed the first two men in just three months. It seemed Aleksei was taking to it, this deadly profession, rather well.

He had to get out of here as quickly as possible. Aleksei decided to leave via the basement: this way he would not be seen. He took the stairs. Reaching the bottom, he passed by an open door and hesitated, concerned there might be someone inside who'd catch sight of him. He stopped and peered round into the room, which was empty but for hundreds of tape recorders that recorded every conversation in every room.

Outside, in the clear, Katya confronted him once more and asked, 'What have you done, Poppa...again?'

'I'm sorry, I had to...I had to,' Aleksei replied, answering her as if she were really there, standing and facing him outside the hotel.

THREE YEARS, TEN MONTHS, TWO WEEKS EARLIER

8TH JUNE 1949
MOSCOW

About forty political prisoners, Aleksei among them, were led out the back of the Lubyanka in the bright sunshine of a late spring morning and loaded onto the back of a big truck which stated on its side that its cargo was 'Meat and Vegetables'. They were made to sit on long narrow benches, huddled together. None of them spoke. How had it come to this? Aleksei wondered, looking at the other shackled men around him. Like so many, he had been sure that life in the Soviet Union was the correct way to live, its citizens striving to create a fair and decent society, and Aleksei would do all he could to help realise this – this dream of a better country, a better world, a socialist utopia on earth. And was not Stalin motivated by the same end, committed wholeheartedly to Russia's industrialisation and militarisation, acting for the citizen's own good, in the citizen's best interest? He was the people's great protector in a hostile world.

Aleksei attempted to peer through a tiny gap in the lorry's boarded-up sides as it hurtled full pelt down a long narrow cobblestone Moscow sidestreet, the driver, it seemed, choosing to ignore the fact that the cargo he transported consisted of sentient beings not inanimate objects. By the time the truck reached the end of the bumpy road, all the men had fallen off their benches and lay bundled on top of one another like unwanted carcasses.

They clambered off each other and sat once more. It seemed to Aleksei that he, like most Russians, had been lost in a frenzy of belief – in the idea, the man and the mission – and Aleksei for one could not understand how he had once believed in this trinity, this Holy Trinity of Stalinist Russia, and for so long. The Communist project, the ideology behind it, the man to administer it... this had been his religion. Aleksei had believed that humanity could be made good if only it took its medicine, this Marxist trinity, and that through this process, this treatment, it would finally be perfected, transformed.

Off the truck and at the train station, Aleksei and the others were lined up in a column and marched down the platform, led past a huge stone statue, a typical Stalinist creation – a monument to the Great Patriotic War. Masculine and brash, it was neo-classical in form. It portrayed a Russian soldier as if he were a Greek god. The great Soviet warrior, muscles bulging and mouth wide open and roaring, held a machine gun at the ready as he charged into battle. Any man who had fought in a war knew that such a depiction was false, that it was wrong to commemorate war in this way, Aleksei pondered, glancing back at the statue. The men who had led us to war – Hitler and Koba – were hardly notable warriors. The former had been a dispatch runner in the First World War while the latter had been in exile throughout it! They were never knee-deep in the blood and guts of the battlefield, as Aleksei had been, having to kill their fellow man over and over.

When they reached the penultimate wagon, the prisoners were told to kneel, and then were counted, and re-counted, after which all forty of them were crammed inside this hunk of wood and iron wrapped in barbed wire that was meant to hold no more than eight cows. No guards were needed, for they could not escape.

Aleksei looked around him. He suspected the majority to be political prisoners, arrested under Article 58. Their crime – opposition to how they were governed. Their 'Great Leader' did not tolerate criticism well! He might himself have been a subversive and insurrectionary, yet this did not mean he permitted others to be the same. A minority, Aleksei suspected, were probably not even guilty of any dissent, rather had been condemned by association alone. It was enough to be a 'Member of the Family of an Enemy of the Revolution'. All of them had to be made to atone for their lack of faith in the Soviet project. It was dark, the small windows boarded up, and they had to wait here for hours on the station platform before at last moving off.

On their way, they immediately longed for light and for fresh air. If only they could just see out – the beauty of the Russian landscape would have offered them some respite. But no.

The smell inside the wagon quickly became awful, a mix of shit, piss and vomit, and the single stove made it even more pungent. Though there was a sanitation hole covered by a metal grate in the middle, a few already lacked the will to make it there: they needed only travel from the sides of the carriage, just a few steps, yet even this was too far. But then, at least they did not have to suffer the indignity of asking a guard to allow them to relieve themselves.

The first night on the train Aleksei slept just a few hours, the constant clickety-clack robbing him of rest. He had a vivid dream, he dreamt of sweetbread. Sweetbread! How he would love some, he mused.

He woke in the morning, his mouth bone dry. The frenzy of thirst was hard to endure, made worse when the guards failed to give them their daily bucket of water, which they had to ration among themselves. Where were they headed for? Vorkuta, Norilsk, Yakutsk, Magadan…they did not know. Their only certainty was that their punishment, like the millions who had gone before them, would be hard labour, and that many of them would die from this. And what worse punishment could there be for those who no longer believed in the great project than to be forced to work for it, sustain it, make it greater still. What labour would it be? Would he be made to dig a canal, toil in a mine, saw down trees, lay railway track? He did not know.

His memory sustained him as they headed east: lazy summer holidays with the family at the *dacha*; the journey that he and Natasha had made by train to Lake Baikal. It was here, on the western shore, just outside the village of Baranchiki, that Aleksei had asked her to marry him. That day she'd worn a white dress and red cardigan. Her beauty had so enthralled him that he'd been unable to speak. But memory also worked against him, threatening to drive Aleksei to anger and despair: the night he had realised his days were numbered, one of Vladimir Vladimirovich's underlings watching him as he'd stood on the metro platform waiting for a train home, peering at Aleksei from behind the station's many pillars. Aleksei had known that he could see him. The young agent had gone on to tail him on a daily basis as he made his way to and from work. On the fourth consecutive day Aleksei had been so infuriated that he'd confronted the man on the platform and shouted, 'Well... arrest me, then. Go on!' Yet he had simply turned his head and coolly ignored Aleksei, giving his fellow commuters the impression that Aleksei's grievance was somehow imagined, unreal.

On the train, time slowed down, seemed to lose all meaning. Seconds felt like minutes, hours like days, days like weeks. It was unclear to Aleksei how long they had been travelling. One man beside him, Nikolai, helped him through. Aleksei liked him instantly; he was a strong spirit. He had a thick grey beard and intense green eyes, the very same colour as Aleksei's. He had the look of an austere Orthodox priest. In his fifties, he had been accused of spreading religion, an agitator for freedom of religious worship. He was sentenced not even by a kangaroo court but by a troika of officials – a regional NKVD Chief, a Chief Party Secretary and a representative of the Prosecutor's Office – and, like Aleksei, given twenty-five years. 'They judged me to be "a socially dangerous element",' he quipped. 'In this assessment, they even managed to rid me of my humanity, reducing me to no more than an elementary particle.'

Nikolai went on to confide in Aleksei that he had been a priest in Moscow – Aleksei's intuition was right – with a very small congregation of no more than a hundred or so people, a consequence of his refusal to kowtow to the Party and to the local authority. 'If I had cooperated, they would have allowed me a bigger church, a bigger flock. But I refused to. I just spent all my time praying for the death of Stalin! Perhaps I should have been less stubborn, less principled. Then I wouldn't be here now,' he said, managing to summon a wry smile. 'This heart of global atheism, the Soviet Union, where every religion is considered no more than a delusion, an opiate, has the unfortunate habit of making its inhabitants crave for something spiritual, immaterial. Science and rationalism are not enough to sustain man, it seems,' he continued, stroking his beard thoughtfully, then looking over at the heavily tattooed young man opposite, perhaps the only real criminal among them. 'Russia is full of *bezprizorni* like him, orphans of Stalin, children of his great terror. And this new orphan generation is lost, rootless. It's not enough just to be a Soviet citizen. They might have built this new socialist system, but they're not happy. And thus, from being the victims, they become the victimisers. There must be something else which binds us, be it nationality, religion or culture,' Nikolai concluded.

Aleksei tried to imagine the forest beyond the carriage – vast and endless. He recalled when he and Natasha had taken the train to Baikal. For days and days all they saw was forest, the *taiga*, birch after birch, their beautiful slender white trunks. These trees had hypnotised them. The Empire, it was truly vast, Aleksei thought. This train, it went on and on, its wheels thundering against the tracks. He dreaded to think how many before them had died building this railway line that had no end. This journey into excommunication, their removal from Soviet life, was a long one. They were headed all the way to Vladivostok, he and Nikolai suspected.

The elderly man in the corner – neither Aleksei nor Nikolai had spoken to him yet – had the look of an old Russian peasant. Such men had been disappearing, forced collectivisation having obliterated them, kulaks in the '20s and '30s either shot or imprisoned. Aleksei remembered his father's fury over the terrible famines in Ukraine in '32. He had been just twelve. Millions had died. 'He doesn't look too good,' Nikolai said, getting up from beside Aleksei. 'Let me see how he is.'

'Yes, of course,' Aleksei mumbled, wishing he had thought the same. Our own suffering could make us terribly selfish, he reflected, clearly disappointed with himself.

Natasha and Katya, their faces were constantly etched on his mind's eye. How he loved them! When would he see them again? Life had to be harder. He was sure that some neighbours were already being cruel, shunning and humiliating them. For had not the man in their house been shown to be a traitor to the people! Why else would he have been arrested and sentenced? And yet Aleksei knew they both loved him, that they would be loyal, would not denounce him in spite of what others might say. He remembered at this moment how Katya used to squash her face against the bathroom window, press her nose until it was almost flat at the end like a piglet's, and her lips, until they were flush with the glass, giving her the appearance of a sucker fish, this image drawing a rare smile out of him, which he savoured.

A person's disintegration in here, this cattle wagon, was public: grown men were sobbing and shitting themselves in front of one another. In fact, it soon became evident when one of Aleksei's fellow exiles was about to die: he pissed and shat himself. Every few days they dragged another body out of here before giving the prisoners their food, a bucket of raw fish that they grasped at like animals. Their numbers were dwindling fast.

The elderly man in the corner was dying. Peering through the half-dark car, Aleksei stared at him: he sat huddled, knees to his chest, shivering and in pain. Nikolai had been with him all morning and it was now Aleksei's turn. His face had lost all colour, his complexion grey. 'Is there anything I can do?' Aleksei asked, kneeling down in front of him.

'I was late for work,' he said. 'The damn *kolkhoz*.'

'Sorry, what's that?' Aleksei replied, confused both by his answer and the fact that he looked too old still to have been working prior to his arrest.

'That's why I'm here,' he replied. 'I let down the collective, you see.'

'Right.'

'My crime was tardiness.'

People were arrested for anything, Aleksei thought, for taking a stalk of grain or spool of thread.

He stayed with him, sensing the elderly man wanted him to.

Night set in. When everyone else was asleep Aleksei caught him gnawing in the darkness on the inside of his wrist and realised he was trying to get at the vein. 'What are you doing?' Aleksei asked urgently.

'Isn't it clear?' he responded.

'Yes, but…'

'But what?'

Aleksei did not say anything.

'I've had enough.'

'Yes.'

He then passed Aleksei his jacket, which covered his chest and knees, and whispered, 'Can I ask that you smother me when I'm asleep?'

'What!?'

'I'm so sorry to ask,' he said, 'but I'm in a lot of pain … and I can hardly ask your friend, the priest, now can I?'

'No…' Aleksei replied, and it was clear from the way he looked at him that there was little point in challenging the elderly man. He had made his decision.

'Let's face it, it's not as if I've something good waiting for me at the end of this journey.'

Aleksei put his arm around his shoulder.

'And rest assured,' he continued, 'I won't put up a fight,' and with these words the elderly man laid on his back and stared up at the roof of the carriage.

Aleksei took his hand, held it, and waited for him to fall asleep. Next he laid the jacket over his face, to cover his nose and mouth, then holding down the elderly man's arms and shoulders he leaned his upper body, its whole weight, over his head and face so as he could not move. He put up no resistance.

Aleksei stayed like this and held him for a few minutes, until he could no longer feel the breath at his chest, then rolled off him.

He wanted to cry but was unable to.

He closed the elderly man's eyelids and laid the jacket over his chest.

Then Aleksei slowly got to his feet, leaving the dead man's side, and returned to his precious spot beside Nikolai, who was fast asleep.

Aleksei was too angry and sad to sleep. The thought of how it had come to this – he having to put an old man out of his misery – plagued his mind. And so he sat there wide awake, his friend Nikolai gently snoring in his ear.

Off the train at last, Aleksei and the other survivors – more than half of those who first boarded had died – were herded like cattle into a camp, a transit camp. All of them struggled to walk after being forced to sit, to lie down, for so long. They were in Vladivostok. It seemed their end destination was Magadan after all.

There were thousands here, all waiting to be transported. Aleksei and Nikolai stayed close as they shuffled into the main zone, a vast open space populated by men and women of all ages, all 'enemies' of the regime.

It was evident right away that sickness was rife in this place, particularly typhus and dysentery, the symptoms showing themselves on the faces and bodies of many. They were fed salt herring and given water. Aleksei wondered whether what he had just eaten and drunk might be infected, but then, he had to eat and drink.

He looked around. There were guards everywhere, rifles hung over their shoulders, and some of them resembled old Bolsheviks. 'They've never been able to tolerate dissent,' Nikolai whispered in his ear, 'have dealt with it brutally from the moment they seized power.'

He was right, Aleksei thought, his comment reminding him of Lenin's declaration on gaining control: 'Today is not the time to stroke people's heads. Today, hands descend to split skulls open.' Lenin had ensured that all 'unreliable elements', as he referred to them, were locked up in concentration camps, the vast camp network born out of his commitment to crush all opposition, any hint of counter-revolution or sabotage. These unreliable elements, these parasites, were anyone who did not believe in the Communist project.

It was getting late; the sun was setting. Aleksei, Nikolai and the others were obviously due to spend the night here, though it was unclear where they would sleep. Aleksei hoped it would be in the open, under the night sky. Vladivostok was far south, at least by Russian standards, and it was summer. It was wonderful to be outside after weeks of confinement, to be able to walk, and since getting off the train Aleksei had found himself taking large gulps of air, savouring the sensation of breathing, and taking bigger and bigger steps, like a toddler finding his feet for the first time. His legs were becoming accustomed to movement again.

He turned to Nikolai, who watched a group of three young women, no more than eighteen or nineteen years old, with five or six guards on the other side of the zone. 'What are they doing?' Aleksei asked, squinting in the dwindling light.

'It looks like they're having sex,' Nikolai replied, unnecessary for him to clarify that these young women were only doing this in exchange for food. Their youth and beauty was a curse here. He continued, 'Some of these men look old enough to be their fathers,' and with these words he crossed himself and muttered a short prayer.

Though there were boarded tents behind them they were left to sleep under the stars, on the dust and earth.

In the morning, they were led down to the seafront as the sun shone, and they boarded the boat, an old American cargo steamer it looked like. Perhaps the authorities had chosen this specifically for them. They would feel at home on a Yankee boat. 'We'll go past Sapporo, through the Tatar Strait and into the Sea of Okhotsk. If only it were winter...' Nikolai mused as they were marched along the lower deck.

'Why d'you say that?' Aleksei asked.

'Because then I don't think they'd be able to get us there. Up in Okhotsk the sea would be frozen over.'

It appeared they were to be kept in the hold, below deck, the authorities perhaps concerned that they might be spotted by 'foreign spies', this their favourite expression, as the boat passed by the coast of Japan.

The boat pulled away from the dock. It was terrible down here, as tenebrous and cramped as the train's cattle wagon. None of them knew how long the journey would be to Magadan. The only consolation was that it would not be as long as the one from Moscow to Vladivostok.

They had to sleep on long wooden shelves, tens of them lying in protracted rows. Aleksei's hips and buttocks hurt, his sciatic nerve, he thought. No wonder really. Half starved, he was all skin and bone. The sea was rough and they all suffered from awful nausea.

Aleksei, Nikolai and a few others found themselves, for most of the voyage, trying to protect four women seated next to them from the clutches of a large, rowdy and violent gang of men at the other end of the hold. The gang consisted of *urki*, it looked like, the Soviet Union's professional criminal caste, and its leaders appeared especially vicious. Aleksei and Nikolai managed to pull two of the women to safety, the two youngest, both in their early twenties, though they could not help the other two, their mothers, it transpired. There were too many criminals, they were too violent, and it seemed both women were willing to sacrifice themselves in order to spare their daughters. They were raped repeatedly, and the convoy guards stationed above, clutching their machine guns, did nothing. In fact, these particular guards appeared more indifferent than most. They were likely annoyed and bitter that they were mere convoy guards, Aleksei concluded.

The hold was eventually opened. 'Are we here?' Nikolai asked, staggering to his feet, and he and Aleksei emerged out of the darkness and walked into beautiful blue skies. They had been allowed on deck.

The boat had entered a natural harbour, before it was the port of Magadan, this dock built by prisoners, by men like Aleksei and Nikolai. The boat slowed and there was extraordinary quiet on board, everyone transfixed by the surroundings – the still blue sea, the cloudless sky, the grey-green rocks on either side – as they sailed effortlessly, carried by the gentle current, towards the shore. Was this really hell? Aleksei wondered.

Off the boat they were lined up in front of a few men, various camp commandants in search of the healthiest prisoners – those least likely to die in the first few weeks or months. The commandants needed workers to try and meet government output targets. Aleksei, Nikolai and the rest of them were told to undress, their stinking bodies inspected – prodded and pulled by women in white coats – to determine the amount of flesh on them. It was like a slave market: they were to be exploited, commodified and worked to death – and this was official policy, government policy. There was an appalling reason and logic at work: better that they were made to contribute to the Soviet project before being killed by it. For Koba, prison labour, obviously, still had immense value.

He, Nikolai and about twenty others were shackled to one another, loaded onto the back of a truck and driven deep into the forest. Their predecessors had not been driven; rather they had walked, and had had to build the road as they went. It had not been enough that they'd been consigned to a hard labour camp for ten years, twenty years, perhaps a lifetime. No, they'd also had to make their own way there.

They drove for the whole day and arrived late at a roadside barracks. Ordered to get out, they were fed – boiled fish heads, black cabbage and old potatoes. Aleksei consumed every part of the head until nothing was left, he was so hungry. Food, he had thought of nothing else the past four hours. Nikolai remarked, 'Not quite like the Kremlin cafeteria, eh! Our great leaders might be feeding us fish heads but they're feeding themselves only the very best grub, which they import from all over the world, in particular from the immoral, capitalist, cosmopolitan West!

'It's funny, isn't it. All Soviet authority seems to be based upon breaking established rules, and yet it has nothing to offer but hypocrisy!' Nikolai concluded.

They were made to walk the last leg of the journey, their clothes no more than thin rags now. Aleksei looked back over his shoulder, and all he could see was never-ending forest and mountains. Where could he flee to but into the boundlessness, the nothingness? Perhaps this vast land beyond the Urals was always destined to be the home of expulsion, he reflected.

Exhausted after three full days of walking, Aleksei finally spied a rainbow in the distance: if only it were real, but it was artificial, made of plywood – the entrance to the camp. 'Are we really headed for the rainbow?' he asked Nikolai, then looked at the other weary men around him.

Nikolai was too tired to respond.

A banner hung from it, and when they got closer he was able to read it: 'Labour in the USSR is a matter of honesty, glory, valour and heroism!'

They had reached their end destination…a hard-labour camp deep in the heart of Kolyma.

THE THIRD KILL
14TH MAY 1953
SALEKHARD
(1122KM NORTHEAST OF SVERDLOVSK)

He stood in the centre of Salekhard, this remote far-north town towards the Arctic Circle, home of his third victim, Grigory Stepanovich Zhdanok. A former camp commandant, he had murdered Ivan Ivanovich's brother-in-arms, Aleksandr Mikhailov.

Aleksei had had to wait over a week to receive the file on him, precious time he could ill afford to lose if he was to complete the mission in the allotted time. He had hated waiting, it affording him too much time for reflection, which he had done incessantly, chewing over whom he had killed so far and what he was becoming in a rather obsessive manner. Such periods of doubt and rumination he did not want, he'd realised. Rather he wanted, quite simply, to act, and alongside this to cultivate the conviction that the mission he had undertaken was right and defensible. For was he not carrying out justice on behalf of the many innocent victims of a few evil men, men who would certainly not be brought to account by anyone else, by the new troika of Malenkov, Molotov and Beria that had replaced Koba – a pro-Stalinist bunch, part of the evil few? Yes, there had been the great amnesty just one month after the monster's death, however this was politically, rather than morally, motivated, evidenced by the fact that the majority to go free were career criminals not politicals. Perhaps Beria intended to destabilise the Union to such an extent that he, by virtue of his leadership of internal affairs and security, would be able to seize control and become the new undisputed leader, an even greater monster than Stalin, if this were possible. Aleksei's mission was utilitarian, therefore, motivated by the greater good. He had to see it through, Aleksei told himself, for Ivan Ivanovich, for the good of the Russian people, and in order to prevent further cruelty and suffering. He was not solely doing it to avenge his own suffering, Vladimir Vladimirovich in last position proof of this. Thus, even though he had lost some time, it was still only the middle of May, which meant he had a further eight-and-a-half months to assassinate the remaining four men. He did need to ensure, however, that he wasted no time now here in Salekhard and got the job done as soon as possible, as Boris Andreyevich had warned him to expect much more opposition from numbers four, five and six on the list.

It was as an orphan on Moscow's mean streets that the young Ivan had first learned the thieves' trade with fellow orphan Aleksandr Mikhailov, and though he ran with a number of other kids it was only Aleksandr whom he had really trusted to watch his back no matter what. Ivan Ivanovich had spoken very fondly of him during their late-night conversations in the camp barracks, Aleksei recalled. He'd recounted on one occasion how, when he was eight years old, he was tailed by a group of five teenagers who had seen him swipe a wallet and wanted to claim it as their own. They'd cornered him in a dead-end alleyway at the back of a hotel and Ivan was sure he was done for, that was until Aleksandr had come to his rescue, hurling empty vodka bottles at the gang from a first-floor fire escape, hitting two of them on the head, both of whom fell to the ground wounded and unconscious, then tossing other bottles so quickly and ferociously that another two simply fled the scene, overwhelmed by the assault. The final teenager had stood his ground, and Aleksandr, though he could have dispatched him in the same manner as the others, tossing more bottles, decided to go head-to-head with him despite being just half his age and size. He leapt down from the fire escape, three metres to the ground, and went straight for him. The teenager was flabbergasted by Aleksandr's sheer courage, and before he knew quite how to respond his diminutive opponent had planted his right boot firmly into his genitals. Ivan would have had a real hiding that day had it not been for the bravery of Aleksandr, and he'd promised him then that he would never forget this. Thus, when he discovered his old friend had been killed – held, beaten and starved in isolation for fourteen days until he went mad and killed himself, biting off his own tongue and then deliberately choking on it – he resolved to avenge his death no matter what.

Just as with Anichkov and Ivankov, Aleksei needed to be sure that he was killing someone who had inflicted terrible suffering on others also. According to the file, before his retirement a few years ago Zhdanok had been responsible for the deaths of hundreds of prisoners in isolation. If these men had not died by suicide, like Aleksandr, they had died by beating or starvation. He'd often participated in the beatings himself, and relished them. Carrying the blubber of a whale this had been his opportunity to have a workout, to shed a few pounds, yet he never lasted long, and more often than not retreated from the cell hot, sweaty, flustered and hyperventilating in order to nurse his bruised knuckles and sore feet, and of course to catch his breath.

In his mid-sixties now, comfortably living out his days with his wife and receiving frequent visits from his children and grandchildren, he would be difficult to get to, Aleksei soon discovered as he started tailing him. For he always had company.

He might be a former camp commandant and mass murderer, but he was also a pillar of the community, a respected member of the authorities, playing happy families. Did they, his fellow residents, know what he had done!?

His wife was always at home, and on the rare occasion that she was not other family members were, so Aleksei decided the only viable place to get to him was in the *banya*. He went there three times a week an hour before closing, when it was quieting down, and lay right by the edge of the green-tiled icy pool, sprawled out like a giant walrus. This meant that when his obese body got too hot and needed cooling he simply had to heave his hulk a metre or so to the right and roll into the cold pool. A short wiry attendant kept vigil outside, making it impossible for Aleksei to enter unless he posed as another bather and stripped naked but for a towel. It would be difficult to get past him with a gun or knife, so Aleksei concluded he would have to kill Zhdanok with his bare hands. As a boy and a young man Aleksei could not bear immersing himself in the icy pool of a *banya*, though now he could tolerate this with relative ease. It was since Kolyma. Zhdanok would often use the shoulder of another man to haul himself out – he would never stay in the pool for more than a minute or so, it was so cold – and Aleksei realised this was the most opportune time to make his move. He could grab Zhdanok round the neck, force him back down under the water and drown him.

Over the next fortnight Aleksei went to the *banya* the same days as Zhdanok, and remained there, on each occasion, until the very end, until they were the last two men bathing. He offered Zhdanok his shoulder each time the former camp commandant dragged himself from the pool – sadly, he couldn't roll out of it as he could roll in – and he grunted and nodded at Aleksei, the wobbling flab of his chin signalling his gratitude. This was the extent of their discourse. The attendant brought Zhdanok tea about fifteen minutes before closing, and it was when he left them for this final quarter of an hour that Aleksei would strike, when Zhdanok got into the pool for the last time.

Today was the day, Aleksei decided, as he got to the *banya*, only to discover that it was closed, a sign on the door announcing that, 'The boiler is broken and repairs are being carried out.' Typically, this explanation was not accompanied, first, by an apology of any kind, and second, by any indication of when it, the boiler, might be fixed. Aleksei was furious. Another delay. He had to find out when it would be repaired, as he knew this was his only way of getting to Zhdanok.

He managed to locate the short wiry attendant in town, lounging in a grotty restaurant, who informed him that it would be at least two weeks – they had to wait for parts from Moscow – and even this had been expedited further after pressure from Zhdanok, aggrieved that he would be without his precious *banya*. Perhaps he should start his daily surveillance again, Aleksei considered. There must be another way to get to the former camp commandant, he thought, though knowing deep down that there wasn't. Zhdanok's only private time was the *banya*, and without this he simply languished at home with his wife and grandchildren.

The next two weeks were difficult for Aleksei, his mind turning inwards once more, and despite the local library, the contents of which provided some respite from his thoughts, he could not wait for the *banya* to re-open in order that he could assassinate Zhdanok and get the hell out of Salekhard, this far-north town which reminded him too much of Kolyma and the horrors he'd had to endure there.

It was over three weeks before the boiler was eventually repaired and the *banya*'s doors opened again, and both men were immediately there, one in search of heat and relaxation, the other justice. However, in light of the fact that it had been closed for some time it was busy even in the hour before closing, Aleksei noticed. He'd have no choice but to sit it out for another week, until things returned to normal, he told himself, as he lay there in the steam with Zhdanok and a few other men. It was the middle of July now, and all he could think about was how fast he'd have to move to get to the location of his next victim. But no, he must not do this, think about the fourth man on the list until he had dealt with this one.

The following Tuesday evening and it did appear to Aleksei, as he arrived at the *banya* for what he hoped was the last time, that things were as they had been before. An hour later, and he was alone with Zhdanok as he was brought his tea and the attendant exited. He had gone through his now familiar ritual in his hotel room before leaving today – he was thoroughly prepared – even preparing his gun in the event that he had to use it when he fled the scene. Aleksei got into the pool and waited for Zhdanok to join him. He followed soon after. 'How are you?' the former camp commandant asked, settling down beside Aleksei.

He had not tried to engage him in conversation before, and Aleksei was reluctant to talk to him, not least because this would merely delay, and quite possibly jeopardise, what Aleksei planned to do in about a minute, when his intended victim went to lug himself from the pool, and so he replied succinctly, 'I'm okay, thanks,' and looked away.

'Where are you from?' Zhdanok persisted, determined, it appeared, to talk.

A Russian man will always talk freely in a bathhouse, Aleksei thought. He was unable to ignore him. For this would only antagonise him, and perhaps make him suspicious. 'Novosibirsk,' Aleksei answered.

'What are you doing all the way up here, then?'

'They want me to help them get at some of the mineral deposits.'

'Right…so you're working at the new site on the river.'

'Yes,' Aleksei replied, unsure where Zhdanok was referring to. He hadn't spent long enough in Salekhard to answer this question.

'Found anything?'

'No, not yet.'

'How long you here for?'

'Until I find something.'

'It's funny, you don't sound like you're from down there.'

'I'm not. I live there because of my wife. She was born in Novosibirsk.'

'I see…' Zhdanok answered, sounding for the first time like he didn't quite believe him, and he looked to his right, down at Aleksei's left hand, something seeming to catch his eye, perhaps the tattoo of the star on his little finger, which Aleksei had managed to conceal on previous occasions.

Now Aleksei, now, he urged himself – he could not wait any longer – and he slammed his elbow hard and violently into Zhdanok's face, hitting him square on the nose, then brought his arm around his blubbery neck and forced his head down into the water…though he could not get it under, Zhdanok managing to push it back, onto the side of the pool, by locking his legs to the floor…and so Aleksei realised he was going to have to strangle him if he wanted to kill him, and thus tightened his arm around his neck, then pulled on it with the other one as if tugging a thick rope, then rolled his naked body onto Zhdanok's, his back and buttocks pressing against the former camp commandant's sagging breasts, the breasts of an old woman, and his gargantuan stomach, his vast weight providing the necessary resistance as Aleksei tightened his grip…and Zhdanok eventually started to choke, his cheeks swelling like a giant toad's until they were bright red.

'Ivan Ivanovich sent me. Look at me,' Aleksei said, twisting Zhdanok's neck even more until he was able to see into his bulging, bloodshot eyes.

Zhdanok, unable to look away as his predecessors had done, simply closed his eyes.

'Open them. Look at me!' Aleksei demanded. 'Into my eyes.'

As he opened them Aleksei loosened his grip slightly, looked at Zhdanok searchingly, even though on this occasion he was sure of his guilt, then with a sharp thrust upwards tightened his grip once more until his victim's cheeks swelled to the point where they appeared that they might burst like two small red balloons…but then suddenly deflated, the air rushing out of them, his whole body becoming limp.

Aleksei loosened his grip and rolled with Zhdanok under the water, letting him go and watching him float facedown to the surface.

After this, getting out of the icy pool, Katya confronted him again, asking insistently this time, 'Did you really have to do this, Poppa, did you?'

'Yes, I did, Katya. He was an evil man!' Aleksei snapped back impatiently, then left his daughter standing there as he set about concealing the dead body and making his escape.

21ST JULY 1949
BUTUGYCHAG, KOLYMA
(5696KM EAST OF MOSCOW)

First things first, Aleksei and the other prisoners were led into an empty stone barracks and stripped naked – the authorities' modus operandi to ensure they had not forgotten they were the lowest of them all! Women then appeared with razors and shaved them until they were hairless, which made Aleksei feel like a baby again, after which they were sprayed with a bitter-smelling liquid, de-louser he presumed, and washed down with icy-cold water. Aleksei stood cold and shivering, and wondered whether they would inform Natasha that he was here.

They were held in a sanatorium for a week, all of them without exception very frail, and were quarantined, the authorities concerned they might pass on infection or disease. They were fed well and permitted to sleep, and furthermore on a mattress with bedding. Then they were discharged and another selection process ensued. Lined up, a camp major walked down the line, assigning each of them to different workplaces within the camp. Some were sent to the mine, others to the forest. Aleksei and Nikolai were sent to the latter.

Both men were given camp-issue uniforms – quilted trousers, jacket, felt hat with ear flaps, fleece-lined mittens and rubber-soled boots (they were being prepared for the bitter winter already even though it was still summer) – then assigned to a brigade and sent to their barracks. Aleksei's jacket and trousers carried his prisoner number, K-891: he had even been stripped of his name, he thought. He was a *zek*, no more. At least they were not expected to build their own sleeping quarters: their predecessors had not been so lucky here either, even tasked with incarcerating themselves, unrolling the barbed wire and building the watchtowers. And then, after all this, they'd had to feed themselves too.

The barracks consisted of a long rectangular ramshackle wooden building, and inside rows and rows of rickety double-decker bunk beds, some of which were rotting. Two slept on each level. About two hundred men were crammed in here, Aleksei figured, as he looked around. The floor was sprinkled with sawdust and wood chippings, and beneath this the earth, the tundra – the thick permafrost of the north. The walls were flimsy, sufficient for the summer, Aleksei supposed, though he dreaded to think how they would fare in winter. 'We should be grateful we're not in an earth dugout,' Nikolai said, facing him. 'That's what I thought we'd end up in.'

Aleksei sat down on the hardboard bunk. He must write to Natasha and Katya, had to know they were all right. What were they doing at this moment? he wondered. How he wanted, needed to be with them, his 'beautiful' (he referred to Natasha as just this, this single adjective alone sufficient to capture her, her spirit and essence) and his 'little sucker fish'. He fell asleep with them in his thoughts.

A loud siren woke him the following morning, this intrusive sound signalling his first day of hard labour. Aleksei was fed breakfast in the mess hall, a small bowl of watery porridge which provided little sustenance, and after this a second siren sounded, marking its end. He lined up with all the other prisoners in the centre of the compound. Brigades and workers were counted and frisked by warders, then led off to work, urged on by a small band which played triumphant-sounding Soviet military music, escorted by a number of convoy guards in short fur jackets with dogs and machine guns. There was one guard for every five men. Prisoners had to march heads lowered and hands behind backs.

Aleksei quickly discovered that any slight deviation from the line constituted an attempt to escape when a man three rows in front of him, straying too far to the right, was suddenly shot in the back by a convoy guard. Aleksei stopped dead in his tracks and stared at the dying man sprawled on the ground, before being ordered to 'march on' as if nothing had happened. He looked to the great forest, this mass of trees in front of him, and forced himself to wonder at this natural beauty, which he prayed would sustain him.

He and the other men in his brigade, including Nikolai, were set to work in the forest felling trees. There was no modern logging machinery to help them: they worked with saws and axes. The organisation was poor, typically Soviet. He had been assigned to the heavy-work regime, his political class, KRTD (counter-revolutionary terrorist activity), ensuring this. Thank goodness he was not classed KRTTD (counter-revolutionary Trotskyite terrorist activity), he thought. He might be judged a cosmopolitan democratic recidivist, or some such, beyond reform, but a Trotskyite was beyond redemption. It was evident right away that the authorities considered this the ultimate punishment for someone like Aleksei, a bloody intellectual who spent all his time in his head. Now he would know what it was to be a working man, a member of the masses – to do real labour! It appeared they had decided to forget his brave military service as an officer on the front, first on the outskirts of Moscow when Hitler had invaded, then in Stalingrad from the summer of '42 until January '43. He would have fought on had he not been wounded. There had been days during the fighting when the whole city was ablaze, fires burning across it, everything reduced to sand and rubble. Yet it was on such days as these, Aleksei recalled, when the dust of destruction hung thick in the air, that it had been safe to go out in the open, the German snipers unable to see them. And better this than travelling through the sewers, shit everywhere, in order to avoid the snipers' preying eyes.

It was hot today, twenty-five degrees, the air clammy and thick with midges, and as the morning progressed Aleksei longed for meal break. When he paused for breath, Rafik, his brigadier, reprimanded him, shouting, 'No rest till noon!' He was a tough work-gang boss, though not cruel, Aleksei sensed.

When meal break finally came they were fed three ounces of fish and a few drops of oil. The camp authorities fed prisoners enough simply to keep them alive and working. Some of the men were so hungry they ate the bones as well, Aleksei noticed. Though the country was not afflicted by famine any more, its prison population was. The brigade ate together, silent and downcast.

Lunch over, they were made to work hard the next few hours, Aleksei's whole imprisonment, it seemed, geared towards productive labour. He had to toil, that was all, for the good of the state, the people, Communism! 'You're required to produce at least six-and-a-half cubic yards of logs by the end of the day, this your work norm,' Rafik informed him bluntly.

In the late afternoon, when the sun was losing its power, the mosquitoes came, thousands of them, to feed on them as they continued to work. Here Aleksei was, paying his debt to society, though it was not apparent what debt was due.

Only when it got late were he and the other prisoners rounded up like sheep and returned to the camp, given half an hour for supper, lined up and counted once more, then returned to the barracks for the night – secure under lock and key and padlock and chain, windows barred.

He had better get used to these men, his brigade, Aleksei considered, while lying on his bunk that first evening. From here on he was going to be doing everything with them. He and Nikolai slept by the slop bucket, the special privilege for the new arrivals. The fumes from the kerosene lamp helped make the smell slightly less foul, fortunately. They were not permitted to sleep until eleven o'clock, however, just one hour from midnight, and when this hour eventually came they had to endure lice and bed bugs, which fed on them through the night, Aleksei's sleep made even worse because he worried that someone would steal his boots, which he had taken off and left at the end of the bed. He retrieved them and held them tight in his arms, as if cradling a child.

The night was white; it was not dark here in summer, the sun refusing to set. Last night at midnight it had still been light, Aleksei recalled. It reminded him of his visit to St Petersburg as a child – he would not call the great city by its Communist name, Leningrad, any more. Then he could not sleep, and now, likewise, he was only able to sleep for a few hours, from two to four in the morning, these few hours when darkness faintly settled. At least he had the luxury of a mattress, he considered, albeit a thin one stuffed with wood chippings, and a pillow made of sawdust. Some men in his barracks did not sleep at all. They had started to lose their minds, it appeared to him, moaning strange utterances through the night, becoming lost and delirious in the never-ending light. However, Aleksei knew he must cherish this light while it lasted. For soon it would be dark, and this darkness would last a lot longer. He dreaded the onset of winter already, and he had only just got here.

Within the first few days, he and Nikolai realised they would do well to join a group if they were to find some safety from the criminals. It was a cultural melting pot in here, with people from all over the Union, so many different nationalities, ethnicities and religions. It was no wonder the Russians had a predilection for violent nationalism, Aleksei mused. Under Communism, these cultural differences were not acknowledged, since a citizen of the Union had to be defined by one thing alone, his Sovietness, possessing no other identity than a Soviet one. Jews were not Jews, Caucasians not Caucasians, Mongols not Mongols, Tartars not Tartars. All were Soviet, and specifically Soviet Russian. And yet, in spite of this, it seemed to Aleksei that everyone here was unable to let go of their national, ethnic and religious identities. Poles stuck with Poles, Jews with Jews. Some also grouped according to what city they were born in – there was a recognisable group of Muscovites, as there was St Petersburgers. However, there did appear to be one mixed grouping in the barracks, consisting of about eight men, a disparate collection of former teachers, scientists and academics from Moscow and St Petersburg, which, Aleksei sensed, he and Nikolai could find a home with, if these men would have them. One of the group, Anatoly, a tall and lean man in his mid-forties with a slender neck and large Adam's apple, a former scientist from St Petersburg, had been here for fifteen years, Nikolai learned. Another, Mikhail, the opposite in stature, short and stocky with a thick neck and quintessentially Jewish, had a very similar story to Aleksei's – he had fought in the war, then taught in Moscow, literature though, not history. He had most likely been picked up simply for being Jewish. Koba was after them again!

While waiting for dinner, Aleksei asked Mikhail about letter entitlement, and was informed that they were allowed to send two a year. And what about receiving mail? Aleksei enquired. Yes, this was permitted, Mikhail confirmed, though all correspondence was read by them first. Aleksei hit it off with Mikhail right away, not least because he reminded him of his Poppa before his stroke, so energetic and full of life in spite of his predicament. 'You'll quickly see how obsessed they are with our work capability,' Mikhail explained. 'It's meant to determine every part of our existence – how much we eat, how we are dressed, how much we sleep. If only they didn't take themselves so bloody seriously. They're obsessed with rules and directives. Maybe opium would calm them down a little!

'There are a few men who work very hard, but they sure as hell aren't motivated by Stakhanov – yes, the great Aleksei (your namesake, how unfortunate!), the notorious prison miner who believed that a man could re-forge himself, reform his bad character through honest, hard labour,' he said sarcastically. 'As far as I'm concerned the very notion of 'corrective-labour' is perverse. No, these men are just driven by their appetites. They simply want to eat more, that's all!'

Mikhail possessed a bitter honesty that Aleksei was instantly drawn to. Truthfulness had become a rare quality in Soviet Russia. 'Take a look at the old poster near the kitchen,' he went on, pointing to it. '"For the best workers, the best food." However, do these few men really think they're better off because of this? They might get more food, better food, and yet they need it because they work so damn hard. Look at them, they're bloody knackered!' And with these words Aleksei laughed, he noted for the first time in a long while.

Food had immense power in here, and the camp authorities knew this all too well. In fact, it appeared to be one of the principal ways in which they maintained control over the men. For without it, of course, they would die.

'You must try and get hold of your own bowl,' Anatoly said firmly to Aleksei, giving him his after he had finished eating. 'If you keep on having to wait, you'll get the scraps only.'

'Right, thanks…' Aleksei replied, and Anatoly walked off.

'Don't worry about him,' Mikhail said. 'He can be a moody bugger at times, but he has a very good heart. He's telling you this for your own good.'

'Yes, I can see that,' Aleksei answered.

'Chop-chop, then,' Mikhail said, urging Aleksei to go and get some food before it was all gone, which he did.

He returned moments later with scraps, a measly mash made of no more than crushed grits and carp bones. Mikhail looked at his bowl.

'Yep, enough said,' Aleksei went on.

'Make sure you give your whole attention to it. Savour every bit,' Mikhail said.

'I will, though I'm not sure "savour" is quite the right word,' Aleksei replied, taking his first mouthful and wincing. He then stopped talking while he ate.

'Use your bread to mop up every last scrap. You'll need it,' Mikhail said as Aleksei took his last mouthful. 'Rafik's alright, by the way, as brigadiers go.'

'Why d'you say that?' Aleksei asked.

'You seem a little wary of him, that's all.'

Aleksei did not respond to this comment.

'Don't worry, I'm not a damn informer,' Mikhail went on.

'It's not that,' Aleksei answered. 'I'm just trying to figure him out.'

'He tries to ensure that all his brigade members work as much as one another, and he's to be commended for this. Many don't, you see. He tries to make things fair, albeit in a system which by its very nature is profoundly unfair. And at least we don't have someone like Stepan, who insists that his men work hard "for the good of the Motherland." Stepan remains a committed Communist in spite of the lunacy he sees all around him, and blames his incarceration not on a malevolent Soviet state but on the work of foreign agents looking to undermine the great utopian project!'

'Okay, thanks for letting me know,' Aleksei replied, looking around. 'Anatoly?'

'Don't worry, he'll be back,' Mikhail said.

'No, it's not that. It's just, well, he's been here so…'

'Yep, since the early '30s. I can't imagine spending that long in here. I've done just four years. It's a miracle he's still alive.'

'I heard that!' Anatoly said, appearing once more. 'What, you'd rather I were dead?'

'I can see you're fishing for a compliment, my old friend.'

'Always, my dear Mikhail. Always.'

'How was it back then?' Aleksei asked, turning to Anatoly.

'Well, the criminals were less dominant.'

'Right…'

'The work regime was worst during the war. But it's still very hard. The camps became harsher in '40 when Beria took over. The man's even crueller than his predecessors, Yagoda and Yezhov. Rumour has it that he personally supervised many interrogations, and still does. He relishes them. We old-timers were sure that when the war ended things would get better.'

'Just make sure you keep talking,' Mikhail said, patting Aleksei on the shoulder.

'Yep, and this one knows all about talking,' Anatoly quipped, prodding Mikhail. 'It's all he does.'

The siren sounded.

'It's that time,' Mikhail said, and the three of them turned and ambled slowly back to their barracks.

THE FOURTH KILL
22ND AUGUST 1953
TOMSK
(1473km SOUTHEAST OF SALEKHARD)

Andrei Edmundovich Smidovich had learned his trade from Vasili Blokhin, Koba's Chief Executioner, and working alongside him he'd killed with relish, particularly during the purges. Smidovich had displayed a particular contempt for intellectuals, beating many to death with the butt of his gun – his preferred method of execution – and Aleksei, as he read his file, was forced to wonder whether it was this man who had terrorised his father while he was under arrest at the Lubyanka, Smidovich's place of work for over fifteen years. If so, the sadist was likely full of regret, not for what he had done but rather for what he hadn't: he'd failed to kill the man with the butt of his gun, Aleksei's father's stroke getting in the way of this. Ivan Ivanovich had seen Smidovich murder his fellow thief-in-law, the Historian – Pavel Borsky's nickname, the man a lover of history like Ivan Ivanovich – when he was held with him in the Lubyanka for four days, it being only the intervention of a less pugnacious *apparatchik* that had saved Ivan Ivanovich from also being pummelled to death by Smidovich.

Aleksei found it extraordinary that this mass killer remained alive. Stalin had typically got rid of such accomplices, he thought. Smidovich now lived alone in Tomsk, returning to his mother's side after Koba's death, only to see her die a few months later.

Perhaps she'd been unable to live with the blood on her son's
hands, Aleksei wondered. Smidovich would never have told her
what he had done – the thousands of skulls he'd smashed in with
his precious gun – though his mother would have known deep
down yet never said anything, unable to accept what he, her son,
had become: this small delicate boy she'd given birth to all those
years ago who was now big, burly, tactless and abominably cruel.

Permanently drunk and slowly losing his mind, Smidovich, a
virtual recluse, barely left his home on the edge of town, Aleksei
discovered, as he started observing him, and when he did, it
was only to stagger in a forlorn and pathetic state across the
road to an abandoned factory, which he did most nights, for
an hour or so. Once inside, he'd lumber across the vast derelict
floor to a small secluded space at the back of the building which
housed a filthy old armchair and rusty projector, and from
there, he'd watch footage, projected onto a bare wall, of some
of his atrocities, which he had perversely committed to film.
Aleksei's observation did not enable him to see how Smidovich
responded to what he watched, but he suspected that it gave
him some pleasure, this dark and macabre nostalgic routine.

Back in his hotel room in the early morning, Aleksei confident
of when and where he would strike – at night, in the abandoned
factory – he looked out over Tomsk's small skyline, still out of
breath. He had had enough of this place, which had been his
home the last few weeks. How could he call it this, his 'home',
he wondered, looking around its small, brown, grey interior. It
possessed none of the warmth, history and culture that his home
with Natasha and Katya had possessed. Though its exterior and
common parts had suffered from the terminal neglect so typical of
Soviet-era housing – grimy walls, damaged floorboards, leaking
pipes and the accompanying stench – once inside it was as if you
had walked over the threshold into another world. Colourful
rugs from Iran and Afghanistan had covered the old parquet

floor; Far Eastern blankets were draped over sofas and chairs; incense burned, giving it the smell of an Orthodox chapel. These things had made up for the dilapidation of everything else – the rickety furniture, peeling wallpaper, cracked plaster, old pipes. And this damn hotel room, it was the antithesis of this, a drab and colourless place void of life, which represented everything he despised about the Soviet system – its self-conscious humility, its mediocrity, its blandness, its functionalism, all these profoundly Soviet characteristics. It was a home fit for a fugitive, no more, a place simply to sleep and work.

And what was his work? Aleksei asked himself at this moment, walking away from the window towards the bed. He killed. He killed to settle accounts, Ivan Ivanovich's accounts. There were no women or children on the list, thank goodness, and had there been, Ivan Ivanovich knew Aleksei would have refused him this. *Nomenklatura* only, the most reprehensible, this was Aleksei's rule. He sighed heavily.

Anger, revenge and justice drove him, he mused, standing at the end of the bed now, but also a special kind of desperation – that which only comes from a broken heart. He began to undress, removing first his sweater then his sweat-drenched T-shirt. A large part of Aleksei had died when he knew he would never be with Natasha and Katya again, he reflected, staring blankly ahead as he laid his clothes down. He had assumed a number of different identities these past seven months, forever living in the shadows, and what was most difficult about this life, Aleksei found, was that he was often terribly lonely and found himself yearning to talk to, to be with, others. He no longer asked himself why he had taken to it, this deadly profession, quite so well. On the battlefield and in the camp he had seen what man should not see, and that he had survived both, well, this was what made him quite so dangerous. Aleksei had learned to fear almost nothing.

He began to work out, using the furniture in his hotel room, the end of the bedframe serving as the most suitable, and stable, surface from which to do push-ups, working his chest, biceps and triceps, performing ten sets for each muscle group, and fifty repetitions per set. He then performed squats and lunges, working his hips, legs and calves. After this Aleksei lifted the bed on its side and leaned it against the wall – freeing up as much floor area as possible – in order to practice his fighting techniques, which he did for a further hour. He had become extremely fit and well-trained since the start of the year, running every morning for an hour in the pre-dawn darkness – as he'd done this morning, this the best antidote to his insomnia – before working out. His leg ceased to trouble him also, he having successfully built up enough muscle mass around the old injury to compensate for any former weakness.

Aleksei continued to be extremely thorough, almost neurotic, in his preparation before every assassination. The moment he cut corners, became complacent, was the moment he got caught or killed. And he continued to follow the same ritual in the hours leading up to every kill, as he started to follow here, now, in Tomsk. In his drab hotel room – they were always drab – he spent the morning preparing the gun he intended to use, scrubbing the inside of its frame and cylinder, wiping away all the dirt and grease, cleaning the barrel and oiling the moving parts. Then he prepped his back-up pistol in the very same way – he made sure he carried one, in a mini-holster on his right shin – and sharpened his knife, the one which he had killed the Azerbaijani with. After this he ironed his shirt and trousers, polished his leather jacket and boots, then laid out his clothes and weapons on the bed – he needed to see everything before him. Aleksei spent the afternoon lying in the bath – he always made sure the room he took had one – savouring the silence, watching the steam rise and evaporate, and listening to his breath. Then later, standing naked before the small bathroom mirror, he shaved, then stared at his reflection, the face he observed hard and cold. As evening fell he strolled into the bedroom, sat naked on the bed, his clothes laid out beside him, and observed the wall above the bureau, his master guide, studying its contents one last time. After this, he dressed, then reached for his leather coat, which he ensured always hung in its customary position on the back of the bedroom door. And with this last act, of putting on his coat, Aleksei was ready.

He stood outside Smidovich's house and waited. He was sure he would leave the relative safety of his home soon enough – he always had his front door locked, never failing to lock it in spite of his inebriated state as long as Aleksei had observed him – and head for the abandoned factory across the street in order to indulge his morbid ritual. And yet two hours later, no sign.

Aleksei's better instinct told him he should abort the kill and try again same time tomorrow, yet there was a recklessness about him tonight, an impatience, not least because he needed to kill Smidovich quickly in order to get back on track, to give himself sufficient time to deal with the final two men on the list.

He knew that the front door would be locked, and thus he'd have to force it open – Aleksei could not pick the deadbolt lock Smidovich had on it – which would alert his target right away, and give the old executioner time, even if he were drunk, to arm himself with something, and yet Aleksei did not care.

He kicked at the door hard, eventually forcing it off its hinges, until he stood in the hallway, then headed straight for the living room, hurling the door open, pistol in hand. Smidovich was ready for him, however, smashing something hard into his face, right between his eyes.

Aleksei fell to the floor and before he knew it Smidovich had scrambled on top of him and straddled him, pinning Aleksei's arms to the floor with his knees. Smidovich held his throat with one hand and a gun with the other, perhaps the very bloodstained instrument he'd killed those thousands with, Aleksei thought. The old executioner's size and weight made it very difficult for him to move at all: Aleksei was trapped.

'I knew you'd come for me soon enough,' Smidovich said, holding the butt of his gun above Aleksei's head, in preparation, it seemed, to smash someone's face with it once more.

Smidovich had hit him clean on the bridge of his nose, which already throbbed. He'd broken it badly, Aleksei realised, tasting the blood in his mouth which streamed from his nose. 'Yes,' Aleksei replied, still managing to answer Smidovich, in spite of the pain.

'All those traitors I killed deserved to die. They were weak.'

'Is it true you killed thousands?' Aleksei asked.

'Yes, and now it seems I've been granted one more victim – you,' he growled, and extending his arm slightly in preparation to thrust the butt of the gun down on Aleksei's head again – which caused him to twist his body ever so slightly, his left knee lifting a fraction from the floor – Aleksei was able to wriggle his right arm free.

Without hesitation he aimed straight for Smidovich's Adam's apple, hitting him hard there, which caused the old executioner to choke and his grip loosen.

Aleksei grabbed the side of his neck and thrust his head downwards, then punched him hard in the side of his face, throwing three fast and clean left hooks, his other arm free now, then rolling on top of him.

Smidovich struggled to breathe and gasped for breath. Aleksei gripped his Adam's apple with his index finger and thumb.

'Are you sorry?' Aleksei asked.

'No,' Smidovich muttered, Aleksei surprised by this answer. His victims up until this point had been cowardly, full of false repentance. 'Who sent you?' he went on.

'Ivan Ivanovich sent me. Look at me,' Aleksei said, looking hard into Smidovich's dark, bloodshot eyes. He did not need to search for this man's sin. It was clear enough. 'How do you feel when you sit opposite and watch them, watch yourself doing what you did?' he continued.

'I feel good,' Smidovich replied.

Aleksei was silent. What could he say in response to this? he wondered.

'You think you can kill me, the great executioner?' Smidovich went on.

'Yes,' Aleksei said.

'Why don't you kill me as I killed them?' he asked, his eyes looking to his precious bloodstained gun, which lay on the floor.

'Because I'm not cruel like you are,' Aleksei answered bluntly, and drawing his back-up pistol from his shin he grimaced with anger then pulled the trigger, shooting Smidovich straight between the eyes.

As he turned to leave, Aleksei saw a small bust of Stalin that stood in the corner of the room, and taking aim at its head he fired. The first shot did little more than take the eye out, and so he fired again, and again, shooting Koba in the head continuously until his face was completely disfigured and barely discernible. Just three years before this he'd met a man in Kolyma who'd been sentenced to ten years for hanging his jacket on one such bust: the man had been unable to find a cloakroom.

Walking outside the house Katya confronted him again, asking probingly, 'Was he a bad man also, Poppa?'

'Yes,' Aleksei answered coolly, leaving his daughter standing there as he hurried off down the road, eager to get to the fifth man on the list.

Aleksei worked efficiently now, always departing the scene quickly once the job was done, as he'd done tonight, yet his conscience – the face of Katya he saw after every killing – had begun to haunt him again and rob him of sleep. He was sure, in fact, as he made his way back to the hotel at this moment, that he'd be unable to sleep tonight after this kill, and would likely soon be up and running in the pre-dawn Tomsk darkness, as he had done the previous night, before taking the first available train out of here. It seemed that his anger could not obliterate his conscience after all, as he had hoped it could after the third assassination. He might not be killing the kind, humble, decent working man, he thought, but rather his opposite, the cruel, vain, dishonest, privileged one, however he was being plagued with doubt once more, with dread. And why? Well, because beneath the endless patter of conviction and self-justification, the numerous philosophical arguments he had used and continued to use to explain why he was right in doing what he was doing, he knew deep down that he was not entitled to play God, that no one was, as Nikolai had maintained when he killed the Azerbaijani. Aleksei knew this, yet he continued to kill.

Was he a protector or a predator? Aleksei asked, back in his hotel room. He did not know. He sat down at the bureau, crossed the name of his fourth victim, Smidovich, off the list, then returned it to the brown envelope. After this he stared at his dark reflection in the window: his nose was badly broken, his face bloody, bruising already forming around his eyes after his vicious fight with Smidovich. He'd need to clean himself up. His reputation as a cold-blooded assassin preceded him now, Aleksei knew this. He was distinguishable by his two tattoos: he did not just have the star on his left little finger but also 'Kolyma' written on his right hand. For he never wanted to forget the horror of the place and what it symbolised – the very worst of this damn regime's brutality, its contempt for humanity, for freedom and happiness. He stared at this tattoo, then looked to the telephone, which sat on the bedside table, knowing that it would ring soon enough with details of the fifth job, the next kill. He put his palm to his chest. He could feel his sin in his work, in his heart. Still, he was yet to find God, as Nikolai had hoped and prayed that he would. Was he not most likely to find Him through sin? Aleksei wondered. He doubted it. Rather, it felt like he would never find Him.

His morality was skewed, yes, and yet the whole of Russia's was.

He, Aleksei, had become a bad man in a bad country.

4TH AUGUST 1949

BUTUGYCHAG, KOLYMA

Aleksei was acutely aware how little stimulation there was in here: no newspapers, no books, no radio. The intellectual personality struggled, perhaps more than others, because of this. It also struggled because it was typically assigned general work, which normally involved hard labour – pulling, pushing, carrying. Aleksei wished he had a specialist skill. Being an academic and ex-army officer counted for little. Political prisoners were made to work hard. In fact, the political was judged and punished more harshly than his criminal counterpart – for he posed a greater social danger, according to the authorities. The criminal might be a thief, his crimes motivated by social inequality and injustice, yet he could be reformed. Worse still, the criminal might be a rapist or murderer, but still, he could be changed, made a productive member of society, a useful Soviet citizen. The political, on the other hand, could not be rehabilitated unless he renounced his opposition to the Soviet way and, instead, wholeheartedly embraced it. The rapist or murderer might threaten a few individual citizens, but what was this compared to the effect a political might have on the whole of society, so the topsy-turvy logic went. God forbid a political achieved revolution and affected everyone as Lenin had done! Politicals were incarcerated because of who they were, not what they had done. But if they could not be re-educated, reformed, rehabilitated, then why incarcerate them? Aleksei asked. Would the authorities not have been better off simply taking them deep into the *taiga* and shooting them? Perhaps they wanted rather to humiliate them, see them suffer more, make them contribute a little to Soviet ideals before killing them. But who was this political prisoner, this enemy, under Koba. Maybe it was everyone? Aleksei wondered. Though Kolyma was meant to be home to only the very worst Soviet citizens, it appeared everyone was here, from every level of society.

In the barracks this evening, Anatoly explained that there were fewer political prisoners than there had been a decade ago, even a few years ago. 'Immediately after the war, six in ten prisoners were political. But now I reckon it's about four in ten,' he said to Aleksei and Nikolai. 'The vast majority of these are not real counter-revolutionaries or agitators. I hardly need to tell you that! No, they're simply victims of this mad regime, arrested under Section 10 for telling an inappropriate joke about our 'Great Leader' or some other Party boss. And many are former inmates too. Mikhail's sure that the NKVD is working its way back through the alphabet!' Anatoly concluded.

'The criminals do best in here,' Mikhail interjected, 'and grab most of the privileges going. The leading ones live by their own rules, mete out their own justice, operate like a cabal, a close-knit brotherhood. During the war, they were utterly dominant, according to Anatoly, but these days less so. The prisoners coming through the gates now are tougher after their war experiences.'

'Thank goodness!' Anatoly interjected. 'The Poles and Chechens in particular seem to be growing stronger. The latter were brought here in '44, hundreds of thousands of them deported, and tens of thousands must have perished in transit.

It appears Stalin is trying to eradicate the entire Chechen nation, just as he did entire classes.'

'A few of the criminals,' Mikhail resumed, 'are thieves-in-law.'

'Yes, I've read about them,' Aleksei said, recalling a paper a university colleague of his had written about their emergence in Tsarist Russia. 'They live by a specific set of rules.'

'The thieves' code,' Mikhail confirmed, 'which includes forsaking one's relatives, not having one's own family, never working, and having nothing to do with the authorities.'

'The last two don't sound too bad!' Aleksei quipped.

'Mikhail is utterly fascinated by them,' Anatoly remarked dryly.

'Why's that!?' Nikolai asked, with more than a hint of moral judgement in his voice.

'I wouldn't call it fascination,' Mikhail responded.

'What would you call it then?' Anatoly enquired.

'Interest,' he answered. 'And well, at least they're providing some opposition.'

'Opposition?' Nikolai queried. 'I'd hardly call it that. Their resistance is solely about themselves, for their own benefit. It's not as if they're acting for the greater good. They're brutes, the lot of them!' he concluded, huffing, then joined Anatoly on his bunk.

It appeared the two of them wanted to talk about something other than the criminals they had to cohabit with.

But Mikhail was a blessing, as far as Aleksei was concerned. He admired him for his vivacity, which he suspected, though he had only just met him, was present against all odds – against the coldness, the indifference all around them – and for his rather wicked sense of humour. For unlike Aleksei, who was easily prone to pessimism and too readily retreated into himself, Mikhail seemed to have realised that his survival depended on his optimism, his benevolence, his wit: he would not be beaten by the boredom, humiliation, overwork and deprivation. No! And he clearly cherished the solidarity within the group. For this is what kept him alive, Aleksei felt – this camaraderie, togetherness.

Aleksei looked over at the criminals on the other side of the barracks. They sat there with their shirts off, proudly bearing their upper bodies, which carried tattoos, marks of their crimes, a clear record of their criminal history. There was a hierarchy among them which seemed to be determined by the number of tattoos each one had: the more he had the higher up he was, Aleksei presumed. 'Each tattoo has been authorised,' Mikhail made clear, 'and an unauthorised one, one which has not been earned, is punishable often by death. There are two thieves-in-law in the camp with stars on both chest and knee,' he told Aleksei. 'They're the leaders. One's from Russia, the other Azerbaijan.'

The Russian was in their barracks. 'He was first sentenced to a tenner, ten years for extortion, but after he escaped, only then to be recaptured, his sentence was extended to twenty-five,' Mikhail went on, pointing him out.

He sat on his own, on the only single bed in the barracks, surrounded by a number of men.

Mikhail continued, 'He then went on to murder a guard – who was allegedly a rapist – with his bare hands, and though the Rostov camp authorities didn't execute him in retribution, they did serve him with four quarters, a one-hundred-year sentence, and ship him off to Kolyma.

'Rumour has it that he, Ivan Ivanovich Bessonov, despite his imprisonment, still has enormous power and influence on the outside, and continues to control his interests from inside here. Among other things he makes a lot of money supplying bootlegged vodka to the depleted tribes of the north, the Nentsi,

Khanty and Komi, a valuable commodity to them, and in return gets mammoth ivory and furs that he knows will fetch a very good price in Moscow and St Petersburg.

'He is able to settle disputes with a few words, he fears no one, and tolerates neither insults nor any challenge to his authority.

'A middle-ranking thief was put on trial by the thieves' court recently, then executed with a big metal file on his order. Vasily, one of Ivan Ivanovich's henchmen, was his executioner. He is distinguishable by his mouth, which carries a full set of gold teeth, his peakless leather cap, and his distinctive walk, always taking small steps, legs slightly apart. An assassin with a fifty-year sentence, he's hardly worried if they decide to give him another quarter.

'He might be incarcerated, the state might be punishing him, yet Ivan Ivanovich persists with his criminal activities, standing proudly aloof from the normal world,' Mikhail said, as Aleksei stared right at him, this thief-in-law, across a sea of bunk beds.

'He doesn't work, but is allocated a full ration. In fact, he can have just about anything he wants, within reason, even fried potatoes. The one thing he can't have, however, is his freedom. That single bed he sleeps on, it's iron not wood, the only one in the whole camp. And those five men standing around him, they're his henchmen. They guard him day and night.'

Aleksei looked over at them, all formidable in stature, tall and muscular.

Mikhail continued, 'He wears an aluminium cross around his neck. I'm not sure if you can see it, we're too far away, but it's this which marks him out as a thief-in-law.'

'I'd better make sure Nikolai doesn't spot that,' Aleksei replied. 'Christ, this really would be, for him, the ultimate sacrilege. He'd probably try and take it off him.'

'He wouldn't?'

'He would.'

Aleksei moved to the end of his bunk as Ivan Ivanovich got to his feet and addressed one of his henchmen. He had a far better view of him now: he faced Aleksei. His face was hard and weathered, strewn with scars – these marks of his criminal ascendancy – and it was clear there were more blemishes behind the brown stubble which covered his cheeks and jaw like a thick rug. Piercing blue eyes appeared like gems out of this hardness, like perfect sapphires. They were almost beautiful. When he spoke, his mouth barely opened, he grumbled, and the gold crown on his front tooth gleamed.

There were just two female barracks, they hardly saw the women who inhabited them, and Ivan Ivanovich, according to Mikhail, had his pick of the most beautiful. 'It's said, Aleksei, that while we work a warder will bring them to him and he'll have sex with them in the empty barracks. Petrov permits this because he's terrified that Ivan Ivanovich will order another strike, and he can't afford this, as there's so much pressure on him to meet the production targets set by Moscow. These women can't refuse him. Many are the wives of former Party bosses, the daughters of intellectuals, who'd never dream of having sex with a man like Ivan Ivanovich – but if they're to survive they have little choice. He's not meant to be abusive or violent, however. Quite the contrary, in fact. Almost gentlemanly, some say. However, Vasily also has access to the women, and he's meant to be the opposite, often violent, treating them with contempt.'

'That's him there?' Aleksei asked, pointing with his index finger.

'Yes, that's Vasily,' Mikhail replied. 'You see the tattoo on his chest?'

'Yes...'

'It reads, "There is no happiness in life."'

'So he's a depressive as well as a misogynist,' Aleksei said, looking at him closely.

'Yes, it seems that way,' Mikhail answered, at which point Vasily noticed Aleksei's intense scrutiny and gestured with his two middle fingers, bringing them to his throat, then pointing them at Aleksei. 'He's threatening you,' Mikhail went on. 'Stop staring at him,' which he promptly did.

'Ivan Ivanovich's meant to be a traditionalist, an old thief-in-law,' Mikhail continued. 'He doesn't cooperate with the authorities nearly to the extent that the Azerbaijani does. The latter assists the guards with meeting work targets. Christ, he sometimes even has his boys overseeing the work, normally of politicals. What better way to punish us for our lack of faith in Communism than to have our work overseen by criminals!

'This thieves' world has existed on the margins of Russian society for hundreds of years. Its methods were so successful, in fact, that the Bolsheviks assumed many of them in order to gain power, and then retain it: harsh discipline, secrecy, the defiance of conventional culture. And yet these very same men then went on to deny, in true deluded Soviet style, that this criminal society even existed – for how could it in a socialist society! But in reality it thrives in the shadows, driving the black market economy and working with corrupt state officials.

'The Azerbaijani also exploits the most vulnerable, who must pay him for the privilege of not being beaten or murdered. He eats very well because of this, the big, dark-skinned, hairy Central Asian, almost closer to a bear than a man.

'Yes, the cruelty of the strong towards the weak thrives here. A group of the Azerbaijani's boys escaped a few years ago and they took a political with them. In the event that they could not find food, there was always him. The first thing they did was wreak their vengeance on a young soldier they came across, whom they took to be a bounty hunter: they garrotted him.

'Most try and escape in the summer,' Mikhail continued, 'the best time of year to do it. They can find mushrooms and berries to eat, and if they're good hunters – rabbits, chipmunks and squirrels. But they'd better make sure they don't get caught. If the dogs don't finish them off, the authorities will. And when they get their dead bodies back to camp, they'll hang them from the gatepost as a grim warning to future would-be escapees,' he concluded.

Aleksei thought of 'the shed' – its name preceded it – this building of the dead which he had only seen for the first time today when Anatoly pointed it out to him. It had been locked, of course, but Aleksei had imagined its inside, bodies stacked like lumps of meat, and numbered. Death in Stalingrad had been far nobler, he remembered, bodies burnt in the snow, not left to rot. Only when it was full did they load the bodies onto sledges and transport them to the forest, where they buried them, nameless, in ditches. 'The way you get through this, Aleksei, avoid ending up in the shed, is simple,' Anatoly had said to him. 'Keep your head down, don't cross any criminal, don't get ill, don't work any harder than you have to, and eat as much as you can.'

The real criminals were, of course, the authorities – the troika of the MVD, the MGB and the Soviet Procurator's Department – whom millions of comrades worked for, and millions more sustained. They were the policemen, the agents, the informers, the inspectors, the guards. The list went on. How could so many be complicit in this great deception of good governance, fair governance, decent governance, benign governance? Aleksei wondered, finally returning to his bunk for the night after bidding Mikhail good night. And yet perhaps this was what the Russian people required – strict social controls. They were unable to handle too much freedom, and beyond this did not believe in it.

Morning, and before Aleksei was marched off to work, he at last got his letter off to Natasha and Katya – he couldn't wait for them to receive it, to hear from him, to read him – and after this had to stand in the yard and listen to the neat black-haired camp commandant Petrov deliver a long litany of ideological drivel about the valour of hard work. Grisly and xenophobic, he represented an age-old Russian who clearly despised all the prisoners from the Caucasus and the Steppes, 'all black vermin' as far as he was concerned. Colonialism remained, it was clear to Aleksei, and the demands of Communism – which insisted that the people treat one another fairly, decently and equally – had little sway. Petrov was not much fonder of the prisoners from the former Nazi-occupied territories either – the Poles, Estonians, Lithuanians and Latvians. Special contempt was reserved for the Poles. He had obviously still not forgiven them for their short occupation of Moscow in 1610! Aleksei thought, smiling to himself. According to Anatoly, 'There was also an American here for a bit – the intellectuals wanted to know all about his life in the West – but Petrov was clearly concerned about the effect he was having on them, so he put the man in isolation and he died within a week.'

Aleksei looked up at the main watchtower, the highest in the camp. The bulk of the compound was open to view and, of course, fire from here. The Mongol was there, he held his rifle, wore a long sheepskin coat. 'The man is a sadist,' Mikhail warned him, 'driven by rage, and occasionally shoots a prisoner for sport.' This was obviously why Petrov tolerated him, in spite of his ethnicity. A sadist like him must be an asset in a place like this. 'The Mongol cannot help himself,' Mikhail explained, 'and always seems to feel better afterwards.'

'The vicious prick!' Anatoly grumbled. 'He'll get his comeuppance one day.'

It looked as though he might shoot someone this morning. Aleksei moved out of his range.

Petrov's sermon eventually came to an end, and Aleksei, Mikhail and the rest of the brigade were led off to the forest for the day under the watchful eye of Vadim, another cruel man. Short, muscular and only semi-literate, he wore a bear-fur coat even though it was summer, had permanently drunken eyes, and always held a machine gun close to his chest as if clutching the love of his life. Aleksei had begun to notice that if they failed to meet their work targets then Vadim liked to cut their rations, and today he seemed to be in particularly vicious spirits as he watched over them – Aleksei, Nikolai, Anatoly and Mikhail, and one other man, Viktor. He shook his head, clearly not happy with the output of one or all of them. Rafik spotted this and attempted to lessen his frustration by managing their work more closely. But no, it seemed that whatever he, their brigadier, did, Vadim the petty tyrant would not be satisfied. Ultimately he lost his cool and decided to single out Aleksei, shouting his number and insisting that he come over right away. 'Yes, you, K-891. Get over here!' he screamed, scowling at him. 'And the rest of you, get on with your fucking work!'

'Be careful,' Anatoly whispered as Aleksei laid down his axe and walked towards him.

'I haven't spoken to you yet,' Vadim said softly, as if trying to regain his composure, and it appeared he did not want anyone else to hear.

'No,' Aleksei replied.

'No...what!?'

'No...sir,' he answered, straining to call Vadim this, to show him any deference.

'You need to be working harder. And I don't want to have to remind you again.'

'Yes...sir,' he added reluctantly.

'D'you have anything else to tell me?' Vadim asked, and Aleksei knew right away what he was getting at.

'No, I don't.'

'You sure?'

'Yes.'

'There's nothing wrong with informing on others. It's your Soviet duty to.'

Aleksei said nothing. The last thing he wanted to do was become a stool pigeon, a grass.

Vadim continued, 'You know your family will suffer more if you don't.'

'I don't have one,' Aleksei replied.

'Don't lie to me,' he said flatly. 'And I'm not just talking about your mother.'

This quip implied he did know something about Aleksei.

'Your family…' Vadim persisted.

'What about them?'

'You do have one, don't you!?' he said. 'You can't lie to me.'

'Yes,' Aleksei answered reluctantly.

'Yes…what?'

'Yes…sir.'

'So how are your wife and daughter, then?'

'You…'

'What, K-891?'

Aleksei stopped himself.

Vadim continued, 'I won't get to them, but someone else will,' this prompting Aleksei to think of Vladimir Vladimirovich. 'And anyway, if I were you I'd forget about them. You're in here for a quarter, they'll forget about you soon enough, just wait and see,' and with these closing words Vadim smiled at him and said, 'You fail to show me sufficient respect again, and I'll put you to the bench. Now, off you go. Back to work!' He saw off Aleksei with a dismissive swipe of his hand. 'And your remaining rations for the day…they're halved.'

Vadim was forever eager to punish any man he could, be this through a ration reduction, beating or torture, and he always delighted in calling their number prior to administering punishment, his eyes gleaming with anticipation. Aleksei suspected he had failed in the NKVD and so had wound up here – and it was this failure that made him quite so malicious. He called no one by name: the prisoners had no self. Some had become slaves to him, either weak or broken men, running around after him, hoping that their obsequiousness would be rewarded with the occasional scrap of sausage. In no other line of work would Vadim have had men revering him. No, he would only have had men despising him, Aleksei concluded.

'Be careful,' Anatoly mumbled as Aleksei picked up his axe once more. 'Neither pride nor defiance goes a long way in here.'

'What's "to the bench"?' Aleksei asked.

'You're forced to sit on a pole suspended high in the air the whole day, the pole high enough that your feet don't touch the ground, with heavy boulders tied to your legs. By evening you're crippled, and can only make it back to camp on a stretcher.'

The work targets they were set were impossible to reach. However, this was deliberate. Aleksei remembered what Anatoly had told him a few days ago. 'During the war, we were made to work fourteen, sometimes sixteen hours a day,' he had said, 'some sentences indiscriminately extended to twenty-five, and we were given just one rest day a month.' They were not being worked to this extent, Aleksei realised, yet he had had just two rest days so far and had been here almost three weeks. Still, better this than simply being executed by firing squad or gas chamber, the authorities surely concluded. For at least this way they actually got something from their enemies.

'Most men are broken after the first month,' Anatoly said to Aleksei later on as they walked back to the camp, traipsing through thick mud, which squelched underfoot. 'The Yakuts fare better than most, these iron men of the north.'

'It seems they're prisoners for little more than their ethnicity.'

'Yep, sounds about right. But they're tough as hell. Mikhail reckons I must have some Yakut blood in me as I've lasted so long.'

'Yes, and let's hope I've got a little too,' Aleksei replied.

In the barracks this evening before bed one of Ivan Ivanovich's henchmen approached them as they sat and talked. Mikhail spotted him as he neared the bunk, whispering in Aleksei's ear, 'His name's Igor and he's the youngest.'

Nikolai was the first to speak up, confronting the young henchman immediately. 'We're not looking for any trouble,' he said. 'Please, just stay away.'

'I'm not looking for you, old man.'

'Well, then who are you looking for?'

'Him…the professor,' Igor replied, staring at Aleksei.

'Which one?' Nikolai asked. 'We're all educated men here, you see,' he added.

Ignoring this jibe, Igor answered, 'I'm looking at him.'

'What, Mikhail?' Nikolai asked.

'Are you blind? No, the history man,' he replied, pointing at Aleksei.

Well, he knows a bit about me, that's clear, Aleksei said to himself. 'Can I help you?' he asked Igor.

Nikolai interjected, 'No, he can't!'

'It's okay, Nikolai.'

'No, it's not,' he said. 'Why would you want to talk to him, this…' Nikolai continued, waving his arm disparagingly in Igor's direction though not looking at him.

'Nikolai, please…' Aleksei interjected.

'I'm not afraid to tell you what I think of you, young man,' Nikolai said, getting to his feet and addressing Igor.

'You're a thug and a coward, who dedicates his life to serving a murderer.'

'Listen, Old Believer…' Igor said.

However, Nikolai would not let him speak. 'I might be a believer, but I'm not an Old Believer. And do not speak of God. You have no right!'

Aleksei stood up and took Nikolai's arm, 'Nikolai, sit down.'

'Do what the professor says, old man,' Igor said.

Aleksei pulled his arm hard and pushed down on his shoulder, forcing Nikolai to sit. 'You don't intimidate me!' he concluded.

'Sorry, what do you want?' Aleksei asked Igor, taking a few steps away from Nikolai, trying to create some distance between the two of them.

'The old man… he's brave,' Igor said, pointing at Nikolai.

'Yes,' Aleksei replied.

'I have a gift from Ivan Ivanovich,' he said, handing Aleksei a generous helping of tobacco.

'Oh right…'

'You're not going to accept that, are you!?' Nikolai butted in again.

'Nikolai, please, this is none of your business,' Aleksei said firmly. 'Thank you, that's kind,' he replied to Igor, accepting the gift. 'Please, pass on my thanks.'

'I will,' Igor answered, nodding his head, then turned and walked slowly back to the other side of the barracks.

'I'm disappointed in you,' Nikolai said, wasting no time.

'Come on, give him a break,' Mikhail interjected.

'You would say that, wouldn't you? You have a perverse admiration for them.'

'It's not "admiration".'

'Well, you know what I mean.'

'What makes you holier than thou?' Mikhail quipped.

'Oh come on, Ivan Ivanovich isn't some small-time crook. He's a thief-in-law, he's utterly ruthless.'

'And the system we live under isn't!?'

'It might be wrong, but it isn't criminal.'

'You sure about that?' Aleksei asked Nikolai.

'So what are you and Mikhail saying, then? That it's better to be a criminal than a Communist!'

'Not quite,' Mikhail replied.

'What then?'

'Let's just leave it, okay,' Aleksei appealed to Nikolai.

'You know, I don't understand you sometimes,' he said, full of frustration, huffing and sighing. Nikolai turned his back on them, and laid down on his bunk as if in a sulk.

'Why the gift, anyway?' Mikhail enquired. 'Perhaps word got back to him how you stood up to Vadim,' he speculated.

'Hardly,' Aleksei replied.

'Or maybe he just wants to talk history with you!' Mikhail quipped, leaving Aleksei to ponder quite why the notorious thief-in-law had shown an interest in him.

THE FIFTH KILL
17ᵀᴴ NOVEMBER 1953
IRKUTSK
(1331ᴋᴍ SOUTHEAST OF TOMSK)

So here Aleksei was, in Irkutsk, about to kill the penultimate man on Ivan Ivanovich's list, Pavel Maximilianovich Kalegaev. The journey here had taken too long, hindered first by internal travel controls which meant he had to wait for Yakov to produce more papers, then by faulty trains. He had a little over two months to kill the last two men on Ivan Ivanovich's list, after which he could finally devote himself to getting his revenge on Vladimir Vladimirovich. What he would do after this he did not know.

Kalegaev had been one of the leading figures in the Katyn Massacre, an obvious candidate to lead this mass murder of Polish nationals in light of his pathological hatred of Poland and her people. This deep-seated contempt sprung from his Polish stepfather, a drunk who'd beaten his mother black and blue throughout his childhood. The youngest of the men on the list, just thirty-eight years old (Kalegaev had been a young man when he carried out the massacre), Ivan Ivanovich held special scorn for him as he had killed a dear friend of his, Oskar Bielski, a man who'd saved his life not once but twice: he had met the Pole during his first incarceration in Rostov. A leading Communist in the region, what made Kalegaev even worse was his narcissism. Tall, powerful and handsome, and an ex-heavyweight wrestling champion, he had married a local beauty queen whom he smugly called his 'princess', and himself her 'prince'. The proud Communist was an aspiring royal. Prince Pavel and his beautiful pampered blonde young wife lived in an enormous apartment in the centre of Irkutsk and were the talk of the town, the city's golden couple, and he its most powerful son.

Aleksei had little idea how he'd kill him. Kalegaev was always with somebody, be this his adoring princess or his many sycophantic admirers. The best time to get to him was at night, as it always was, yet even this was problematic, Aleksei realised, as he lived in the very centre of the city, which was never as quiet as it needed to be. Kalegaev went every morning to the gymnasium, where he trained with local wrestlers. Aleksei had been watching him for six days in a row now, sitting discreetly at the back of a small spectators' gallery. In his tight-fitting red wrestling singlet, the hammer and sickle adorned brazenly across his broad chest, Kalegaev would strut, in front of the large mirror there, like an obscenely proud giant male peacock in the midst of a mating ritual, eager to make clear to all other males present that he was utterly dominant – that there could be no challenge to his virility, his potency, his throne. This arrogance reminded Aleksei of his nemesis, Vladimir Vladimirovich. Those men who did challenge Kalegaev to wrestle he made short shrift of, and afterwards, when victorious, stood in front of the mirror smirking at, and flirting with, his reflection – yes, the man was indeed in love with himself. And today was no exception as another challenger stepped forward and Kalegaev challenged him.

However, there seemed to be something wrong with Kalegaev today. He did not possess his usual self-control and restraint when fighting a lesser man. Instead he was angry and reckless, the heavyweight Kalegaev charging over to his middleweight opponent and rather than beginning with an introductory grapple simply picked him up and hurled him violently to the floor with a throw of such force that he lay motionless and unconscious for a number of minutes – all onlookers fearing that Kalegaev had killed him – until he finally stirred and regained consciousness.

Kalegaev, the victor, was unrepentant, and stormed around the mat demanding another challenger, shouting that all of them were 'Cowardly motherfuckers!'

The defeated smaller man was helped to his feet and led away, all the assembled men – past challengers and would-be challengers – promptly leaving also, their disapproval of Kalegaev clear enough. He clearly could not contain himself, maintain that princely cool all the time, Aleksei thought, slowly getting to his feet.

'You there!' Aleksei suddenly heard these words behind him.

He looked up to see Kalegaev marching towards him. 'Who are you? Look at me!' the big man demanded.

But Aleksei did not want to – he had to maintain his anonymity – and so, head down, started heading for the exit. He heard the sound of scampering feet, the barefoot Kalegaev sprinting on the wooden gymnasium floor towards him.

'Don't run away from me!' he shouted.

The hunter was now being hunted. What should he do? This had not happened to him before. Think, Aleksei urged himself, think.

It was just he and Kalegaev here. The other men would not return, not after what Kalegaev had done. Perhaps this was the most opportune time to kill him after all, Aleksei considered, swinging round to confront him. It would also give him more time to assassinate the last man, Valuev.

Aleksei was not armed, carrying neither his guns nor his knife. For he had not anticipated killing today. He'd have to do it with his bare hands.

Kalegaev was too big to attempt to grapple with, Aleksei swiftly concluded, not least because he was a highly accomplished wrestler. In fact, he was sure that Kalegaev would attack him with a chokehold or nelson, and Aleksei immediately realised that his best chance of taking him down was a powerful punch to the heart, which would hopefully stun him, enabling Aleksei to get him against the wall and then employ a swift, hard, cold-cock punch to his face, which would likely drill the back of his head against the concrete.

'Who the fuck are you!?' Kalegaev demanded as he neared him, just five metres away from him.

'Ivan Ivanovich sent me. Look at me,' Aleksei said, looking hard into Kalegaev's eyes as he stopped dead in his tracks at the very mention of the thief-in-law's name.

This would be Aleksei's only opportunity. He had to attack first.

'What does the great thief-in-law want from me now?' Kalegaev asked.

'Your life,' Aleksei said, and in one swift motion was upon Kalegaev, hitting him firmly in the heart, then slamming him against the wall, after which he punched him hard and fast, just once, in the face, his skull smacking against the wall.

Aleksei watched the big man's knees give way and his whole body slump to the floor.

His body was motionless, and Aleksei stared at the blood which slowly seeped from the back of his head.

Aleksei knelt down and reached for Kalegaev's windpipe in order to ascertain whether or not he was still breathing.

He was dead.

Aleksei had to get out of here. For all it took was for one of the formerly assembled men to return.

He dragged Kalegaev behind the wall of the spectator gallery. This would buy him more time, he calculated, likely postponing the discovery of the dead body.

Then Aleksei took a deep breath and walked slowly out of the gymnasium.

No sign of Katya, he thought, as he made his way back to his hotel, that is until she suddenly appeared again, walking out in front him as he stood waiting to cross the main road. But before she even had time to speak, to confront him again with what he'd done, Aleksei dismissed her brusquely with the words, 'Katya, don't say anything, please.'

He could feel the sin in his heart now, no longer needed to be told to look for it. He carried it with him, and it became ever more painful.

Before he left and took the long train back to Moscow he wanted to go to Baikal, to the spot where he had proposed to Natasha. He would make time for this, as it would cost him just one day. Though she was no longer a part of his life, he still cherished this particular memory of her, in spite of what she had done to him, because it possessed such warmth, such happiness. How beautiful she had looked that day in her white dress and red cardigan, Aleksei recalled. He had been so overwhelmed by her he could not speak.

Was Koba's malign and gloomy presence really fading? Aleksei wondered. The system remained cruel and corrupt as its new leaders continued to battle for control. Khrushchev and Zhukov might have got rid of the sadist Beria, yet this hardly pointed the way to a new era of benign and compassionate governance. For Comrade Khrushchev had helped the monster with his purges! Aleksei could already see what would likely happen. The people needed to hear an apology for the terrible abuses of the last thirty years, and were this apology to be given then the blame would be planted firmly at Koba's feet, not least because he was unable to respond to the charges. Yes, he was the perfect scapegoat because he was dead, and the new leadership would use that for all it was worth. He, Comrade Stalin, might have been awful, but we are not. We will care for you. We will look after you. Trust us! This is what they'll say, Aleksei speculated. However, the people were not as naïve, as ignorant, as uninformed as their rulers thought they were. They all knew what a monster Koba really was, Aleksei thought, that he had turned Russia into one vast prison complex. The majority of them just had not said anything, because they were too damn afraid to.

He took the bus to the west shore, just sixty kilometres away, driving through thick forest before being struck by the dazzling blue of the lake, this blue which seemed to articulate the divine. When would amnesty be granted to the most serious political prisoners, the twenty-fivers like him? He thought of Mikhail, Anatoly and Yuri. What of them, then? And even if this final reprieve were granted it would be too late for so many, who had already suffered irreparable emotional damage and would never be able to return to their former lives. Off the bus, not far from Listvyanka, Aleksei walked past a small fish market selling omul, this fish unique to Baikal, then kept on heading west towards the village of Baranchiki. It was exactly as it had been. It seemed that man was yet to ravage this place as he had so many others. Aleksei knelt down and drank from the lake, and after this carried on towards the spot, which he recalled was marked, first, by a vast pine tree, and second, by a tall mountain peak which loomed over it like a benevolent spirit. Perhaps he should end the mission, he asked, not kill the sixth man on the list? For maybe his country could become good now. But no, how could it, when it was still governed by this mad ideology, enforced by a bunch of authoritarians serving a totalitarian regime.

Aleksei stood on the shore and looked out over the lake, which due to its immense size appeared more like the sea. It was here, yes, in this very spot that he had asked her. He closed his weary eyes, then opened them. She, Natasha, stood before him, tall and graceful, the speck of yellow in her blue-grey eyes shining in the bright light of the afternoon sun. He was transfixed by her stare, which drew him in, offering a sense of serenity that had been absent for too long. He felt no anger towards her, no sense of betrayal, rather just love. She reached out and touched his face, her long slender fingers caressing his cheeks, as if exploring them for the first time. Perhaps he appeared to her as a dream, and so she needed to be sure that he existed, that he, Aleksei, did stand before her. Did she love him again as he loved her? Was she no longer with Vladimir Vladimirovich? She looked at him with such devotion that he had to look away, could not bear it, because he knew she was not really there, that she was nothing more than an appearance to his troubled mind. His head slouched to the ground, he felt an excruciating sadness, a sickness of sorrow. Aleksei began to cry, then howl...

FOUR YEARS, THREE MONTHS, TWO WEEKS EARLIER

20TH AUGUST 1949

BUTUGYCHAG, KOLYMA

The work was getting harder, and this evening when he was fed Aleksei longed for a good piece of bread, this food that was so sacred to all Russians. He was tired of the black, wet, heavy stodge he was given every day, and yet he should be grateful that he was at least being fed, he thought. 'During the peak years of the war, '42–43, sometimes prisoners were not fed for days, and many died of starvation,' Anatoly had told him. While he ate Aleksei overheard one man in his brigade – he did not know his name – insisting that 'Comrade Stalin will realise the authorities have made a terrible mistake' and free him. His wife 'has written to Him, our "Great Leader". He will read her petition, it is only a matter of time, and order my release,' he maintained.

This prompted Aleksei to think of Natasha. Had she received his letter? Had she written back? It was far too soon to expect a reply, he knew this. He had to be patient. Though how he longed to hear from her! He recalled what Anatoly had said to him this time yesterday in the mess hall, urging him to stop thinking about Natasha. He'd advised, 'The sooner you get used to being without her, the less you will suffer. Take it from me!' Should he stop thinking about her? Aleksei asked. But no, he could not, because he loved her. If only there were some way he could find out about her, at least have confirmation that she was alive and well, that Katya was alive and well. He finished eating. How would he survive the winter with so little food? he wondered. He continued to dread its arrival. Then his attention returned to the man in his brigade whose wife had written to Koba.

'But what if your wife's letter has been intercepted by Beria,' another man butted in, 'or by some other sadist? What then!?'

Aleksei smiled at this, not because he was unsympathetic, rather because this statement seemed to imply that Stalin was not a sadist and that if only he read the letter personally justice and goodness would prevail. He almost had a better chance finding grace with Beria than with Koba. However, this man was nevertheless brave to have said what he just had. For just as on the outside there were informers everywhere, everyone spying on everyone else, the air thick with denunciations and counter-denunciations. You could not be anti-Soviet on the inside either. Any criticism of the way things were was not tolerated. Even reality was denied, Aleksei thought. Good men became bad in order to survive – they informed, cooperated, collaborated. And yet this was hardly surprising. For as a 'trustie', life was much easier. Better to be a foreman, a norm-setter, a cook, a dishwasher, a clerk, an orderly than be consigned to hard labour, felling timber or working in the mines.

Aleksei was exhausted tonight, yet was not permitted to sleep: the criminals in the barracks made a lot of noise as they played cards by the light of the smoky kerosene lamp. They played this game precisely because it was forbidden, and placed bets on different hands in order to win bread, tobacco, clothes and shoes. Igor, however, was more interested in Aleksei, and approached him once more, much to Nikolai's annoyance and suspicion. Sitting down on Aleksei's bunk, the two men immediately hit it off and set about discussing many things, though it seemed Igor was most interested in history. Perhaps Mikhail had been right after all! Aleksei mused. Igor revealed a particular fascination with the age-old relationship between Russians and Tartars, and Aleksei enjoyed recalling the lectures he'd given at Moscow State about the Mongol invaders – the Golden Horde – who ruled all of Asia until the latter part of the fourteenth century. Igor seemed to relish hearing him expound on this period, and was quick to seize on Aleksei's analysis as reason for 'Stalin's distrust of all things Tartar.'

'Yes, thank God for Grand Prince Dmitry,' Aleksei remarked sarcastically, 'and his victory at Kulikovo Pole. For this was the Russians' first step towards liberation from the Tartars, which they finally achieved a century later. Perhaps we must blame Ivan III for this rampant Russian nationalism. Yet it was his brutal successor, Ivan IV, who declared himself the "Tsar of all the Russians".'

'You'll get on with the boss, that's for sure,' Igor said smiling. 'He shares your love of history and is always complaining that he's no one to talk to who's read as much as he has.'

Vasily had just lost a hand and was furious, since he'd bet his boots. He pointed to a man in another bunk close by and declared, 'Let's go again. I bet his boots.'

The man did not challenge him. For he knew that if one of Ivan Ivanovich's men needed to bet with someone else's belongings, then that was what he would do. Were he to challenge him, he would most likely be killed.

They played the next hand, and this time Vasily won.

Then he won again … and again.

His opponent, a smaller man with a tattoo of Koba on his chest, had lost just about everything. He sat there in no more than his underwear.

However, Vasily wanted revenge and would stop at nothing until he had got the ultimate prize.

There was quiet, before he suddenly banged his hand on the floor and declared, 'I want one of your fingers!'

With this pronouncement Igor immediately got to his feet, excused himself, and returned to his side of the barracks.

Vasily's opponent did nothing at first, then reluctantly nodded his head.

The whole barracks were silent as the subsequent hand was played out.

It was not clear which of them had the stronger hand. Their faces gave nothing away.

Vasily was dealt his last card...

Then the other man...

And Aleksei watched the latter's head sink as he saw what his card was.

'Yes!' Vasily shouted, laying his winning hand down, then held up his left hand, which had a missing finger, and, pointing to it, his gold teeth flashing, said determinedly, 'Let me take back what I lost!'

Aleksei could not bear to watch, yet still had listen to the screams of Vasily's opponent as his finger was hacked off with a piece of sharp wire.

There was a brutal gamesmanship at work in this place.

When winter did finally come, its arrival was abrupt and violent. Aleksei had been right to fear it. This morning it was ten degrees below zero. 'But this is nothing, it will get colder still. Far colder, in fact,' Anatoly warned Aleksei, rubbing his cheeks with his palms and taking short rapid breaths through pouted lips.

'You sure about that?'

'Yes, I'm sure.'

'Well, that's something to look forward to,' Aleksei quipped.

'Yes,' Anatoly replied wryly.

One of his boots had a hole in it. Aleksei had wrapped it in birch bark yesterday, on Mikhail's advice, in an attempt to stop it leaking, but still snow and damp had got through. It would help if he had another pair of warm foot-cloths, he thought. The foot was becoming infected – it looked like Aleksei had something akin to trench foot. He prayed he did not get frostbite.

Still nothing from Natasha. Why did she not write? Why!? How could he get word of her? he fretted.

He looked to Anatoly and Mikhail as they lined up after breakfast to be counted. Anatoly had a rag tied around his face while Mikhail had double-fastened his jacket with string. Both men knew the secrets of keeping warm, it seemed. They jumped up and down on the spot, swinging their arms from side to side and slapping their chest and thighs. It was plainly an imperative to keep moving now it was cold, a cold that penetrated their skin, and which, in a month or so, would penetrate their bones too.

Today they worked in an early-winter blizzard, a *purga* blizzard, which whirled and whipped and howled. It tore right through them, snow sticking to their faces, cheeks, eyes and nose, making their breathing difficult. The axe seemed heavier, Aleksei struggled to swing it, and when it hit the trunk it felt like stone not wood that he was cutting. Soon he was knee-deep in snow, but still had to work. The work norm had to be met.

All Aleksei thought of the whole day was dinner, the soup they would be fed – he longed for it, its warmth. He wore the winter clothes they had given him when he first arrived, the felt hat with ear flaps and the fleece-lined mittens, yet these were inadequate.

When the blizzard let up, he looked out of the forest past the great arches of pine and birch at the barren landscape, beyond the trails of barbed wire, and glimpsed a little beauty – a sea of never-ending whiteness, the snow a perfect white, so white.

The one advantage of winter: workdays were shorter. As they walked back to the camp, he shivered. This had been the coldest day yet. He needed that soup inside him as soon as possible.

'Now it's winter make sure you dunk your bread in the soup before you eat it, you'll feel fuller this way,' Anatoly said to Aleksei as he took his first mouthful.

'And make sure you eat quickly, otherwise it'll freeze over,' Mikhail added, wolfing down his portion, soup dribbling from the sides of his mouth and smearing his chin, which he promptly mopped up with a piece of bread and stuffed in his mouth.

This was difficult – since being here Aleksei had learned to eat slowly, to chew bread thoroughly, as this way he felt he had eaten more.

'Also, make sure your lips don't touch any part of your bowl,' Anatoly advised. 'Because you've got a small metal one, they'll stick to it, it's so damn cold.'

'Any more advice, gentlemen? If I have to listen to one more recommendation I might die of hunger!' Aleksei quipped.

'For your own good, Aleksei, your own good,' Anatoly insisted.

'I know, I know,' he replied, patting his friend's forearm and smiling warmly.

As the weeks dragged on Aleksei grew tired of the snow, the snow. There was so much of it, and it kept on falling. Maybe he would ultimately vanish in it, evanesce.

It was dark all the time. When he left for work, it was dark; when he returned, dark. The sun did not rise until half past ten and set at half past two. Just four hours of light. The lack of it induced a kind of madness in him, forcing him inward, towards endless reflection, thinking becoming his enemy, until he was lost in the labyrinth complexity of his mind. The dark, it weighed heavy on his soul.

Every day Aleksei worked now his body was in great pain. And yet his mind was worse: it reeled and screamed. He was plagued by thoughts of injustice. What was my crime!? I do not deserve this! What they are doing to me is wrong. Natasha did receive the letter but has chosen not to reply because she no longer loves me. Perhaps she has denounced me. No, maybe she did not receive it. Are she and Katya dead? And yet such thinking was fruitless, and he started to wonder for how long he could continue to bear such inner turmoil. But why should he have expected reason amidst all this madness. Perhaps this camp was indeed the natural order of things, Aleksei speculated.

He gained some respite from the vicious whirl of his thoughts when he was conscious of his breath as he sucked in the cool, still air. He felt almost drunk on it. But this feeling never lasted long. Mikhail's humour, Anatoly's pragmatism, Nikolai's spirituality – all were vital to him, Aleksei realised. He also continued to enjoy visits from Igor, who had proved himself an avid student of history. The practical benefits of this relationship were clear enough, messages passed between different criminals not to steal from, curse at or harm Aleksei and his small band of men, though the morally righteous Nikolai was hardly grateful for this protection despite Aleksei's continued assurances that he would not get too close to the young criminal, always keeping him at a distance. Rumours, however, had begun to circulate that Ivan Ivanovich himself was interested in speaking with Aleksei, and though he was worried about what he might be getting himself into, Aleksei remained intensely curious, not least because the thief-in-law represented perhaps his best hope of finding out about Natasha and Katya.

Vadim was particularly noxious today: he was gaining increasing pleasure from watching the prisoners work through the bitter winter months as they heaved and retched through exhaustion. This afternoon he sat slovenly on his chair, patting his portly belly as he ate sausage and cheese. For he knew they found it almost excruciating to watch another man eat, especially food such as this that they had not tasted for so long. His laziness and greed made him even wickeder, Aleksei thought. He usually tormented the emotionally vulnerable, and today was no exception. He had singled out Danila, a young man no more than twenty or twenty-one, slight of frame, a little effeminate and profoundly shy, who worked next to Aleksei, Nikolai and the others. Vadim goaded him from his chair, 'Get on with it, you queer!'

Nikolai was kind to Danila, and the last few evenings had encouraged him to join the rest of them in the barracks before bed. Aleksei's dear friend Nikolai, he was very perceptive, and knew that the young man was becoming increasingly isolated.

'You weak fucker!' Vadim continued.

Nikolai went to say something, to defend Danila. However, Aleksei quickly put his hand over his mouth, urging him to be quiet.

'If you don't fell four more trees in the next ten minutes,' Vadim went on, 'then I'm going to have you put in the cooler.'

'He can't handle this,' Nikolai muttered urgently to Aleksei.

The target he had set the young man was almost impossible, only the very best lumberjack could reach it, and yet this was surely the point. Though they were cutting just birch, Vadim knew the young man was neither strong nor quick enough. But still he tried, exploding into a frenzy of work.

At first, Danila swung the axe fast and frequently, and a few of them wondered whether he might just do it. Vadim kept a close eye on his watch, calling out each minute that went by. 'Two!' he announced, as the first tree fell to the ground.

'He's on target,' Nikolai said excitedly.

However, then his work rate started to slow, his breathing became heavier.

The minutes went by, and they found it ever more difficult to watch.

'Six!' Vadim shouted as the second tree fell.

'It can't have been this long,' Nikolai mumbled. 'Oh God, please help him…' he continued, realising this one had taken him twice as long.

Danila's legs began to wobble, as did his arms, each swing of the axe becoming more awkward and pained.

'Eight!' Vadim pronounced smugly, sure now that he would fail.

He could no longer lift the axe.

They heard Danila mumble, 'I can't…I can't…'

'Yes you can,' Nikolai called out, urging him on.

He managed to swing it again, though only a few times.

'Nine!' Vadim declared.

Then, turning to Nikolai, Danila looked at him blankly, put his left wrist and palm flat against the trunk and, summoning one last morsel of energy, swung the axe with his right hand, bringing it down on his wrist.

Everyone was silent as his left hand fell to the ground with a dull thud.

'Oh God, no!' Nikolai uttered.

Anything to avoid isolation, Aleksei concluded.

The barracks were quiet tonight, everyone in sombre mood, even, it seemed, the criminals. Aleksei lay on his bunk and thought of Danila in the sanatorium. How was he? he wondered. His thoughts, however, were interrupted by the arrival of Igor, who, placing his left hand on the bunk right in front of Aleksei's eye line, asked, 'How are you, Professor?'

'Okay,' Aleksei replied wearily, staring at the cross the young thief had tattooed on his left ring finger. 'Why did you get this?' he enquired.

'Like Jesus I've been oppressed and sentenced by the authorities,' Igor answered soberly, his explanation, even though melodramatic and inappropriate, sounding almost poetic. 'And what about your mark?' he continued, pointing with his right index finger at the scar on Aleksei's throat, this mark which suggested he was more than a *muzhik*, an ordinary guy.

'No, it doesn't point to a criminal past, I can assure you,' Aleksei answered.

'You sure about that?' Igor pressed him.

'Yes, I'm sure. Like my limp, I got it in the war.'

'What's on your mind?' Igor asked. 'The kid?' he continued, referring to Danila.

'Yes, and my wife and child,' Aleksei replied. 'I'm desperate now to know they're okay.'

'The boss might be able to help you here,' Igor said.

'I was hoping you'd say that.'

With these small words of hope, Igor wished Aleksei a good night's rest and returned to Ivan Ivanovich.

Left on his own Aleksei's mind moved without hesitation to Natasha, as it always did before sleep. How he longed to see her: her blue-grey eyes – each one containing a speck of yellow, so striking – which at times looked like they were either lost in a dream or in search of the divine; her light-brown hair, brushed and clipped behind her ears, giving her high cheekbones even more prominence; the grace of her long slender legs, these beautiful delicate limbs; the sway of her hips and buttocks when she walked, this gentle movement always mesmerising him; her soft, pale complexion, the few pockmarks on her face seeming to, if anything, emphasise her beauty even more; and those lips...those lips, small and exquisite. He used to love watching her in the morning as he lay in bed. She would stand naked over the sink in the bathroom and wash her face and comb her hair. He could watch her do this all day. It had never bored him.

6ᵀᴴ DECEMBER 1953
LAKE BAIKAL
(4340ᴋᴍ SOUTHEAST OF MOSCOW)

'**D**on't cry, please don't cry,' Natasha whispered over and over in his ear, continuing to caress his cheeks as he wept uncontrollably into her hands.

Could this really be her, his Natasha, after all this time? Aleksei asked. He had to be dreaming, surely. He would wake at any moment and find himself no longer here, by the shore with his long-lost wife, but in another hotel room on his own.

'I can't believe it's you,' he sniffed through spit and tears, still looking down at the snowy, pebbly ground beneath him. 'Look at me, will you,' he said, choosing to indulge his illusion – yes, Aleksei was sure it was just this, it had to be! – revel in this dreamscape, which offered such happiness.

Aleksei lifted his head slowly and she looked once more into his gentle, discerning and loving green eyes, then put her open palms to his broad chest, clasped either shoulder, and placed her feet squarely on his, encouraging him to walk with her balanced precariously on top, as she used to when feeling playful, and he did this, took her wrists in his hands and walked with her, taking a few clumsy steps forwards until she was leaning not against the bedroom wall as she used to, but rather against the trunk of the vast pine tree, and opening and closing his eyes at this moment he realised that he was awake, that this wasn't an apparition in his mind and that Natasha was here with him.

Natasha held him close, embraced him, did not want to let go. The feel of her body against his – he'd forgotten how she felt, how she held him – and feeling her pressed up against him he wished, despite her betrayal, they could stay like this for eternity, that this moment be frozen in time. And yet what of her betrayal? Aleksei wondered. Why was she here in Irkutsk and not with him, the bastard, in Moscow? They stood and held one another for a number of minutes, neither of them speaking, just savouring each other's touch in the cool winter air.

'Where have you been?' she asked gently, at last breaking the silence, looking into Aleksei's eyes.

He didn't answer, looked to the floor.

'Aleksei, please look at me.'

He lifted his head slowly.

'Where have you been?' he asked her now, accusingly.

And it was she who now looked to the floor.

Aleksei sensed that her reticence, though a reflection of her guilt, was also present because there was simply too much to say – for he felt the very same – and before he knew it she was kissing him, this woman who had wronged him and broken his heart, her tongue touching his, and then she reached for his fly, unbuttoned it.

'What the hell are you doing!?' he uttered, disgusted by her, pushing her away, and yet she ignored his rejection, instead turned him round until his back, rather than hers, was against the trunk, then pushed him downwards, pulling at his trousers and underwear, forcing them down around his ankles while at the same time removing her tights and knickers and hoisting her dress up. When his buttocks touched the floor and nestled into a thick bed of pine needles, she spat into her hand, grabbed his penis and squatted down hard, forcing him inside her. And Aleksei did not resist.

It was she, Natasha, who started to cry at this moment as she straddled Aleksei, holding his head to her chest, pushing her torso down hard, wanting to feel all of him, it seemed, and he came quickly, almost right away, then went to lift her off him, but she held him there, keeping him inside her until he became hard again, and this time she moved slowly on top of him, and still weeping she built herself to an orgasm, and only when she came did her tears at last subside.

Natasha rolled off him and lay down, her head in his lap, then stared up at the branches above, these long beams spiked with thousands upon thousands of green needles, then sniffed the cool air, their scent so rich. Aleksei looked at her, struggling to understand what had just happened between them. He suddenly felt repulsed by Natasha, this slut who had betrayed him. 'I saw you in Moscow…I…' Aleksei insisted anxiously, breathlessly.

'Sorry…?' she enquired.

'I saw you, Natasha.'

'What are you trying to say, Aleksei?' she asked.

'I saw you!' he bellowed, pushing her off his lap and jumping to his feet, then glaring down at her, this woman who had fucked that bastard, betrayed him, driven him to kill.

'What d'you mean you saw me? When?'

'When I first got out.'

'Where?' she asked, shaken, it appeared, not just by the extent of his anger but also by his answer to her last question.

'Outside our apartment.'

'And? That's where I was living. What are you talking about, Aleksei?'

'That's where you were with…'

She interjected, 'Why didn't you come to me then, when you saw me? Why!?' It was she who had anger in her voice now.

'I…' Aleksei struggled to speak, sensing that perhaps all had not been as it had seemed on that fateful day in Moscow when he first returned after the years of hell he'd endured.

'Why, Aleksei!?'

'You were with…'

'With?'

'Him!' he finished off.

She couldn't deny it any more, Aleksei thought. Yes, he was right. Yes, he had been justified. The bitch.

However, Natasha surprised him again, getting to her feet and facing him. 'You don't understand, I…'

'How could you!?' he interrupted, his brow creasing heavily as if holding back a wealth of pain that was on the verge of exploding out of him. He wanted to hit her.

'How could I?' she asked.

'Yes,' he replied, unable to look at her.

'You mean, how could I demean myself with such a man?'

'Yes.'

'And with him of all men?'

'Yes!' he shouted.

'I don't know, Aleksei,' she muttered. 'Maybe because I thought it might help you, might protect Katya, might…'

'Help me!?' he yelled. 'By fucking him!'

'Let me finish, Aleksei, please. He made it almost impossible for me to resist.'

'What did he do? Dress up nice…tie you up, huh!? Tell me!' he shouted, angry that she had the gall to suggest what she just had.

'He did what you'd expect a man like him to do. He made sure he had me, then offered me just a little hope.'

'What d'you mean?'

'If I stayed with him he'd see if he could secure your early release, he'd not throw Katya into state care, he'd not…'

'He did?' Aleksei asked, his voice all of a sudden softening.

'Yes, but then I also went along with him to save myself.'

'He threatened to send you away as well?'

'Yes, and I'm ashamed how I reacted to this. You see, this final intimidation scared me more than anything else, I…' and Natasha started to well up, turned away from him.

Aleksei didn't say anything. Her honesty here about her own cowardice pointed to some truth, he knew this. What choice had she really had!? he asked. A man like Vladimir Vladimirovich Primakov didn't give you choices. He simply made you do things, things he wanted. Had Aleksei misjudged Natasha? Had she actually betrayed him? Or had she simply been given no choice but to?

She continued, 'I was so selfish, weak, I…'

She could not speak any more, just cried.

He left her standing there, walking slowly off down the road.

7TH JANUARY 1951
BUTUGYCHAG, KOLYMA

Over a year on and it was Christmas Day according to the Julian calendar, and nature here in Kolyma had become malevolent. Aleksei longed for the sun, a bit of warmth. The sky was an impenetrable grey, the sun plainly not welcome. He felt like if he did not see it soon, he might go mad. For he had had enough of the dark. Yet winter seemed to last forever, and he was not even permitted to cry: it was too cold for tears.

Nothing from Natasha. Aleksei had given up waiting, given up speculating what might have happened to her and Katya. He had hoped that, after what Igor had said, Ivan Ivanovich might help. But no. Nothing.

None of them resisted the brutal regime now: they simply cast their heads down and worked out each day. This was perhaps not dissimilar from how they were much of the time before, Aleksei thought, before they were incarcerated, many of them living in a trance, a trance of belief in a system that they still thought could be decent and fair. Perhaps the Russian man was predisposed to live under strong authority and thus accepted the terrible abuses of a totalitarian system. Perhaps he believed that his ability to endure it, his suffering – sometimes he seemed actively to pursue it – would provide him with salvation. But also, convinced of Mother Russia's great destiny as the dominant global power – she needed to be mighty and authoritative! – he was willing to suffer on her behalf. Still, it was a wonder how they kept going, Aleksei pondered. It had to be the Russian in them. For without this, they would surely have given in. This Russianness, this unique quality of endurance, was what had ultimately defeated Hitler. The Russians had not conquered, so much as outlasted, him.

Aleksei returned at the end of each day weak and exhausted, cold and hungry. In fact, this had become his perpetual state. It was as if he would never again be strong and energetic, warm and well fed. He was becoming little more than an animal, he felt, yet he did not possess an animal's vigour, an animal's will to live. He worried he might die from one of the diseases that were rampant here – tuberculosis or pneumonia. Yet exhaustion, or rather despair, was the greatest killer. Men were broken, got to the end point where they had just had enough. And if they then had to wait for the final departing of their bodies, suicide became irresistible. Last week a man had not even needed a rope: he'd just hanged himself in the fork of a tree, Aleksei recalled. Nikolai had insisted they hold a service for the poor man. In the barracks that night, Nikolai had put a sheet over his shoulders – assuming the garb of a priest – lit a candle and chanted prayers for the dead man. A number of them had wept.

Sleep was vital, as was warmth. In the barracks Aleksei was now nearer the fire, the privilege of survival, and though the smell was still rank – a heady mix of the slop bucket, kerosene and dirty clothes – he was so shattered by the end of each day that nothing stopped him from sleeping, not even the howling and barking of the dogs in the cold of night, these poor creatures that encircled the camp, consigned to living on chains.

This morning, as they lined up to be inspected, Igor approached and handed Aleksei a note. The Mongol spotted this.

Aleksei immediately looked to Igor, who said coolly, 'Don't worry, he won't punish us. He knows the note is from Ivan Ivanovich.' He then walked away.

Aleksei opened and read it. Ivan Ivanovich wanted to see him this evening.

At last, he thought.

'It's a damn freak show!' Nikolai quipped.

'What are you talking about?' Mikhail asked.

'The notorious thief-in-law wants a meeting with the history professor.'

'That's a bit harsh, Nikolai,' Yuri cut in.

'Is it? Come on, Yuri, Aleksei's no more than a novelty, a curiosity for him. He wants to know how it is that a man like Aleksei gets by in here.'

Aleksei suspected that he, Ivan Ivanovich, knew already. He was most likely as angry with the system as Aleksei was, knew full well how anger could sustain a man through terrible hardship.

Nikolai continued, 'But he'll grow tired of you soon enough,' and he addressed Aleksei now, 'and then will simply spit you out.'

Aleksei answered, 'I don't care, as long as I can find out about…'

'Don't use him for this!' Nikolai demanded, not letting his friend finish his sentence.

'You almost sound jealous!?' Mikhail retorted. 'And why not?'

'Don't ridicule me,' Nikolai shot back. 'And why not… because then you'll be indebted to him, and you don't want to be indebted to a man like Ivan Ivanovich Bessonov.'

'This is for me to decide, Nikolai, not you,' Aleksei replied resolutely.

The rest of the day Aleksei could barely think about anything else, and Mikhail confessed he was almost excited for him, while Nikolai was furious and refused to speak to him. Aleksei wondered how Ivan Ivanovich would be face-to-face, quite how menacing.

When evening came it was Igor who summoned him to meet the thief-in-law, raising his hand from across the barracks.

Aleksei got to his feet and walked slowly over, and there was a hush of expectancy around the barracks as he, a political, entered Ivan Ivanovich's inner circle, walking past, first, small-time crooks, then highwaymen, after this hardened criminals, and lastly his five henchmen, Vasily scowling at him. Igor pulled back the sheet which hung across the bunk in front of the single iron bed, and Aleksei found himself standing in front of a seated Ivan Ivanovich.

The thief-in-law did not wear a shirt or vest but was bare-chested, his upper body broad and powerful, the stars standing proudly on either pectoral muscle. At first he stared intensely at Aleksei, the scarring on his face even more striking close up, as were his blue eyes. Next he rubbed his thick brown stubble thoughtfully and stretched his neck, swooping it in a circle clockwise then anti-clockwise, and after this rolling his big shoulders like a prize fighter preparing for his next bout. Only after these slow deliberate actions did he at last open his mouth, the gold crown on his front tooth gleaming, and speak. 'Aleksei Nikolayevich … pleased to meet you,' he said, his voice extraordinarily deep and gravelly.

'You too, Ivan Ivanovich,' Aleksei replied.

'Call me Ivan,' he said, and invited Aleksei to sit opposite him, which he did.

There was silence between the two men, broken by the thief-in-law. 'Lenin and now Stalin, they have made Gods of themselves, haven't they, these men who so despised God.'

'Yes…' Aleksei answered hesitantly, slightly taken aback by Ivan Ivanovich's opening words, their eloquence and intensity.

He continued, 'The notion that they, and other Party leaders, would not misuse the power they hold, as their feudal predecessors had done, has been proved false. For they have abused it just as much.

'The Party exists above the law, its ruling district elites throughout the Union acting in its name as racketeers and extortionists of the tribute system. And what makes their abuse worse is their duplicity – their insistence that greed and inequality could never find a place in a Communist system. They might have been inspired by noble ideals, but they have not exercised them.

'Rather they have become what they so despised – feudal masters! Stalin and his Politburo members rule over us from inside the walls of the Kremlin, rarely venturing out, and when they do their faces are barely visible, obscured by the great red turrets that straddle the walls. Were they not meant to be our fellow comrades, walking with us on the righteous path towards equality and utopia!?' Ivan Ivanovich insisted, then paused, seeming somewhat preoccupied at this moment as he stared at Aleksei and looked away.

Aleksei was wary what to say in response, not because he was being asked to confirm his dissent too, rather because it was unclear why the notorious thief-in-law was giving him his analysis of Communist abuses. However, it soon became apparent that it did not matter what Aleksei's reply was. Ivan Ivanovich was working something through, and Aleksei was sympathetic to this process. For he possessed exactly the same trait, of sometimes being consumed by thought.

He continued, 'I apologise, Aleksei Nikolayevich, I got rather carried away. You see, it's been a long time since I talked to a man as educated as you.'

'Thank you,' Aleksei answered, accepting Ivan Ivanovich's compliment even though he, Aleksei, had not actually said anything of interest. It was Ivan Ivanovich who had done all the talking thus far, and he was not yet finished.

'Men such as me,' the thief-in-law went on, 'outsiders, are an inevitable product of this great upheaval, this great betrayal, this great abuse. We are orphans, and there are millions of us, victims of the Revolution, the Civil War, collectivisation, industrialisation and the Second World War,' and his words made Aleksei recall the thousands of lost boys who had wandered the Moscow streets while he taught during the last two years of the war and beyond.

Ivan Ivanovich continued, 'So much fear, anger and chaos is bound to produce a formidable criminal caste, vengeful and cruel, hell-bent on living apart from the Soviet consensus – disrupting it, undermining it, mocking it and flouting it whenever and wherever possible.'

'Yes, it is,' Aleksei said in acknowledgment, and the thief-in-law smiled at him, making him feel very welcome, nodding his head gently a number of times.

It became clear to Aleksei, as he continued to listen to Ivan Ivanovich, that the authorities had provided him with a justification for his outsider status, his criminality. However, it also became clear that the thief-in-law would never be as criminal as they, the authorities, were.

The two men went on to talk late into the night.

Over the following weeks Aleksei and Ivan Ivanovich spent a number of evenings talking together, and only when the former was confident that he would receive a positive response did he ask the latter whether he could help him. Ivan Ivanovich assured him he would do what he could to get word of Natasha and Katya. The thief-in-law possessed a formidable mind,

Aleksei realised, and was also, as Igor said, very well read. For though he had spent much of his life in prison or in camps, Ivan Ivanovich had managed to obtain books: his status had enabled this. Petrov and the guards, including Vadim and the Mongol, had a grudging respect for him. For they knew that their uniforms offered little protection: the thief-in-law might be a prisoner, but this did not mean he could not have any of them killed on the outside if he so chose.

Aleksei found that the more he got to know him, the more he liked him. Ivan Ivanovich was clear about his place in the world, and Aleksei suspected that even if he were free he would live humbly. 'For a true thief-in-law,' according to Mikhail, 'is not meant to live in luxury.' His life was characterised by a fierce almost fanatical independence, and possessed little warmth and affection. He had no wife, no children, and his parents and siblings he renounced when he was anointed. Ivan Ivanovich told Aleksei that mistresses had entertained him during those periods when he'd not been incarcerated, and yet even here such exchanges had been practical first and foremost. They certainly had not involved love of any kind.

Aleksei learned about the Scabs War, which began in '48. Some thieves had been, and still were, intent on punishing those within the ranks who had supported the war effort – they had broken the code, they had to be excommunicated, they were now 'bitches', 'traitors' – yet Ivan Ivanovich had not been, and was not, one of them. 'For I love my country,' he told Aleksei, 'even if I hate the men who run it.'

A new generation of thieves was emerging out of this internal war, however, thieves no longer willing to bow to tradition but rather intent on working with the authorities in order to obtain money and power. The Azerbaijani had proved himself to be one such thief, which explained his willingness to act as enforcer for Petrov and ensure that all the gangs met their work targets. He had also, according to Mikhail, been muscling in on some of Ivan Ivanovich's operations in the Steppes, though it was not quite clear to Aleksei how his friend knew this. As far as the Azerbaijani was concerned, Ivan Ivanovich, the white imperialist Russian, should keep his nose out of Central Asia. His people had been interfering for too long. 'Look at what Moscow did. It tried to turn the whole of Central Asia into one vast cotton plantation! It was inevitable that the land would dry up after a few years,' the Azerbaijani had told Ivan Ivanovich. 'I will fight for my clan, my people!'

Ivan Ivanovich had proposed they work together – he was a practical man – but the Azerbaijani was not interested. 'He has balls, that's for sure,' Mikhail remarked to Aleksei, 'if he's prepared to stand up to Ivan Ivanovich…and I suspect the Russian partly admires him for this.'

The camp authorities started giving orders to the men to work additional hours – they were behind with their targets – and soon they were exhausted.

Today they were hit by a winter storm, and despite the cries of Vadim, who insisted they carry on in spite of it, Rafik told them to lie down on the ground until it passed. They lay like this for over an hour in the freezing cold huddled together, before getting up and being ordered to resume work once more.

When they were escorted back to camp at the end of the day, Nikolai was unable to hide his frustration with the Azerbaijani, cursing him, out of earshot of the guards, non-stop. Earlier on he'd received confirmation that the reason why they were being made to work so hard was because the Azerbaijani had promised Petrov that he would meet his month-end targets no matter what, as he was now under real pressure from Moscow to deliver. 'If we were being made to work like this for the good of the people, then okay,' Nikolai grumbled. 'But no, we're slogging our guts out in order to line the pockets of a ruthless Central Asian gangster and we're propping up a ghastly commandant who'll do anything to stay in charge.'

'Be quiet,' Aleksei warned him, concerned that someone might overhear and squeal, yet Nikolai carried on regardless. But then, would the Azerbaijani really waste his precious time on the ranting of a religious prisoner? Nikolai, of all people, was hardly a threat, Aleksei reasoned.

Nevertheless, an hour later in the mess hall, one of the Azerbaijani's boys approached their table while they were eating, leaned over the back of Nikolai and hissed in his ear, 'I'll cut your fucking tongue out if you say anything else!'

He said this loud enough that the rest of them could hear, then walked away.

'Satisfied!?' Aleksei and Mikhail remarked to Nikolai in unison.

The force of this threat had shaken Nikolai; he crossed himself.

'You know, you can be a bloody-minded fool sometimes!' Aleksei demanded, shaking his head from side to side.

The fog was thick the next morning, like a great white cloak suspended in the air, and were they not chained together they would have disappeared in it, been enveloped by this cloak. Aleksei noticed Nikolai was getting weaker as he walked beside him. He could not handle the increased workload, it was clear. The last few days he'd been failing to meet his targets, and had been eating less. He had also struggled to get up this morning, needing to lift his legs with his hands before standing. 'I'm feeling dizzy a lot of the time,' Nikolai told Aleksei as they neared the forest.

'Right...' Aleksei replied hesitantly.

'And last night I couldn't see anything.'

'Of course.'

'No, I mean anything,' Nikolai stressed.

Aleksei knew these symptoms well; he had seen them in the war. Dizziness and blindness in the dark – the signs of a starving man. There were other signs as well: the body typically became covered in sores, the legs swelled, the lips turned blue, the teeth fell out. The criminals referred to such a dead man walking as a 'wick', his body shrinking like a candle until all that was left was the wick, and then even this stopped burning, was extinguished. And once dead, they would fight over his clothes.

Aleksei leaned over and sniffed Nikolai. He smelt bad, had stopped washing.

How could he not have noticed his deteriorating health sooner? Aleksei chastised himself.

He could not bear the thought of losing his dear friend. What would he do without his mumbling prayers every night? Aleksei might not have believed in his God, yet he loved his prayers, found immense comfort in them. Nikolai, more than all the other men, had been able to retain his spirit, his faith, a very difficult thing to do when forced to live like an animal, Aleksei pondered.

They began work and Aleksei made sure, with the blessing of Rafik, that he paired with Nikolai rather than Mikhail, Anatoly or Yuri. He would need to double up today, to do most of Nikolai's work as well as his own. Between them they had to produce sixteen cubic yards, three more than normal. He started to fell, and left Nikolai to tidy – to remove the branches only. However, even this he struggled with. He was simply too weak.

It was clear Aleksei must try and shield him from Vadim, who had already shown himself to be in mean spirits this morning. He'd snatched a piece of bread out of Mikhail's hand earlier and stuffed it in his mouth – punishment for not working hard enough. Mikhail often saved a small piece at dinner, which he would eat mid-morning to help him through till meal break. Not even a criminal would steal another man's bread, Aleksei thought. For bread was the one thing you had to let a man have.

From the comfort of his chair Vadim stared at Aleksei, then at Nikolai. This was the second time he'd looked over at them in the last five minutes. Aleksei turned to his dear friend, 'You must try and keep going,' he insisted.

'I'm trying,' Nikolai replied. However, it was no use. He was still managing to remove a few branches, though his progress was excruciatingly slow.

Vadim looked over again, and this time smiled at Aleksei while shaking his head from side to side. 'Oi, priest. Slow today, aren't we!? You better hit that fucking target!' he shouted.

Nikolai looked up, yet said nothing.

'Have you got anything to say?' he went on.

Nikolai remained silent.

'Well, you must have some explanation for why you're doing fuck all!?'

'Why do you think!?' Nikolai snapped back.

With this retort, everyone stopped what they were doing and waited to see how Vadim would respond.

'Insubordination!' he screamed, jumping to his feet.

'He didn't mean it, he's okay,' Rafik interjected, trying to calm him, but to no avail.

'You'll get the death penalty for this, you know that!?' Vadim bellowed.

With these words Nikolai smiled broadly and answered, 'Death at this moment would be my liberation from all this.'

'Well then, you shall not be executed!' Vadim replied. 'Everyone, get back to work…and that means you too, you fucking Yid!' he snapped at Mikhail.

Vadim walked right up to Aleksei and Nikolai. No one dared look at him.

He said in a low voice, 'Your friend here, the priest. Stop helping him! You're getting another two for this.'

Helping someone meet their work targets was forbidden, and thus Aleksei's sentence was to be extended, just like that. What was another two years when you had been sentenced for as long as he had? Aleksei asked. He felt at this moment as if he inhabited the theatre of farce, and that at any moment the sheer ludicrousness of life in here would be exposed. But no. The authorities had even made a vice of trying to save someone's life.

Vadim continued, 'He's going to be swilling slop before too long, he's going to be a shit-eater!'

After this, he addressed Nikolai directly. 'Father, dear father, don't worry. I'll make sure you're not executed. Instead, I'll work you to death!'

Then he hacked up some phlegm, spat it at Nikolai's feet, and returned to his chair.

Aleksei looked at Nikolai, at his frail frame, his drawn face. If he did not eat properly in the next few days he would die. Grace did not exist here, the logic brutal and unforgiving. The system thrived off any weakness and eradicated it. 'If I die and you get out of here,' Nikolai whispered, 'make sure you say a prayer for us all at the foot of St Vasily's.'

But, his friend had to live, Aleksei would make sure of this. Without Nikolai's spirit, his companionship, Aleksei would not have found the will to last as long as he had.

The next few days he was Nikolai's shadow, always with him – watching him, feeding him (Aleksei gave him some of his rations, as did the others), working for him, talking to him, simply being with him. Also, Vadim was absent, and these days without him were crucial. His replacement was a decent man who permitted Nikolai to rest. He also ensured that he was fed well, given chalk to keep his food down, and lots of cups of hot water.

By the time Vadim returned, Nikolai had turned a corner.

He would make it, he would live on. Thank God, Aleksei thought, even though he still did not believe in Him.

6TH DECEMBER 1953 CONTINUED
LAKE BAIKAL

A few hours had passed; they hadn't spoken. Natasha had followed Aleksei as he'd walked off down the shore, away from her. His heart broken, he'd killed all those men, sure that his wife had betrayed him. Yet now, her betrayal was less clear. He finally turned round and addressed her, 'I should've known…should have thought otherwise.'

She was silent.

He went on, approaching her. 'I did know deep down why you were with him, yes…but then I couldn't bear seeing you with him that day,' he confessed.

'Yes,' Natasha replied, anger in her voice, Aleksei noticed.

And was she not entitled to be angry? he thought. Angry that he, the love of her life, had not stopped to consider the extent to which she had been coerced by Vladimir Vladimirovich, threatened by him.

He continued, 'I left Moscow shortly afterwards.'

'You were released in the amnesty immediately following Koba's death?' Natasha asked.

'Yes,' Aleksei grumbled, instantly uncomfortable with the fact that he was already being forced to lie to her. Would she not find him out? he fretted. For this first amnesty, on 27 March, had mainly applied to prisoners with five years or less, and Natasha surely knew this.

'Where have you been the last eight months?' she asked. 'What have you been doing?'

'Not now,' he whispered, eager to get her off this question, and took her in his arms, pulling her towards him and holding her tight.

Natasha held him less eagerly, however. She must have sensed he was trying to hide something, Aleksei thought. It was as if she didn't quite believe him.

How could he have been so black-and-white about her betrayal? he wondered. And what right did he have, of all people, to judge her so harshly? The extent of his crimes was far greater than hers.

Again, there was silence between them for a while, which Aleksei eventually broke, asking, 'How is Katya?'

'She's well,' Natasha replied.

'I...I want...' he struggled to speak.

'I'm sure you want to see her, yes.'

He nodded.

Natasha went on, 'She's at ballet school in Irkutsk for the night but will be back tomorrow.'

'She's still dancing, then?' Aleksei asked, realising with this question quite how long it had been since he'd last seen her, his precious daughter. It had been over four-and-a-half years. He pictured her now, with her mother's hair, eyes and face, and her slender and graceful body, also like her mother's, though not as tall – this a good thing, however, in light of her pursuit of ballet. Her mother had been judged too tall to be a ballerina.

'Yes, of course she is, and she'll be heading for Moscow soon, probably the Bolshoi.'

'I never thought she'd make it all the way there...'

'It looks like she might,' Natasha replied.

'Right,' and with this short exchange they were silent again, and stood here by the lake, shivering slightly underneath a tree, until the sun began to set.

'Would you like to come with me?' Natasha asked as if they'd just met.

'Yes,' Aleksei answered.

'I live just down the road.'

'You came to live here?' he enquired, sounding surprised.

'Yes,' she replied succinctly, and Aleksei did not ask her how and why for now, rather just let her lead them slowly back to her home here in Baranchiki.

Their first steps inside were awkward, tentative. Aleksei looked around the living room as if scouting the place out, in search of his next victim, though after this his gaze settled on the small silver-framed photograph above the fireplace. It was the picture his mother had taken of them outside Lomonosov, Moscow State, when they were just married. He walked over to it as if entranced, like it was some kind of sacred object, picked it up and studied its image closely, and then sighed, this sound heavy with sadness.

'When did you get out?' Natasha asked.

'I'm not sure I can do this…' Aleksei mumbled.

'Right.'

'Is it too long?'

'I don't know.'

'Can we start again?'

'Maybe,' she answered quietly.

However, he looked at her unconvinced and sat down on the sofa.

She joined him.

He went to speak again, but she put her hand over his mouth, urging him not to.

Natasha yawned, and Aleksei followed.

Both of them were all of a sudden very tired.

They fell asleep.

Morning, and they sat in her cramped kitchen at her tiny table eating breakfast, this table which was only really fit for one – and Natasha could not help but laugh at the spectacle of Aleksei and her seated here, his big frame rendering the scene, almost absurd. He held his elbows close to his ribs and awkwardly sipped his tea.

'Well, I'm pleased you find it so funny,' he quipped.

'It looks like I'll need a bigger table.'

'Or kitchen,' he replied, laughing too.

There was a brief silence between them.

'You didn't tell me when you left Moscow?' he finally asked. He'd been itching to ask this question.

'I managed to get away from him not long after the monster died.'

'He didn't come after you?'

'No,' Natasha answered, and got up to fetch some more hot water. 'He was offered even more power by Beria and couldn't resist. The promotion kept him there, stopped him from following me. Katya should be back soon,' she went on, sounding eager to change the subject.

Was she telling the truth? Aleksei wondered. Vladimir Vladimirovich was obsessed with her, would not have let her go, even with greater power. He would have made sure, rather, that he could have both, Aleksei thought.

'Did you hear me? Katya's back soon,' Natasha said again.

'Err…yes…I should have a wash, get ready,' Aleksei said, sounding a little flustered, which he was, first because of his suspicion of Natasha's explanation, and second of the thought of seeing his daughter again after all this time.

'Are you okay?' she asked, relieved, it seemed, that his mind was occupied by something other than her explanation.

'No, not really. I mean…she's almost eighteen now. I haven't seen her since she was thirteen. Will she even remember me?'

'Of course she will, Aleksei, you're her father and she's never stopped loving you.'

'But…'

'No buts. She knows you should not have been arrested, she knows how much you've suffered being apart from her. You're a good man, Aleksei,' Natasha said, though he looked to the floor, reluctant to look at her when she said this. 'Aleksei?'

'I'm sorry, yes of course, I know there was nothing I could do.'

'Yes, Aleksei.'

'I'll go and get ready,' he said, getting to his feet, squeezing past her and heading for the bedroom.

Natasha watched him as he made his way – Aleksei could feel her eyes on him, which made him wonder whether he was right about what he'd thought yesterday, that they could not do this, in spite of their love for one another, that too much had passed between them, that Natasha was lying to him. And could he really entertain the idea of staying anyhow, in light of the fact that there was still one man left on Ivan Ivanovich's list and he'd assured the thief-in-law that he would complete the mission in full. Yet surely Ivan Ivanovich would understand. He was back with the woman he loved, and was about to see his daughter. There was nothing more important, Aleksei concluded.

But what of Vladimir Vladimirovich? he thought. Did he still want to kill the bastard?

2ND FEBRUARY 1952
BUTUGYCHAG, KOLYMA

A cold morning, and Aleksei was handed a letter, the first he had received since being here, which he immediately knew was not from Natasha, as it was in type, but rather from Moscow, some official correspondence. The envelope bore the stamp. He opened and read it. It informed him that his 'mother died on 29th December last year, the cause of death suicide'. That had been more than a month ago, he thought. The letter offered no condolences. In fact, it contained no sentiment at all. It was just one sentence, a statement that she was dead, and that she had killed herself. That was it.

At first, Aleksei did and felt nothing. In fact, time almost ceased. He stood there with the letter in his hand, motionless.

Nikolai approached. 'Eat, my friend. You mustn't miss out,' he urged, gesturing for Aleksei to go and fetch himself some breakfast, some morning gruel.

He did not reply.

'Aleksei?'

He felt unable to speak.

'Aleksei?' Nikolai pressed him. 'What's the matter?'

'She's dead, Nikolai.'

'Who?'

'My mother,' and Aleksei handed him the letter, which he read.

'I'm sorry,' Nikolai said.

Aleksei stared at him blankly.

'Are you…' Nikolai went on, 'do you need me to do anything?'

Aleksei shook his head.

'How can they do this?' Nikolai asked irately, his sympathy quickly turning to anger.

'I don't know,' Aleksei muttered.

'In this way!'

'Why not?' Aleksei replied. 'Need it contain any more than this. For am I not an enemy of the people?'

'No, but with no compassion at all!' Nikolai insisted.

Aleksei felt extraordinarily tired and no longer wanted to speak.

'What if it were them that had to endure this, the loss of their mother?' Nikolai went on.

Aleksei was silent.

Nikolai looked to the letter again, this time reading it aloud, 'cause of death… suicide.' He said this word again, 'Suicide.'

'Do not judge her, Nikolai,' Aleksei said quietly.

'I wasn't.'

'Yes you were.'

'Don't be silly, Aleksei.'

'I'm not. It's just that I heard some disapproval in your voice.'

'Well…'

'Well… what? Are you disappointed that your dear friend's mother did not die a noble death?' Aleksei asked.

'Aleksei… don't, please,' Nikolai appealed to him.

'That she was weak and took the coward's way out?' he continued. 'Do you judge her final act to be selfish, against God? If only she'd respected the sanctity of life, I hear you say. Our

Communist leaders might disapprove of suicide because it's not in the interests of the greater good, the good of the people, the Soviet good, but at least they don't apply moral censure to the extent that our former Christian leaders did. God, they were a self-righteous bunch, those Orthodox priests! And do you...'

'Stop it,' Nikolai interjected.

'Let me finish,' Aleksei went on. 'And do you not believe that it is a greater sin to betray God's will than the Soviet will?'

It was Nikolai who was silent now.

'Well, do you!?' Aleksei shouted. 'Yet you, like them, did not know my mother, and thus cannot judge her. You can never judge her!' With these departing words he stormed off.

'Momma, my dear Momma...how I will miss you', he muttered to himself as they were marched off to work. It was the system that had killed her, that had driven her to take her own life, he thought. She had never been able to accept Poppa's death. After his stroke he'd recovered and returned to the university, but had taught less. Like his family, his colleagues and students were able to see that he was no longer the man he once was. He possessed none of the former passion and vigour. He'd died just weeks before Operation Barbarossa, and Momma had blamed his premature death on his arrest four years earlier.

Aleksei hated the squalor she'd lived in during and after the war, the dilapidated nineteenth-century mansion block he was brought up in, a building that under Tsarist rule had been home to the intelligentsia. Poppa told how well it had been maintained before the Revolution, but that after it, when Aleksei was growing up, it had become increasingly neglected, until its corridors and stairwells were thick with dust and grime and the stench of urine. It seemed to Aleksei that the Bolsheviks wanted to punish them, the intelligentsia, for what they had been, the bourgeoisie, even though the majority of them – particularly Aleksei's mother and father – had been supportive of their cause. Perhaps Lenin, their upper-middle-class leader, had actually been punishing himself. The self-loathing prick! Aleksei thought.

'Momma, my dear Momma…how I will miss you', he muttered these words again like a mantra as he looked up at the mountains, their murky brood, and wished that if he only made it to the other side then life would be different, and though he would not see his mother again he would be reunited with his beloved Natasha, his beautiful Katya. And yet these mountains had no end, he knew this. He would perhaps never get beyond them, back to his family.

Consumed by grief, his melancholy quickly became seductive. Aleksei knew this sentiment all too well. It possessed a determination that he, Aleksei Nikolayevich Klebnikov, in true Russian spirit, had to survive the very worst of life. And though he, like his mother, might have wanted to take his own life, he urged himself to carry on, to try and retain some hope, even though his will to live dwindled, even though he still had no news of Natasha and Katya. The men who died here, the 'goners', were the ones who stopped bathing, and so Aleksei dragged himself to the bathhouse – to this cold, damp, mouldy, foul-smelling place – and waited, for hours as usual, to be given a wooden tub, a cup of hot water, a small piece of soap. How he would have loved a long hot bath, Aleksei mused. Bathing used to provide respite, though not any more. He stared at his reflection in a small cracked mirror and realised he had not seen his face for months. His complexion had turned a grey-yellow. He also forced himself to take some of the bitter-tasting pine-needle drink which was supposed to make him stronger, help him fend off illness. However, perhaps he would have been better off in the sick bay, he wondered.

Many in here said you could not survive the camps: for if you did make it out, you were brutalised and mad, and hence better off dead. It was not even clear to Aleksei that he was in the Soviet Union any more. Kolyma, this oasis of suffering in the vastness of this continent, it seemed to exist on its own, in its own ghastly world. What purpose was there to all this suffering? Aleksei asked. It was not clear, but then, should it be? Need man's cruelty to man have a reason?

My Natasha, my Katya, still nothing from Ivan Ivanovich. 'Will I ever hear from, see them again? Would I!?' he screamed in his sleep.

7ᵀᴴ DECEMBER 1953
BARANCHIKI, PORT BAIKAL

'I knew it was Poppa straight away, I just knew,' Katya said to her mother excitedly, holding her father's arm, swinging it back and forth, as the three of them sat together in the living room. She was no longer a girl but a beautiful young woman, Aleksei thought, admiring her, his precious daughter.

It was noon and two hours earlier they'd finally seen each other again, father and daughter. They had met by the woodpile in front of the house, while Natasha had been inside finishing off some seamstress work.

Katya went on, 'I still can't believe it's you, Poppa. You look the same, but also different, if that makes any sense.'

'What's the same?' he asked.

'Your eyes, your body, your voice … yes.'

'What's different then?'

'Your face … it's harder.'

'What d'you mean?'

'It's … '

'I think you mean older,' Aleksei said.

'Yes, but also … oh, I don't know … ' she replied, and her observation prompted Natasha to look at his face too, to try and ascertain what Katya might have meant.

Aleksei was well aware of this physical change, he had noticed it himself, the slight harshness, the wrinkles round his eyes, the frown across his brow. But then, after what he had been through in the camp, such change could hardly have been a surprise to Natasha and Katya, surely. Who would not have changed as a result of this horror?

'Can you tell me about the camp?' Katya asked.

'I don't think Poppa wants to talk about that right now,' Natasha interjected.

'No, it's okay,' he said, putting his hand tenderly on his daughter's knee, 'Katya should know what it was like, and she's old enough to.'

'Sorry, I just thought you didn't want to talk about it so soon, that's all.'

'Well, I have to sometime.'

'Yes.'

'I was thousands of kilometres away.'

'In Kolyma, I know,' Katya said, and Aleksei wondered quite how much Vladimir Vladimirovich had told them, his wife and daughter, about his incarceration.

'It was extremely hard. They made us work twelve hours a day, sometimes longer, either cutting down trees or working in the mines. In winter it was unbearably cold and the clothes we had were inadequate. Many died, either from the cold or from hunger. They fed us very little, they were very cruel.'

Natasha struggled to listen to Aleksei as he spoke – he noticed this right away – as he described the dreadfulness of the place. Katya, however, listened intently, still possessing the curiosity of a young woman naïve enough not to comprehend fully this suffering, this awfulness. She asked another question: 'What were the other prisoners like, Poppa?'

'Many were just like me, politicals.'

'Were there others as well?'

'Yes, criminals.'

'Murderers?' Katya asked rather ghoulishly.

'Katya!' Natasha interrupted.

'Yes,' Aleksei answered.

'Really!?' Katya exclaimed.

'I think that's enough for now,' Natasha insisted. 'Come on, let's eat.'

It was wonderful for Aleksei to be reunited with Katya. They were so happy and serene in one another's company. Natasha watched them this afternoon, from the shore, as they drifted slowly in a small fishing boat on a patch of lake which hadn't frozen over, their shadows cast faintly in the still water. Katya lay between her father's legs, as she used to when she was a little girl, and he stroked her hair while she held a line in the water and waited patiently for a bite. Aleksei knew Natasha wished she could accept his return as Katya had. His daughter asked fewer questions, took Aleksei as she found him, whereas Natasha was incapable of this, of being quite so welcoming and open-minded. She seemed sure that he was keeping something from her, which of course he was, something that he knew he could never disclose to her. She, on the other hand, had been rather more forthcoming. She'd told Aleksei that she had to get as far away as possible, though Katya was still furious with her for dragging her away from school, her friends, her ballet classes in Moscow.

'And why so far, Momma, five thousand kilometres away?' she'd asked incessantly.

'To get as far away as possible from him, of course,' Natasha had replied.

'And why here, in the middle of nowhere, this small village on Lake Baikal?' Katya had gone on.

'Well, because this was the place where your father proposed to me,' Natasha had answered. A hopeless romantic, she knew this, she admitted to Aleksei, and yet if she could no longer be in Moscow, then the only place she'd rather be was here, she'd concluded. But it had also made sense to get as far away as possible to ensure that he, Vladimir Vladimirovich, never found them. She'd rented this small *dacha*, sufficient for Katya and her, and though it was rather rundown, some of its exterior beams hanging loose, window frames rotten and floors creaking, it had two bedrooms, affording each of them some privacy – vital for a young woman, of course – and the most wonderful garden, great poplar trees looming over the house like sentries, shading it from the glare of the sporadic sun, hiding it from the prying eyes of passers-by, and tall shrubs encircling the rickety perimeter fence. Natasha told Aleksei how she loved to sit on the little bench on the porch, wrapped up warm, and admire this flora, its patches of green and brown, which in the summer had offered up far more colour, reds and yellows and blues. She had had to get work almost as soon as she'd arrived. For though she'd taken all that she could with her when she left Moscow, she'd sold most of it within a few weeks just to get by. This is what came from living in a Communist country – she had few possessions, and those that she did have weren't worth anything! Life as a single mother had been tough right away. The main industry here was fishing, which seemed to be the sole preserve of men. She could hardly go back to teaching, she'd realised – there was not much interest in Chagall or Kandinsky on these shores – though instead had managed to get some seamstress work, and the old baker in the village, Pavel, a kind man with a thick white beard who'd welcomed her warmly the very first day she'd bought some bread from him, gave her a few days a week also; he clearly needed a helping hand. There was a good local school that Katya started attending, which had a comprehensive library, and Natasha was sure she'd be able to continue her ballet somewhere, even if it meant her travelling to Irkutsk. Among the few villagers whom she'd met was Marina, a charming, educated bright-eyed redhead in her early thirties who seemed rather out of place here – from St Petersburg, she had met her husband in the village while on holiday and had remained ever since. Natasha had otherwise thus far managed to keep herself to herself, and knew that this was best. The fewer questions she was asked the better. She'd got her story straight, she told Aleksei. She was a widow from Moscow – Natasha could not hide the fact that she was an educated Muscovite with a daughter – and had chosen to settle here for a few years to overcome her husband's death. He'd died of a stroke. She told Katya it was better this way, that people thought Poppa was dead rather than knowing he was a political prisoner. And why here, if they asked. 'Well, because this is where Poppa proposed to me,' she told Katya to tell them. This part of her story, at least, she could be honest about! Aleksei thought, as his attention again returned to the present moment here on the lake with his daughter.

Aleksei opened his mouth, leaned over and put his lips to Katya's neck. A farting sound reverberated across the lake, accompanied by Katya's playful giggles, as he blew hard on the skin of her neck. He did it again until he was red in the face, and this time Katya guffawed loudly. This had always been her favourite game with Poppa, and even though she was no longer a little girl she still loved it, Aleksei could tell. 'Do it again, will you? Please?' Katya shouted, and he did, almost right away.

'You're not going to catch a fish that way,' Natasha called to them. 'You're scaring them away.'

'I know, Momma, but it's funny.'

'Well, I'll leave you be. I'm going to head back to the house,' she said, and got to her feet and walked slowly away, leaving the two of them, father and daughter, lost in one another.

Days and weeks passed and their lives together, the three of them again, began to assume some kind of normality, though this was perhaps the wrong word for it, Aleksei realised. For how could there be 'normality' after what had happened? Perhaps one should say familiarity or routine, he thought. No word from Ivan Ivanovich. He'd hear from him soon, no doubt – one of his men would come – and upon seeing him reunited with his long-lost wife and daughter would immediately understand why he had not killed the last man. Natasha still seemed to love him as intensely as she did before – Aleksei continued to make her weak at the knees when he stared into her eyes, he noticed – yet there was something different about her love for him, though he struggled to articulate exactly what this was. He knew he was less intellectual now, his voracious appetite for reading and debate having clearly diminished, and he was more introspective, seeming often to lose himself in his own thoughts, hardly surprising after the extreme hardship of camp life. However, he was also more present when he was not in the grip of introspection, seeming to be at one with all that was around him. When he was with Katya it was as if there were no one else – he was truly with her – and she adored him for this, this precious attentiveness. Whereas before he would become bored and look to return to his books, to the latest academic paper he was writing, now he relished her, his daughter, simply wanted to be with her for as long as possible.

There would come a time soon when Natasha would need to know more of the truth, Aleksei knew this – it was difficult to love someone fully when you felt they were keeping some great secret from you – just as he would need to hear the truth from her, quite how and why she had left Vladimir Vladimirovich, yet for now he wanted to try and savour his reunion with Natasha and not form any great expectations of what the future might hold. Every morning when he woke to see Natasha beside him and every night when he came inside her still felt like a dream – and may it last, Aleksei thought.

2ND AUGUST 1952
BUTUGYCHAG, KOLYMA

Summer. Morning. Again, for three months, it would not get dark, the days never-ending, the nights short and white. Rumour had it that other camps were striking. One in Kolyma had even had an armed uprising. But nothing happened here. The Azerbaijani would rather they worked, and Ivan Ivanovich, for the time being at least, continued not to challenge him, did not impose a strike.

It was hot this morning, and Aleksei and the others had to work in a swarm of midges and gnats. Fresh from the tundra pools and vast in number they almost suffocated them. There was little camaraderie between the men today, and so when meal break came Mikhail urged them all to link arms – he, Aleksei, Nikolai, Anatoly and Yuri. They did this, stood in a phalanx, and sang, though to what none of them quite knew. A few other prisoners looked over at them bemused, smiling faintly; the spectacle of the five of them singing must have appeared somewhat surreal, Aleksei mused.

After they had finished eating Aleksei and Nikolai elected to sit in the sun, on a large log that overlooked the forest, waiting to be summoned back to work. 'You know, I can't even stand the sight of this forest any more,' Aleksei said. 'I used to love the smell of pine. Now I hate it.'

'There's only so many trees a man can cut down,' Nikolai replied.

'I no longer even like the white birch,' Aleksei grumbled, then started laughing.

'What's so funny?' Nikolai asked.

'That they've even made me hate trees. How is that possible!'

'For them, anything is possible!' Nikolai declared, laughing too. 'But the beauty's still there, my friend, you just have to look closely.'

'I know, I know,' Aleksei replied.

'You know, if you ever do find God, I urge you to go and see Father Iosif,' Nikolai said.

'You see, you are a purveyor of religion, an Orthodox recidivist! They were right all along!' Aleksei quipped.

'Of course I am. But seriously, if you ever do, go and see him. Sitting here reminds me of his monastery, I'm not sure why. Perhaps it's the light today, its brightness, intensity. It's in the Altai Mountains, near the southern slope of Mount Belukha, an old monastery derelict throughout the nineteenth century that Father Iosif settled in and restored. When the sun shines up there you feel God right beside you, He is with you.'

'It's on the Katun river?'

'Yes, it overlooks it, and as I trust you implicitly, my dear Aleksei, I want to tell you about it. I spent two years there immediately after the war. Should you ever get out of this awful place and want to find God, I urge you to go there. Just follow the mountain path up the southern slope and you'll come to it.

'It's a small monastery, with no more than twenty or so inhabitants at any one time, and Father Iosif chose its location very deliberately. In the middle of nowhere, in extremely harsh terrain, the Godless Communists would have to be remarkably determined in their atheistic mission to seek it out and close it down.

'Father Iosif helped me a lot. I was having a crisis of faith and needed a man like him to see me through it. Clearly, I should have stayed longer – for then I would not have been arrested, as they would never have found me! – but my small yet perfectly formed congregation wanted, needed me. To maintain one's faith in the face of such unrelenting opposition is extremely difficult.'

'You know what, I might just go, my dear friend, if I ever see the outside world again.'

'You're just saying that.'

'No, I'm not,' Aleksei replied. 'I have the feeling I might need someone like Father Iosif after all this!'

'Yes,' Nikolai said, and patted Aleksei's knee, then held his hand there, and Aleksei put his hand on his, and the two men smiled at one another, before hearing Vadim's vicious bark ordering them to resume work.

In the afternoon a woman arrived, a prisoner from the female barracks, and went over to Vadim. She must have been ordered to deliver something. The degenerate ogled her from his chair as she handed over a package, and when she turned to leave – this blonde-haired, blue-eyed woman in her mid-twenties – Vadim leaned forward, threw his hands up her skirt, grabbed her hips and sank his head in between her buttocks. 'Aaaggghhh … aaaggghhh … ' he groaned, and panted like a dog on heat. 'Look at that arse. I want to eat it!' he exclaimed.

A few of the other guards guffawed as she dragged herself away from his clutches, pulled down her dress and escaped red-faced. Aleksei looked to Vadim. He had no doubt had sex with her already. He was notorious for his abuse of women prisoners, ensuring that he and Petrov had their pick of the most beautiful, and he was more than willing to play second fiddle to the big boss, he only having his fun with them once Petrov was done. Vadim had a long line of bedmates, and yet still he was never satisfied and remained cruel, loveless. As soon as a new batch turned up he was always right there, sitting behind his small desk, ordering each woman – dumbstruck and wounded by the loss of her family – to strip and parade naked in front of him. Modesty was not permitted, and should one of these poor women try and preserve her own by crossing her arms over her breasts and genitals, he promptly ordered her to drop her hands. On one occasion he had reportedly said to a terrified young woman, 'There's no room for prudery here, my girl. And listen, if I don't choose you, then someone else will. And you'd better hope it's not the Mongol. He'd rather beat you than fuck you!'

Aleksei looked away from Vadim towards the blonde-haired, blue-eyed woman who passed him now, shaking and breathing heavily, and he could see her clearly, her eyes and face. Poor woman, he thought, and though he wanted to empathise with her, share her humiliation, he could not help but also regard her as a sexual object. He had not seen a woman for so long. He thought of Natasha. What he would do to make love to her, his beautiful wife! To run his fingers through her hair, caress her skin, kiss her lips, stroke her neck, put his arms around her waist, and enter her, be inside her, Aleksei mused. And yet, she'd surely be repulsed by him, by his foul-smelling body that he's rarely permitted to bathe and by his sexual desperation, he concluded.

Evening, and Aleksei sat on the ground in the compound staring up at the sky.

'Ivan Ivanovich finally has news of your wife and child,' Igor said, walking up to him.

Aleksei did not respond.

'Did you hear me, Professor?' Igor went on, pressing him for a response. 'The boss has it from a reliable source, from Boris Andreyevich no less.'

This was a name Aleksei had heard mentioned a number of times, a thief-in-law in Moscow who worked with Ivan Ivanovich, according to Mikhail, and who had access to State Security.

'What?' Aleksei exclaimed, at last grasping the magnitude of what Igor was saying.

'Yes, Professor,' Igor replied, and Aleksei jumped to his feet, held the young henchman's hand, shook it a number of times excitedly, patted him on the back, embraced him, and hurried back to the barracks.

'Ivan…Ivan…' Aleksei called, entering, and made his way across the floor towards him.

'Aleksei, please sit down,' Ivan Ivanovich said.

'You sound serious,' Aleksei replied, setting himself down opposite him. 'I thought you'd given up.'

'How could I, with something as important as this? I'm sorry it took so long.'

'Well, it's good news, isn't it?'

'Not exactly.'

'But they're alright, they're together, they're safe?'

'Yes, they are…but your wife was seen with another man.'

'What?' Aleksei asked. 'What man? What d'you mean!?'

'In bed one night with another man, Aleksei.'

'No…' and he instantly felt lightheaded, nauseous. 'Maybe it wasn't Natasha?'

'It was,' Ivan Ivanovich answered coolly. 'Boris Andreyevich would never be wrong about something like this.'

'I…I…'

'He was NKVD.'

'No…' Aleksei mumbled.

'Vladimir Vladimirovich Primakov.'

'No!'

'Yes.'

'But Natasha wouldn't do this…'

'Why not?'

'He was my arresting officer.'

'The one who sent you down?'

'Yes.'

'My God...'

'But that's why...if she slept with him...it must have been because she had to.'

'What are you saying?'

'Yes, perhaps he threatened to take Katya away if she didn't denounce me. Maybe that's it!' Aleksei said, suddenly sure of his explanation.

'Okay,' Ivan Ivanovich said, trying to calm him, encourage him to think clearly.

'Yes, he forced her into it. Natasha loves me, she'd never denounce me, and so he made her sleep with him.'

'But could she have been saving herself, Aleksei?'

'No.'

'What if he threatened to charge her as well?'

'No, Natasha's a selfless person. She'd only have done it for the sake of others.'

'You mean to protect Katya, because he threatened to take her away?'

'Yes, and my honour, because she'd never denounce me,' and Aleksei was now sure of this.

'Look Aleksei, it's possible, but what I omitted to tell you, which I feel I must at this point, is that...' and he paused.

'What Ivan?'

'She didn't just spend that one night with him.'

'What are you saying?'

'He's there a lot, in your apartment.'

'What?'

'Yes, the four of them. She and Katya, and the NKVD and his son, Dmitri, who's about Katya's age.'

'No, this can't be,' and Aleksei's chest hurt and he gasped for air, felt like he was drowning.

'Boris Andreyevich wouldn't get this wrong, Aleksei.'

'The four of them…together?'

'Yes,' Ivan Ivanovich answered. 'I had her followed for two full weeks in order to be sure. All the surveillance suggests she's with him because she wants to be, that the kids are close, the…'

'Enough!'

'I'm sorry.'

'It doesn't add up…'

'It's okay…it's okay,' Ivan Ivanovich said, putting his hand on Aleksei's knee and holding it there paternally, seeking to console him.

Aleksei stared blankly at the barrack floor and began to cry.

'Igor, can you get one of the men to go fetch Aleksei some tea?' Ivan Ivanovich continued. 'Our friend could do with it.'

During the night Aleksei did not sleep, his mind tormented by the narrative of sexual betrayal: Natasha naked astride Vladimir Vladimirovich, thrusting, screaming with pleasure; he penetrating her from behind, patting his belly while first admiring his handsome face in the gilt-framed mirror which hung above the bed, and second staring with contempt at the small silver-framed photograph of Aleksei that sat on the dresser adjacent to the bed. He could not bear these images, which populated his mind, full of jealousy and hate, and kept opening his eyes in a bid to lessen their power. Next, he had to contend with doubt, his mind asking incessant questions to which there were no definitive answers. Had Boris Andreyevich got it wrong for once? Was Ivan Ivanovich lying to him? But if so, why? Had Natasha ever really loved him? When had she first betrayed him? How could she be with a man like Vladimir

Vladimirovich? Had this bastard come after him in order to get at her? Aleksei remembered one of the final gestures Vladimir Vladimirovich had made before arresting him that day. He'd taken Natasha's knickers from the bed and sniffed them and said, 'How I'd love to fuck her!' Aleksei could not bear it.

When morning came he did not get out of bed as the rest of the group made its way to the mess hall for breakfast. He was dejected, exhausted, and punishment would follow soon should he fail to make morning parade. It was as if he had endured all this for nothing, Aleksei felt. Had not his reasons for going on been proved false, nothing but a sham!? His wife and daughter had not been distraught without him; Natasha had never been waiting for him; and neither had Katya, who had another father now. His suffering here, on the boat, the train, in the Lubyanka, it had had no purpose. It had no purpose. 'Aleksei...' he heard a tender voice behind him say. It was Ivan Ivanovich. Aleksei did not answer. 'My friend...' he continued.

Aleksei could not find it in him to speak.

Ivan Ivanovich sat down on the bunk opposite, leaned forward, rested his elbows on his knees and looked at Aleksei warmly.

'What do we live for?' Aleksei asked quietly.

'We decide that for ourselves,' Ivan Ivanovich replied.

Aleksei was silent.

'I have some idea of how you feel,' Ivan Ivanovich continued. 'When I was nineteen I fell in love with a woman. Her name was Anna. I was mad about her, felt I couldn't live without her. Five months after meeting her I was sent down for three years. She promised she'd wait for me, that she'd never abandon me. But while inside I learned that she'd betrayed me for another man. He was from a rival gang and had been responsible for my arrest. He'd tipped off the police,' and Ivan Ivanovich sounded desperately sad and stopped speaking, and Aleksei wondered whether this was because his voice was about to break and he was close to tears.

'Ivan, thank you … for …' Aleksei said.

'It's okay,' Ivan Ivanovich mumbled, nodding gently. 'This is why I'll always live alone, even if I get out of here. You see, life in the zone is the best way to live.'

'Yes,' Aleksei replied, contemplating this 'zone', this place outside the ordinary, the everyday, on the outside. 'What did you do on your release?'

'I killed him,' Ivan Ivanovich answered, then turned and walked away.

Aleksei lay here, wondering if he should do the same.

He managed to get up and take himself to work, though he failed to eat breakfast. Vadim's horse struggled as they were led off, and the petty tyrant became increasingly frustrated with the poor animal. An old mare, she was suffering from arthritis.

As Aleksei walked, his sadness and rage grew with every step. His life, he thought, had been characterised by unending violent upheaval. His country during his childhood had changed radically under the Soviets, beyond comprehension. First collectivisation, then industrialisation. The peasant majority decimated, the proletarian minority fortified, expanded. The late '30s, his father had been dragged from his home in the middle of the night, threatened and brutalised. The early '40s, he was made to leave his wife and child, and fight. He had been wounded. The mid-'40s, he was compelled to fight another battle, this one against the state. For he could no longer live under a totalitarian regime. The late '40s, he had been arrested, beaten and tortured for his beliefs. He was separated from his wife and child, exiled and incarcerated. And yet his life was not exceptional. Many others had suffered, and continued to suffer, just as he had, pulled along by Russia's harsh and extreme history. Why was she like this? Need she be like this? he asked.

'This stupid horse!' Vadim suddenly screamed like a petulant child, dismounting the mare in a rage. He stomped around her, as she stood tired and weak and breathing heavily.

Aleksei looked to her, this noble creature, as she exhaled through her nostrils, her warm breath filling the air. She seemed unaware of the wrath of her master, appeared almost peaceful.

He, that monster Koba, Aleksei thought. Tens of millions of us, his beloved people, died in defence of Mother Russia. Yet what was our reward? Not freedom. No, the opposite. Enslavement! We defeated one totalitarian regime in order to make another stronger. Aleksei's mind was reeling, and he was unable to halt its stream of furious thought.

Fucking Vadim. Fucking Stalin. Fucking Communism. Fucking camp.

More were drawn to stare at the old mare and admire her – her calm, her being. A rare sense of serenity was upon them all. Some even smiled, Nikolai taking Anatoly's arm and urging him to look.

However, Aleksei was far from peaceful. He was tired of this shit, tired of everything. So tired. Of not laughing. Of cutting down trees. Of being told when he could and could not eat, sleep, piss and shit. Of living like an animal. Of being treated like one. Of acting like one, a submissive sheep. Of not being able to say what he thought. Of being no more than a unit of labour. Of having no name. Of…

Vadim then shattered the tranquillity of the rest of the men in an instant, as he marched towards the mare, put his arm around her neck and shot her in the head with his pistol.

She let out a terrible neigh, her legs wobbled and she fell to the ground.

She did not die right away, but writhed in pain, hyper–ventilating.

He did not end her agony with a second shot, rather just watched her as she suffered. Perhaps he had not intended to kill her immediately, Aleksei thought, staring at the dying mare.

They watched her silently as she lifted her head a number of times and looked over at them, as if appealing for one of them to do something, help her.

At last Aleksei could not bear it any more and shouted, 'Will you just put the poor creature out of her misery?'

Vadim shot her in the heart several times until she was motionless.

Everyone was silent.

'What did you fucking say, K-891?' Vadim demanded, swinging round to confront Aleksei, strutting over to him and shoving his gun in his chest. 'How dare you tell me what to do?'

Aleksei stumbled backwards, and after that, before he quite knew what he was doing, he had retaliated, disarmed Vadim, got him on the floor, and was pounding him in the face with his fist as hard as he could.

'Stop it! Oh God, stop it!' Nikolai cried, hurrying over and pulling Aleksei off him, and in his voice Aleksei heard the dread of what he knew would come.

'You're going to rot in the cooler for this!' Vadim uttered through a bloody mouth.

8TH FEBRUARY 1954
BARANCHIKI, PORT BAIKAL

Aleksei and Natasha sat outside the house, wrapped up in warm winter clothes, on the small wooden bench on the porch. He wouldn't have done this before, sat peacefully and observed his surroundings, and yet this is what Natasha had found him doing when she returned from her shift at the bakery an hour ago. He would've considered such a pursuit insufficiently dynamic or challenging, but now he relished it, its ease and simplicity. They heard Katya's footsteps before they saw her, hurrying up the garden path towards them. She called out, 'Poppa, a girl in school today said she didn't believe you were in Kolyma.'

'Katya, you know the rules!' Natasha shouted, getting up from the bench and confronting her.

'But I thought things were different now...' Katya replied shakily, startled by her mother's hostility.

'Why would they be different?'

'Because of the amnesty,' she said tentatively.

The village had asked questions as soon as Aleksei had arrived, and Natasha had therefore decided to come clean right away, to change her story. Her husband had not died, but was a political prisoner, and was only released in the amnesty which immediately followed Koba's death. The majority would fully understand why she had lied. In spite of the monster's end and the apparent thaw that seemed underway, any association with a political prisoner still carried a terrible stigma, the associate consigned to a miserable outcast life. It was still yet to become clear to the average Russian citizen that many political prisoners had not been enemies but rather victims. Thus Natasha had told Katya, on Aleksei's return, that she should not discuss her father at school. She still had to be discreet, to say as little as possible about him. For, like Aleksei, she was distrustful of the new openness shown by the authorities, and was not convinced that it would last. A return to repression was surely not far off.

'Katya, we're not sure if the amnesty applies to your father,' Natasha said. 'And you know what I told you about not discussing him at school.'

'Why?' Katya asked.

'Because he escaped!' Natasha shot back angrily.

'Can we discuss this later?' Aleksei interjected, as Natasha finally let slip what Vladimir Vladimirovich had told her. She'd known all along that he'd lied about this, his release.

'I thought you were released?' Katya addressed her father.

'Look, there's nothing to discuss,' Natasha said bluntly. 'I know, Aleksei, okay.'

He didn't dispute this, instead looked to the ground. How much did she know, he wondered anxiously, what exactly had Vladimir Vladimirovich told her?

Natasha turned to Katya. 'Just as you don't talk about me at school, the same goes for your father. It's the only way.'

'But I don't…' Katya mumbled, her voice breaking. She was becoming tearful.

If Vladimir Vladimirovich had let her leave, then why need she be so secretive? Aleksei wondered. Perhaps because she was concerned that Vladimir Vladimirovich might decide he wanted her once more, and come in search of her, drag her back to Moscow.

'Katya, all you need to know is that if you do talk about us it's likely we'll be in danger, that your father will be arrested again.'

'You're scaring her, Natasha,' Aleksei said, taking his daughter's hand.

'I'm scaring her?'

'Yes.'

'Well, shouldn't I be?'

'What are you talking about?'

'It's not as if we're safe now, in the clear.'

'What d'you mean?'

'There's still a bloody State Security out there, a government that'll do anything to stay in power.'

'I know, but...'

'But what, Aleksei? You're on the run.'

'Katya, please go inside,' he said.

She didn't move, just held his hand.

'Please Katya,' he insisted.

She reluctantly let go of his fingers, scowled at her mother and stormed into the house.

'Why didn't you tell me the truth?' Natasha asked. 'Why d'you lie to me?'

'He told you, didn't he?'

'Yes.'

'What else did he tell you?'

'That you killed someone...someone in the camp, and a guard when you escaped.'

'Right,' Aleksei replied. 'Anything else?' he asked bluntly.

'No.'

He was silent, considering whether he should deny or admit this. It felt like a long time.

'Well, did you?' she pressed him.

'Yes,' he eventually answered, and before he confessed to Natasha he took a deep breath, as if preparing himself to re-live what he had done, confront his conscience again.

She watched him closely, Aleksei noticed, as he shuffled on the bench, presettled his position, placed his hands on his knees. He felt like he had just taken the stand in the witness box and was preparing to make a full confession. Natasha did not sit beside him, instead settled down in the rocking chair, a piece of junk furniture normally the exclusive domain of Katya.

Aleksei finally began, 'When I learned of your apparent betrayal, I simply couldn't take it any more. My punishment for attacking Vadim was isolation, "the cooler", as they called it. I might have told you about my other experiences in the camp, but not this, what happened to me in there. You see, I find it very difficult to speak of it, as I suffered so much. But, in short, something changed in me, which enabled me to do what I then did,' and he paused for a moment, closed his eyes and felt his breath through his nose, then continued. 'I was stripped bare and held in the punishment block, in a cell made of grey stone, Kolyma stone. It was not enough that they rid me of my clothes, they also rid me of my humanity – my classification had gone beyond "enemy of the people": I was now deemed a "malicious element", and my anger with the system, my lack of faith in it, constituted this malice. The cell was just a few metres square, big enough for one man, and I was chained up like a bear. It was empty but for a slop bucket and a narrow bench, and dark and damp. I was too big to lie on the bench, so had to lie on the grimy stone floor.

'I remember the first night. Staring up at the ceiling, I waited for nightfall. It was pitch black and I listened for her song, Momma's song, and heard it faintly, that old Russian folk cry. "Momma, is that you?" I asked out loud. "Yes," she answered.

"I remember how you used to sing to me in the bedroom," I said to her. "Lie here, you would say, rest your head in my lap, and you would gesture for me to come, and I would sit down beside you, lower my head onto your stomach, and you would stroke my head, run your slender fingers through my hair, and I would listen, enchanted by your voice. Oh Momma, I wish I had been there for you. But no, they had taken me…and you, Momma, were left to die alone. How can I forgive them this?" I asked.

'The next morning I was fed a "Stalin ration", the name they gave it, 300 grams of black rye bread, no more, and I ate it quickly, urgently. I recalled what Anatoly had told me about isolation when I first arrived. "Most are dead after fifteen days, killed by the cold and hunger," he'd said. At least it was not winter, I thought. "There was an Orthodox priest during the war, a religious prisoner," Anatoly had said, "who lasted eighteen days, but that's the longest I've heard." I did not know how long they intended to keep me here. Some were held for a week, sufficient time to scare them into submission, others for longer. I knew they judged me to be a threat, but the question was how much of one.

'There was little stimulus in the main camp, yet here in the punishment block there was none. No people, no work, no exercise, no tobacco. I found myself reciting the single verse of the Pushkin poem, "Message to Siberia", over and over. Do you remember it, Natasha? I had studied it as a teenager, its rather grand, morose and melodramatic sentiment appealing to me, and had not recalled it until this point. "Entombed beneath Siberian soil," it began, "be proudly patient in your pain; your soaring vision and your toil, will not have been in vain." It is strange what can emerge from the depths of one's memory. I recited it less as a stimulant for my mind, more for my heart. I was starting to feel an appalling darkness there, you see.

'As the days went by I became increasingly lonely. I lay on my arm until I could no longer feel it, then laid it on my chest. For a few seconds I was sure it was someone else's touch, perhaps yours, but soon discerned it as my own. The two warders who watched over me were not violent. However, Vadim was. He let himself in at night and had his fun, cursing and beating me. I continued to recite the Pushkin verse – I must have said it ten, twenty thousand times – and when I was permitted to sleep I dreamed of Katya and heard her voice in my ear whispering, "Poppa...Poppa."

'A week had passed – I'd been marking the days on the wall with my thumbnail – and I felt like I had reached the bottom of life, that I had become an abomination, my body so filthy, mind morbid. I was not sure I could go on. Something had to give. I closed my eyes and screamed in the dark until I was too tired to any more.

'I woke the following morning and felt that something inside me had snapped, turned sour, that I would never again be the man I had been. There was simply too much anger and bitterness in me. Many here, so imprisoned by the system, almost fell in love with their predicament: slavery. However, I would not, I told myself. My hope, my idealism, had gone. I could not be a priest, so perhaps I should be a criminal, I thought. For the whole Soviet system was an enormous black market, the whole of Russia a camp! Stalin had become more terrible than Ivan IV, determined to persecute everyone. Had my suffering ennobled me? I wondered. No, it had not.

'I refused to carry on as every other good Soviet citizen did – not asking questions, minding my own business. I was tired of this, Natasha. This is the true nature of the Soviet man: he is not a silent hero but a submissive coward. I would become a free man, I resolved. Mother Russia might have been massive, powerful and serious, yet Soviet Russia is not. She is weak, small-minded and foolish, drowning in corruption and hypocrisy, of her own making. I hate the poverty she inflicts on her people, which in turn breeds apathy and indifference. Perhaps Ivan Ivanovich had seen this long ago and it was this insight that explained the life he'd chosen. For him, crime was a way out of this dishonesty, this malaise. There exists in the Russian soul a special intimacy between law-abidingness and criminality, holiness and sin. "Dostoevsky knew this," Poppa always told me.

'Though my body was weakening I now felt an urgent need to stay strong, and my anger fuelled this want. I ran up and down on the spot, did this for hours, and did press-ups, thousands of them. I trained like a fanatic for the next three, four, five days, and could not believe that my body was able to keep going. Neither could Vadim, who continued to visit me each night. My rations were reduced further, to just 150 grams of bread a day. I was being practically starved yet I continued to fight, to endure.

'After a fortnight my body was too weak. It carried the same signs of exhaustion and starvation as Nikolai's had done, my lower legs swollen and skin marked with purple blotches. I prodded the few boils that had appeared, these ugly growths of blood and pus. I felt nauseous day and night, and had diarrhoea. I could not smell my own body but I was sure it reeked of death – the dying man is foul-smelling. I stopped eating.

'Five days later, and still I had not eaten, just took sips of water, and after three weeks I was too weak to stand up and relieve myself in the slop bucket, so did it lying down, my body covered in shit and piss. Every night Vadim continued to come, yet he finally got to the point where he didn't beat me, instead kneeled down and asked, "Have you had enough?" to which I replied, "No, I haven't." Only on day twenty-five was I at last dragged out of there like a dead carcass and handed over to the camp doctor. It was unclear why they had not left me there a few more days to die,' and Aleksei stopped at this moment and looked over at Natasha, who held her head in her hands and quietly wept, overcome by the awfulness that Aleksei had had to endure.

He waited for her tears to subside, then continued, 'I woke up in a hospital bed, was sure that I was dreaming. The ward I was in was clean and white; there were five other beds. I did not know how long I'd been here. The smell of boiling vegetables filled the air. Carrots and potatoes, I thought, sniffing eagerly. I fumbled for my mouth and ran the tips of my fingers over my lips. I expected old saliva and dried snot, but found them to be clean and smooth. Next, I ran the end of my tongue around my front teeth, upper and lower, anticipating scurvy, yet not finding it. Rather, my teeth felt as though they had been brushed. Then I reached for my eyes – formerly sunken, bruised and closed, the victims of Vadim's countless beatings – letting my fingers gently explore them. The lids had lifted, the skin was soft, they were wide open. What of my bashed ribs and swollen legs, I wondered. I lifted the bedsheet and blanket and saw that they had been dressed and bandaged. And my filthy body had been scrubbed and washed, its rancid odour gone. A nurse entered with a trolley carrying food, plates of boiled vegetables, carrots and potatoes. I was right. There were also green peas and turnips. The other patients and I were fed, and given white bread as well. I was not dreaming, I realised. "It's a miracle you're still alive, that you lasted as long as you did," the doctor said, standing over me as I ate. I nodded my head. "And that you're recovering so well," he went on. "For most it's too late by the time they get in here, there's nothing we can do for them. But you…" He looked into my eyes, as if trying to see behind, beyond them. "You must be blessed," the doctor mumbled in conclusion and walked away. I smiled wryly at the word he chose, "blessed", in view of what I had been through. I had just survived twenty-five days in solitary.

'It was clear to me, as I looked around the ward, why some ran the risk of the punishment block in order to get in here. They refused to work, demanded medical attention, yet often, rather than being sent to the sanatorium they were sent to isolation instead. I finished eating and, turning to the man beside me whose hand was wrapped in thick bandage, I asked, "What happened?" my voice weak and croaky. "I cut off three fingers," the man answered matter-of-factly. "That guy over there," he went on, gesticulating with his good hand, "he went one further. He nailed his balls to a tree stump." Koba's approach had always been very clear, I thought. If the people would not work willingly for the Communist system – this great method and organism which was humankind's only salvation – then he would force them to, even if it killed some of them, and one day, they, the survivors, would thank him for it. For Uncle knew best, eh! Yet you know my view well enough, Natasha. A political system built on fanatical theory and dogma is always destined to be harsh, intolerant and unforgiving, since it does not acknowledge the complexity of human nature and how human beings seem, by their very nature, to perpetually resist categorisation.

'I was kept in the infirmary a full week before being discharged. When I was returned to the main camp I looked around and felt as though I had been away for a very long time. I was returned to my barracks and told to wait there till the evening, till the others returned from work. I walked over to my bunk and sat down. I had really missed Nikolai and the others, the madcap Mikhail and grumpy Anatoly. A few of Ivan Ivanovich's henchmen looked over at me, Vasily among them, from the other side of the barracks; the thief-in-law was absent, as was the young Igor. The criminals' faces did not carry the usual look, part ambivalence, part contempt, whenever they saw a political, I noticed, even one that was liked by their boss. Rather, they almost conveyed respect. Perhaps I had become an object of interest after my lengthy spell in isolation. They might not have admired me for my dissidence, my conscience, but they did for my resistance to the Soviet regime, my ability to make a bloody nuisance of myself. One thing I did know from Ivan Ivanovich was that their greatest contempt was reserved for the authorities. They consequently let me be, and I spent the afternoon lying on my bunk and resting.

'When evening came I was anxious to get to the mess hall to see my dear friends, and as I entered they were all there, bent over their bowls getting their evening feed. I fetched some food and walked over to them. I remember, I appeared to be a figure of curiosity in here too: a number of men stopped eating to look at me. My friends, however, did not see me, so engrossed were they in their food. I walked behind Nikolai, rested my hand gently on his shoulder, bent over and whispered in his ear, "My dear friend, how have you been?" Nikolai immediately recognised my voice and called out excitedly, "Aleksei... Aleksei..." then got to his feet and embraced me, wrapping his arms around my chest, holding me tight. "It's good to see you too, my friend," I said over and over, until Nikolai at last let go of me, after which I greeted Mikhail, Anatoly and Yuri. "We thought you were dead," Nikolai said. "So did I," I replied. "How are you?" Nikolai asked. "I breathe," I replied. "I'm so sorry about..." Mikhail said, looking to console me about your alleged betrayal. "Yes, you don't need to say any more," I replied, cutting him off. "How did you last so long in there?" Anatoly asked. "The thought of seeing us again!" Yuri quipped. I smiled at this. Nikolai looked into my eyes, and I felt compelled to look away, wary of the scrutiny of his gaze. For Nikolai would be the first to sense the change in me, I knew that. "Let's eat together," I said, and took my place in between Nikolai and Mikhail.

'The following day we were set to work in the mine, the hardest job of all. It smelled of blood and iron down there. If solitary had not killed me, this surely would, I thought. All this coal and gold that lay beneath the frozen tundra, how it had contributed to Koba's Five-Year Plans, I mused. Only he, the monster, had had the foresight to colonise Komi and Kolyma, these far north republics. Nikolai, however, was furious that we were being made to work down there, and after thirteen straight days with no rest we were exhausted. He blamed it on the Azerbaijani. "I'd bet it's him again!" Nikolai shouted. "Aleksei, why don't you have the other thief-in-law stop it? I saw you with him again the other night. Surely the Azerbaijani's a threat to him, no?" he enquired. He was vociferous with his criticism, did not even attempt to hide his anger, much to the dismay of Mikhail and Anatoly, and at the end of the workday, as they entered the compound, Nikolai was approached by one of the Azerbaijani's boys, the same one as before, who said matter-of-factly, "Did you forget what I said last time, that I'd cut your fucking tongue out if you carried on moaning?" Nikolai, rather than keeping quiet, immediately faced up to the threat, quipping back, "No I didn't, young man, and why don't you tell that boss of yours that I'm not intimidated by him, just as I'm not intimidated by you, and that I will say what I want, when I want." To which came the curt reply, "Well, then you're a fucking dead man, aren't you!"

'Back in the barracks, I went straight to Ivan Ivanovich and asked whether this threat should be taken seriously, to which the thief-in-law replied succinctly and without hesitation, "Yes," then walked off to talk to Vasily. Igor went on to tell me a little more about the Azerbaijani. "He's a pederast, and a violent one at that." It transpired he had developed the habit of biting off the tips of young men's noses once he'd had his way with them. "He likes to mark them out as his boys," Igor explained. "He also drinks too much *chifir*, he's hooked on the stuff." "Right..." I replied. "The Azerbaijani calls the boss a 'bitch' because he refused to punish those thieves who helped out during the war. You know the boss loves his country. But the Azerbaijani's the real 'bitch'. It's he who does their dirty work now, he who kills for them, he who ensures production is maintained and the camp's run smoothly." Ivan Ivanovich returned. "You have a problem, Aleksei Nikolayevich. The Azerbaijani will kill your friend Nikolai. He, of course, will not do it himself, but rather will get one of his boys to do it." "Well...what do I do?" I asked. "You kill him first," Ivan Ivanovich answered flatly, flicking his right thumb against his teeth and moving it in a circle around his chin. I watched this deliberate gesture closely, which Igor noted, then stared at the tattoo on his hand, of an eagle with talons. "I can't do that..." I said. "You're going to have to, if you want to save your friend," Ivan Ivanovich replied. "There must be another way?" I asked. "Well, I can't see one," the thief-in-law said. "Neither can I," Igor added.

'I left both of them and returned to my bunk. My mind was all over the place. Thank goodness Nikolai was asleep. I could not face him at that moment. Mikhail stirred and asked me why I was so long with Ivan Ivanovich, what was I talking about. Nothing, I insisted, go back to sleep, which he did. If the Azerbaijani was challenging Ivan Ivanovich's authority, then why did he not just get rid of him? Was it because Ivan Ivanovich still had a grudging respect for him? I wondered. Or because his collusion enabled Ivan Ivanovich to position himself as "the good thief-in-law", if indeed there was such a thing? And yet he had just told me that I had to kill him if I wanted to save Nikolai. I did not know where I was going with this. Could I do it? The Azerbaijani had threatened to kill my dear friend, he was a pederast, and he colluded with the authorities. Were these not reasons enough!? But no, how did I know the threat was serious? Christ, maybe it was just talk, bluster. I needed to calm down, needed to rest.

'The following morning I stood with Nikolai in the yard waiting to be counted. We were the first there. "You look tired, Aleksei," Nikolai said. "Yes, I am," I replied. "It's no wonder. You were up late with him again," he quipped angrily. "Not now, Nikolai, please…" I appealed to him. "You're just his little mascot! He likes having an intellectual around, someone he can talk to, who isn't coarse and illiterate like all the lackeys who dote on him. Who does he think he is? He's just a hoodlum. Look at what his men do. They steal, intimidate and rape. None of them work. He's as bad as…no, worse than they are. At least they believe in something, be it unattainable. He believes in nothing!" At this moment I saw over Nikolai's shoulder the young man from the mess hall yesterday. He was about fifty metres away and walked fast, heading straight for us. I grabbed Nikolai and started pulling him towards the barracks. "What are you doing, Aleksei?" Nikolai demanded. "Trying to save your life, you bloody fool! Now hurry up," I answered, and Nikolai looked round to see the Azerbaijani's boy hot on our heels. "Oh God!" he muttered. "God's not going to help you now," I responded, the barracks still some thirty metres away. Nikolai was slow, and we were not going to make it. I stopped, pulled Nikolai behind me and turned round to face his assailant. Right at this moment I heard the barrack door fly open, its great metal lock slamming against the wooden wall, and snatching a glance back over my shoulder I saw Ivan Ivanovich's men charging towards us, their leader right among them. Grabbing Nikolai by both arms I hurled him towards them, then turned to face the Azerbaijani's boy.

Spotting the charge of Ivan Ivanovich's men, he stopped dead in his tracks just a few metres from me, turned on his heels and scurried back across the compound towards his own barracks. Ivan Ivanovich, Igor and the rest of the men came to a halt. I hurried over to Nikolai, kneeled down beside him and lifted his head up. He breathed heavily, did not speak. "Is he okay?" Ivan Ivanovich asked. "Yes, thank you…he is," I replied. "Just very shaken, that's all. He'll be alright." "You know what you need to do," Ivan Ivanovich said, gently nodding. "Come and see me this evening." And with these words he turned and walked with his men back to the barracks.

'I spent the whole day thinking about the Azerbaijani's murder. My immediate concern was how long I had. Would the Azerbaijani not try again tomorrow morning, same time, same place? Ivan Ivanovich assured me he would not, as long as I heeded his advice. "Don't go out into the yard until the very last minute, and make sure you stand as close to the barracks as possible. He won't attempt another hit if he risks being caught by one of the warders or by us. He'll know we'll be waiting for him just behind the barrack door." "Okay," I replied. "I'll make sure my men keep a close eye on Nikolai for the next few weeks, but you need to be ready to carry out the killing within a fortnight. Igor will provide you with the weapon, a knife, and I'll show you how to use it. I'm sure you had knife training as an officer, but killing a man this way is different. You're not killing him in battle, you're executing him. The best time to get to him is when he's in the guards' bathhouse. He's there at two o'clock every Thursday afternoon for a couple of hours, his special arrangement with Petrov. The Mongol lets him in. You'll most likely find him with his trousers down getting sucked off by a young political that his boys have smuggled in. You'll find him at the back, the hottest part. He'll be sitting on a bench with his back to you. If you can get into the bathhouse without being seen, and you're light on your feet, the only thing that might cause you a problem is if the boy kneeling between his legs spots you. It's hot in there though, there's a lot of steam, and if he's going down on him he'll most likely not see you. Once you're behind him, draw the blade and plunge it hard and deep through the back of his neck. It's crucial that you do it right, and this is what I'll show you. You won't get a second chance. And finally, Aleksei, make sure you don't tell anyone about this, especially Nikolai."

'I started planning right away. As Ivan Ivanovich had made clear, preparation was everything. Igor delivered me a knife, big and sharp enough to penetrate the Azerbaijani's neck, and I began to train with it. I practiced hand-to-hand knife combat in the barracks with Ivan Ivanovich for an hour every evening, and my military training helped me a lot. For a man in his mid-forties Ivan Ivanovich moved with great speed, I noticed. He also demonstrated exactly how and where to place the blade before thrusting it into the victim's neck, and how to hold the head. I hid the knife in the same place each night, in a small hole in the underside of my mattress.

'Ivan Ivanovich had arranged for me to do a dummy run. It was Thursday and he had spoken to Rafik and told him he must do without me today. We stayed in the barracks till midday, then made our way over to the guards' bathhouse, waiting behind the guardhouse for the Azerbaijani to show. The first arrival was a young prisoner, a boy no more than seventeen or eighteen years old, escorted by two of the Azerbaijani's henchmen. They were met, a minute later, by the Mongol, who turned up at exactly two minutes to two. The henchmen left the boy with the Mongol and returned to their barracks. The Azerbaijani appeared dead on the hour, accompanied by a single henchman, a fellow Azerbaijani, Ivan Ivanovich informed me. The camp was all but empty this time of day, and so he required little protection. The Mongol let the Azerbaijani and the boy in, and after this returned to his watchtower. Meanwhile the henchman sat on the bench outside. "I've got to get past him, then," I said to Ivan Ivanovich. "And the Mongol," he replied. "He has a clear view of the entrance to the bathhouse from his tower." "And how will I do that?" I asked. "For the next two hours while he's in there, I'll watch the Mongol and you watch his heavy outside," he answered. We sat and waited. After about half an hour the henchman fell asleep. "He's nodded off," I said. "Keep an eye on him," Ivan Ivanovich replied. "You need to see how long he sleeps for." Another half hour passed. Still he slept. Ivan Ivanovich spoke again. "It seems the Mongol's a creature of habit. For ten minutes up until three o'clock he glanced at his watch every couple of minutes, and then, bang on three, he turned and fixed himself another tea. You've got about a minute to get from here into the bathhouse." "But what if his man outside doesn't fall asleep?" I enquired. "Well, then you have a problem," he said bluntly.

'I spent the next six days continuing to train with Ivan Ivanovich, who insisted I prepare for every possible scenario. What I would do if the henchman woke up as I was entering the barracks? If the Mongol saw me? If the boy alerted the Azerbaijani to my presence once I was inside? If the boy screamed when I killed him, thus notifying the henchman outside? "You must plan for every outcome," Ivan Ivanovich insisted. We also discussed my escape from the bathhouse once I had killed him. I had to put on the Azerbaijani's long sheepskin coat, his bearskin hat, and leave with my head down. And I had to make sure that I went before the boy.

'It was Wednesday night. Again, Ivan Ivanovich had spoken to Rafik and informed him that I would not be at work tomorrow. He was concerned, however, that Vadim, in the pay of the Azerbaijani, might become suspicious, as this was the second Thursday in a row. Thus my mission had to succeed, as I would most likely not get another opportunity. Lying in my bunk, listening to the gentle snoring of Nikolai, who remained unaware of what I was about to do, I was suddenly terrified, and wondered whether I should go to Ivan Ivanovich and just tell him that I was unable to go through with it. He would understand, surely, that it was very difficult for a man like me to do such a thing, even if it was to a man like the Azerbaijani. I had killed enemy soldiers in battle, but this, as Ivan Ivanovich himself said, was different. But no, what would be the point? I thought. Ivan Ivanovich was not the one making me do this. Rather it was the Azerbaijani. Perhaps I could wait for Ivan Ivanovich to kill him. From what Igor had said, this was looking increasingly likely. But then he might not, and I could not afford to wait.

'I got little sleep and woke the following morning tired and overwhelmed. I was unable to eat breakfast. I spent the morning lying on my bunk, wide-eyed and breathless. Midday arrived, and Ivan Ivanovich came over to me. "The first time is the hardest," he said. "I'm terrified," I admitted, to someone other than myself. "I know, as I was," he said. "Do I really need to do this?" I asked. "Yes," he answered. "I know…" and there was a brief silence before Ivan Ivanovich spoke again. "I understand what you're struggling with most, Aleksei. You feel that a man such as you, a former army officer and university professor, should not do this, should not take justice into his own hands and kill a man, other than on the battlefield. However, you are faced with extraordinary circumstances and you are living in extraordinary times. Your dear friend's life is at risk and your intended 'victim', if you can call him this, is a violent pederast and colludes with this awful regime that you must live under and which keeps you captive. Why should you be expected to do the morally right thing, let justice, divine or otherwise, take its course, in a country and system which by its very nature is profoundly immoral? And lastly, you perhaps might want to ask yourself whether you are that man any more, that good, decent and noble man, after all that you've been through. How can you be? You hate them as much as I do; you want to break them as I do. Good luck, my friend," Ivan Ivanovich finished off with his characteristic nod, then handed me a watch. "You'll need this," he added, and returned to his side of the barracks.

'I got up, retrieved my knife from inside the mattress, and headed out. I waited in the exact same spot as Ivan Ivanovich and I had waited last week, behind the guardhouse. Events proceeded as expected. First, two of the Azerbaijani's henchmen showed with a boy. Second, the Mongol. Third, his henchmen left. Fourth, the Azerbaijani and his compatriot appeared. And fifth, the former looked the boy up and down and took him into the bathhouse, while the latter got comfortable on the bench outside. Now I had to wait for the henchman to fall asleep. I kept a close eye on the watch. Time moved very slowly. Half past two, and still he remained vigilant. Quarter to three, no sign of him sleeping. Five to, still no sign. If he did not fall asleep in the next few minutes it was going to be too late. His head started to droop. Yes, he was nodding off. I turned and looked up at the Mongol, who glanced again at his watch, his lips thirsty now. One minute to three. The Mongol readied himself to make a fresh cup of tea. The henchman was at last asleep. I moved too soon, before it was exactly three, and the Mongol sensed something and jumped to his feet. I dived back behind the barracks. Did he see me? I wondered. My heart raced. The Mongol waited, scanned the area in front of the guardhouse and bathhouse, did it thoroughly a number of times, and after this went to make his tea once more. Now, I said to myself, and made my way again, all the time watching the henchman. I reached the door – he had not stirred – opened it just a little, slid inside, then gently closed it behind me as I saw the Mongol resume his watch.' Aleksei paused for a moment, in the midst of his account, and Natasha looked at him impatiently, hanging on his every word, eager for him to carry on.

So he continued, 'It was hot in there. I made my way slowly towards the back, the steam becoming thicker. The sound of heavy breathing, and groaning. I stopped and waited, peering through the thick hazy white clouds, and caught sight of the Azerbaijani. He appeared to be sitting just as Ivan Ivanovich said he would be, his dark-skinned burly body slouched on a bench with his back to me. The boy I could not see, yet I heard him, the sound of him gagging. The Azerbaijani held the top of his head with both hands and thrust his penis into the boy's mouth, causing him to choke. I pulled out the knife and tiptoed towards him. Just a few metres away, and I was right behind him. I drew the knife, wrapped my forearm around the Azerbaijani's forehead, and put the tip of the blade to the back of his neck, pressing it firmly against the skin. "Fuck," the Azerbaijani mumbled, and at this moment the boy looked up and saw me. "It's okay," I said quietly, "don't make a sound." The boy did not. "Let me see your face," the Azerbaijani said, and craned his neck back to look at me. "I want to see the man who dares do this to me!" We stared at one another, and I looked searchingly into his eyes, and then the thief-in-law hissed through gritted teeth, "Fuck your mother!" With these words I plunged the blade hard and fast, his skin and flesh splitting, and, recalling Ivan Ivanovich's instruction, repeated the action to ensure death,' Aleksei said, Natasha's mouth wide open, this physical gesture capturing the horror of what he had done.

He went on, 'There was blood everywhere. I let go of his head; his chin flopped against his chest. I looked to the boy again, his face pale and expressionless. "You wait here until I leave, okay?" I told him, and turned and headed back towards the entrance. I fetched the Azerbaijani's coat and hat from the bench by the door, put these over my own clothes, and then, with head bowed, left quickly, not looking up. The Mongol did not make a sound. I had thought he might call out the Azerbaijani's name. I headed for the dead thief-in-law's barracks first, in order not to arouse suspicion, and after that, once I was out of sight of the watchtower, I removed his jacket and hat, then made my way slowly back towards my own barracks. You came to mind then, Natasha, I remember. If you could see what I had just done, what I had become, I thought. And yet did it matter what you thought any more? I concluded, in light of your betrayal.

'Word spread fast that the Azerbaijani was dead and that I was his assassin. In the barracks that evening I was treated very differently. My fellow prisoners might have been intrigued by me when I came out of isolation, but now they were in awe. And what had I done to deserve this reverence but kill a man? Nikolai immediately confronted me when I entered after dinner. "What have you done?" he asked. I looked up from my bunk and answered quietly, "I had no choice." "Yes you did, Aleksei!" he insisted. "Do you forget what happened a fortnight ago, Nikolai? You've been a marked man ever since!" "Yes, maybe, but I didn't ask you to intervene." "Nikolai, he wanted you dead, and you just put your head in the sand!" I maintained. "No, I put my faith in God!" he replied. "No, Nikolai." "Yes, Aleksei," he insisted. "And who did you put your faith in but Ivan Ivanovich? Did he just use you to do his dirty work?" he asked. "No," I answered. "You had no right to take another man's life, to act as judge and executioner." "Was I just meant to stand by and watch you get killed, then?" "Let God do His work," Nikolai said. "How can you say that? It's not about God in here, Nikolai, how can it be in such a godforsaken place? You've simply got to do whatever it takes to survive!" "This is Ivan Ivanovich's way, and is precisely why it must be about God," he said, and turned his back on me.

'It was clear right away that Ivan Ivanovich's authority was now unchallenged, and Petrov, all too aware of this and concerned how he would maintain order and discipline from here on, summoned him for a meeting. He knew that Ivan Ivanovich held him in contempt, and so needed to find a way to win him over, make it worth his while. I suspected what Ivan Ivanovich would push for, if he were to help Petrov, was the free flow of information between the inside and outside. According to Mikhail, this is what had prevented Ivan Ivanovich from running his interests as well as he wanted to.

'After Nikolai had said what he did, I realised I had to choose between the two men, Nikolai and Ivan Ivanovich. The benefits of choosing the latter were clear enough. No more hard labour but easy work, and no more paltry rations but double helpings, plus numerous other perks. Yet so were the disadvantages. I would lose my dear friends, and I would be abandoning once and for all the conviction that goodness and justice would, in spite of everything, ultimately prevail.

'My decision was made for me, however, when Ivan Ivanovich returned from his meeting with Petrov and informed me that it had gone well, to the extent that he might now be able to find a way to get me out, should I want to take my revenge on Vladimir Vladimirovich,' Aleksei said, looking into Natasha's eyes when he said this, as if this were a key part of his confession, his desire for revenge. Natasha looked away, uncomfortable, it seemed, with what he had just told her. Aleksei prepared himself for what would inevitably follow, her desire to know whether he had taken revenge or not once he'd escaped. He went on, 'So that night I moved over to the other side of the barracks.

'I sat with Ivan Ivanovich; it was the middle of the day. "You know, Aleksei, had you not led a life outside the code, working and serving the people, the state, I suspect you'd have been anointed one day, made a thief-in-law," Ivan Ivanovich said, as I studied the second finger on his left hand, which carried a tattoo of the cross. "Yet I can perhaps trust you more because of this, because you know what it is to lead the ordinary, the conventional life, even though you've finally renounced it," he said through his deep, grizzled voice, which at this moment possessed a striking authority. Looking into my eyes, Ivan Ivanovich held his stare, then went on, "I'd like to give you a tattoo, a star on your left little finger, the mark that you'll never again bow to Soviet authority. Our code, our way of life, was around long before the Communists, and will be around long after too. That cunt in the Kremlin, the Georgian, he thinks he can break us. Never!" he concluded. "Do you accept, Aleksei?" "Yes, I do," I replied, and with my acceptance Ivan Ivanovich summoned Sergei, the tattooist.

'After this, life for me became very different. I ate well, occasionally even got herring, and had the luxury of two mugs of hot water twice a day. I was also able to get tobacco whenever I wanted it, slept near the window next to Igor, close to Ivan Ivanovich, and was far away from the slop bucket. I was assigned a job in the small library, which only the camp employees and trusties were given access to – Ivan Ivanovich honouring my love of books – and I savoured my time here away from the clamour of the barracks to contemplate and reflect. Furthermore I did not have to show up for work if I did not want to. In fact there were no consequences should I stay in the barracks for the day, those closest to Ivan Ivanovich afforded this privilege, which was perhaps the ultimate reward for what I had done, the decision I had made: I no longer had to contribute to the system I so loathed.

'I started to learn the thieves' language, this language that was defined by sex and violence, and to understand the hierarchy more, which was determined, in part, by the offence committed. A Moscow bank robber was going to carry a lot more respect than a Siberian small-town thief. Many of these lowly thieves aspired to be bank robbers or more, and thus served the higher criminals as valets and messengers. Vasily found it difficult to accept me, however, and was envious of my friendship with Ivan Ivanovich, who treated me as an equal rather than as one of his men. Yet there was little Vasily could do, and I was not a direct threat to him in light of my unique status: I was not an aspiring thief-in-law.

'The following weeks I did not attend work – I refused to, could not even bring myself to maintain this small library used by a handful of warders and trusties. For why should I help anyone in uniform, anyone who collaborated, anyone who contributed to the system? I even found myself judging my former friends for this, though they had little choice but to contribute.

'Some days I wondered if it might help me to go and see Nikolai or Mikhail. Might their kind hearts diffuse some of my anger and bitterness? I still missed them. However, I did not. Rather I sat quietly with Ivan Ivanovich and contemplated my revenge, how I would get to Vladimir Vladimirovich.

'Thus when Igor and I were dispatched to bury four bodies one morning, I immediately realised that this was my chance to escape – Ivan Ivanovich had arranged it – and that I had to take it. And though I knew the consequences, should I be caught, were awful, I was not afraid. For I had nothing more to lose. Igor would accompany me, as he had work to do for Ivan Ivanovich on the outside. "Take this," Ivan Ivanovich said to me as we stood in the compound and waited to be escorted, handing me some smoked fish wrapped in newspaper. "You'll need it for the journey ahead. And don't worry, Vadim won't search you, I've made sure of that," he assured me. "Okay," I replied, opening my felt jacket and shoving the package of fish beneath my undershirt. I was wearing winter clothes even though it was still autumn. "Don't forget to take his pocket compass. And keep heading south," he advised. "Right." "You're carrying?" he asked, turning to Igor. "Yes," Igor replied, lifting his shirt to reveal a large blade tucked into his trouser hip. "And you have the money I gave you?" Ivan Ivanovich enquired. "Yes," the young thief answered. "Good luck on the outside, Aleksei. It's an even bigger prison zone out there," he said. "Here's Boris Andreyevich's address. Go and see him when you get to Moscow," he added, handing me a knife, the address carved into the wood of the handle. "Thank you, Ivan," I replied, lifting my shirt and slipping the knife into the same place as Igor's. "My pleasure," Ivan Ivanovich said with his distinctive nod.

'Vadim approached and we were led off. We first collected the cadavers from the shed, depositing two per barrow, then wheeled these into the forest. He made us walk for about an hour before eventually ordering us to stop and set the barrows down. "Now get on with it. Take the shovels and dig!" Vadim shouted dismissively. I knew we must conserve as much energy as we could for the big journey ahead – the railway, the Trans-Siberian, was two thousand kilometres away – so if we were to kill him it had to be right away. Igor and I turned our backs on Vadim, as instructed, and, shovels in hand, we commenced digging. We waited for him to light a cigarette – when Vadim did this he would temporarily let go of his rifle, which he carried instead of a machine gun, and I would have time to swing round, take one big step forward and smash him over the head with the end of the shovel, and then Igor would finish him off with his knife. We dug for ten minutes, and nothing, though it would only be a matter of time, as he was a heavy smoker. However, he spoke before he smoked. "Dear Father finally died, by the way," Vadim grumbled, "your old fucking friend. Last night. The prick never stopped believing!" I was not prepared to wait any longer, for the sound of the match to flare, rather rolled my shoulders and turned on one leg like a discus thrower as my arms flew round and the shovel smashed into the side of Vadim's face. It did not hit it square, but side on, the sharp edge slashing his cheek.

'At first Vadim looked no more than mildly affronted as he held his hand to his cheek, but then, removing it, this quickly turned to outrage as he felt his slashed right cheek slimy and bloody in the palm of his hand as if he were a butcher holding a freshly cut fillet. Igor did not pounce on him immediately, I didn't know why, instead hesitated, perhaps overcome by this almost unreal spectacle, and Vadim, though his knees were buckling, managed to grab hold of his rifle, which still hung from his shoulder, and fire it, hitting Igor in the head and chest. Igor did not stand a chance, and died instantly.

'He turned the gun on me now, but I managed to swing the shovel again, this time hitting Vadim square on and with such force that he collapsed face-down in the snow.

'I leaned over and reached for his wrist to check his pulse. Vadim was dead. I slumped beside Igor, stroked his face, and sat like this for about a quarter of an hour in a daze of grief, for him and for Nikolai, before eventually deciding I must bury him – I could not leave him to the wolves. We had dug no more than twenty centimetres, and so I took the shovel and worked flat out until the hole was about a metre deep. I could not afford to go deeper than this. I laid Igor's large muscular body in the grave, took the small bundle of rouble notes Ivan Ivanovich had given him, closed his eyes, then filled in the hole.

'After this I went over to Vadim, stripped his body and fashioned a sack out of his undershirt and long johns, into which I put his compass, his tobacco, his hat and gloves, Igor's knife and money, and a small axe which lay in the bottom of one of the barrows.

'Then I set off,' Aleksei concluded, his lengthy confession at last at an end.

He sighed heavily. It was dark now. Natasha had said nothing all this time.

He watched her get up from the rocking chair, walk over to the bench and sit down beside him, putting her arms around his broad shoulders and holding him in the cool winter night air.

14ᵀᴴ APRIL 1954
BARANCHIKI, PORT BAIKAL

It had been over two months since Aleksei had confessed to Natasha about his killing of the Azerbaijani and Vadim, yet it was now he who wanted a confession from her, still unsure of quite how she had got away from Vladimir Vladimirovich, how she'd managed to leave Moscow. There were simply too many unanswered questions, his doubt even greater in view of the fact that she'd failed to ask him, as he was sure she would, whether he'd taken his revenge on Vladimir Vladimirovich.

Since the confession, he'd spent time remembering his escape from Butugychag, his journey south all the way to Chita. It was October when he'd at last escaped. He recalled how, when the smoked fish Ivan Ivanovich had given him had run out, he'd been forced to hunt, killing first a deer, then a bighorn; and how, when Yakutsk had come into view, after he'd walked for hundreds of kilometres without seeing anything but *taiga*, he'd felt like a beast that had just come in from the cold. He'd had to avoid two local policemen as he headed for some hot food: he might no longer have been wearing his camp-issue felt jacket, but they would have immediately known where he'd come from, that he had to be an escaped convict. For prisoners were never released: they either escaped or died. There had only been two dishes on the menu, Aleksei remembered, a choice of raw frozen pony liver or boiled reindeer, and he'd eaten the latter. When he had finally got to Chita, having hitched a ride from a truck driver, he'd then taken the train back to Moscow, from where he had been dragged over three years before. He'd climbed into an empty wagon at the end of the platform, and the first thing he had seen had been an old metal grate in the middle of the floor, which had made him shudder, this the giveaway that the cargo had once been human not animal: for only the former had been able to escape through the sanitation hole. Yet other than this, all evidence of its past use had been scrubbed and washed away, the dark wood and iron concealing countless atrocities. And the stench of death, well, this had long gone, the wagon's open door allowing the Siberian air to do its cleansing work. The journey had gone on and on, the landscape before him huge, the vast *taiga* harsh and striking like the Russian soul, and he had not arrived in Moscow until December.

He had imagined that his confession would bring Natasha and him closer together, but of course how could it, as he had withheld what he then did afterwards. He had assassinated five men in cold blood. Aleksei was yet to hear from Ivan Ivanovich, which surprised him. He'd expected by now a visit from one of his men. He'd asked Natasha, on several occasions, to elaborate further, yet every time she'd been elusive. Aleksei did not want to force the issue. For he was reunited with her, his beautiful wife, and that was all that mattered. The last thing he wanted to do was jeopardise their reunion. Yet his doubts persisted.

Maybe it was this, her inability to be straight with him, which kept them at a distance, Aleksei considered, which prevented them from loving one another as they used to. And this separateness, this detachment was so hard because being reunited with her was what had sustained him all those years in the camp, Aleksei being sure that once they were together again they would be perfectly happy. That they were not together pained him.

He did acknowledge, however, that it had to be difficult for Natasha to be with him again. He'd changed a lot. Though Aleksei still possessed a formidable intellect, he did not exercise it. Rather he had got work on the shore maintaining the fishing boats. He faced the same predicament as she did – there was little demand for an academic in Baranchiki, a former history professor about as useful as a former art historian – yet whereas Natasha continued to indulge her knowledge of, and passion for, art when she was not working in the bakery or as a seamstress, the local library a lifeline in this respect, Aleksei was content to abandon his academic discipline, his love of history, altogether, in favour of his practical work on the shore. And he enjoyed it, this menial work, principally because he could do it at his own pace, able to rest when he needed to, this the antithesis of his working life in the camp, where everything had been prescribed, monitored, controlled. Christ, he hadn't even been able to pause for just two minutes without risking the wrath of Vadim! he recalled. He also liked to help Yevgeny, a local fisherman, with his catch, hauling the wooden crates of omul up the pebbly beach, taking the load, feeling the heavy weight in his back and knees as he braced himself and then made the short, awkward walk back up the shore. Taking small rapid steps, his legs slightly bent, buttocks protruding, he resembled a giant crab, much to Yevgeny's perpetual amusement.

Natasha, conversely, often tired of the work she now had to do, and so had started to draw and paint again, this clearly sustaining her, Aleksei could see, as did the beauty of the place. She'd started doing landscapes, which she had never done when she was in Moscow. Only nudes and portraits interested her back then. When Katya was at school and she was not with Pavel at the bakery or busy with seamstress work Natasha headed for her favourite spot on the lake. She came here not just out of hopeless sentimentality, but also because it was the ideal vantage point to work from marked first by a vast pine tree that she found herself wanting to depict over and over, this thing of natural beauty that her eye never tired of, and second by a tall mountain peak which loomed over her like a benevolent spirit, a spirit she hoped would keep her and her family safe. Natasha always maintained to Aleksei that beneath the historian was an artist: for how else could he have chosen such a place? Her friendship with Marina was also vital to her, Aleksei realised. Marina, another former city girl, shared the same need as her – the clamour of large numbers of people, which Baranchiki would never provide, and without this stimulus the two of them spent hours remembering their lives in the city, these recollections seeming to keep something alive within them that might otherwise have died. Marina's love was not art but literature: she was obsessed with Tolstoy, whom she had read over and over, all his works, including his essays on social reform and religion. Her favourite novel was *Resurrection*. She would have got on with Poppa, that's for sure, Aleksei thought, though he of course would have maintained that Dostoevsky was the greater novelist. 'For who better captured the startling contradictions in men's souls than Fyodor,' he used to say to Aleksei over and over. That he might have, Aleksei mused – though he knew Marina was better qualified than him, as an historian, to make the judgment about which of them was the better writer – though in his estimation Dostoevsky was not as interesting a human being as Tolstoy, nor as likeable. The former responded to his own human failings rather predictably and unconvincingly: he became a conservative – politically, socially and religiously. In truth, Aleksei found this more than just unconvincing. He had contempt for it! Tolstoy's conversion had far more depth and sincerity to it, as far as he was concerned, the aristocrat renouncing wholeheartedly his nobility, his decadence, his intellectualism, in favour of spiritual transformation, which gave birth to a message of universal love. But then he would romanticise Tolstoy, his mystic fervour, wouldn't he!? Natasha insisted. Forever the contrarian!

Their reunion was also difficult because Aleksei was unable to live under his real identity – the former professor and brave war veteran – but had had to assume another if he was to elude the authorities and preserve his freedom. He had not been released but had escaped, and had killed a guard in the process. And even with his made-up status as a returnee, released in the first amnesty, reintegration was hard. Despite the monster's death, still the returnee was shunned, distrusted, judged harshly.

In one respect it was as if his arrest and imprisonment had rid him of his belief in the importance of history, and though on one level this was hardly surprising in light of the fact that the Communists had so utterly ignored its lessons, on the other it was surprising because he'd maintained to Natasha right up until the day he was dragged off to the Lubyanka that history must always be explored and consulted, its lessons invaluable. Natasha hated them for this, she told Aleksei, that they'd robbed him of his precious subject, his way of seeing and interpreting the world.

But why could she not accept that he had changed? Aleksei asked. Perhaps such personal change only occurred when someone really suffered. The majority of people plodded through life retaining the same character, personality, demeanour. Life was relatively easy. They were not challenged, did not evolve. However, real adversity visited a few, forcing this small number to think and act in exceptional ways, in ways they never would have dreamed of. The hardship got inside these few, altering them, and sometimes completely transforming them, Aleksei thought.

It was a warm spring evening and they lay on a rug in front of the house and ate dinner, some smoked omul, which Aleksei had brought back from work today. Katya was in Irkutsk for the night. There was a strained atmosphere between them.

'We're not happy together, are we?' Aleksei suddenly announced.

'What are you saying?' Natasha asked.

'Well, just this. You seem not to love me as much, as much as you used to.'

'Where's this coming from?'

'From you, Natasha. I sense it, feel it.'

She took a slow breath before speaking. 'Things are different, aren't they?'

'Yes, and you seem like you can't accept that,' he said.

'I'm finding it difficult. I just keep on thinking about how we were.'

'You can't do this. If you do, we've no chance.'

'Have you changed that much?' she enquired, staring into his eyes.

'What d'you mean?'

'I think you need to get back to academia, to teaching.'

'How can I?' he asked incredulously, sitting up on the rug and straightening his back.

'You can go to the authorities, confess, tell them what you told me. They'll pardon you, I know they will.'

Aleksei knew she would not have dared suggest this if she knew the full truth, what he'd done once he escaped. 'You don't honestly believe that, do you?' he went on.

'Why not?'

'Come on, Natasha, think,' he demanded. 'It seems to me that if anyone's frustrated, if anyone's hankering for a return to the comfort of the past, to the way things were, it's you. Why don't you go back to teaching!?'

'I can't.'

'Why not, Natasha? I mean, he hasn't come after you, it's been ten months since you left Moscow.'

'I know…'

'If you'd be happier returning to Moscow, to teaching, then you should.'

'What about us, then?'

'What about your happiness?'

'Look, I just can't, okay. Let's leave it!' she shouted.

'Why!?' Aleksei demanded, determined for the truth now.

'I killed him, Aleksei…I killed him!'

Aleksei was speechless at first, and Natasha silent also. She stared off into the distance, lost, it seemed to Aleksei, in the pain of her revelation – the pangs of conscience and difficult memories, which Aleksei knew all too well.

They both sat in silence for some time, eluding one another's gaze, before she at last spoke.

Natasha began, 'I still remember so clearly that first week after you'd been taken. It was awful. I was going out of my mind, pacing frantically up and down our small kitchen, night after night. "Where were you? How could they do this!?" I asked these questions over and over. And Katya kept on asking where you were too, and each time I simply told her that you'd be back soon. But I didn't know this, of course I didn't. You might never come back! Katya had struggled to sleep with you gone. What was this doing to our daughter? I wondered. And at such a tender age!? That bastard Vladimir Vladimirovich came to my work, to the Institution, while I was in the middle of giving a talk on Chagall. He deliberately sought to embarrass me in front of my students and colleagues, insisting that it couldn't wait, that he needed to talk to me right away, that it was about my husband. They all knew then that you'd been arrested. In my office he looked me up and down like I was a whore, kept sniffing as if he was hungry and wanted to consume me, his eyes all over my body, stare seeming to penetrate beneath my very clothes. Urgh, he repulsed me! He didn't admire me like you did, through gentle, discerning and loving green eyes. Rather his hazel eyes were hard and hateful. He next told me that you were "done for" unless I cooperated. Did he really think that I'd denounce my husband? I asked. How could he think that!?

'And I next recall him in our living room after you'd been sentenced. Katya sat in her small wooden rocking chair opposite, swaying gently back and forth, while I sat on the worn and weary sofa next to him. Vladimir Vladimirovich held my hand sympathetically as I stared blankly at the floor. He said for the second time, "I'm sorry, Natasha," and again I was silent, said nothing. "Did you hear me?" he asked, pressing me for an answer, a response of any kind, though I knew that if I did permit myself one it would be an eruption of anger, and so I gritted my teeth, pressed my lips together, in a bid to contain myself, to remain quiet for just a little longer, because then he'd go, leave me alone once and for all. For I'd had enough of his visits, he came all the time, and I hardly needed to receive him any more now that your fate had been sealed. "Look Natasha, if I'd had it my way," he persisted, "I would've had him released without charge, but I had no choice, it went above me. They judge him to be a serious threat, you see. And anyway, he confessed." "Of course he didn't! Come on!" I eventually shouted back, pulling his hand away from mine. "And how can you really suggest he's a 'serious threat', a counter-revolutionary? You know he isn't! He doesn't like you-know-who, but then, who does. Yes, he's critical, but it's his job to be." "He's a historian not a politician," Vladimir Vladimirovich insisted, "and you'd better watch what you say, especially in front of Katya." "We don't have politicians, just Party members. Katya...please go to your room," I said, and waited for her to leave before addressing him again. "What...you going to arrest me now as well!?" I asked. "Enough of the wisecracks, okay," he replied. "I know you're high up enough to have got him off if you'd really wanted to," I said. "Then why didn't I?" he asked coolly. "I know why..." I responded cautiously. "Well, tell me..." "Because..." and I could not say it. "Because I like you, Natasha. Yes, that's it. Say it..." he answered his own question matter-of-factly, and I was rendered speechless, this time by his sheer audacity, that he'd practically confessed to constructing your guilt, consigning you to a quarter of a century in a labour camp because he wanted me, your wife, for himself.

'While he stared at me I summoned the courage to speak again. "You like me?" I asked abruptly, getting to my feet. "Yes," he answered, and stood as well. "You mean you want to fuck me," I said. "That as well," he replied, smirking. "And so you went after my husband like a crazed dog." "Look, he's an enemy of the people!" Vladimir Vladimirovich insisted. "Are you mad? One minute you're telling me you simply concocted his guilt because you want me for yourself, the next you're insisting that he's actually guilty of something," I maintained. "Of course he's guilty of something. He's guilty of not believing, of not supporting Stalin, the people, the common good," Vladimir Vladimirovich demanded. "No, he's guilty of possessing too much courage, standing up to sheep like you," I retorted. "Look, you'd better give me what I want because I can make things even worse for you, you hear me," he said menacingly, facing up to me. "What have you got up your sleeve now, then?" I asked. "I'll make sure that Aleksei doesn't get the chance to work out his sentence but is executed, that you're thrown in a camp in the arsehole of nowhere like he's just been, and that Katya rots in state care for the rest of her miserable young life." I was silent. "So be nice then, Natasha," Vladimir Vladimirovich concluded, stroking my cheek, kissing me on the lips, then leading me into the bedroom, our bedroom.

'Those first few months you were away, Aleksei, I felt like I was in the midst of a nightmare and that I'd wake at any moment and it would be over. But days, weeks passed and I was yet to wake up. I hated myself for letting him fuck me. Did I give in too easily? I asked myself this question repeatedly… no, more than that, incessantly. I felt as I did when my mother, and then my father, died. Utterly lost! I still didn't know where they'd sent you. The most I'd got out of Vladimir so far – yes, I referred to him by his first name now, "the bastard" was becoming familiar – was that you'd been sent east to a camp. This, of course, meant hard labour. I prayed not in Kolyma. I knew I must do all I could to find out where you were, to help you. If I could secure your early release, get you out in ten, even fifteen, then that would be something. I could not even comprehend what was surely going through your mind. Twenty-five years! This must have seemed like a lifetime. I struggled to grasp, let alone accept, it.

'How could I wait this long? "But I can, I will, because I love Aleksei," I said out loud, I remember this, while laying on the floor of your study, on your favourite Persian rug, the orange and red one, in the early evening summer sun, which beamed through the small window in front of your desk. I gazed up, squinting through the rare sunlight, at your countless bookshelves, these great towers of learning that lined every wall, almost encircling me. When I had got home from work that day, worn out after a full day's teaching, I'd taken myself straight there, to your study, because I missed you desperately and needed to be with you, to feel you beside me, at your desk, reading and writing, immersed in your beloved history. I'd sat on your old leather-backed desk chair and stared down at a brown monochrome photograph propped up against the window ledge of the two of us taken a few years before outside Moscow State Art Institution. Was this the only hint of colour left in my country? I'd wondered. Then my mind turned to Vladimir. He'd told me the previous night that he loved me. How could he say that!? He threatened me, then forced me to have sex. He compelled me to enter into a relationship with him, giving me no choice but to comply. And he called this "love". How could he give it this name? It was perverse, wicked! I thought, sitting up then and bringing my knees to my chest, clutching them like a little girl seeking to comfort herself. However, at the same time he said he could help me, that he'd try and get your sentence reduced, that he'd ensure nothing happened to Katya and me, the family of a serious political prisoner. How could I trust him? Yet what choice did I have, I speculated, remaining seated on the floor, swinging my legs gently from side to side, this motion consoling me as the sun began to fade and set.

'I longed to hear from you. I recalled the day in August '49 when I stood outside waiting for Katya after her ballet class, outside the big iron gates to the summer school. Evening, and I had really missed her. Other waiting mothers mingled, trying to engage me in conversation, ask how I was, how Katya was, when she would next be performing, and in which ballet, but my mind was elsewhere. If only you and I could at least correspond with one another, I thought. Though you had been told that you could receive mail, you in fact could not, this part of your punishment, Vladimir informed me. For you had been "deprived of the right to correspond", in the words of the state. As your crimes were of a very serious political nature, constituted a real threat to the security of the Soviet republic and its peoples, you could not be trusted with any correspondence with the outside world. But what if you wrote to me, if your letters were censored, contained no political references, were of a personal nature only? I asked him. Surely this was permitted! Well, you could write and send such a letter, Vladimir told me, but I'd never receive it. Then why let you write such a letter in the first place!? I demanded. Why not simply tell you there's no point in writing it as I won't receive it? Again, part of your punishment, Vladimir maintained. Just as you were allowed to think you could receive mail, so you were allowed to think if you sent it I would receive it.

'This was cruel! All it did was make you suspect me even more. That you never heard from me, never received a reply to one of your letters, meant that I had surely betrayed you. Perhaps I should verify with someone what Vladimir had told me, I wondered then, and looked to the three gossiping women who stood next to me, and speculated as to whether they might know, but of course they would not, I thought, and would scarcely say if they did, as this was hardly a conversation to be having at the school gates, how difficult it was to correspond with one's husband when he was consigned to hard labour. I simply had to accept that I had no means of communicating with you.

'Vladimir continued to maintain that your crimes were real, that you deserved to be punished for your criticism of Stalin and the Soviet system. It seemed that even though he'd constructed your guilt out of fiction, this had now become fact in his mind. He was utterly deluded! You might be allowed to receive mail in the future, however, Vladimir suggested, and though I knew he merely said this to give me hope, I had to believe him, for the time being at least. For if he was in a position to ease your suffering, then I had to appease him, stay with him, use him.

'How I hated the position Vladimir had put me in, this bastard, whom I had to demean myself with night after night – he on top of me, thrusting away, desperate to please me even though he couldn't and never would, not least on account of his incredibly small penis that would struggle to satisfy even a sex-starved mouse. I was stuck with him, had nowhere to go. For it was not as if I could report him to the authorities! And I could not run away either. He'd covered off this eventuality as well, telling me that if I did he'd find me, and that before he did he'd have you executed.

'When that first winter came, I wondered how on earth you would survive it. Stalingrad might have been cold, but Kolyma – this was where you were, I was sure of this by now, though he hadn't told me – was something else. I remember one particular night when I couldn't sleep. The dream that had woken me two hours earlier still preoccupied me. I'd dreamt I was standing in a barren field, only to realise that it was vast and had no end, and that I might never find my way out. I got up and ambled around the bedroom. I missed you dreadfully, longed to wake up beside you. I sniffed the air. Your smell, which I know and love, was fading. One of your jackets still carried a faint whiff, but other than this, nothing. I hurried to the wardrobe and buried my face in it, the fabric of this jacket, sucked it up ecstatically, as if inhaling an exquisite perfume. I uttered your name several times, yes, I remember, had to preserve this last bit of you. I took the jacket off its hanger and stuffed it in the small wooden trunk at the foot of the wardrobe. It had been more than six months since I'd last seen you. I'd dreamt the previous night that Vladimir had destroyed the drawings, paintings and few photographs I had of you. The dream had been so compelling in fact that I'd got out of bed at three o'clock in the morning and gone in search of them, these things of yours, needing to be sure that he hadn't, that they were still there, underneath Katya's bed. They were, thank God, and so the next day I'd taken them to the Institution, sure that they'd be safe there. I could not let Vladimir have these last pieces of you. You see, he wanted to eradicate you, was sure that one day I'd finally see the light and express my undying love for him instead. Vladimir was driven by this pathetic fantasy till the very end. And that night, in order to preserve you, I decided to draw and paint you…yes…needed to be with you, to understand how you were, feel your suffering at that moment. And by drawing you, by painting you, I could do this, be with you. And maybe help you too, lessen your pain. I hurried to the living room, pulled an old sketch book out of my desk drawer, some willow charcoal and some black and white paint, and began to draw and paint you from memory, using my hands and fingertips, no pencils or brushes…and I was with you again, if only for an instant.

'The first Christmas for Katya without you was terrible. I insisted on celebrating it despite it being banned, and according to the Gregorian calendar – and Katya was tearful. She spent the whole day pining for you, sitting in her bedroom, and after that at the kitchen table quietly murmuring, 'Poppa…Poppa.' In the evening, when she had at last fallen asleep, I sat on my own in the living room and stared at the shoes and dresses that Vladimir had bought me, which lay on the Persian rug at the foot of the sofa. Even Vladimir Vladimirovich, the committed Communist, had bought into the Christmas spirit – though he had done it not out of goodwill but self-interest. He was not with me but with his mother – this woman who had given birth to such a vile man. He'd spent a small fortune on me, sure that he could buy my affection. The shoes, three pairs of them, all high heels, were Italian, and the dresses, another three, were French and made of silk and satin. A high-ranking member of State Security, he could get hold of anything of course. He might have been working to uphold all things Communist, yet this did not stop him buying goods that were inherently capitalist. Like all *nomenklatura*, he was a Communist only when it suited him to be one. For what was most important was power, not ideology! I had refused to

try on any of them all day – he'd dropped them round in the
morning – but now I did, the red heels and red silk dress, then
hurried into the bedroom and stood in front of the full-length
mirror in order to admire myself, running my hands excitedly
down my chest, over my stomach, onto my hips and down my
legs, until my fingers were touching the floor. The sensation of
the dress on my body was beautiful, so tight and smooth, and
the shoes magnificent, making my legs even longer, and I felt
wonderful, for the first time in ages. Yes, I was still a slave to this
particular bourgeois compulsion – the need, the desire, to wear
beautiful clothes. Shame on me! However, when I stood upright
and looked at myself once more, I was instantly horrified by
what I saw, that I, Natasha Sokholova, wife of Aleksei Klebnikov,
was delighting in these gifts bought for me by my husband's
nemesis, Vladimir Vladimirovich. How could I!? I tore at the
dress, ripping one strap and pulling it off me, then kicked off
the heels, both hitting the mirror hard. And lastly, my knees
buckled and I fell to the floor, sobbing uncontrollably, disgusted
with myself, staring at the peeling wallpaper which hung limply
from the wall, and then beyond this, into the hallway, at the
screw-back 'Distinguished NKVD Employee' badge – Vladimir
continued to wear this despite the security service's name change
– on his jacket that he'd left that morning, which hung on the
lopsided coatstand by the front door.

'Over the next year-and-a-half we seemed to fall into some
kind of domestic normality, Vladimir and I, and this frightened
me. Was I starting to finally accept my perverse relationship with
him, this man who was my captor, my tormentor, but who also
shared my bed? He'd started bringing his son Dmitri round, who
was a year older than Katya. Dmitri and Katya got on very well.
He had the very same face as his father – this was what I noticed
about him when I first met him, and yet his demeanour was
softer, kinder, thank goodness. He lived with his grandmother.

According to Vladimir, Dmitri's mother had walked out on them a number of years before. She, of course, had walked out on him, not her son, ultimately realising the kind of man she'd married, had a child with. God, maybe he'd murdered her? I wondered. The man was clearly capable of anything!

'He continued, throughout this period, to tell me that he loved me, that I was "the most exquisite, the most beautiful woman in the world," in his words, and that he'd "love me forever." Yet while he said these things he penetrated me from behind like a dog, held my head down against the pillow, his palm pressed hard against my cheek, and thrust into me as if he had contempt, not love, for me. However, what was most awful, Aleksei…I'm sorry, I have to be honest with you now, I must be…was that part of me relished this, being fucked by Vladimir in this way. I had always had contempt for the notion that the captive sometimes falls for the captor. But look at how so many had fallen for Koba. He might have been their jailer, but they, his prisoners, the Russian people, loved him!' Natasha said, looking right at Aleksei at this moment, into his eyes, though he was unable to meet her stare, so unsettled was he by her honesty.

She went on, 'When you told me how you had suffered in solitary I wept, and this was in part because I'd felt you the day you were sent there, after you attacked Vadim. I know I might sound mad saying this, but I recall the moment vividly when, on a bright Moscow afternoon, the sun shining strongly through the classroom window and the sky a pale blue, while standing before the students discussing the work of Kandinsky I was all of a sudden struck by the strong sense that you were in grave danger. I immediately lost my train of thought. Where was I? I had no idea. I knew what I was talking about generally, the artist's path to pure abstraction, but specifically, no, not a clue. "So, pure abstraction, yes, why would an intense theorist seek to…look to…why would someone like Kandinsky go in search of…" and the face of the pocket-sized young man in the front row, I cannot recall his name, said it all, that I was well and truly lost, and that however much I mumbled in general terms about abstraction – how very apt! – I was not going to find my way again, but rather was simply going to dig myself an even greater hole to clamber out of. "Oh fuck it, excuse me… sorry," I at last exclaimed, openly confessing my predicament, "just give me a few moments, okay…" and I walked out of the classroom and closed the door behind me. I stood up against the wall outside, out of view of all the students, and took deep breaths to calm myself. But I could not. Why? Because I felt you at this moment, and knew that something awful was about to happen to you…

'The relationship with Vladimir changed significantly in the autumn of '52. I remember that time well because there had been talk in Moscow that Stalin was sick, though I was sure the rumour was false, spread by his numerous enemies. As far as I was concerned the monster was immortal! Seventy-four years old and he was still going strong! On the front page of *Pravda*, however, he had looked more like a grey ghost than an all-powerful phantom, hardly a good thing for someone who could only live with absolute power. How he relished the latter image, the fear and awe it inspired, as if he, Iosif Vissarionovich Dzhugashvili, the former cobbler's son and street urchin from Gori, was in fact not of this world but a powerful awesome phantasm. He was rarely seen in public towards the end, in fact did become a virtual recluse, a problem for a man so vain, such a monumental narcissist, who thrived off public appearances and needed them, the adulation they brought. So I wondered what would happen if he really was sick and did die. Might you be released, Aleksei?

'I was not sure how much longer I could wait, continue to appease and tolerate Vladimir, and one morning, over breakfast,

I eventually confronted him. He was tetchy as soon as I asked him if he had news of you. Rarely here at this time of day, thank goodness, he preferred, rather, to treat me like a whore, turning up late at night to fuck me, then returning to his own place where he drank himself to a stupor before passing out on the sofa. It seemed he possessed sufficient self-awareness to realise he was virtually incapable of actually living with anyone: cohabitation did not accommodate self-contempt well, and he was full of it. Yet occasionally he did try to lead the normal life, and so here he was now, sitting beside me, eating bread and cheese with his son, his captive and his captive's daughter. One big happy family, the four of us! "Why are you asking me this now? Why?" he blurted out. "You know why. Because you'd promised me some news, and you owe it to Katya to let her know how her father is," I replied. "Don't put it on her, Natasha," and he pointed at Katya dismissively. "It's you who really wants to know!" I shot back, "Of course I want to know, you know I do, but right now I'm more concerned about Katya knowing something." "Look, I'll make some enquiries, okay, just leave it with me," he mumbled. "This is what you said last week, and the week before that," I maintained. "What d'you expect me to tell you, huh? That he's not dead yet, that he's going to be out next year. I mean... he's a twenty-fiver!" Vladimir insisted. "You..." I went to say. "Dad, that's not fair, Katya misses him so much..." Dmitri interjected. "Shut up, okay... just shut up..." Vladimir shouted, and he grabbed his son by the collar and clouted him round the head. Sometimes his sharp tongue eluded him and violence was the only other response he was capable of.

'Dmitri looked horrified, then wiped a tear from his eye. The enduring innocence of a child, I thought, even though Dmitri was now a young man. He knew all too well that his father was often violent towards him, yet still, every time he was, Dmitri looked at him as if it was the first time. There's nothing more powerful than the righteous indignation of one's children, yet even this did not deter Vladimir. "Shit, I can't deal with this," Vladimir sighed, pushing his plate away and getting to his feet. "You can't deal with it. Then what about your son, who you just hit?" I retorted. "Look, I know, I know…I'm sorry, son, I didn't mean it," Vladimir said, appealing to him. "You always say that," Dmitri replied. "It seems your son knows you better than you know yourself!" I quipped.

'Vladimir surprised me at this moment. He did not respond as he usually did when justly criticised and condemned, becoming offensive and abusive, but started to cry and then could not stop, embracing his son and next me, insisting he was sorry, so sorry, that he wished he could control himself, wished he could drink less, wished he could show how much he really loved us all. He finished with, "I must go, I'm sorry again, really. Dmitri, please forgive me. I'll never lay another hand on you." Then to me, "Look, I'll find out about Aleksei, I promise, see if I can get him out sooner. You know why I haven't done this, because I'm terrified what will happen should he be released. You'd leave me, of course you would, and I simply couldn't live without you. I couldn't."

'I found myself touched by him for the first time that morning as he walked out the door, so fragile, so vulnerable, because I felt that I'd at last seen some truth in Vladimir, this quality which you possessed so much of, Aleksei, which had made me fall in love with you.

'News did come soon that you were alive and well, and though I knew I'd be foolish to suddenly trust him, part of me wanted to. Vladimir said he was certain that when Stalin died things would change, everyone in State Security said so, and consequently your sentence would be reduced with a new leadership in place – and he'd make sure of this, for Katya's sake at the very least. I went over his words again and again, my mind churning like a broken record. Was he just holding out false hope for me? I wondered. Koba might live for another ten, twenty years! However, ever since Vladimir had cried that morning he had been different, and in light of this I was inclined to believe him, because he'd at last admitted to himself how wrong he'd been and that he'd be lost without me and without the love of his son. He possessed a helplessness, a frailty, finally, and with this always came a certain decency, truthfulness.

'I remember that same night after he told me your whereabouts he held me with great tenderness after he'd come inside me, and for a long time. Again, I hate being this frank with you, Aleksei, but I must be. He didn't simply roll off me or push me aside as he normally did. And when he eventually let go, he lay his head down opposite mine and stared adoringly into my eyes and stroked my cheeks, and I was struck by how handsome he was, and though I'd never allowed myself to acknowledge this – how could I, after what he'd done – I did at this moment. Though he still insisted that you would've been given twenty-five irrespective of the fact that he was the arresting officer, Vladimir went on to tell me, in a hushed and sad voice, how ashamed he continued to feel about what he'd done – how he'd threatened me in order to keep me – but that he'd done this out of love, however perverse this might seem. He confessed that this was "an awful love", in his words – abusive, cruel, obsessive – and yet "a love all the same". He ended by saying, "I want to try and earn your love now before it's too late, and though part of me knows it most likely is too late, that Aleksei might be out soon, that you can never forgive me for what I've done, all I've said, I can at least try if you'll let me." And lying there, in the black of the Moscow night, still unable to sleep, these words of his continued to niggle, trouble and preoccupy me, until I was losing my mind. How could it be that I suddenly felt for this man, cared about him? How?

'I remember that it was the very end of the year when I thought I saw you. In fact, for a brief moment, I was sure it was you, and that Vladimir's recent transformation was therefore nothing but an illusion, one further falsehood. At Kirovskaya, I stood on the escalator as it descended into the bowels of Moscow. I thought about the week before, 21 December. A few other work colleagues and I had had to celebrate Comrade Stalin's birthday – always something obscene about this. For though the majority of us knew that he was a tyrant, as you well know, still we celebrated him, some out of coercion, others freely. We were made to stand in front of the Institution and were instructed to sing happy birthday. "Enough of Koba!" I remonstrated, and returned my attention to where I was, looking down the escalator and admiring the tall lanterns which illuminated this underworld. I gazed down, letting my eyes follow the parade of lights all the way to the bottom, their end marked by a small metal cabin in which sat, no doubt, a surly station attendant.

'I looked across at the other escalator, which ascended this great burrow and saw one other passenger, a lone man, some way off. The way he stood, hands in pockets, head cocked thoughtfully to one side, reminded me of you. I waited for him to come closer, and, as he did, as he neared me, I looked at him intently. He didn't have your well-built frame and his face was obscured by a thick beard, yet it could still be you, I thought. I leaned over, almost losing my footing, and as I came up parallel with the man I stared right at him, hoping to look into his eyes, your eyes, but he didn't reciprocate my gaze, rather looked away awkwardly. Were his eyes green? I was sure they were, yes. But not gentle, no, but then, how could they be if it was indeed you, after what you'd been through. I was instantly sure that it was you and so shouted, "Aleksei, Aleksei!" But you didn't turn round, no, just looked straight ahead like you hadn't heard me. "It's you, isn't it? Aleksei? Aleksei!" I screamed.

'The attendant – yes, there was one installed in the cabin at the bottom of the escalator, and as expected she was surly too – was roused from her stupor of ennui, of civic duty, by my frantic cries, and called out, 'What are you doing? What are you doing?' over and over. At first I ignored her and continued to shout after you. Only when you reached the top of the escalator did you finally turn round, and though you were too far away now, you seemed to look at me as if you did know me after all, were my lost husband, were Katya's father, were my true love…Aleksei Nikolayevich Klebnikov. But then you disappeared out of sight.

'The attendant bellowed into my ear, "Have you gone mad?" "It's nothing to do with you, okay," I shouted back, stepping off the escalator. "Yes it is, when you're making a show of yourself and disturbing other comrades." "Look around you! There are no other comrades!" I insisted. "What am I then?" she asked. "Oh, just get back in your bloody box, will you?" I walked away, onto the platform, worried that the attendant might follow me, report me, but she didn't, she let me be. Perhaps, for her, sisterhood preceded Soviethood. Was it you? I asked myself again. No, it couldn't have been, you were in a labour camp. Had you escaped, Vladimir would've told me. If it were you, you would have acknowledged me sooner, would've come to me. No, it wasn't you, I concluded. And yet I felt you here in my heart,' and Natasha touched her chest at this moment, her memory so vivid, and Aleksei was forced to wonder whether it had been him. For he remembered this period well also, the month when he'd finally seen Natasha's betrayal for himself. Had they been reunited then, he would not have agreed to Ivan Ivanovich's mission.

Natasha continued, 'A train was coming, I heard its murmur growing louder. I was talking of you like I was with you again, like you'd never left. Though you didn't leave, but were taken. Why did I feel you again? There had to be a reason,' and Aleksei swallowed uncomfortably when he heard these words, knowing that her intuition had been right.

She went on, 'The train pulled up alongside the platform. I got on. However, was I not deluding myself with this feeling? Perhaps my heart had concocted it, and it represented one last desperate bid to bring you back even though you were never coming back! I rubbed my forehead with the tips of my fingers, vainly hoping that this physical gesture might relieve some of the pressure of my thoughts, lessen their power, their effect. The woman sitting opposite gazed at me with a worried look, as if observing someone on the verge of a nervous breakdown, and I did feel close to mental collapse at that moment.

'It was only when the monster eventually died that I had to accept what was becoming increasingly inevitable, that Vladimir was still lying to me and always would, that he wasn't a reformed character, hadn't had a great change of heart. When the news broke, he sat at the kitchen table looking pale and stunned, whereas I, what did I do, but start to cry. 'It was last night,' Vladimir said, his voice flat, monotone. "Right…" I mumbled through heavy tears. "Why are you crying?" he asked. "I don't know…" I replied. "You hated him," Vladimir said. "Yes…" I answered. "I told you he wouldn't be around forever." "Yes, you did." "I'd better get off," Vladimir said, getting to his feet. "Okay…" I muttered. "To the office?" I enquired. "Yes, I'll see you later, okay," and he went to leave. "Will Malenkov take over now?" I called to him. Taking in this question, Vladimir stopped by the front door and turned round slowly before speaking, "Why d'you ask?" "I'm just curious, that's all," I replied. "How should I know?" he said, sounding hostile for the first time in a long while. "Well, I thought you would've heard something." "And why's that?" "Well… because you're a senior officer in State Security," I said. "Are you thinking about who'll be best for Aleksei?" he asked.

"Yes…I am," I confessed, "but I also just want to know who'll succeed Stalin." "I hope it's Beria," Vladimir said smugly. "No, he'd be awful, the man is a…" and I hesitated now. "What, Natasha?" "Err…nothing." "What is he, Natasha?" he asked threateningly. "You know what he is, Vladimir!" I insisted. "Former NKVD Chief and now Deputy Prime Minister," he replied. "Not that!" I shouted. "And this is why he'd make a good leader. He's tough, ruthless," Vladimir answered his own question bluntly. "The Russian people wouldn't stand a chance under him. He's crueler than Stalin." "You mean, Aleksei wouldn't," and with this final remark he closed the door behind him, leaving me alone to speculate.

'That spring, however, and the place did feel different. I remember the first amnesty of political prisoners, freedom given to those with five years or less, and also to women and children. And who had effectuated this first amnesty, but Beria, the sadist. Could you believe it? There was even an exhibition of the avant-garde put on, yes, featuring works by Malevich, Gonchorova and Popova. I couldn't wait to see them, these works which Lenin and Stalin so despised because they had no obvious function or purpose – this, of course, making the prospect of viewing them even more wonderful! I was also excited since I'd had my fill of socialist-realist shows, which, as you well know, typically included Malevich portraits of leading Communists (how he must have hated painting those!), such appalling kitsch works a betrayal of his great talent. There's only so long an artist can deceive himself. It's no wonder Mayakovsky committed suicide! And so perhaps Vladimir was right after all, I thought. Yet would he, Beria, would they, the authorities, grant the same reprieve to those in Kolyma, where you were, this home of *katorga*, the twenty-fivers? I was not so sure…

'It was on 3 June 1953. It was early morning, Katya had just left for her ballet class and I lay in bed, Vladimir bedside me.

My mind was on you. It jumped from one thought to the next, desperate for an answer, wanting to know why, if so many had been released since Koba's death, you still hadn't. Reeling from the perpetual doubt about your fate, I needed some certainty, and so sat up, pulled at Vladimir's shoulder, shook it, and asked him straight out, "Where is he?"

'Vladimir stirred in his sleep and rolled over, bleary-eyed. "What are you talking about?" he grumbled. "Where is he?" I asked again. "Who?" he shouted. "You know who." He paused for a moment, then said coolly, "I didn't tell you at the time…" "What?" "He escaped." "What?" I asked again. "Yes, last year in October," Vladimir said flatly. "What are you talking about?" "I just told you, he escaped." "How could you not have told me this?" "Why would I?" he responded matter-of-factly, sitting up in bed and leaning against the headboard. "Why? Because you said you'd changed, because he's Katya's father, because you claim to love me." Vladimir said nothing.

'I sat on my knees, looked into his eyes, and went on, "I don't believe you." "Don't then," he shot back. "Well…why would he?" I enquired. "What?" "Escape." "What d'you mean 'why?' He was sentenced to twenty-five," Vladimir responded. "Where is he now, then?" I asked. "How should I know!" "You know everything, it's your job to," I replied. "Well, I don't know that." "If he escaped he would have come back to Moscow, to find Katya and me." "But he didn't, did he?" "He's dead, isn't he, worked to death like all the rest!" I insisted, all of a sudden overcome with dread, sure of your fate. "You've just strung me along all this time, haven't you, so you can carry on fucking me and playing happy families once in a while!"

'I felt hot, my cheeks flushed and burning, mouth dry. "No," Vladimir answered. "Why didn't you tell me sooner? Why?" I screamed. "He's not dead…he's on the run." "Why, Vladimir?" "I'm sorry, Natasha," he replied, seeking to calm me, caressing my shoulder, and I saw that I'd got to him again. "And you know why," he went on. "Do I?" I asked. "Of course you do. You know I did it to protect you and Katya." "To protect yourself, you mean. As always you were looking out for yourself first and foremost." "No," he rebuffed. "Yes. You love me only because you cannot live without me." "But I can't." "That's not love, Vladimir." "What is it, then?" he retorted. "Self-preservation," I answered. "What is love, then?" "What I feel for Aleksei."

'Vladimir paused, then said coolly, "Fuck you, Natasha!" "And you've known that all along," I responded immediately, "that in spite of all that's passed between us I'm only with you because of Aleksei, because of Katya. It's all for them, it's always been just for them." "You bitch!" he snarled. "What you did to my husband, to me, and you thought you could simply have me once you'd got rid of him, and that I'd eventually forgive you this and end up loving you for it?" "Shut up," he cut in. "You know how mad you are?" I persisted. "Shut up," Vladimir said again. "A woman doesn't love any man, Vladimir, she loves a particular man. And I loved Aleksei, and still love him. I could never love a man like you."

'He stared coldly at me at this moment, wanting me to acknowledge…no, more than this…to feel his indifference, before speaking again. "Your good Aleksei…he's not so good any more." "What are you talking about?" I asked. "He's a murderer." "You'd say anything at this moment." "No, really, he is. He killed a fellow prisoner, knifed him in the back of the neck, and when he escaped, a guard." "Aleksei wouldn't do that." "Well, he did." "No…" I hesitated. "So I am protecting you, you see. I'm protecting you from him, from what your beloved Aleksei has become." "Stop it, Vladimir," I said, as he then climbed on top of me, forced my legs apart with his own, and entered me. "You see, we're one and the same, Aleksei and I, we're both monsters, both carry a darkness inside us. The only difference is that I always come out on the winning side." "Get off me," I insisted. "You must have a thing for cunts!" he said through gritted teeth, thrusting hard. "Get off!" I screamed, and pushed violently on his chest with both hands, but this failed to budge him, and so I slapped him hard across the face, and as he clasped his cheek I managed to escape from under him, rolling off the bed and onto the floor, hitting it with a dull thud.

'I got straight to my feet and ran into the kitchen. He followed. Grabbing the iron from the sideboard, I held it in front of me. "Get out, Vladimir, get out. I never want to see you again!" "If you throw me out, Natasha," he said angrily, standing before me, finger pointing wildly, spit coming from his mouth like venom, "you know exactly what will happen. You've heard it before, but let me say it again for you. I'll make sure that Aleksei is recaptured and executed, that you're thrown in a camp in the arsehole of nowhere like he was, and that Katya's miserable young life is ruined." And before he knew quite what had happened I'd swung my right arm, which held the iron, back over my shoulder and brought it down with all my might on top of his head.

'My arm stopped abruptly, I heard the crack of his skull, saw his head split open and blood ooze from it.

'I let go of the handle, the iron dropped to the floor. He was silent but for a gentle moan and whimper.

'I watched Vladimir take his last breath and die, there, on the kitchen floor,' and with these closing words Natasha at last stopped speaking and fell silent.

Aleksei stared at her in the darkness, then down at the half-eaten food in front of them. Night had fallen. He was silent too.

Then she began to weep, softly at first, and then violently.

20TH MAY 1954
BARANCHIKI, PORT BAIKAL

He was shocked when she first told him what she had done. The first thought Aleksei had was that he wished he had killed Vladimir Vladimirovich before the others because then Natasha would not have done. Carrying the murder of someone on one's conscience, even if this person was cruel and wicked, was extremely difficult, and the last person he wanted to endure this, this mental anguish, was his beloved Natasha. The face of the person you've killed never leaves you, Aleksei thought, you see it over and over, and though the frequency becomes less it always haunts you. God, how he knew this! He still saw all their faces, and had seen them even more since being with Natasha and Katya again. Love, in this respect, was probing, harsh and unforgiving, opening him up, laying him bare, forcing him to confront himself.

Aleksei vividly remembered the sound of Natasha's voice as she described what had happened that fateful morning, flat and monotone at first, yet by the end extraordinarily expressive. He also recalled her endless tears when she had finished, she'd wept and wept, Aleksei forced to wonder whether her tears might never stop. He had considered then if he should tell her about the others, but no, he could not. It was one thing to kill someone in a fit of rage and despair, or in order to protect a dear friend, quite another to kill a number of men out of righteousness. It was then that he'd decided to get rid of all evidence of the assassinations, and so had fetched his old black leather suitcase, which he kept underneath the bed, and burned the file on Valuev, the last man on the list.

Natasha explained she'd found it so difficult to confess to Vladimir Vladimirovich's murder because, in spite of him, the terrible things he had done, she was still riddled with guilt and shame, and the fear that she might lose Aleksei again once he knew what she had done. 'Is it not worse for a woman to kill than a man?' she'd asked. 'And did I not kill in a fit of rage!? I was hardly acting nobly as you were, protecting the life of a dear friend,' she had concluded. Was she harder now, like Aleksei, since killing someone? And would she ever get over what she had done? Would she ever be able to forgive herself? And would he? Aleksei didn't know.

What have I done? Aleksei asked himself this same question every morning when he woke up. Justice had not solely motivated him but also contempt. Ivan Ivanovich knew how much he loathed the system, and after Aleksei had seen Natasha with Vladimir Vladimirovich that day it seemed to legitimise, to crystallise this hatred. He continued to question why the noble thief-in-law had not got word to him that Vladimir Vladimirovich was dead. Had Aleksei been informed of his nemesis's fate, Natasha his killer, then he would have gone after her right away, would most likely have stopped the mission there and then. Ivan, he must surely have known, Aleksei considered. But then, perhaps not.

He prayed that no person or thing would disrupt them any more. He continued to wait for Ivan Ivanovich's man, who'd want to know if Aleksei still planned to kill the last man on the list, though he would surely know that Aleksei could not, now that he was reunited with his family, and would understand this. And the authorities, it was unlikely they would find him here. As he'd worked his way through the list he had learned to cover his tracks extremely well.

Natasha was very loving now, and had been this way ever since she'd told him about Vladimir Vladimirovich. The truth, it seemed – however hard it had been to express – had liberated her and their relationship. She seemed settled, content, no longer yearning for what was, no longer struggling to recreate the past. Their mutual status as murderers on the run had afforded them a certain clarity and shared purpose, Aleksei thought, and they had to make the most of this second chance they'd been given, and, unless forced to up and leave, stay put in Baikal on these quiet shores.

Katya had finally left for Moscow and the Bolshoi, having won a place, though she was due to return late summer for a brief visit. He knew Katya was happy – she'd missed her former friends terribly – and understood that Baranchiki was hardly the most thrilling place to spend your late-teenage years: there was little excitement here. It was better suited to those who'd had enough excitement in their lives and now wanted peace. This was why he loved the place so much, why he at last felt so settled. He was so lucky to have Natasha, Aleksei realised, and found himself loving her more and more, day after day, week after week. Those nights when he was unable to sleep – his mind full of the horrors of the past, those committed by and against him – it often helped to open his eyes and look at her, this beautiful woman beside him, and when his mind was particularly restless and troubled she woke and held him, sharing his suffering and looking to soothe him. Natasha told him on several occasions, after comforting him in this manner, that the vividness of his dreams, or rather nightmares, surely pointed to the fact that he was still keeping something from her. She revealed how his eyelids fluttered rapidly, his unconscious clearly at work, expressing that which his conscious mind could not, and how his face twitched, his whole body shaking, like he was in the grip of some painful experience, his forehead creasing and cheekbones lifting. 'What did you do after you saw me with him, that year in between?' she asked him. Natasha admitted that she didn't think she'd feel this after she confessed – she thought he'd tell her everything – but no. 'You continue to be laconic, enigmatic about this period, urging me to leave the past behind and just get on with the present,' she maintained. And this was exactly what Aleksei did do. For what else could he do or say, he thought, other than tell her the whole truth?

29TH JUNE 1954
BARANCHIKI, PORT BAIKAL

Midday, and Natasha stood in front of the bathroom mirror staring at her shock of hair. Head on it looked like a wild lion's mane, and from the side a poor bird's nest raided by magpies. Rather the former, surely, Aleksei thought, as he walked into the bedroom.

'Who was that?' she asked him.

'Nobody,' he answered.

'Well, you were talking to him for some time.'

'You were watching me?'

'I…yes, I was.'

'Not dressed yet?' he said, looking to change the subject.

'No, I've been lost in that book which Katya got me the last time she was in Irkutsk. You know, the one on Turner, the British painter.'

'Right.'

'He's not from around here, is he?'

'Who?'

'The man you were talking to.'

'No, he was lost.'

'Lost?'

'Yes.'

'Right…okay,' Natasha answered hesitantly, and Aleksei could hear in her voice that she didn't quite believe him, if anything because his explanation did not fit with what she'd seen. For the man had approached him as if he knew him. They hadn't greeted one another like strangers. He had taken off his jacket as he stood there in the morning sun, his arms laced with tattoos, the marks of a criminal. And Aleksei hadn't once gesticulated with his hands as if giving directions. Rather, it was like he'd been expecting him. And he had been.

The man's name was Georgi, and he had come to ask Aleksei first if he was still prepared to kill Valuev, and second whether he wanted to continue working for Ivan Ivanovich. He'd come at last, Aleksei thought.

Aleksei had told him to relay to the thief-in-law that in light of the fact he'd been reunited with his wife and daughter, he was no longer prepared to kill the last man on the list. For if he did, he'd only be putting his family in jeopardy. This extended to other work also. He could no longer undertake it. Georgi was very gracious, assuring him that Ivan Ivanovich wished him every happiness, irrespective of his decision, and that he would fully understand. And Aleksei, on hearing this, realised that he should have expected nothing less. For Ivan might be a leading thief-in-law who could be very ruthless when he needed to be, yet Aleksei had always held a special place in his inner circle, the exception to his code, his law.

'You're not telling me something. You are like Mother Russia sometimes, Aleksei. Impermeable and mysterious,' Natasha went on.

'Natasha, please!'

'But you're not!' she persisted.

'Leave it, okay.'

'But…'

'Natasha, if I was in danger, I'd tell you.'

232

'Would you?'

'Yes.'

'And what about Katya and me? Are we in danger?'

'No.'

'Are you sure about that?'

'Yes.'

'How can you be sure?'

'Because I am.'

'And you? Are you in danger?'

'I've already said. No!'

'Can I believe you?'

'You're going to have to, Natasha.'

Aleksei proved to be right. She could believe him. Time passed and there was no threat to them. Natasha admitted she continued to have the feeling that she was in love with a different man, and yet she accepted this where before she had not. The human character or personality is not static, Aleksei knew this now. Man wants it to be, he reflected, this fulfilling his need for certainty, honouring his resistance to change. However, it is not. Instead, it's forever moving, changing, Aleksei realised. There was now an immediacy to everything he did. He was more present. Evenings on the porch with Natasha, sitting beside her on the small wooden bench, caressing her neck and chin, running his fingers through her hair, stroking her arms with the tips of his fingers as if he was discovering her for the very first time. And he savoured this, this gentle and seductive exploration, every time he performed it, seeming to find something different on each occasion. Whereas before it had been he who'd become impatient after a while and looked for other stimulation, which he normally found in a book or an essay, his intellect his default position as it were, now it was she who became restless and looked for something else to occupy her. Why must man always seek distraction? Aleksei wondered. Why cannot he, quite simply, be with things? Aleksei finally had the presence of mind to be with people, experiencing them as they were in any given moment, fully and without judgment. Perhaps it was only possible to experience life in such a way when one had truly suffered. Such a mind, one which had confronted suffering head on, was no longer seduced by happiness, grasping at that which offered it and pushing away that which did not. Rather, it elected to do no more than fully experience things, be they good or bad. Aleksei was someone who had put enormous emphasis on his intellect. It had been this human faculty, above all else, that was most valuable. He was brilliant, driven, ambitious, his intellect at the forefront of his being. But now he was almost distrustful of it, his great gift. And was this really surprising? For how had it helped him when Vladimir Vladimirovich had interrogated him and when he had been incarcerated in Kolyma. It had not. If anything, it had worked against him. This was why he no longer believed in the value of intellect, instead the value of direct sensory experience. Historical analysis had been rendered meaningless by the Communists as they seemed to have ignored every lesson it had offered. Unless one was prepared to be an historian simply for the sake of being an historian, there was little point. This was Aleksei's view. He no longer wanted to be caught up in the melodrama of human history. And this great dismissal was not the product of petulance, ambivalence or defeat, but of wisdom.

Katya had joked with him, before she left for Moscow, that he was possibly the most politically disengaged person she knew. 'Did he believe in anything political?' she'd asked. To which Aleksei had replied, 'Communism is the only thing I categorically don't believe in.' He'd gone on, 'Though I might be disengaged with the internal wranglings of our Communist leaders, their incessant in-fighting, their love of power, when their authority is threatened, well, then I become interested.' He was looking forward to seeing her again. Natasha thought she'd fallen in love, 'call it a mother's intuition', as she described it. She suspected Katya had fallen for the young man in Moscow whom she'd been writing to ever since they'd left for Baikal. This is why she'd been so devastated about her mother dragging her here, Aleksei pondered. 'A childhood sweetheart, no less!' Natasha had exclaimed. Perhaps it was Varlam or Isaac, both of whom doted on her at school, Aleksei recalled. According to Natasha, prior to leaving for Moscow Katya had kept the young man's letters in an old shoebox in the bottom shelf of her chest of drawers. Natasha had often been tempted to take a peek, she'd confessed to Aleksei, though had resisted. For she had no right, and should respect her daughter's privacy, just as he should, Aleksei thought. He missed her terribly; she seemed so young to be there on her own. He knew why he'd struggled so much with her departure. For he'd doted on Katya since being reunited with her, doing this consciously and deliberately, wanting to savour her as much as possible, having been separated for so long. He didn't want to be wrapped up in things as he'd been before, the ambitious young professor consumed by his work. No, he wanted to be with her, Katya, his daughter.

Their life here together on the lake, it was strange, Aleksei considered, as he sat underneath the gazebo at Natasha's seamstress table, her woollen shawl wrapped around his shoulders, and stared at the dress which she had promised a woman in the village and that was now late. This gazebo – built by Aleksei, something he surely would never have done, and not been capable of doing, had he remained a professor, an academic in Moscow. And this dress – made by Natasha's very own hands, which she would not be making were she still in

Moscow, an art historian. Their lives had changed irrevocably – this was what made it strange – and yet the same could be said for the majority of Soviet citizens. Their Communist leaders would not cease until they were one, Aleksei mused, all carbon copies of one another, all labouring and striving for the same goal, the common good of the Soviet people: Aleksei, the Soviet man in his flat cap, and Natasha, the Soviet woman with her red scarf.

Did he miss what they were before, the lives they'd had, before the state elected to turn things upside down? Aleksei asked, looking to the heather that encircled the perimeter fence. Aleksei had his professorship, Natasha her teaching post, which also enabled her to practice as an artist. They were both ambitious, both had promising careers ahead of them, their lives rich with friends, academia, students, museums, galleries, and so much more. Look at them now, the odd couple, man and wife felons, one a boat builder and repairer, the other a baker-cum-seamstress, marginalised and living on the fringes of society.

And yet they had found a real happiness here, and with this thought Aleksei smiled broadly, stretching his arms behind his head, looking to the garden once more. The red lilies would be in bloom again soon, he thought.

28TH AUGUST 1954
BARANCHIKI, PORT BAIKAL

Aleksei walked home slowly after work – it was the middle of the afternoon, and he felt very peaceful. He thought of Natasha as a gust of wind whooshed past him, brushing his cheek. She had at last accepted him for who he was, and for this he loved her, perhaps more than he ever had. He ran his fingertips over his cheekbone, as if searching for a mark left by the wind. She had ceased questioning him about what he'd done last year, and he was extremely grateful. He had found it difficult not to tell her everything, and part of him longed to, he thought as he walked past their vast pine tree, its needles in this light possessing a violent glint of green.

Aleksei looked ahead, down the long road leading back to the house, this winding road that encircled the great lake. He had missed her today, his 'beautiful', he mused, glancing down at the two large omul in his right hand – a gift from Yevgeny, the finest of his catch – that swung back and forth, propelled by the momentum of his strides down the shore. He'd cook them on the wood fire this evening, he decided, gently smoke them. Natasha loved them this way. Back from Moscow briefly before she headed for Chechnya – she was due to perform for two months there, before returning to her studies in Moscow – Katya was in Irkutsk for the night and so he had Natasha to himself. He wanted to make love to her as soon as he walked through the door; she fulfilled him so completely. Aleksei felt comfortable with her, at ease, she no longer judged him, and appeared even more beautiful, the blue-grey of her eyes seeming to capture her very soul. He never thought he would have believed in this notion, of the immaterial, the spiritual, after a lifetime of Soviet propaganda and its dogmatic creed of dialectical materialism, of atheism, though he was starting to. Nikolai would have been proud of him.

There was a lightness in his step as he approached the halfway-home point, marked by the tatty fish stall of Akop, an eccentric fellow in his fifties whom Natasha affectionately described as 'possibly the hairiest, and smelliest, man in the world.' It was a wonder he sold anything, all his own catch. A few did buy from him, however, mainly out of sympathy, as Aleksei had done in the past, though not today, as he already had his fish for the evening. Aleksei held his breath – a trick that Natasha had taught him – and nodded as he walked past Akop, who raised his hand and shook it wildly, his wave always the same, displaying an almost demented affection as he smiled broadly, showing off his toothless mouth. Aleksei didn't breathe out until he was some way past him, and when he eventually did he savoured it, relishing the clean air, sucking it in, taking a gigantic gasp and letting it fill his lungs. Aaaggghhh. Natasha's love was helping him forgive himself, yes. He had felt bad, unworthy, ever since the first killing. How could someone love him after what he'd done? He was a heartless killer. These thoughts had plagued him. But it seemed he had been afforded a second chance, the opportunity to redeem himself, be a good man again, and he had to embrace this. Aleksei knew he would continue to have sleepless nights, be riddled with feelings of guilt and shame, until he confessed to Natasha, told her exactly what he had done.

And why don't I! Aleksei urged himself at this moment, looking up at the late afternoon sky, a vibrant blue. Might I risk losing her if I do? he wondered. Maybe, but I should take that risk, because I owe it to her to tell her the truth. For I want Natasha to know all of me as she did before. My liberation rests with her, yes, and I'm almost excited at the prospect of telling her, he thought. Aleksei quickened his stride, he wanted to get home, could not wait.

He spied the roof first as he always did, the tip of its triangle that Natasha had painted a bright blue. During winter she had been struck by the building's absence of colour, grey predominant, the poplar trees bare, the heather non-existent, and so had decided to paint a small part of it a single bright colour, give it life. How dare she do such a thing, make her house colourful! For was this not anti-Soviet? It was not the colour in itself that was ideologically wrong – though of course the authorities would rather the roof was red! – but what it represented. For suddenly her house was different, separate, unique. One blue-roofed house amidst many grey ones. Everything had to be the same, or not exist at all! Did she, Natasha Sokholova, consider herself exceptional!? Why must everything Soviet be monotonous and clichéd? Aleksei thought. Why can nothing Soviet take on an individual character? He always smiled, therefore, when he saw her dazzling blue roof. For this was the primary reason why she'd painted it this colour, to lessen the sky's gloom, which sometimes felt like it might remain grey forever.

As Aleksei got closer he admired the house itself, peering through the thick flora of the garden at its log walls, a deep brown, standing out against the grey of the surrounding poplar tree trunks. But when he saw that the garden gate was open he knew immediately something was wrong: for Natasha never left it open, and Katya was not here.

He stopped in his tracks, his chest felt tight. Standing by the parade of tall heather that lined the old fence, he was reluctant to go any further.

Walking slowly up the path towards the porch, Aleksei climbed its few old wood steps, which creaked and moaned, to find that the front door was also ajar.

He stepped inside, into an ominous silence: Natasha might have loved the silence, though this was another kind, possessing no serenity.

Looking to the bedroom he knew right away that this was where he'd find her.

He did not head there immediately, rather stared down at the bedsheet that lay crumpled on the floor in the doorway, the fading light of day, which streamed through the window, illuminating it, casting on it a vibrant white.

Aleksei closed his eyes and saw her now, his beautiful Natasha, sitting on the end of the bed and smiling at him.

However, when he opened his eyes she was not there. He remained standing motionless in the front room.

His legs shuffled reluctantly across the floorboards towards the bedroom.

He peered round the door towards the bed, and there she lay, naked, on her back, legs apart, blood strewn over her face and body.

As he got nearer he saw her face, its expression one of horror. She had not been killed quickly, but had been raped, it appeared repeatedly, then beaten to death.

Something lay on her chest, an old NKVD badge, a screw-back 'Distinguished NKVD Employee' badge, of the type which Vladimir Vladimirovich had proudly worn on his left breast.

31ˢᵀ AUGUST 1954
BARANCHIKI, PORT BAIKAL

His grief felt unbearable, coming at him in waves, and when each wave reached its peak he was sure he could not endure another, the pain of loss cutting right through him, making it difficult for him to breathe, his head pounding, eyes aching, nose riddled with snot. Oh God! Aleksei had not slept since he'd found her. Katya had sat with him last night, stroking his head and urging him 'to rest, just a bit', whispering these few words over and over, though his mind would not let him, and did not let him now either, as he got up from the sofa and walked into the kitchen. She was strong, like her mother. She might be devastated yet he could already see in her that she would be okay, would find a way through her grief. He, on the other hand, suspected he might be consumed by his, lost in it for good.

The funeral was small, attended by Marina, Pavel, Yevgeny and a few others. Aleksei found it hard to stand during the service, using Katya's shoulder to prop himself up, though it got to the point where she could no longer support his weight and nodded to Yevgeny to help her, which he did, stepping forward, taking Aleksei's arm and holding him tight.

The service concluded with Katya reading her mother's favourite poem, Baudelaire's 'The Fountain', and the final chorus she repeated:

The wisp of water rises,
wavers, reappears:
a white bouquet
whose flowers sway
until the moon releases
showers of bright tears.

Later, standing by the grave, Aleksei continued to hear Katya's recital, heard it over and over. He was sure she was still uttering it and so looked to her, but she stood there silently, staring straight ahead, her eyes heavy and red with tears. The verse no longer contained any beauty. Rather, it haunted him. He closed his eyes and squinted hard, as if hoping that when he opened them again the verse would cease, though it did not.

'Are you okay, my friend?' Yevgeny asked, sensing his distress and coming to his aid.

'Yes, yes…I'm alright,' Aleksei replied falsely, it abundantly clear that he was far from alright, but was being torn apart, his mind ravaged by loss.

Marina walked beside Katya as she turned, head bowed, and left her mother's graveside, this special place they had chosen for Natasha to rest by the vast pine tree on the lake's shore, which symbolised her and Aleksei's love, and Katya's conception.

The men went to walk away as well, Yevgeny and Pavel, though Aleksei remained rooted to the spot, staring down at the black earth.

His legs wobbled, then gave way, and he fell to his knees.

He sobbed uncontrollably at first, gasping, choking and spluttering, then roared like a great bear.

Katya could not tolerate seeing her father like this, and looked to Pavel, the oldest among them, who urged Yevgeny to help him. 'Go to him, he needs you,' Pavel told him. 'But don't hurry him, let him get it out.'

'I don't think he'll...' Yevgeny mumbled to Pavel, then walked further away from Katya in order to ensure she couldn't hear. 'Christ, how can he carry on...after losing her like this?'

'I don't know...' Pavel muttered. 'Don't know what I'd do if I were him.'

'That's what I'm worried about,' Yevgeny said flatly.

'Pavel, shall we...' Marina called to him.

He interjected, 'Yes...take Katya back to the house. We'll come in due course.'

As the two women walked away Katya looked at Pavel, who stared intensely at Aleksei as Yevgeny went to him, and in his face she saw a kind of horror, as if the old baker knew the vengeance that her father was about to wreak.

At home, Aleksei did not sit with his friends, these other mourners, instead retired to the bedroom. In the fading light of the late afternoon he listened to a crow caw, and slowly seduced by this baleful birdcall, his mind, after three days of grief, at last turned to revenge: it had to be one of Vladimir Vladimirovich's former colleagues. Again, the authorities were looking to destroy him, ruin his life.

Early evening, and Katya came to see him after everyone had left. 'They all say goodbye, Poppa,' she said, sitting down on the bed beside him.

'Thank you,' he replied.

'I'm exhausted.'

'Yes, you must be...and you need to rest. You've got a big journey ahead of you.'

'What are you talking about?'

'You leave for the Caucasus tomorrow.'

'Poppa, I'm hardly going to leave now, am I, so soon...'

'Why not?'

'I thought that would be obvious.'

'Look, I'm okay…you don't need to worry about me,' he assured her.

'You sure about that?'

'Yes.'

'And what about me?' she asked angrily.

'Well, I…I can see that…'

'That what, that I'm okay!' she shouted.

'I didn't mean it like that.'

'How did you mean it, then?'

'That though both of us are in pieces we have to get on with our lives,' he said quietly, not looking at her but gazing at a small wood framed photograph of Natasha on the bedside table, which he'd taken recently with Yevgeny's camera.

'But Poppa, I don't want to leave you so soon,' she insisted, clutching him by either shoulder and urging him to look at her. 'I mean…what will you do without her?'

'I don't know, my darling…but I have to get on, I have no choice…and so do you, you have your whole life ahead of you.'

'I know that…I'm just saying that I postpone my trip for a week or so, so we can spend a bit more time together.'

'This will hardly be the best start. It's your first public performance with them.'

'In light of what's happened, I think they'll understand.'

'I think you should just go.'

'You seem like you don't want me here,' she said, standing up.

'It's not that…Come on…' he said, appealing to her.

'It's like you're in a rush or something and want me out of here.'

'Enough Katya, okay!' he demanded, sitting bolt upright in bed, finally losing his temper with her.

She immediately started to cry, feeling utterly rejected – Aleksei observing her as if she were all of a sudden a little girl again – then stamped her feet, the floorboards rattling loudly, and stormed out of the bedroom.

He did not follow her, but remained where he was, seated on the bed in the darkness of the room, fixating on the framed photograph of Natasha.

6TH SEPTEMBER 1954
MOSCOW

Aleksei stood, as he had done many times before, outside Boris Andreyevich's office, in the corridor with one of the thief-in-law's blue-eyed crew-cut Slav henchmen, the foot-tapper, breathing down his neck. Any second now the door would reopen and the other henchmen, the toothpicker, would nod and summon Aleksei inside. He might not have been here for eighteen months, yet things were exactly as he'd left them. He entered Boris Andreyevich's inner sanctum to see him, Ivan Ivanovich's deputy, sitting in his customary large black leather armchair, wearing a black shirt, black trousers and black shoes no less, his eyes possessing that familiar violent glint.

'Please, sit down, Aleksei Nikolayevich,' he grumbled in his customary low, coarse voice.

'Thank you,' Aleksei replied, taking a seat opposite him.

'It's been some time.'

'Yes.'

'I didn't expect to see you back here.'

'Neither did I.'

'You run out of money?'

'It's not about money.'

'It never was with you, was it? That's why Ivan Ivanovich valued you so much.'

'Yes.'

'Why are you here, then?'

'I need information.'

'About what?'

'Natasha was raped and murdered last week. I need to find out who did it,' Aleksei said matter-of-factly.

Boris Andreyevich was silent, glanced down at the floor.

Then he looked up, stared into Aleksei's eyes. 'I'm sorry,' he said.

'So am I,' Aleksei replied.

'Who d'you suspect?'

'One of Vladimir Vladimirovich's men maybe. There was an old NKVD badge placed on her body.'

'A little obvious, no.'

'Maybe. You heard anything?'

'No,' Boris Andreyevich replied. 'Might it be a revenge killing, one of your victims' families or associates?'

'Perhaps…'

'How long's it been since the last?'

'Kalegaev was last December.'

'You must be missing it,' Boris Andreyevich quipped.

'No,' Aleksei answered flatly.

'Okay.'

'It was the same month I was reunited with Natasha.'

'You forgave her?'

'Yes.'

'I couldn't have done,' Boris Andreyevich said.

'She had little choice,' Aleksei replied.

'She didn't have to fuck him.'

'She didn't have to kill him, either.'

'What are you talking about?'

'I didn't kill Vladimir Vladimirovich,' Aleksei said. 'Natasha did.'

Again, Boris Andreyevich was reduced to silent reflection.

'Yes, he attacked her,' Aleksei went on, 'and she hit him in self-defence, killing him.'

'Right,' Boris Andreyevich uttered, at last responding to the revelation.

'Where's Ivan Ivanovich? Still in Kolyma?'

'Yes, it looked like the new authorities might grant him a reprieve. However, the great trail of blood you left made them suspicious, and then he murdered Petrov with his bare hands the day before the commandant was due to be given his marching orders. Petrov had been so cruel under Koba he had to go. Rumour has it they leaked his dismissal to Ivan Ivanovich as they knew full well what he would do, that he'd be sure to say goodbye in his own inimitable thief-in-law way, give the arsehole a proper send off. He wrung his neck like a chicken's.'

'Will he still be able to help me, then?'

'Of course. He's Ivan Ivanovich. He can do what the fuck he wants. The only thing he can't do is walk across the Urals. The one thing they still won't give him is his freedom.'

'That probably doesn't bother him so much,' Aleksei remarked. 'He always said it's an even bigger prison zone on the outside.'

'Yes,' Boris Andreyevich nodded gently. 'You have money, somewhere to stay?'

'I could do with a place to put my head down.'

'I have somewhere. And I'll get hold of Ivan Ivanovich as soon as I can. Leave it with me.'

'Thank you,' Aleksei replied, and stared down at the dark wood floor.

The apartment which Boris Andreyevich found him was, like the place he first put him in when he arrived in Moscow after his escape from Kolyma, dreary and devoid of life. A warm late-summer's evening in the capital, just four days since he'd seen Boris Andreyevich, and Aleksei sat naked in the dark on the end of the bed after a long slow bath. He stared out of the window, eight storeys up, across the vast city skyline, and imagined where Natasha's killer was hiding. He was sure he was here, in Moscow. Next, he listened to his breath, before his right hand, the one which bore the mark of Kolyma, started to massage his left. He pressed and rubbed every finger methodically until he reached the last, the little one, the one marked with the star, this image that Ivan had awarded him, which symbolised his decision never again to bow to Soviet authority. Lifting up his right hand and scratching his stubble, he spied his reflection in the mirror adjacent to the bed: a big brooding naked man intent on revenge. Momentarily detached from this image, viewing it as if it were not him, he saw something ugly in it, but also something perversely beautiful. He did not want to kill again, yet how could he not after what had been done to Natasha. He was desperate for news of her killer.

The days dragged, and still nothing. Aleksei could no longer sleep, the pain of anticipation fuelling his insomnia. His only real pleasure now was the small *banya* he went to not far from the apartment block in Tverskoy. He went there late at night for a good steam, taking with him his own eucalyptus oil, which he added to the rocks, sitting by the furnace until he could see nothing in the scalding steam, then plunging into the icy pool. He spent at least two hours here, moving back and forth between the steam and pool at fifteen-minute intervals. The attendant, little more than a boy, seventeen or eighteen years old, watched Aleksei with fascination. It seemed he knew exactly what Aleksei was waiting for, and then what he would do. Do I have the look of a killer? Aleksei asked himself. To some, yes, but only the very perceptive, insightful.

It had been over a fortnight, he'd been patient, yet he had reached the point where he had had enough. Aleksei returned late from the *banya* angry and restless. Walking through the dingy apartment's front door into the living room he was greeted by Boris Andreyevich, who sat quietly in the grubby brown armchair in the silence of the night. 'I let myself in,' he said.

'Yes, I can see,' Aleksei replied, immediately sitting down opposite him.

'How are you?' he asked.

'Please, it's been a long time, Boris Andreyevich…I need to know.'

'Patience, Aleksei. Patience is fortitude, remember.'

'I have neither patience nor fortitude for this kill. I just need to do it.'

'Okay…okay,' Boris Andreyevich mumbled, readjusting his position in the chair, sitting up a little, before finally revealing what he had discovered. 'Ivan Ivanovich has found the culprit.'

'Who?'

'Dmitri Vladimirovich Primakov.'

'Vladimir Vladimirovich's son?'

'Yes.'

'Is Ivan Ivanovich sure?'

'Dmitri's the only one who could have known the truth.'

'That Natasha was his father's killer?'

'Yes,' Boris Andreyevich answered, 'and who had reason enough to track her down in Baikal.'

'It's revenge, then?' Aleksei asked.

'Yes, he was devastated when his father was killed. Poppa might have been an evil sonofabitch, but he was nevertheless his father.

'He was also furious with Natasha for ruining what they had. For the young Dmitri felt like he was part of a family once more, albeit a rather contrived one.

'And he was furious with her for taking Katya away,' Boris Andreyevich concluded.

'What about Katya!?' Aleksei demanded.

'Well, Dmitri had fallen in love with her.'

'But he's a kid. I mean…he's the same age as Katya!' Aleksei insisted.

'He's a year older than her, Aleksei, and he's a young man now. He's twenty-one. He never stopped thinking about her.'

'How d'you know this?'

'Because he kept in touch with her while she was in Baikal. He waited for her.'

'What!?' Aleksei exclaimed, jumping to his feet.

'We found a box full of letters in his apartment, the apartment he now shares with Katya.'

'No! That's not possible. She's in Chechnya.'

'Here are some of them, and some pictures too,' Boris Andreyevich said, handing them to Aleksei. 'The photos were taken a few days ago, in Moscow.'

'How? I don't…' Aleksei stuttered, first looking at some of the pictures, of Katya and Dmitri arm-in-arm and embracing, then reading one of the letters, which was dated 10 September 1953.

'Is he really in love with your daughter? I don't know.'

'She lied to me. She told me she was performing for two months in Grozny. Four days after her mother's murder, she… she left for Moscow…'

'To be with her mother's killer,' Boris Andreyevich concluded.

Aleksei did not speak; he was engrossed in thought.

'Has he simply been with your daughter in order to get to your wife?' Boris Andreyevich went on.

Aleksei had to grapple with this question.

'And is Katya in danger now?' Boris Andreyevich raised yet another troubling query.

'Look, all of this doesn't add up,' Aleksei blurted out. 'I mean, Ivan Ivanovich says it must be Dmitri because he's the only one who could have known the truth, who was close enough, and yet he wasn't there when Natasha killed Vladimir Vladimirovich.'

'Are you sure?'

'I remember what Natasha told me. It was early morning, they were there in the apartment on their own. Katya had left for ballet, Dmitri was…'

'Where?'

'He was…'

'He was there, Aleksei. He heard everything,' Boris Andreyevich said coolly.

'No, Natasha would have told me.'

'Would she? That she killed a father in front of his son.'

'I…I…'

'The young Dmitri was there. He heard the screams, he saw Natasha hit his father, he watched his Poppa die there on the floor.'

'Oh God!' Aleksei uttered.

'This isn't about God, Aleksei, it's about you doing what you need to do…taking revenge. Natasha didn't kill Vladimir Vladimirovich in cold blood, she was defending herself. However, Dmitri killed her in cold blood, and raped her first.'

Aleksei gazed ahead, saying nothing, and though looking towards the window out of which could be seen the Moscow night, some lights still glowing gone midnight, he was not observing this nighttime scene but rather staring blankly into space, lost in his darkening mood, his thoughts of revenge, his need to act. He finally said, 'Where does he live?'

21TH SEPTEMBER 1954
MOSCOW

He stood on ul Bolshaya Ordynka, outside a blue and white church, the Church of St Nicholas in Pyzhi, close to Dmitri Vladimirovich Primakov's home, and waited. Aleksei wore his old uniform: his grey cotton shirt, black trousers, dark-brown leather boots and three-quarter-length dark-brown leather coat. Yet other than his attire, he had not planned for this killing in the manner he used to, meticulous and obsessive in his preparation to the very end. No, he did not want to prepare for it, rather just to do it, and as soon as possible.

He had rung on the bell when he first got here, but there had been no answer. Might Katya be with him when he returned home? Aleksei wondered. They were living together, after all. He did not know. Assuming Dmitri Vladimirovich was on his own, he would follow him inside the large building block, push him through the door of his apartment as soon as he put his key in the lock, and kill him right away.

Aleksei knew he was out of control, that he was experiencing too much emotion, this likely to jeopardise the success of his mission, but he did not care. He was feeling such rage that he simply had to act.

He knew it was him right away as he saw a young man stride purposefully up the street. Dmitri Vladimirovich might have been taller than his father, more slender, yet he had the very same handsome face. Whereas this handsomeness had jarred with Vladimir Vladimirovich, however, his pot belly and foul character almost precluding such physical beauty, it sat well with his son. Aleksei could see why Katya had fallen for him: he possessed a certain confidence, poise and grace. In fact, on the face of it, he appeared the very antithesis of his father. Yet beneath this pleasing posture, this attractive deportment, Aleksei was sure he was the very same man, no less vicious and cruel.

When Dmitri Vladimirovich walked past him on the other side of the street, Aleksei waited a few moments before crossing the road and tailing him. He listened to the crisp tap of the young man's heels on the pavement as he made his way towards his home. Aleksei counted these paces down. For at any moment he would come to a halt and turn and enter his apartment block.

There at last. He stood outside the big ugly concrete entrance, pausing briefly and looking over his shoulder before going inside. Aleksei followed close behind, Dmitri Vladimirovich, for the time being at least, having no idea that he was being pursued. Aleksei waited, saw the young man reach the end of the corridor and mount the stairs, then followed, as if he were just another building resident.

First floor…second…third. When he reached the fourth-floor landing Dmitri Vladimirovich stopped and turned round, still hearing footsteps behind him and wondering whether they belonged to one of his neighbours. Aleksei, rather than looking away in a bid to conceal his identity, stared right at him, acknowledging Dmitri Vladimirovich as if he were a fellow resident. Aleksei knew he was less likely to arouse the young man's suspicions this way, and hoped that he did not recognise him (Dmitri Vladimirovich must surely have seen a photograph of him, Aleksei thought). He then looked back down at his feet and continued ascending the stairs. He must not engage him more than he needed to.

Another flight…and another, Aleksei moving slower now, lighter on his feet, like a leopard stalking his prey. The eighth floor and Dmitri Vladimirovich walked to the third door on the left along the corridor and put his key in the lock. He turned it, the door opened, and before entering he turned to the stairwell, this moment of caution, ironically, affording Aleksei the very opportunity he needed. He pounced, hurtling down the corridor with lightning speed, grabbing Dmitri Vladimirovich's arm and twisting it behind his back, then forcing him inside and slamming the door shut behind them both.

'What are you doing? Who are you!?' Dmitri Vladimirovich demanded, his voice strikingly different from his father's, Aleksei noticed immediately.

'Shut up, just shut up,' Aleksei insisted, whispering in his ear, concerned that another occupant might overhear. 'Voice down, or I'll kill you.'

'You want money, you want…'

Aleksei did not let him finish. 'No, it's not money I'm after.'

'What then?' Dmitri Vladimirovich appealed to him.

'Justice,' Aleksei said.

'What are you talking about?'

'Justice!'

'What? I don't understand…'

'I thought you might have the courage to confess.'

'I haven't done anything,' Dmitri Vladimirovich stressed.

'If only!' Aleksei said, as if in conclusion.

'Show me your face…look at me,' the young man appealed to him.

'This is for my Natasha, my Katya, my everything!' Aleksei said through gritted teeth, and without a moment's reflection plunged the blade, the one which Ivan Ivanovich had given him all those years ago with Boris Andreyevich's address carved into its wooden handle, hard and fast into the back of Dmitri Vladimirovich's neck, his skin and flesh splitting like the Azerbaijani's had done.

He then thrust it again, as he had done with the Central Asian thief-in-law, to ensure he was dead.

There was blood everywhere.

Aleksei let go of his head, and his chin flopped, lifeless, against his chest.

He hadn't demanded that Dmitri Vladimirovich look into his eyes before he'd killed him, Aleksei realised at this moment, as he had done with all his previous victims. Rather his victim had requested he look into his.

Standing there in the hallway, smeared in the young man's blood, the carpet and walls spattered red, the front door suddenly opened and Katya stood before him.

She was silent at first, it seemed unable to comprehend the spectacle before her, and after this started to scream, and could not stop.

THE SIXTH KILL
18TH OCTOBER 1954
MOSCOW

Mid-afternoon in the drab apartment which Boris Andreyevich had put him in just under six weeks ago, and Aleksei lay in the bath, in the silence, watching the steam rise and evaporate, and listening to his breath. Then later, standing naked before the small bathroom mirror, he shaved, next stared at his reflection, the face he observed hard and cold.

As evening fell he strolled into the bedroom, sat naked on the bed, his clothes laid out beside him, and observed the wall above the bureau, studying its contents. After this, he dressed, then reached for his leather coat, which hung on the back of the bedroom door. And with this last act, of putting on his coat, he was ready…to kill again.

However, when he left the apartment he did not head to the home of the last man on the list, Sergei Ilyich Valuev, but to Boris Andreyevich.

'I cannot do this,' he exploded, walking into the thief-in-law's office and addressing him in his large black leather armchair.

It had been a month since he'd killed Dmitri Vladimirovich, and while Aleksei had prepared to assassinate Valuev, he continued to be haunted by what had transpired that day. Katya had refused to accept that Dmitri was her mother's killer, and though Aleksei had pleaded with her that evening, covered in the young man's blood, that it had been him, that it could not have been anyone else, she would have none of it. Katya had insisted, 'Dmitri was not Momma's killer…you've killed the wrong man…and you've killed me too. I loved him more than anyone, Poppa, and he loved me back. He would never do this, he was not his father.' And with these words she had rejected him, he was sure for good.

He did not know what she had told the police, as there'd been no body to inspect – Aleksei had taken it, left with the dead young man slung over his shoulder. He had heard Katya's parting words over and over, could not get them out of his head, 'I'll never forgive you, can never forgive you this.' And he heard them now as he stood in front of Boris Andreyevich, tired and desperate.

Aleksei continued, 'How can I be about to do this again? I am not this man, no!'

Boris Andreyevich, still sitting in his armchair, looked up, and, holding his hands together as if he were about to commence prayer, the tips of his fingers pressed determinedly against his mouth, started to speak. 'They killed your father, made you fight for them, and ruined your career as a respected historian,' he said. 'Next they stole your wife, separated you from your daughter, threw you in Kolyma, killed your mother, and left you to rot in isolation,' and with these words he took a deep breath, pausing for a moment, before continuing. 'Then, still not satisfied, they returned, raped and murdered your wife, and now your daughter has rejected you forever.' He looked searchingly into Aleksei's eyes, and concluded with, 'And you ask me how you can do this again?'

'But he, Dmitri, he was not really one of them, was he? He was not *nomenklatura*.'

'He might not have been in a position of power, yet he was the son of a man who was, who abused his authority terribly.'

'Yes, but he was also exploited, according to the file on Valuev...was a victim too!'

'He raped and murdered your wife, Aleksei,' Boris Andreyevich said coolly. 'Is this not reason enough to do what you did to him?'

'But Valuev, he...'

'And this is why you need to kill him as well.'

The file on Sergei Ilyich Valuev had indeed made for dismal reading, the man the personification of the dark, strong pull of selfish, greedy, impatient, unscrupulous ambition. Aleksei had studied him in depth the last month, Boris Andreyevich having given him a replacement file, the old man's life story and countless photographs of him lining the wall of his dingy apartment. Valuev had been very fond of his protégé Vladimir Vladimirovich, who, like him, had had a formidable propensity for violence. Yet Valuev's predilection was far worse: he was an out-and-out sadist. In the early years of the Revolution, he had been responsible for recruiting street orphans into the Red Army, such youngsters ripe for political indoctrination and military conscription. He used to catch them foraging like rats through the rubbish tips in Moscow desperate for food. He was only interested in the boys, however, and they had to be pre-pubescent. Before getting them ready for active service Valuev would beat and sodomise them. Valuev had been offered a position in the Cheka shortly afterwards, which marked the beginning of his illustrious career as a State Security operative. He had served first under Dzerzhinsky, then Yagoda, during Koba's purges, the latter's tenure providing him with an official licence to be cruel, which the career-minded Valuev took up with relish, his sadism suddenly legitimised, made good. Though mainly ensuring the fate of political opponents of Stalin, responsible for the arrest and execution of thousands, he had also targeted Ivan Ivanovich mercilessly during this period, ensuring his arrest and subsequent torture in the Lubyanka, where he'd narrowly avoided being beaten to death by Smidovich. Valuev had also been responsible for furthering the careers of a number of fellow sadists during his time in the Cheka, NKVD, then KGB, including Vladimir Vladimirovich, whom he'd brought under his wing in the post-war years before Koba's death. Though in his sixties by this point, Valuev had lost none of his appetite for cruelty. On one occasion, so incensed was he with a particular prisoner, Svechin – a man with a big burly frame the very opposite of his own diminutive stature, and reportedly a great lover of women, profoundly heterosexual, which Valuev, the bitter homosexual pederast, resented deeply – that, when he'd been unable to elicit a confession from the poor man, had thrust a burning-hot ramrod up his anal canal. Valuev had been deeply affected by his young protégé Vladimir Vladimirovich's death, vowing to find his killer no matter what. A violent paedophile, the prospect of killing Natasha had not excited Valuev. He'd needed someone else to do it. And who better than Vladimir Vladimirovich's son? The young Dmitri had been unable to come to terms with his father's murder in spite of the latter's occasional violence towards him, seeing this single tragic event as catastrophic and irreparable, and Valuev, well aware of this, had known that the fragile and impressionable Dmitri was therefore best placed to take revenge.

Boris Andreyevich continued, 'He deserves to die, Aleksei. There's no remorse in the old man. He's just like the others you killed. Another bad man who doesn't give a fuck, who feels nothing, and will hurt others if he's not got rid of.'

'You don't have to say any more,' Aleksei said, and walked purposefully out of the room.

Gone eleven o'clock at night, and Aleksei closed the large oak front door to an old mansion house, its exterior worn down and unremarkable yet its interior opulent and majestic. He looked up to see an enormous ornate chandelier which hung from the high ceiling in the hallway, glistening in the darkness, then mounted the grand staircase, beautifully carpeted, admiring the many gilt-framed oil paintings that lined the wall as he ascended each stair. This was not the home of a noxious European–American capitalist but of a leading member of the State Security forces, Sergei Ilyich Valuev.

Aleksei reached the top of the staircase then walked softly down a short, poorly lit corridor towards an open door at the end, from which came light and a little music, Mahler, he thought, though he could not be sure. He peered through its frame to see Valuev sitting with his back to him, in a red velvet armchair, holding a large silver goblet, which he sipped from as if he were a king. So much for the end of aristocracy, Aleksei mused, and entered the room.

'I have been expecting you, Aleksei Nikolayevich Klebnikov,' he called out, it unclear to Aleksei how Valuev knew he was standing behind him, until he spied the old man's face, his distorted mirror image, in the side of the goblet, which must have offered up Aleksei's reflection too.

Aleksei was silent.

'Please do not be shy, my friend,' Valuev continued. 'Come and sit down.'

Aleksei walked across the room and round in front of the armchair to face him. He drew his gun from his trouser belt and put it coolly to Valuev's forehead. Staring at him hard, he said, 'Ivan Ivanovich sent me. Look at me.'

Valuev did not squirm and look away, but held Aleksei's stare and spoke calmly. 'I know he did. None of us can escape being corrupted. I knew the devil would catch up with me one day.'

'You got your revenge, then!?' Aleksei demanded, discon-
certed by his intended victim's composure.

'It was not I who killed your wife,' Valuev said.

'I know. You didn't have the courage to do it yourself, so
you got that weak son of his to do it for you.'

'No, I did not.'

'And all in the name of Vladimir Vladimirovich Primakov.
Was his life really worth avenging?' Aleksei asked urgently. 'I
need you to confess to what you've done before I kill you.'

'I have done many awful things, the majority of which I
am sure you know about – his files on his intended victims are
always thorough – though one awful thing I have not done is
murder your wife. That was his work!'

'What are you talking about?' Aleksei asked, again
discomfited by Valuev's response.

'He did not count on me speaking out, yet I have nothing to
lose now, do I? If you do not kill me after I have revealed the
truth, then he will.'

'Go on…' Aleksei said, taking a deep breath, lowering his
arm and letting his gun rest against his hip.

'Your friend Ivan Ivanovich, the noble thief-in-law, is not
quite the man you think he is,' Valuev begun. 'Here is a man who
saw the potential for such anger and hate in you, such contempt
for the authorities, that he knew right away you would serve as
the perfect servant – the distinguished assassin – if only he could
nurture this hatred, validate it, then get you out of Kolyma.
For no one would suspect a political – the brave soldier, former
professor and married family man. He has fostered and used
your suffering – how the state betrayed you – solely to further his
own ends, to maintain his position as a leading thief-in-law.'

'What are you talking about!?' Aleksei demanded.

'The men on the list, all those you killed – yes, they were
as contemptible, as reprehensible, as Ivan Ivanovich led you to

believe they were,' Valuev went on, 'but he did not want them dead on account of their awful deeds against him and those he loved, the terrible abuse of the power they held, but because they were no longer doing what he wanted them to do, were asking for too much, had become greedy, were questioning his authority.

'Ivan Ivanovich was motivated by money and power, Aleksei, and cared little for the lives he told you you were avenging, those of Anna Dementieva, Maria Akhmatova, Aleksandr Mikhailov, Pavel Borsky and Oskar Bielski. And likewise, he cared little about how their killers – these servants of a wicked regime – had abused their power, had terrorised the decent and innocent, had betrayed humanity. No, rather he worked with them, had them in his pay, used them to further his own ends.'

'No,' Aleksei insisted.

'Yes,' Valuev answered succinctly, then went on, 'In the pay of Ivan Ivanovich for more than five years and high up in the Moscow Communist Party, Anichkov had made it possible for the thief-in-law to extort money from a number of business cooperatives. Lavrenti Romanovich had become greedier, however, demanding a greater share of the profits. Ivan Ivanovich decided to get rid of him.

'Ivankov, responsible for many of the factories that had relocated to Sverdlovsk during the war and anxious to profit from the goods they produced, had struck a deal with Ivan Ivanovich, knowing that the thief-in-law had a thriving export business in Soviet-manufactured goods. But, like Anichkov, he'd become too greedy, and when Ivan Ivanovich's man on the ground, the Iset, named after the river that ran through the city, was found dead the thief-in-law knew that the time had come to dispose of Ivankov, the Butcher of Ukraine.

'Kalegaev had managed to monopolise all criminal activity in Irkutsk, which included Ivan Ivanovich's significant illegal trade in gold and aluminium, where the thief-in-law made most of his money. In fact, he had been utterly ruthless, befriending a number of Ivan Ivanovich's key lieutenants with promises of protection and immunity, only then to kill them off one by one. He had to go.

'And then there is me. Granted, I did have my way with the young Ivan when he was a boy urchin on Moscow's streets, and he should have punished me for this, for my abuse, yet he chose not to, instead wanted to have me work for him, as he did the others. He was not going to tell you, pardon my language, that he'd had my cock up his arse. The devil would not admit to this, which would hardly help his standing as a leading thief-in-law!

'He is a businessman, a pragmatist, first and foremost, and I, a leading member of State Security, was far more useful to him alive than dead. For I could tell him about anyone, my eyes and ears everywhere. Yes...and this includes you, your wife, your daughter. However, he did not always relay this information correctly.

'Ivan Ivanovich knew the truth about Natasha, that Vladimir Vladimirovich had forced himself into her life, threatened her, given her no choice – I told him this, for God's sake, told Boris Andreyevich – yet because he wanted you to kill for him, he needed for you to be utterly betrayed. For only then would you do what he wanted, when you had nothing else to lose. Thus he withheld the truth from you – the extent of Vladimir Vladimirovich's coercion – long enough to let your anger grow, then revealed "evidence" of Natasha's betrayal when you were at your most vulnerable, right after your mother's death.

'Your first kill was not Anichkov but the Azerbaijani. Once one of the Central Asian's boys had threatened your dear friend Nikolai, Ivan Ivanovich decided that this would be your initiation, your training ground, and if you carried out this first assassination with sufficient skill and courage, then he'd use you again. You proved yourself to him here, Aleksei, you were a loyal and committed student, and he was sure after this that he'd found his man, his perfect assassin. However, you proved to be such an asset – you worked your way through the list with extraordinary proficiency and determination, Aleksei – that he could never accept your killing days were over once you were reunited with Natasha and Katya. Rather, he was ready to give you another list right away, once you had killed me of course, your sixth kill.'

Aleksei grunted, clearing his throat, which felt as dry as a canal in the midst of a drought, the horror of Valuev's words, Ivan Ivanovich's alleged duplicity, rendering him speechless.

Valuev continued, 'Ivan Ivanovich tried to get by without you, yet the other contract killers he used were clumsy and inept by comparison, and failed to kill me. He did not graciously accept your decision to no longer work for him and to live out your days quietly on the shores of Lake Baikal, as Georgi led you to believe he did. Rather, he was furious with you for not completing the mission, and so waited reluctantly, impatiently, letting other matters occupy him, all the while, however, determined that he would have you back one day to finish the job. And what better way to do this than to reignite your rage, make you angry and vengeful again.

'Aleksei, he had Natasha raped and murdered, then fed you false information once more, getting you to believe that her killer was Vladimir Vladimirovich's son. In truth, Dmitri was nothing like his father, would never have done this. He was a kind and decent young man, deeply in love with your daughter.

'And now he has concocted my complicity in your wife's murder. I, Vladimir Vladimirovich's dear friend and mentor, used his weak-minded son Dmitri to get the revenge I had hankered after. And look how easily you were convinced.

'You are a brave man, Aleksei, and a very intelligent one, but you are a fool... so desperately naïve. He's played you perfectly.'

Aleksei grimaced long and hard, his head ached. He did not know what, or who, to believe any more. He still could not find it in himself to speak.

Valuev was not yet finished. 'So here you are, sure of my guilt –
"For how can it not be me!" Boris Andreyevich insists – and once
you have killed me then you are his again. A political prisoner, an
escaped convict, a prolific assassin, and now a widower whose
daughter has rejected him for good – I would say that after you
have executed me, a leading State Security operative, there is no
turning back. You will be forever his, in his pay.

'Why does Ivan Ivanovich want me dead? Why was he
adamant that you complete the mission in one year? Why was
he so furious that you failed to kill me, the last man on the list?
Well, because he is desperate for his freedom, and I have been
blocking his release. For I do not want him to wreak further
havoc on the world. My final act of goodness, if you will. I had
to perform one before I died, didn't I? My deputy is in his pay
now, however, and will ensure Ivan Ivanovich is released once
I'm gone.

'So Aleksei, are you going to get rid of me, as he has planned,
or do I have to wait for another one of Ivan Ivanovich's lackeys
to walk through the door?'

Aleksei glanced at his gun by his side, then gazed into
Valuev's eyes. He mumbled, as if to himself, 'I can't do this…
despite what you say, what you've told me.'

'You cannot?'

'No.'

'But I'd rather you kill me than let him do it.'

'I won't do that, cannot bear another man's death on my
conscience.'

'Even a man such as me.'

'Yes,' Aleksei replied.

'I don't even have the courage to do it myself,' Valuev said,
for the first time sounding afraid. For he knew his death at the
hands of another of Ivan Ivanovich's men would not be quick.
The thief-in-law would make him suffer.

'No more killing,' Aleksei said quietly, and walked away from Valuev, back round the armchair towards the door.

'You had better hurry. The devil will be right behind you, now you have failed to do what he wanted,' Valuev called to him.

'I know,' Aleksei replied, and left Valuev sitting there all alone to meet his fate.

He hurried out into the street, onto its cobblestone, and began to run, as fast as he could, back to the apartment. He was sure there was someone on his tail, though whenever he looked round he could not see anyone. The streets were without light, and though he'd functioned perfectly in darkness less than a year ago, like a cat able to find his way almost instinctively, and with great agility (despite being a big man), through the black of night, now he struggled. Moscow, this dark labyrinth, he could lose himself in it, Aleksei thought. As he scrambled clumsily and blindly along, from one alleyway, one street to the next, he wished that his former prowess and intuition would return, and it did, slowly, as he continued to make his way through the city.

Back in the apartment, he knew he must get his things together as quickly as possible. He rushed to the bedroom, pulled out a small holdall, began to throw a few items into it – a shirt, a pair of trousers, some socks. What should he take? Aleksei was not sure. Where should he go? I cannot stay in Moscow, he said to himself. He was not thinking clearly, knew this. Another quality he had lost in the short period in between. Faced with the possibility of capture or his own death, he had possessed the capacity for clear thought: anger had been perhaps the central reason for this ability. In fact, this had been perhaps his greatest asset, and he was without it now and needed it.

He stumbled into the bathroom, stood over the sink, turned on the tap, threw cold water in his face – as if this act might offer him sudden clarity and purpose. Next he stared at his reflection in the small, dirty, broken mirror. Ivan Ivanovich would find him, he knew that. It would only be a matter of time before he disposed of Valuev with the help of somebody else and secured his release via his deputy. And then he would be in Moscow in no time, in search of him. Should he run? Aleksei wondered. Perhaps he should merely stay put, as Valuev had done, and wait for the thief-in-law to come for him.

Looking at his green eyes glistening in the mirror, tears started to well inside them, and before he quite knew it Aleksei was crying, feeling an immense sadness in his heart. He was drawn to the sound of the tap, water dripping from it, drip drop, drip drop, its sound seeming to induce in him even more anguish, as with every new drop he saw another face…a face of one of the men he had killed…and then another…and another. How many!? What have I done? God, what have I done?

He had been brought up in, and been a citizen of, a country that had contempt for this notion of God – that there was something wiser, greater than man. 'There was nothing else but man!' the Communists insisted. 'Man must forge his own destiny!' However, was it not clear, after nearly four decades of blind ideology, that man alone had no idea where he was going and continued to flounder despairingly in the dark? Did not man need to be accountable to some entity bigger than himself?

'Aleksei Nikolayevich,' Boris Andreyevich said, standing in the kitchen and looking through into the bathroom where Aleksei remained standing, in front of the mirror, absorbed in his own anguish.

Aleksei did not answer, did not even acknowledge Boris Andreyevich, but continued to stare straight ahead at his reflection.

'Aleksei Nikolayevich,' the thief-in-law said again.

Still Aleksei failed to respond.

'It looks like he's lost it,' Boris Andreyevich quipped, turning to his two blue-eyed crew-cut Slav henchmen. They said nothing, however. For they remained fearful of Aleksei, this unlikely assassin who had killed with such skill and ruthlessness.

'I've come for you,' Boris Andreyevich said loudly, as if addressing an imbecile, someone who had lost his mind for good.

'You have?' Aleksei muttered, at last speaking, not turning to Boris Andreyevich or either of his men but continuing to look at himself in the mirror, vision blurred, eyes still wet with tears.

'Yes,' Boris Andreyevich replied.

'Why is that?' Aleksei asked.

'I think you know why.'

'I do?'

'Yes, you do.'

'I don't think so.'

'Aleksei, please,' Boris Andreyevich insisted, becoming impatient.

Aleksei was silent.

The thief-in-law continued, 'Look, don't fuck with me, not when I'm standing here with a gun in my hand and my two best men either side of me also carrying, and you standing unarmed and lost in thought like the village idiot in front of the bathroom mirror with no idea of what to do next. Come on, Aleksei Nikolayevich, not even you are that good.'

'What d'you want me to say?'

'The truth.'

'What truth is there in all this?' Aleksei enquired thoughtfully.

'From village idiot to philosopher. Now is not the time to be thoughtful. Did you kill Valuev?' Boris Andreyevich demanded.

'No,' Aleksei answered.

'Why not?'

'Because I cannot do this any more.'

'And what is that?'

'You know what.'

'Kill, you mean,' Boris Andreyevich said, articulating this word with relish.

'Yes.'

'We've been through this already.'

'Look, please, can you ask Ivan to leave me be? I did what I had to do for him back then.'

'Did you kill all those men for him or for yourself, Aleksei Nikolayevich?'

'It's for me to ask that question, not you,' Aleksei answered impatiently.

'Is that right?' Boris Andreyevich replied, smirking and nodding his head.

'Look, that was then and this is now. I can no longer do this.'

'It's not that simple, I'm afraid.'

'What d'you mean?' Aleksei said, fully aware what Boris Andreyevich was alluding to, and yet eager to see whether there might still be a way out. 'I mean…why not get someone else to kill Valuev?'

'It's not just about Valuev any more, is it?'

'Isn't it?' Aleksei asked, still searching.

'I know, Ivan Ivanovich will know, what happened in there.'

'What are you talking about?'

'Don't take us for fools, Aleksei Nikolayevich. Never do that.'

Aleksei did not speak.

Boris Andreyevich went on, 'Now, Valuev…he said some things he shouldn't have, didn't he, about Ivan Ivanovich? I know he did, you see, because I had instructions to listen to you while you were there, and I heard everything. Ivan Ivanovich has been bugging his place for years, care of his unfaithful deputy, and wanted immediate confirmation of Valuev's assassination. And there was the filthy pederast thinking he was too clever for us, that we'd never get one over on him.'

'But why should I believe him, and him of all people?' Aleksei said.

'Well, why not?'

'I thought that would be obvious.'

'Because of who he is?' Boris Andreyevich enquired.

'Yes,' Aleksei replied.

'And who is Ivan Ivanovich then?' Boris Andreyevich asked.

Aleksei was silent.

'I asked you a question,' he continued, pressing for a response.

'He is a thief-in-law,' Aleksei said, giving him one.

'And so does that mean you can trust him more than the *nomenklatura* Valuev?'

Aleksei said nothing.

'That you do not answer my question right away, a very straightforward one, leads me to think that you do believe him.'

'Do it then!' Aleksei demanded.

'Do what?' Boris Andreyevich asked.

'What you've come here to do.'

'The great assassin submits so easily.'

'Yes.'

'Do you want to know how the pig squealed when I came for him after you'd failed to kill him?'

'You've got to him already?'

'Yes, I cut his fucking heart out!' Boris Andreyevich said proudly. 'Made a right old mess,' and he opened his jacket to reveal a filthy blood-splattered shirt.

'Right.'

Both men looked intensely at one another before the thief-in-law spoke again. 'You see, though you might not believe a word he said to you, how can I be sure, and most importantly, how can Ivan Ivanovich be sure that you don't? Belief cannot be articulated, now can it?'

'Does he need certainty?'

'I would say that he does. Ivan Ivanovich hates ambiguity, thrives off clarity and conviction. If you only believe part of what Valuev said, then this will provide sufficient motive for you to seek revenge one day.'

'But this is what I've been trying to say, that I've had enough of revenge. No more.'

'And this is meant to offer sufficient assurance that, in spite of what Valuev said about Ivan Ivanovich, and how much of this you might or might not believe, that you will not try and kill Ivan Ivanovich in the future.'

'Yes.'

'Well, I don't believe you.'

'Why?'

'Because you are a man with nothing more to lose. You have nothing left.'

'But I do have something left.'

'And what's that, might I ask?'

'My soul.'

'And you're asking me to believe that?'

'Well, you're not a Communist, and neither is Ivan Ivanovich.'

'And neither am I, nor is he, a sucker!'

'So that's it, then.'

'Yes, that's it,' and he smiled and slowly raised his gun.

Aleksei needed to act. A number of different scenarios played themselves out, at lightning speed, through his mind. It seemed that, just as with riding a bicycle, the skills he'd acquired as an assassin quickly returned. What to do? Think Aleksei, think, he urged himself.

He first considered whether he should hurl himself through the bathroom window. He knew it was big enough. If he held his hands in the air, palms forward, assuming a posture of surrender, and took two small steps backwards until he reached the window, then he merely had to lean back and let himself fall through the glass. He knew the geography of the apartment inside out, having located all escape routes as soon as he'd set foot in it: old habits died hard. Yet the drop was at least ten metres, and though he knew how to break a fall there would most likely be bottles beneath the window – the bar opposite left its crates there at the end of every night – and if he landed on these he might well impale himself. He had to fight.

Boris Andreyevich stood about two metres away from him. His weak spot was clear enough: hubris. He displayed so much of this trait that Aleksei was confident he could disarm him. Were the thief-in-law slightly less sure of himself, and warier of his opponent, Aleksei would not even have considered doing what he was about to do: take one lunge forward with his right leg, swipe hard with his left arm, knock the gun out of his hand, and hit him with his right fist straight between the eyes. He knew, however, that he could not hope to disarm his two henchmen as well. Why? Because they feared him and hence were fully prepared. All he could hope to do was get past them, through the kitchen, slam the door shut on his way into the hallway, and bolt straight out of the front door. Next, rather than head downstairs, he felt he had a better chance going up. Four flights to the roof, and once on it, he could clamber across the two adjacent roofs and make his way down the fire escape onto the street. Aleksei might be a big man, yet compared to these two Slavs he was small, and hence more agile. These great big Russian oaks would struggle to keep up with him!

Now, now, now, he said to himself, and without further deliberation Aleksei made his move, knocking an unsuspecting Boris Andreyevich clean to the floor as he punched him hard in the face, then managing to move with such speed that he eluded the clutches of his two henchmen.

One of them managed to get off a shot, from a Makarov – Aleksei knew its sound well – as he flung open the front door and bolted up the stairs. 'Get the bastard, get him!' he called out, the toothpicker, Aleksei assumed.

Aleksei heard their loud steps and heavy breaths as they pursued him up the stairs. He felt like he was being hunted, which of course he was. Both men sounded hungry and desperate for the kill.

On the roof, afforded some light from the city's skyline, Aleksei found his way in the blackness of the Moscow night and leapt like a big cat, some three metres or so, onto the roof of the adjacent building. Glancing round, he saw one of them, he could not discern which, point his gun towards him and fire off another shot, and Aleksei reacted immediately by throwing himself to the ground, slipping on the lead of the roof, and after this scrambling on all fours across several metres of cement until he reached a chimney stack that offered him temporary cover.

Peering round from behind it, he saw the toothpicker gaze awkwardly over the edge of the apartment's building, far more reluctant it seemed to make the jump than Aleksei had been. 'I can't do this, you go,' he muttered to his colleague, the foot-tapper, who stood behind him. 'I'll head down to the ground, you herd him,' he continued in a whisper, eager not to disclose his tactics, which Aleksei overheard nonetheless.

His colleague was indeed braver, and made the leap, impressive for a man of his size, and Aleksei was on the move again, this time dropping two-and-a-half metres to the next roof and heading for the fire escape, vertical steps on the side of the building leading straight to the ground. He did not look back, as he was eager not to waste time and was sure that the toothpicker would be waiting for him on the ground. He scurried down the fire escape, almost sliding, his feet barely touching each step, as he held the metal balustrade tight and used his powerful arms to carry his weight. Only when he hit the street did he look up and see the foot-tapper, who had barely begun his descent.

Which way? Aleksei could not decide. Come on, come on, do not think too hard, he urged himself, realising that he was procrastinating and could not afford to. The nearest station was Kazansky, with trains heading southeast to Saratov and on to Central Asia. He had to get himself there and on a train.

He sprinted down the backstreet to the main road – there was no other way – peering round the corner only to be met by an oncoming bullet from the toothpicker's Makarov, which he managed to dodge. The enormous Slav was fifty metres away and running straight for him. And behind him he spied Boris Andreyevich, making his way towards him also, albeit clutching his face and staggering clumsily.

Aleksei had to make a run for it. There was a turning to the right about another one hundred metres up the road, and after this he knew he would be in the clear. They would not be able to keep up with him, and as long as he used the backstreets to get to the station would struggle to deduce where he had headed.

Here we go, and he dashed into the road and ran as fast as he could, not heading straight but darting one way then the next, like a deer fleeing a predator, feeling light on his feet, fear driving him.

Shots came from the guns of both men, but he did not look back, and before he knew it he was making the turn and off down this side road into the twilight, towards Komsomolskaya Square.

19ᵀᴴ OCTOBER 1954
RYAZAN

Щ here have the virtuous gone? Aleksei asked, sitting on a train headed southeast, opposite a woman who was the spitting image of the young Alexandra Kollontai, one of Natasha's early heroines, due to her brave campaign for women's liberation. Where has goodness gone? he continued, in reflective mood. 'I've been betrayed by a man I thought I could always trust, whom I was sure was on the same side as me,' he mumbled to himself, which prompted the Kollontai look-a-like to glance at him and wonder whether his mutterings were addressed to her. How could I have been such a fool, he demanded, containing his thoughts now, not voicing them. Why did I not listen to Nikolai, who maintained from the beginning that I risked being seduced by the charismatic thief-in-law? Why did I think that he'd be any less ruthless with me?

He and Ivan Ivanovich, they had been perfectly united in their contempt for Communism, this mad doctrine whose victims they both were, which believed that it could abolish individualism, correct man's behaviour, make all men think, want and act the same. They, Aleksei and the thief-in-law, would resist this ideology to the very end. Aleksei had at first believed in it because some of its aspirations were noble – the end of bourgeois individualism, the beginning of proletarian

276

collectivism – yet never to the extent that it could change the whole world, bring it truth, justice and happiness for eternity, as the Bolsheviks thought it could. For was this not what every religion also claimed – utopia! Aleksei thought. In the early days of the Revolution, to be a New Soviet Man was to be a rational, disciplined and collective being who lived for the greater good, hardly a bad thing. However, the *nomenklatura* Aleksei had encountered possessed none of these characteristics: they were not New Soviet Men, rather the very opposite – unreasonable, utterly without scruple and selfish.

How the New Soviet Man should live his life was, rather ironically, not dissimilar from a religious monastic life, Aleksei considered, now staring out of the window at the barren landscape beyond Moscow. He defined his life through a routine of work, prayer, celibacy and obedience to a spiritual elder. The New Soviet Man worked on behalf of Communism, prayed to it (his new religion) and was obedient to its rulers, the *nomenklatura*. The one thing he did not do, however, was remain celibate. He would not find liberation or purification in sexual abstinence. No, never! The Kollontai look-a-like stood up as the train neared Ryazan, and watching her disembark Aleksei recalled how as a young historian he had believed wholeheartedly in the course of history, its power to affect and shape human nature, yet not to the same degree as Marxist historians, who concluded that historical forces were so influential that man's very nature could be transformed through revolution. This conclusion was not reasonable, no, but extremist, fanatical. It took more than historical development to change man, Aleksei was sure of this. He had likewise been sympathetic to the other Communist obsession, scientific materialism – Darwin had convinced Aleksei from the beginning – though he had not believed in it as much as Communist scientists did, that man must be wholly committed to improving, bettering himself, becoming a new type of man, the perfect species. Man was not a type; he should not seek perfection in this way.

Gazing out of the window, almost hypnotised by the vast swathes of forest, Aleksei suddenly felt an urgent need finally to confess. For who else but Ivan Ivanovich and Boris Andreyevich knew about all the men he had killed. He remembered the stories Nikolai had told him, those Christian men and women who'd gone to exceptional lengths to lead other lives in spite of everything. There was Father Iosif in the Altai Mountains and Nikolai's friend, the Orthodox priest Semonov, Aleksei could not remember his first name, who, after his church had been closed in '32 and he'd been threatened by the League of the Militant Godless, received secret tonsure, severed all contacts with the outside world and lived as a hermit and idiorrhythmic monk for ten years on the shores of Lake Ladoga. He was eventually captured – Semonov had started to receive a few visitors, spiritual seekers coming to pay their respects to the great renunciate, and to pray with him – and sent northwest to the Kola Peninsula, to a camp near Murmansk, where he was killed, frozen to death. Made to stand naked outside in the midst of a bitterly cold winter, they'd poured cold water over him until he had turned to an ice pillar. How the Communists punished the religious! However, according to Nikolai, Semonov was fortunate to escape and have a decade of freedom before his capture. The majority of believers did not. '32 marked the beginning of another of Koba's Five-year Plans, an anti-religion one, in which he'd sought to remove God, an obstacle to the construction of a Communist society, from the Soviet Union. This removal had entailed the systematic closing and destruction of churches, and the exile, imprisonment and execution of priests, monks and nuns. Had he really judged it possible to eradicate God from people's hearts and minds? Aleksei wondered, realising he no longer knew where the train was, quite how long it had been since the last stop. Still, he was not sure where to go. Why must he keep on having to run? he asked. Yet it was as if every Russian citizen was running from something, and kept on running.

He would head for Altai, for Father Iosif, Aleksei decided. He had to confess, yes! For what else was there? He felt the need to retreat temporarily into the spiritual, this notion which Communism, with its fanatical belief in scientific materialism, in atheism, could not accommodate. The Kremlin maintained to the West that it could, that its citizens who were still religious did have freedom of worship, despite the fact that it had successfully closed the majority of churches. Were our cosmopolitan and capitalist friends really so daft and naïve? Aleksei mused. He got off at Akmolinsk and waited for a bus to Altai. There was not one for another six hours, so he found a restaurant to eat, and kill some time, in. Profoundly Soviet in character, neutral, unexceptional, the personification of bland, its walls were painted a stale yellow. Aleksei should not have been struck by such a place any more – for this had been his life under Communism – yet he continued to be. The regime supposed the people had no idea how restaurants were in the West, that many possessed vibrancy and character. Confined to the Union, we were still encouraged, Aleksei thought, despite the Revolution being close to forty years old, to believe that our restaurants were 'better', whatever this word meant. They might be dull and lifeless, but no matter, they were good for our Sovietness, the cultivation of our Communist characters. However, surely the regime had to realise that its obsessive control of information and its total refusal to reveal how others lived in the 'vile capitalist West' made us not less, but more, curious of this other life, which was less driven and regimented by theory and dogma.

At last aboard the bus, sitting there on a broken sprung seat staring out of the window as it headed east, Aleksei was certain that if he kept moving he would avoid detection. The bus stopped in Semipalatinsk, and he had to make the last part of the long journey on foot, following the Irtysh all the way down. He'd suspected this in Akmolinsk, buying supplies after he left the restaurant, including waterproofs, a sleeping bag and a map in an old army-surplus shop, enabling him to get as far as Ust'-Kamenogorsk and then further east to the Katun river. This closing leg was exhausting, and when Mount Belukha at last came into view he was overcome with relief, shouting out loud, 'Yes, yes!' He had just about run out of food. He rested, ate the last can of fish in tomato sauce, and after this made the slow ascent up the slope.

When Aleksei first caught sight of it, the monastery, looming over him in the striking blue of the sky, flanked by perfectly white small clusters of altocumulus cloud on either side, he wondered whether he was dreaming, its location extraordinary and quite beautiful, perched atop a slender pinnacle, surrounded by cliffs and forest. How on earth did he get to it? he wondered. It appeared to be inaccessible, and were it a cloudy day would have given the illusion of a monastery floating in the air. As he got closer, however, he saw that it was accessible by steep steps, at the bottom of which was a small mine – of what kind it was not clear. Up here it could be one of a number of things – gold or copper, lead or zinc, he thought.

The climb up was slow, the back of his thighs and buttocks aching. However, he did not stop and let himself rest, through fear that if he did he would never get going again. The desire to confess drove him now, and as he walked he imagined what Father Iosif would look like. The image in his mind was admittedly a cliché, Aleksei pondered, an old man with a thick white beard dressed in a black cassock and *klobuk*, the archetypal old Russian Orthodox priest. 'How very unimaginative!' he chastised himself. One thing he could be sure of, though, was that Iosif would be old. Might he be dead? Aleksei next wondered. Well, it was quite possible. He was twenty years older than Nikolai, who was with him immediately after the war, and if Nikolai was fifty then, Iosif was seventy. Now more than ten years on, he was going to be in his eighties. 'Please be alive, please,' Aleksei muttered, climbing the remaining few steps until he reached not the monastery but a small narrow bridge leading to it.

It was about ten metres long, made of wood, built between two pinnacles. He crossed it slowly, gazing over the edge at the mammoth drop below. When he reached the other side he had to climb a few more steps, these carved out of the rockface, before he was confronted by a large wooden door. He was here at last. He knocked on it with his knuckles, the noise he generated barely audible, and so clenched his fist tight and banged hard. Aleksei waited. 'Hello. How can I help you?' a monk asked, standing before him, a gangly, lean and intense young man.

'I'm looking for Father Iosif.'

'Father Iosif, our Elder?'

'Yes,' Aleksei replied, assuming that he was referring to the same man, the Elder the monastery's spiritual father. 'Is he still alive?' he asked urgently.

'Well, he was this morning when we met for prayer.'

'Right, thank you.'

'And whom may I ask is calling for him?'

'Aleksei Nikolayevich Klebnikov.'

'Right,' the young monk replied.

'But he will not know who I am,' Aleksei said.

'And why is that?'

'I've never met him. I was recommended to come and see him by a dear friend, Nikolai Korolenko, a former Moscow priest.'

'A former priest?'

'He died in Kolyma.'

'I see…' the young monk said slowly.

'That's where I met him,' Aleksei added.

'Come with me,' he said, Aleksei's honesty, it seemed – he was not afraid to admit to being a former *zek* – granting him access. 'And watch your head,' the young monk added.

Aleksei bent down and walked through a short, poorly lit stone passageway, its appearance medieval, floor cobbled, the two men's footsteps echoing as if they were walking through a small cave. Next, he had to duck down even further, shoulders hunched, to avoid a wooden beam that hung from the ceiling, after which this claustrophobic corridor opened up into a small hall, the narthex Aleksei supposed, and then a far more spacious hall, the nave, big enough, it appeared, to accommodate about one hundred or so worshippers. Candlelit and sparsely furnished, the pale stone of the walls and floor offered a serene but austere place for prayer. There was little of the ornate religious furniture so typical of Eastern Orthodoxy, but for a few icons. Aleksei caught sight of an elderly monk at the end of the nave by the sanctuary, the gold of the processional cross gleaming in a place otherwise absent of bright colour. 'That's not Father Iosif,' the young monk said, and ushered Aleksei on.

They left the nave and walked along another dim corridor, a small door at its end that was partially open emitting light, a lot of it, and as they neared the door Aleksei could suddenly see everything in great detail – the grey stone of the floor, the specks of dust hanging in the air, the small tear in the young monk's cassock. They stopped, they listened – silence – and after this entered not a room but a cave, the two of them bathed in sunlight as the hinges creaked and the door opened wide to reveal an old monk in full habit, on his knees, genuflecting before the mountains, afforded a perfect view of Belukha's two peaks.

He must be a Schemamonk, Aleksei thought. Though he was unfamiliar with the degrees of habit, Aleksei supposed that the hood and intricate embroidery on the old monk's cassock meant that he had reached the highest level, the Great Schema. He did not acknowledge either of them, so deeply was he immersed in prayer, rather stared straight ahead. Aleksei and the young monk had simply to wait until he was ready to address them, and the wait felt long, so anxious was Aleksei to talk to him.

When at last he turned his head, he did so slowly, revealing piercing green eyes, the very same green as Aleksei's, which stared out from a face obscured by masses of white hair that hung long and wavy from his head and grew thick and wildly around his chin and face. He looked searchingly at Aleksei, his expression not conveying censure, rather curiosity, and then he spoke. 'And who might you be?' Father Iosif asked.

'He is Aleksei Nikolayevich Klebnikov,' the young monk answered.

'Let the man speak, Brother Maxim.'

'I've come to you...because...' Aleksei muttered, looking to the young monk, reluctant to confess to him as well as Father Iosif.

The old monk immediately sensed this. 'Leave us be, Brother Maxim,' he said.

However, the young monk did not leave, rather looked to Father Iosif for further confirmation. He was wary of leaving him alone with this stranger.

'Please, Brother Maxim,' he urged him, and the young monk grudgingly left.

Aleksei listened for his fading footsteps down the stone corridor before speaking again. 'Father Iosif, I've come here because...because I need to...I...'

'Aleksei,' the old monk said softly. 'I do not need to know why you've come here.'

'You don't?' Aleksei asked, with the curiosity of a child who suddenly sensed that he didn't have to be wholly honest if he did not want to be.

'No, you are here, and that is that.'

'Right,' Aleksei replied warily, staring down at the floor of the cave, his tone sober now, since implicit in the priest's openness was the sense that he, Aleksei Nikolayevich Klebnikov, had finally to confront himself, acknowledge what he had done. It was not solely about telling somebody else. Yes, the act of confession, of being able to share, to admit what you'd done to another human being, was critical, and yet this act in itself did not provide redemption, no.

He looked to Father Iosif, who observed him intently. He immediately averted his gaze, unable to look at him, his mind going inward. He had killed the Azerbaijani to protect Nikolai. He had killed Vadim in order to escape. He had killed Dmitri to avenge Natasha. But all those others, the men on the list, he had killed out of – say it, Aleksei, say it, he urged himself – he had killed out of indignation, ambivalence, hate.

Those nine months he'd had with Natasha in Baikal, they were a gift, a blessing after what he had been through. Would he have carried on killing for Ivan Ivanovich had he not met her again on those shores that afternoon? he wondered. Natasha had brought him back from the cold, given him a reason to stop what he'd been doing, to give up revenge, relinquish hate, love again. And yet, conversely, this had also afforded him the opportunity not to repent fully.

Though he'd experienced certain aspects of remorse – he had taken responsibility for, and ownership of, what he'd done – he had not acknowledged the hurt he had caused his victims' families and friends. And though he had experienced regret, this was less for the men he had killed and more for what he had become. He had felt no compunction, telling his victims he was sorry and asking them for forgiveness. He had not made a commitment to change, promising that he would never kill again.

He glanced up at Father Iosif, who carried on staring at him with the same intentness and curiosity, before his thoughts consumed him once more, continued to rob him of speech. Why have I not felt full remorse? Why? Aleksei demanded to himself, willing to accept nothing less than the truth. Because the men he'd killed were Communist bastards, all of them, wicked individuals driven by power! Yes! Such men had ruined his life, caused him inordinate suffering. By killing them he was getting back at a cruel and corrupt system, which made it its business to disrupt and ruin people's lives. Was there not something right and noble in what he had done? Was he not acting for the greater good? Aleksei asked himself, looking at this moment to Father Iosif, who maintained the very same expression.

His actions were just and righteous. Yes, he wanted his country, his fellow citizens, to be free of Communist abuses. However, they were also unjust and selfish. He had not judged these men fairly. He'd executed them without trial. And he was not driven solely by utilitarian motives. No, he'd done it to satisfy his own contempt, his own need for revenge. 'Oh God!' Aleksei said aloud at last.

There was silence in the room.

'My son, would you like to stay with us?' Father Iosif asked.

Aleksei stared at the old monk, his eyes watery, and nodded.

The room he was shown to was small and simple, containing a low-slung wooden bed, a single chair and a Bible. This was it, and yet its sparseness did not trouble him. He was used to such meagre accommodation after the Lubyanka and Kolyma. However, its quiet did.

He sat on the chair. He could hear no screams, no tapping heels (the monks wore sandals), no jangling keys, no slamming cell doors. He had come here imbued with the hopeful sense that he would confess and then spend some quiet and contemplative time within these walls. What was I thinking? Do I really merit this after what I've done? he asked himself. The quiet encouraged him to ruminate, cutting through him like a knife, slicing his heart open. It would, perhaps, have been easier to confess to Natasha, he realised. Her love would have at least provided some comfort, though how much she would have loved him having heard the true extent of his murderous rage was questionable. The faces of the men he'd killed floated across his mind's eye like black clouds in a stormy sky, menacing and forbidding. Some smiled at him, others scowled. It seemed his conscience had hijacked his consciousness: he was no longer under any illusion that he was in charge of his thoughts, the contents of his mind. In fact, he was made to relive everything – the look in each of the men's eyes as he'd demanded that they look at him before he had taken their lives. Some had confessed, others had not. Some had pleaded, others had been almost accepting of their fate. Their eyes… blue, green, brown… and Anichkov's, his had been black. All contained horror, in that there was nothing behind them, no sign of conscience or remorse. What had to happen to a man for him to feel nothing when he killed? This absence was of course what enabled him to kill again, and again. Ambivalence was the most deadly emotion, making almost anything permissible. Am I this man? Aleksei wondered. What had to happen to a man for him to express no regret even when he knew that this was it, that he was about to die? The majority had not confessed but had denied what they had done. He remembered their voices, some of them strangely soft and gentle-sounding, betraying the natures of the men behind them. And he remembered their words too, echoing in his mind as if there was nothing between his ears but an enormous hollow space, a giant cave. 'No, it wasn't me. No, I didn't.' He heard these words of denial over and over, then removed his shoes, sat on the bed, leaned against the stone wall, brought his legs to his chest, held his knees as if embracing a child, and quietly wept.

Aleksei did not leave his room for a whole month, Brother Maxim bringing him bread and water, and when he emerged at last he was pale, skinny and bearded, with dark shadows cast under his eyes. His appearance ghostly, he shuffled uneasily down the long low corridor and passed a small window which opened out on to the mountains, the light shining through it causing him to squint and shield his eyes as if he were a nocturnal animal afraid of the sun.

He was encouraged to wash and eat, then joined the monks for prayer in the nave. Sitting here with them, he experienced no prying, no judgment. They were still to learn what he had done, the reason for his thirty days of penance confined to his room, but it did not prevent them from showing him care and compassion. After prayer, Father Iosif summoned Aleksei and asked him if he wanted to become a novice. He'd have to assume the black inner cassock and skufia, monastic hat, and would also be given a prayer rope and instructed in the use of the Jesus Prayer. Dressed in black, he'd be dead to the outside world, Father Iosif explained, wholly committed to his inner spiritual life. Aleksei declined this invitation, telling him he could not make this commitment as he'd made a pledge, at the end of his penance, that he would return to Moscow to face his daughter Katya, and though he knew Ivan Ivanovich would be waiting for him he did not care. And also because it would not be appropriate in light of the depth of his sin. If he were to be permitted to stay a few months longer, however, then he'd have to make himself useful, Aleksei insisted.

He learned that it was gold that was mined below, and the product sustained the monastery more than any other enterprise the monks engaged in, purchased in bulk by Mongolian Buddhists who sold it on the black market. Only Soviet Russia could produce monks who dealt in contraband! Aleksei was reluctant to go down there at first even though he was determined to help the community in any way he could – he was sure that the painful memories of Kolyma would come flooding back – but summoning the courage he descended the ladder until he reached the base of the pit, and once he started working, seeing the mining operation for himself, it became abundantly clear that it was the very antithesis of his prison-camp experience. He'd seen little beauty in the precious metal back then – all it did was sustain a wicked regime – but now he was struck by its softness, its bright yellow colour and lustre. He remembered his father's wedding band, which though gold possessed a reddish hue, on account of the fact that it was twenty-five percent copper. Yes, typical Russian gold!

He worked with a pickaxe, as did two of the monks, relishing the physicality of the work after a month's confinement as he swung at the rock face hard and fast, over and over. The deposits of ore Aleksei dug out he heaped in a pile, and this mined ore was then hauled out of the pit, crushed into small chunks by another two monks with pickaxes, then heaped on a leach pad where it was irrigated with a dilute cyanide solution, the liquid percolating through the heap until the gold could be extracted. Other than being essential to the working of the mine, the mountain stream which ran adjacent to the monastery also provided the monks with drinking and bathing water. The monastery strove to be self-sufficient, perhaps the goal of any monastic community – particularly one whose very existence was a secret – baking its own bread and producing its own milk and eggs, reliant on a hardy herd of Altai mountain goats and a tough batch of chickens.

The more kindness Father Iosif and his fellow monks showed him, the more Aleksei was driven to work in the mine, the former intellectual delighting in the pure practicality of his endeavours, filled with the same sense as when he'd worked on Baikal's shores, producing something tangible rather than immaterial. And when he was not working, which was not often as he worked tirelessly, he spent his time with Father Iosif, the two men sitting in meditative prayer together in the cave. He had fast become devoted to the old monk, who'd shown him such love and understanding, often recalling what he first said to him when he joined him for prayer. 'Aleksei, it's clear why our Buddhist friends judge it to be the gateway to Shambhala, the mystical kingdom of peace and happiness. God is very close here. You'll feel Him soon enough.' The view of Belukha was indeed extraordinary, its peaks, these white pyramids, seeming to point the way to the infinite, the divine. Aleksei found that his concentration steadily improved until he could sit for many hours in the cave without moving, deep in prayer. His victims continued to visit him as he sat quietly, in particular the innocent Dmitri, as did his perpetrators, the thief-in-law Ivan Ivanovich surely still after him. Yet whenever they came to mind he looked to Father Iosif, his spiritual father and guide, expressed his remorse and asked for their forgiveness. The old monk's warmth and compassion was vital to him. However, he did not confess to Father Iosif directly, admit to someone else the true extent of his crimes.

It was Natasha's birthday today, and Aleksei stood at the entrance to the mine and thought of her, whispering his love to her, as the Mongolians paid for the gold. He also thought of Katya. How he longed to see her. His conscience continued to haunt him, it always would, particularly when he considered the effect his murderous actions had had on his beloved daughter. God, how he'd hurt her! The four of them, the smugglers, were in political mood as they discussed the current state of the Union. They held their Communist Russian leaders in even greater contempt than their Christian Orthodox brothers did.

However, they did feel that a genuine thaw was underway, that better governance might be on its way now Koba had gone. 'They all suffer from ribbon sickness!' one of the Mongolians declared, as he picked up another crate and attached it to his horse's saddle. 'They're obsessed with honouring themselves, even the humble Comrade Khrushchev!'

It had always struck Aleksei as a great contradiction that their rulers' primary identity was military. Were they not meant to be promoting freedom? And that they led ostentatious lifestyles and owned lavish Western goods, yet expected the average Soviet citizen to own nothing, possess nothing. They lived in the grandeur of the Kremlin, Aleksei thought, while the people still lived in cramped rooms and tenements, on top of one another, barely able to breathe and now infected with a terrible cynicism in light of their leaders' appalling hypocrisy. No wonder really that the permanent corruption of the ruling elite had given birth to a criminal system in which thieves such as Ivan Ivanovich prospered.

Might Comrade Khrushchev's new brand of socialism really have a human face? Aleksei wondered. The effects of some of his liberalising policies could be seen already. Did he really intend to open up parts of society? He had to realise, surely, what this would mean, the end of the regime. When the people were at last allowed to see beyond the fog of Soviet propaganda – the noble, happy, free and decent life of a Communist citizen – and say what they really thought, talk of the many abuses they had suffered at the hands of the Stalinist system, the regime would surely collapse, Aleksei was certain of this. Would the *nomenklatura* really relinquish some of the power they held? Might justice at last be done? He could hardly seek it against Ivan Ivanovich, even if he wanted to, Aleksei thought. For what would he tell the new authorities? Would he sacrifice his freedom in order to bring the old thief down?

The following day Aleksei and the small community of monks received a visit from a grey-suited man in his mid-fifties wearing a colourful tie, accompanied by half a dozen men in fur-lined leather jackets. Standing in front of them, he declared, 'The mine is ours now!'

'What are you talking about?' Brother Maxim replied rather naïvely.

'You heard!' one of the leather-jacketed men demanded, hacking up some phlegm and spitting it. Solid mucus, it whisked past Father Iosif's face as he stood beside Brother Maxim, and hit the stone wall of the monastery like a soft bullet.

'You can't behave this way in God's house!' Father Iosif demanded.

'Fuck God, and we're not in his house yet!' another one of them shouted, stamping his foot on the doorstep.

'You have one month to get out,' the suited man said with quiet menace. 'I want the monastery as well.'

'No!' Father Iosif said.

Aleksei interjected, 'I'm afraid they can do what they want, Father, unless you want them to kill us all.'

'Listen to your friend, he's a wise man,' the suited man said, looking to Aleksei, past the thick beard and long hair he'd grown these past few months, and into his eyes. He smoked cigars, his breath heavy with tobacco, which made Aleksei squirm, his face pallid, fingers yellow and stained. 'We'll be back in exactly one month and will expect you gone,' he grumbled in conclusion, turning to leave, and his leather-jacketed entourage followed.

It transpired that the suited man was Evsei Babluani, a Georgian gangster. Aleksei went on to explain to Father Iosif that Babluani was a thief-in-law, distinguishable by the tattoos which Aleksei had spied on his fingers and the aluminium cross he wore around his neck, the latter less a demonstration of his faith than a sign that he would stop at nothing to get what he wanted. In fact, the only way to stop him, other than to kill him, was to appeal to the authorities, though it was questionable how viable this was in light of the fact that the monastery operated clandestinely. Might they receive a better hearing in the post-Stalin Soviet Union? Aleksei wondered. Well, they had to try, he urged them, and Father Iosif and Brother Maxim left for Gorno-Altaisk the following day.

They met with the MVD Chief of the *oblast*, Mimtimer Kurultai, a chubby, red- and round-faced local man and prominent member of the Altai Communist Party. He sat in his dishevelled office within the Altai State Security building. A large framed photograph of himself hung on the wall behind his desk showing him dressed in full Communist regalia replete with ribbons, his name and title embossed in gold beneath the photograph, shaking hands with Serov, the current head of the KGB. The MVD Chief made clear, according to Father Iosif and Brother Maxim's subsequent account, that the mine and monastery were the *oblast*'s property not theirs. Father Iosif made the impassioned argument that the former was mined not for profit but for the monastery's survival only, and that he, Kurultai, in spite of being a Communist, should therefore take it upon himself to protect a few good men who'd given themselves to God. Father Iosif also made clear that the *oblast* would, of course, have the same problems that they, the religious order, were having, the thief-in-law still wanting both for himself. Kurultai responded dismissively, 'Yes, but that's for me to worry about not you, and I have the power of the Union behind me, far more powerful than a dozen or so priests! I have nothing more to say on the matter.' And with these final words, he'd got to his feet and shown Father Iosif and Brother Maxim the door, gesturing dismissively with his right arm.

Aleksei considered their account, then responded by telling both of them that he was sure Kurultai was in on it. Rather than openly claim the monastery and mine for the *oblast* – this would be a political disaster and would provoke a public outcry, the removal of these spiritual men from their home and place of worship by the authorities – he'd let the thief-in-law have it and take his cut. Kurultai would benefit greatly from such an arrangement, Aleksei thought. Brother Maxim agreed with this assessment, telling Aleksei he'd suspected as much after Kurultai had struggled to hold Father Iosif's gaze and had looked awkwardly away, his eyes shifting downward and to the side, when Father Iosif had bade him farewell. He had to do something, Aleksei reflected, staring at a rather lost and bewildered Father Iosif now. He could not let him and the other monks be cast out. All of them would be lost without their precious home. 'There's someone I know in Moscow who'll be able to help,' Aleksei announced all of a sudden. 'I'll leave right away.'

He felt a burning need finally to apologise to Katya, to seek her forgiveness. He knew she would be there, in the city, in spite of what had happened there. For she'd never wanted to leave in the first place, never truly forgiving her mother for the 'move to nowhere', as she'd called it, despite Natasha having had little choice but to flee to some backwater after killing a leading member of State Security.

'Must you go?' Brother Maxim asked.

'Yes, he must,' Father Iosif replied, 'in order to see his daughter.'

'Yes,' Aleksei said quietly.

'But surely we can appeal to Babluani though, if Kurultai is indeed in on it? We could continue to mine it and give him a share,' Brother Maxim went on, suggesting an alternative. 'Kurultai would hardly object, as he'd see the benefit also.'

'It will never be enough,' Aleksei replied knowingly.

'But surely we can come to some kind of arrangement with him?'

'It's not being exploited to its full potential, and Babluani knows this. In fact, you've barely scratched the surface of the mine's gold reserve. He'll bring in big machines and dig deep, and he'll want to get at the gold directly beneath the monastery too. He'll use it to accommodate his workforce for a year or so – he'll cram them in here, probably have them sleeping in the nave too – while they work on the open mine, then knock it down when he's ready to get at the gold beneath.'

'No…' Father Iosif began.

'Yes, Father. Why have a few priests work with a handful of pickaxes when he can take full control, bring in a large workforce and machinery, and make the mine enormously profitable.'

'But…' Brother Maxim mumbled.

'No, you cannot appeal to his better nature. He doesn't possess one. I know men like this well,' Aleksei made clear. 'That's why I must go to Moscow right away to speak with one of his own,' Aleksei concluded.

'Do you believe this person in Moscow will help?' Brother Maxim asked.

'Yes, as I have something to give him which he desperately wants.'

Aleksei would give him his life – hand himself over to Ivan Ivanovich – though the thief-in-law would have to ensure the monastery's protection.

'Brother Maxim, I will call you on the day when Babluani is due to return.'

'But this might be too late?'

'Let us see,' Aleksei replied.

'You could always stay and let God do his work,' Father Iosif said.

'I'd rather not risk it,' Aleksei said warmly, taking his slender hand and kissing it gently.

19TH JANUARY 1955
GORNO-ALTAISK

The Mongolians took him on horseback to Gorno-Altaisk, and from there Aleksei decided not to travel through Mongolian territory, as he had done before, but rather to take the bus to Novosibirsk. However, before he got on it, he located a public phone at the station and dialled a number. The line rang. He waited. Then heard the other end pick up. No voice. Aleksei elected to speak first. 'This is Aleksei... Aleksei Nikolayevich Klebnikov.'

'That man is dead,' a low, coarse voice grumbled, the voice of Boris Andreyevich, it unclear whether the thief-in-law was confirming Aleksei's deceased status according to public record or whether he was making a threatening statement of intent – that he'd ensure Aleksei was dead soon enough.

'Where's Ivan Ivanovich?' Aleksei asked purposefully. 'Has he been released yet?'

'Do you suddenly feel guilty, Aleksei? For it was you that prolonged his incarceration, after failing to kill Valuev as you'd promised.'

'I'm hardly going to feel guilty, now am I, after what he's done to me,' Aleksei replied coolly. 'So has he?' he went on.

'He'll be out and back in Moscow within three weeks,' Boris Andreyevich answered, 'and he'll no doubt be delighted to see you again after all this time.'

If there had been any doubt in Aleksei's mind about returning to Moscow, with Ivan Ivanovich on the cusp of being a free man he knew he had to now, and as soon as possible. For though the thief-in-law knew what had happened, that she, Aleksei's daughter, had rejected her father after he'd murdered Dmitri, Katya still posed a threat. Put simply, she was Aleksei's daughter, the daughter of an assassin who'd ultimately failed him, and this was reason enough to kill her.

'Well, this is why I'm calling. I'd like to see him too,' Aleksei said, fighting to gather his thoughts.

'Right,' Boris Andreyevich replied, hesitantly.

'I have one condition, however,' Aleksei said.

'And what might that be?'

'Evsei Babluani. Do you know him?'

'Yes,' the thief-in-law answered.

'He's trying to seize a monastery in the Altai Mountains. There's a gold mine there, and he wants it for himself. He has to stop. Twelve monks live there and it's their home and livelihood.'

'You want him killed?'

'No, I'd rather he were not killed. For there has been enough killing. Evsei Babluani is due to return there in three weeks. When he does, I need him to tell the monks he no longer wants the mine and monastery for himself. It remains their property, their home, and always will. And I need the regional MVD Chief, Mimtimer Kurultai, to do the same, to guarantee that the authorities will not claim it either, now or in the future.'

'And should Ivan Ivanovich fail to make this happen?'

'Then I do not show, do not finally give myself up to him,' Aleksei replied bluntly.

'Okay,' Boris Andreyevich said.

'Once I receive confirmation, I will call with a place and time to meet,' and with these parting words, Aleksei hung up the phone and headed for the bus which would take him to Novosibirsk. He had no time to spare.

Arriving there, in this Siberian city, he ensured he had sufficient reading material for the long journey ahead, picking up several newspapers in the station, and once on board the train he was greeted warmly by a number of fellow passengers. It became clear right away, from a sequence of articles he read in *Pravda*, that crime was flourishing in post-Stalin Russia. The newspaper did not, of course, state this – for how could it, when the authorities still denied the existence of the majority of crime – and yet it was plain to see. Beria's first great amnesty, just one month after Koba's death, had mainly benefited the real criminals, who were released in their droves, leaving the innocent – those political prisoners who had dared question, challenge and defy the system – to languish further in the Gulags. The *urki* had been content to operate in the shadows under Koba – they'd dared not defy him, the greatest and most ruthless criminal of them all! – but since his death they'd been able to assert themselves more, and were relishing it. These men, as Ivan Ivanovich had insisted, were born out of Stalinism and so were tough as hell.

If only the leader he'd lived under had been less cruel, Aleksei pondered, looking over now at the old woman in her eighties who sat opposite him. Wrinkles criss-crossed and lined her pale face, giving it the appearance of a patchwork quilt. A shock of white hair framed her face, and piercing blue eyes stared out across the carriage. She caught Aleksei's eye and smiled faintly, a toothless smile. She wore a tatty old red dress, a bulky green woollen cardigan and dirty yellow rubber boots, her mismatch of dishevelled clothing representative of her emotional state, Aleksei suspected. She whistled to herself, and occasionally hummed, to which particular song it was unclear. What chance did this woman have? Aleksei wondered. What chance had she ever had? The Communist state – the great army of bureaucrats who sat at their desks most of the day – intruded upon, tried to regulate, every aspect of her life, claiming responsibility for all she did. If only it did the most vital thing and granted her freedom, Aleksei mused, Katya coming to mind again. Yet the regime mainly catered for its own, the favoured few – no wonder criminality throve in this prevailing atmosphere of fear and mania, the whole country steeped in black- and grey-market practices. Those that did not succumb to the allure of crime under Communism either held faith in utopia one day or languished in fear and depression like this poor old woman, he thought. And the majority succumbed to the latter, finding solace in a vodka bottle. No one wanted to work for the state, because they disliked it, distrusted it, which left only the most deceitful, the most cunning, the cruelest to work for it. No wonder it was failing, Aleksei concluded.

The train reached Omsk and the scruffy old woman got off, smiling at Aleksei as she did. By the time he got to Moscow, he'd have little over a week before it was time to call Brother Maxim, he realised. The first thing he had to do, however, was to find Katya and ensure she was safe. The old woman's vacant seat was filled by a very well-dressed middle-aged man, the antithesis of her. He wore a grey suit, a full-length black leather jacket and matching French loafers. *Nomenklatura* for sure, Aleksei judged. He managed to sleep a lot the last part of the journey, and when the train at last pulled into Yaroslavsky Station, its clickety-clack after all these days finally ceasing, Aleksei was eager to disembark and go in search of Katya.

He was immediately struck by the women he passed as he made his way out of the station and onto the main street: they were beautiful, their looks dazzled, and yet they seemed to carry the sadness of the Russian people on their shoulders, the occasional harsh look, abrupt comment or shrug of indifference conveying this deep sorrow. Aleksei stopped in order to eat something, entering an old *produkty* store, the place grim and cluttered. He left and walked further down the road until he came to the Central Market and ate some *pirozhki*.

The first location he headed for was the Bolshoi. He was immediately informed, however, that she was no longer in attendance and had left for another school. She had likely struggled to make an impression as neither of her parents were influential Communists, Aleksei thought. Would they ruin his daughter's promising career too? Young aspiring dancers stood a better chance if they were backed by *nomenklatura*, the new ruling class. Yet then he fretted that maybe she was no longer there because Ivan Ivanovich had got to her. He could surely not be in Moscow already! Next Aleksei made his way to the apartment she'd shared with Dmitri, this place where he'd taken his false and misguided revenge. Not here either, the apartment occupied by someone else. And yet how could she be here, Aleksei considered, after what he'd done, live somewhere that held such painful memories. Then he headed for his former family home, where he, Natasha and Katya had found such happiness before his arrest and Vladimir Vladimirovich's subsequent intrusion. Of course she would not be here either, Aleksei reprimanded himself, stopping en route and not going any further.

His best bet was to scour Moscow's dance schools. He'd likely find her at one of them, as she'd not give up on her dream that easily, Aleksei was sure of this. However, before he did this, he passed by Boris Andreyevich's to ensure the thief-in-law had not got to her already. Aleksei observed the entrance to the old mansion block for a number of hours, though eventually gave up. If Ivan Ivanovich's deputy did have her, she'd likely be locked up in one of the apartment's rooms or at another location, and unless he broke in he'd have no way of confirming this. For the moment, therefore, it was best he assume that she was still a free woman. He got hold of a city guide to educational institutions, located the ones that taught dance, divided these into areas, then commenced his search. He would start in the north, and make his way clockwise round the city.

Aleksei started walking the streets of Moscow, map and list in hand, speaking to anyone he could at each school he visited and asking if they knew of Katya. The majority he questioned were not forthcoming, which he attributed to the latent suspicion which still consumed the people some two years after Koba's death.

Each night he called on the kindness and courtesy of a local priest, bedding down in his church for the night – many Moscow churches having reopened since '41 – and it was here, in the quiet of the twilight hours, that he rehearsed what he would say to Katya when he at last saw her again. He would immediately tell her how sorry he was. He would explain why he did it, how he'd been consumed by rage and betrayed by Ivan Ivanovich, then would inform her about his time in the monastery with Father Iosif. He imagined that by the end of it, just as he was about to ask for her forgiveness, Katya would embrace him and tell Aleksei, her dear father, that she loved him. How he needed to hear these words from her.

After six days of searching he had all but given up until he came across a small dance school close to the Church of St Maksim, the one they had allowed to stand in spite of the Bolsheviks' best efforts to knock it down. A small church situated directly between their childhood homes, Aleksei and Natasha used to meet at St Maksim when they'd first met, Aleksei recalled, in the exquisite quiet of the place, sitting on the pew at the front, right by the altar, and holding one another. It had been enough that they were together, skin touching and words exchanged. The recollection of these meetings, their purity and innocence, touched him deeply as he entered the school and was greeted by an old woman mopping the wooden floors of the small single studio after another full day of dance. If only his life had retained this gentle aspect, had not been blackened by revolution, ideology and tyranny, he reflected.

'Excuse me, madam, I'm sorry to disturb you, but I'm looking for Katya...' Aleksei said.

'Sorry, but I don't know her,' she replied brusquely.

'She's twenty years old, slender, has light brown hair, pale skin and...'

'Katya Sokholova?' the old woman enquired.

'Yes,' Aleksei said excitedly.

'Why are you looking for her?' the old woman asked almost protectively, with a probing stare.

'I...I'm...' Aleksei replied, fumbling for his words.

'You're what?'

'I'm her father,' he answered.

'Her father?' she exclaimed.

'Yes,' he responded, and met her gaze, wanting the old woman to see the truth in his eyes.

'She'll be here tomorrow, the whole afternoon,' and with these words she returned to washing the floor.

Full of anticipation, Aleksei spent the night in the Church of St Maksim, and the following cool and windy morning elected to take the metro to the Lubyanka. He wanted to see this place once more before he saw Katya. The metro was just as it had been, brown, drab and grey, the whole place wrapped in a dull and dirty light. As Aleksei descended its escalator, this slow vast descent into the guts of Moscow, he felt, like he had done when he'd first arrived back in the city after he had escaped from Kolyma, as if he were being transported to hell. Commuters, staring straight ahead, tried to penetrate this glumness, pointing to something beyond this symbol of a fallen country, and yet the gloom, despite Koba being gone, remained impenetrable. How different he had felt when he'd first encountered the metro as a young man! Then, it had not horrified but rather entranced him, as he'd stood on the down escalator and made the descent, as if he had been embarking on an enthralling journey to the centre of the world. On the train, vodka seeped from the skin of many passengers, the old and necessary opiate of the people, and when he got off, the man in front of him was so inebriated that he could not even walk down the platform without falling over. The station attendant scowled at Aleksei from her little brown booth as he made his way back towards daylight. Opposite the Lubyanka, he located a public telephone. He dialled the number of the small store at the foot of the mountain on which the monastery sat. 'Hello, it's Aleksei Nikolayevich here. Please go and fetch Brother Maxim? I'll call again in exactly one hour. Thank you,' and he promptly hung up.

Aleksei sat on a bench and looked up: first at the Lubyanka, which appeared as forbidding as ever in spite of the fact that its chief sadist, Beria, had been executed a year ago; and second to the Moscow sky, pure white, promising heavy snow soon enough. He waited patiently, checking his watch sporadically, then returned to the telephone and called again.

'It's Aleksei Nikolayevich Klebnikov once more. Is he there?' Aleksei asked, only to be told that he was not. Aleksei explained he would call again, an hour later, which he did, only to be told the very same. Where was he? Brother Maxim knew this was the day that Aleksei would be calling. Had there been a problem? Had they been evicted after all? Had Ivan Ivanovich failed to meet his request? He could not afford for this to go on too much longer, he realised. He was due at the school this afternoon. For a fourth time Brother Maxim still was not there. Oh God, he was becoming frantic now. He'd wait one more hour, and that was it. This hour's wait was long, and when he dialled the number for the fifth time he spoke urgently, announcing himself without delay.

'Is that you?' a different voice replied eagerly, the voice of Brother Maxim, Aleksei immediately realised.

'Yes, it's me,' he answered.

'They came this morning, both Babluani and Kurultai,' he said joyfully. 'They no longer want the monastery and mine.'

'Good,' Aleksei replied, letting out a long and heavy sigh. 'I'm pleased.'

'We cannot thank you enough. I'm not sure whom you spoke to, what you said, but...'

'You need not say any more...'

'But I do...' Brother Maxim interrupted him, eager to do just this, to express his, Father Iosif's, all the monks' gratitude. 'I...we...'

However, it was Aleksei who cut him short now. 'Listen, I must go,' he said. 'I wish you and Father Iosif continued peace and happiness, all of you there in fact,' and with these words he put the receiver down, took a deep breath, then immediately dialled another number.

'This is Aleksei Nikolayevich Klebnikov.'

'Yes,' Boris Andreyevich's familiar low, coarse voice answered.

'Behind St Vasily, you know where I mean?'

'Yes.'

'Tonight at ten o'clock,' and Aleksei hung up.

Now he had to get to Katya.

Aleksei did not have a lot of time, he realised, had to get to the dance school as soon as he could. He would go on foot. Outside the Lubyanka, the snow falling, he started to run. His mind whirled with thoughts as he made his way. About Katya, how would she be? About Ivan Ivanovich, what would he say and how would he kill him? About his country, which, in spite of Stalin's death, had not suddenly found more truth and justice, but rather remained fierce and corrupt, controlled by the same ruling elite.

He reached the school out of breath, near the point of collapse. Greeted by the old woman again, she immediately informed him that he was too late, that Katya had gone for the day. 'Oh God!' Aleksei cried out loud. 'But where does she live, then?'

'I don't know,' she answered.

'But you must know,' he insisted, suddenly furious with himself that he'd cut it so fine. For as soon as he'd made the call to Boris Andreyevich telling him to meet behind St Vasily's that same night, he knew he had no choice but to see Katya right away, to confess to her, to apologise for what he'd done, to ask for her forgiveness, before ensuring her safe departure from the city. This he had planned already, having arranged for Yakov, the accomplished counterfeiter and smuggler, to take her all the way to Budapest. There was at least some benefit to Mátyás Rákosi's rule in Hungary, the whole country beating to the Moscow drum, the door thus open to all Russians. Yakov could not only arrange papers for Katya to enable her to travel to Hungary, but could also get her out of Russia safely. Aleksei trusted him, principally because in many respects he was like Aleksei, an outsider who'd found his way into the murky world of organised crime by default, forced underground after State Security came after him. He did occasional work for Boris Andreyevich, but out of necessity only. In fact it was likely that the thief-in-law had first recommended him to Aleksei for this very reason: he'd never be part of the trusted circle. And yet this was precisely why Aleksei trusted him to ensure Katya's safety. It was a sixteen-hundred-kilometre drive from Moscow to Budapest, and Yakov would ensure they'd not meet with too much resistance along the way except for the inevitable small number of over-zealous officials and regional policemen in Belarus and Ukraine, who would likely pore over their papers in search of something suspect. And though Katya would have to languish in another Communist country, Yakov was confident he could get her across the border into Austria within six months. He was a resourceful fellow.

However, he was putting Katya in jeopardy, Aleksei realised. Why had he not met Boris Andreyevich the next day? For Ivan Ivanovich would know full well what Aleksei, the morally flawed man, intended: to go to Katya and tell her everything, give her a full confession. And Katya, once in possession of the whole truth, posed an even greater threat to the thief-in-law. There'd be even more urgency for him to get rid of her, Aleksei's daughter.

'Try the church down the road, St Maksim, she often stops there on her way home,' and with these final words from the old woman Aleksei was on his way again, stumbling up the cobblestone street, the falling snow accompanied by a strong cold wind, which beat against his cheeks, his legs too weary to carry him further.

He bounded clumsily and frantically into the church, through its big oak door, slipping on the stone floor as he did, fighting to maintain his balance and grasping the back of a pew to stop himself from falling over. No sign of her. He shuffled down the aisle, his eyes scouring the place.

'No!' he eventually exclaimed despairingly, sure that he'd missed her.

By the altar, breathing heavily, Aleksei slumped down in the front row. He recalled his times in the very same place with Natasha. He was the only person here. Christ loomed over him. He had not seen this particular icon of the crucifixion for so long, the face of Christ expressing such hurt and sorrow. He had always found icons to be lacking something essential, a credibility, a verisimilitude of emotion. However, the Christ image in this church he found, even as a young atheist, evoked tremendous empathy in him: he could literally feel Jesus's pain.

He heard footsteps behind him, and swung his head round expectantly. It was Katya. She immediately stopped in her tracks, her face at first conveying surprise but then becoming critical and probing.

Aleksei got to his feet and approached her.

'I'm sorry, I'm so sorry,' he said, his voice breaking.

Katya did not look at him as she did the last time they saw one another, with recrimination and hate, yet neither did she look at him with forgiveness and love.

Neither of them spoke; they just stared at one another. Aleksei tried desperately to recall the endless rehearsals he'd conducted as he searched her out, though his efforts were futile. He had to explain himself, yet he could not.

'Why are you here?' Katya asked.

'I needed to see you, to apologise,' Aleksei answered, unnerved by the directness of her question.

'And how did you find me?'

'Well…after a long search.'

'What do you want?' Katya enquired abruptly, her voice heavy with accusation.

'I've just told you…to see you,' he appealed to her, his daughter.

'Well, you've seen me now!' she shot back.

'Look, I can't expect you to forgive me, I know,' Aleksei stuttered, unsure what to say. 'The only thing I ask of you is that you do as I say and go with Yakov,' and he looked over her shoulder at the man now standing at the church's entrance.

'What?' she exclaimed, swinging her head round and observing a heavyset man she didn't know, in his mid-forties and with the face of a boxer, a lopsided nose and a pronounced scar across his right cheek, which even from this distance she could make out.

'He's here to take you. You must go,' Aleksei said clumsily, failing to offer her any sort of explanation.

'What are you talking about?' Katya demanded.

'I've arranged for Yakov to take you to Budapest. I trust him, okay,' Aleksei insisted. 'You're no longer safe here and he'll ensure you get there, and then arrange to get you across the border into Austria.'

'What d'you mean I'm no longer safe here?' she asked.

'Ivan Ivanovich, the thief-in-law, is here in Moscow,' Aleksei said urgently. 'If you don't leave right away, he'll get to you!'

'I don't know what you're talking about…this is all too much,' Katya said, her voice breaking. 'I don't understand… why is he here…why will he get to me?'

'He killed Momma, Katya, don't you see! It wasn't Dmitri… I know!' Aleksei shouted, and with these final words he fell to his knees, clutching the side of a pew, and began to weep, holding his head in his hand.

He wept for what seemed a long time, while Katya stood over him silently and Yakov waited patiently by the church's front door.

Aleksei eventually looked up, his eyes red with sadness and regret, face wet with tears and snot. On his knees, he spoke. 'I am not about to tell you this, Katya, because I expect your forgiveness, not at all, but rather I offer it as the truth only, in order that you might understand what drove me, your father, to do what I did. Some of this you already know.'

He took a deep breath – it seeming he had at last found some composure – then began, 'Grandfather was a victim of Stalin's purges. I was removed from my teaching post, wrenched from our home, separated from Momma and you, interrogated and tortured in the Lubyanka. I was convicted under Section 10 of Article 58 – on account of my opposition to a cruel and unjust regime – and sentenced to twenty-five years hard labour.

'I was put on a transport to Kolyma, worked close to death, and forced to endure the suicide of grandmother, who could no longer tolerate the hypocrisy and oppression all around her. Then I was informed that your mother had made her bed with my nemesis, Vladimir Vladimirovich. Thrown in isolation, I was left to rot.

'I emerged full of anger and hate. I escaped from the prison camp having killed two men, a criminal and a guard. Returning to Moscow, I was confronted by Momma's alleged betrayal. She was with Vladimir Vladimirovich after all. Thus, when offered a mission by the notorious thief-in-law Ivan Ivanovich, whom I'd befriended while incarcerated – to assassinate six leading Communists, and therefore take revenge on those who had fed, profited from and sustained the Stalinist system – I took it. My heart broken, I had nothing more to lose, except my soul.

'I assassinated five *nomenklatura* during 1953, and was due to return to Moscow and kill the last of them when I was suddenly reunited with Momma and you. This led me to abandon the mission, and Ivan Ivanovich could not accept that. I had to complete it as far as he was concerned, not least because the assassination of the last man would lead to the thief-in-law's freedom.

'It was he, Katya, who murdered your mother, and who subsequently led me to believe that Dmitri was the perpetrator. After I'd killed him, I prepared to assassinate the last man on the list, yet was unable to go through with it. For I had done enough killing. I fled Moscow and ended up in a small monastery in the Altai Mountains. It was here that I was able to finally come to terms with what I'd done, which meant I had to return to Moscow and face you.

'Anger and hate not only drove me to take revenge on a system I despised, but also justified it – the killing of all these men. I had no right to take their lives, in spite of their sins. And when I killed Dmitri I acted out of blind fury and misplaced righteousness, sure that my nemesis and the system were trying to ruin my life once more.' He had, he realised, at last, after all this time, given a full confession.

Katya submitted, falling to her knees and into her father's arms, and he held her and kissed her head.

She buried her face in his jumper, nestled against his chest like a vulnerable child seeking comfort and reassurance.

It was wonderful to feel her, his precious daughter, in his arms again. May this moment last forever, Aleksei thought, and he mumbled to his daughter over and over, 'I am sorry, I am sorry. I love you, I love you.'

Yet this moment was immediately broken by Katya, as she whispered in his ear, 'But I cannot forgive you for what you did. I can never forgive you that.'

He did not pull away from her, or she from him, as these words were uttered, rather the two of them remained in an embrace. It seemed that Katya wanted Aleksei really to feel her words, not just hear them.

Aleksei at last looked up, peering through a mist of tears in his eyes. 'Katya, you might be unable to forgive me, but you still need to go with Yakov.'

'But why are you so sure Ivan Ivanovich will get to me? And how d'you even know he's here in Moscow?' Katya asked accusingly.

'I had to help the small monastic order in Altai,' Aleksei answered. 'Father Iosif and his monks were being threatened by another thief-in-law – he wanted the monastery for the gold mine that sat next to it – and I knew Ivan Ivanovich could remove this threat. In exchange, however, I'd hand myself over to him. I'm due to meet him at ten o'clock tonight.'

'That's very noble of you, but don't you see what you've done? You've led him to me also!' she shot back angrily.

'No Katya,' Aleksei responded firmly. 'As soon as I heard of his release, I knew he'd come for you. I had to come to

Moscow and ensure I got you out as soon as possible, before he got to you. Why? Because, put simply, you're my daughter – the daughter of an assassin who's failed him, postponed his freedom, and who now knows too much. This is reason enough to kill you. That I'm here now, however, gives him even more reason.'

'Why?' Katya demanded.

'Because you know the truth too, which is the greatest threat of all to him. Just like the system, he cannot tolerate it.'

'Oh God!' Katya was distraught.

'I cannot let him get to you, Katya, do you understand? You must be safe.'

'And what about you?'

'Katya, after what I've done, I have nowhere else to go.'

'But...'

'I know this, and I think you know it too, which is why you're unable to forgive me.'

'This is mad, there must be another...'

Aleksei became impatient at this point. 'No Katya, there is no other way!'

There was silence between them.

'Is that it?' Katya asked, quietly.

'Yes, it is, it has to be,' he replied softly, summoning Yakov, who walked down the aisle to meet them.

Aleksei looked at his watch. It was a quarter to ten. He could not afford to be late. For then Ivan Ivanovich would come in search of him. He had to get Katya out of here right away. 'You must go,' he said, taking her arm and leading her towards the exit.

'What are you doing?' she asked, resisting him.

'You know what I'm doing,' Aleksei answered, pulling her forcefully. 'Is the van right outside?' he went on, addressing Yakov.

'Yes,' Yakov replied, immediately turning on his heels, realising that Katya would not leave of her own accord but had to be dragged, and by her father.

Yakov hurried outside and opened the passenger door, and no sooner had he done that than Katya was behind him. Aleksei faced her, holding his daughter by either shoulder and urging her, 'Get in, just get in!'

'You can't expect me to forgive you!' Katya shouted.

'I know I can't,' he replied. 'Please, Katya, get in,' and she finally did, sitting down and glancing over at Yakov.

'Drive!' Aleksei shouted, and Yakov pulled away.

Katya, realising this was the last time she'd see her father, called out to him, 'But I still love you, Poppa, even if I can't forgive you.'

Aleksei held these words as he stared at her, his beautiful daughter, the van pulling further away until he could no longer see her, after which he was immediately on his way again, to St Vasily's.

God, how he loved her, his daughter, and how he loved Natasha, his wife. He ran as fast as he could, his thoughts of them carrying him in spite of his exhaustion. The snow, which continued to fall heavily, and the harsh wind, which he struggled against, also slowed his progress. But he would get there on time. He had to.

Two men in bulky fur overcoats at last came into view, and Aleksei slowed to a walk, gasping for breath, and waited for them to see him, which they did in no time. They were Boris Andreyevich's men, the two big Slavs.

Was he, Ivan Ivanovich's deputy, with them too? And was Ivan Ivanovich? Aleksei wondered, as he neared them, until a smaller man appeared, as if from nowhere, between the two henchmen, his scarred face, even from this distance, immediately recognisable.

Wearing a long black overcoat Ivan Ivanovich stared hard at Aleksei, his gold tooth offering menace, flashing in the dark of the night, even though his piercing blue eyes were still too far off to intimidate. Then he flicked his right thumb against his gold tooth, then moved it in a slow deliberate circle around his chin.

They reached each other and said nothing. Aleksei was led down a narrow cobblestone sidestreet. Flanked by the two henchmen, Ivan Ivanovich walked a few paces behind them, thick and deep snow crumpling underfoot.

'In here,' the thief-in-law said, pointing to an old rusty metal door, and Aleksei was ushered down the steps of a derelict building into a large basement.

Wiping the snow from his hard blemished face Ivan Ivanovich spoke first. 'It's been a long time, Aleksei. I thought I might never see you again.'

'Yes,' Aleksei replied.

'Is that all you have to say, my friend, after so long?'

'Yes.'

'Well, it's good to see you, albeit under such circumstances.'

Aleksei was silent.

'So, you gave yourself up for the benefit of a few holy men,' Ivan Ivanovich said.

'Yes,' Aleksei answered, only capable of brevity, it seemed, no more.

'The ruthless killer has found God!'

Aleksei did not respond to this jibe.

'How do you know that I won't allow Babluani to take the monastery and mine once I've killed you?' Ivan Ivanovich asked.

'I don't.'

'After what I've done, do you honestly believe that I'll keep my word and protect a few piddly monks living in the mountains?'

'I've taken my chances.'

'You were my best man, you know.'

Aleksei was reticent.

'My distinguished assassin,' the thief-in-law continued.

'Yes,' Aleksei replied.

'You always knew this, didn't you?'

Again, Aleksei was quiet.

'Is the assassin still there, Aleksei, beneath that conscience of yours?' Ivan Ivanovich continued, removing one of his hands from his overcoat pocket – Aleksei presumed the one which did not carry the gun he intended to kill him with – and tugging at its black cloth.

'No, he's not.'

'Are you sure?'

'Yes,' Aleksei answered.

'Not even to avenge your beloved wife's murder?'

'No.'

'Not even to kill your greatest nemesis?' the thief-in-law asked. 'Me!' he then added with relish.

'No.'

'Why not? Why?' Ivan Ivanovich demanded angrily.

'Because I have no right to play God. No one does,' Aleksei replied.

The thief-in-law was reduced to silence, though only temporarily. He went on, 'You were the only one who hated them quite as much as I did.'

'Yes, and yet you also colluded with them, didn't you? These men you hated, who had killed those you loved, you also entered into partnerships with, shared ill-gotten gains with.'

'I didn't collude or partner with them,' Ivan Ivanovich shot back. 'I'm not the Azerbaijani. I owned them, all of them!'

'Did you care about Anna, Maria, Aleksandr, Pavel…?' Aleksei asked.

Ivan Ivanovich did not let Aleksei finish what he was saying, nor did he answer his question. He said dispassionately, 'I did what I had to do.'

'And what was that?'

'I got rid of those who stood in my way, who threatened my power and authority.'

'But I thought you'd got rid of them out of love?'

'Never love, Aleksei. I'm a thief-in-law, you fool. I renounced my heart long ago. How naïve you were, and still are! And yet that's what made you so precious,' and he blew a kiss at Aleksei.

Aleksei did not react to this contemptuous gesture.

'Do you still hate them?' Ivan Ivanovich asked.

'No, I don't hate them any more, Ivan, but neither do I like them. I'll continue to oppose and resist them until the very end.'

'Well, you had best express your final words of opposition now, before I put a bullet in your head.'

'When you pull the trigger, Ivan, I want you to look into my eyes,' Aleksei said calmly.

'I will, Aleksei, I will. You see, for me this is a righteous kill.'

'And how is that?'

'You broke your word.'

'You mean, I failed to kill all the men on the list.'

'Yes, which you pledged you'd do in a year.'

'I had killed all but one of them in ten and a half months, Ivan, before I was suddenly and unexpectedly reunited with my family. What did you expect me to do?' Aleksei asked forcefully.

'Hell, you make it sound romantic. Natasha hardly waited for you, now did she, Aleksei? Didn't I tell you that you'd be better off with just mistresses,' Ivan Ivanovich said smugly. 'You know, I don't know how you stuck it in her, knowing she'd had that NKVD bastard inside her!'

Aleksei didn't respond.

The thief-in-law continued, 'How dare you not kill Valuev, which meant I had to spend more time inside! No one disobeys me, Aleksei. No one, d'you hear!?' he shouted, pointing at him wildly and clenching his teeth.

'But you got your revenge, didn't you, got what you wanted in the end,' Aleksei said.

'Yes, I did, didn't I?' the thief-in-law confirmed almost proudly.

'You're the greatest monster of all, it seems. An even greater monster than Koba,' Aleksei concluded.

Ivan Ivanovich drew the gun from his pocket and put it to Aleksei's forehead. He cocked it, held the trigger. 'So you're prepared to die now, eh?'

'Yes, I am,' Aleksei replied.

'Yet it's not just for the sake of the monks, is it, but also for the sake of your daughter,' the thief-in-law said. 'You know I'll get to her as well, soon enough.'

'We'll see,' Aleksei answered coolly, certain that Yakov was wasting no time getting her out of Moscow, then Russia. Aleksei trusted him, was confident that he'd make sure Katya was safe.

Ivan Ivanovich was quiet now.

'Look at me,' Aleksei went on.

'I am,' Ivan Ivanovich replied.

'No, really look at me.'

'I am!' he bellowed.

'What do you see, Ivan?' Aleksei asked calmly.

Ivan Ivanovich began to sweat, his hand shook, as he continued to meet Aleksei's gaze. It appeared the thief-in-law might not be able to do what he'd wanted to do for so long.

He then looked away from Aleksei, down at the floor.

'You can take my life, but you'll never take my soul,' Aleksei continued.

'I took your soul long ago, when you killed all those men for me,' the thief-in-law said bluntly, still not looking at Aleksei.

'You can't do it if you look at me, can you?' Aleksei persisted.

Ivan Ivanovich did not answer.

'Is this really a righteous kill, Ivan?' Aleksei pressed him.

The henchmen waited. Aleksei waited.

'No,' the old thief-in-law answered flatly, and, head still pointed towards the ground, he pulled the trigger.

With this final word from Ivan Ivanovich, Aleksei collapsed, his body dropping hard and fast.

Lying sprawled out on the concrete, he saw his beloved Natasha and Katya before him and muttered his love to them. He imagined holding them, caressing them, kissing them.

But then they were gone, and the only person he saw was Ivan Ivanovich, who at last met his stare and held it.

The thief-in-law looked down at him as he, his distinguished assassin, struggled to breathe, coughing and choking on his own blood violently until he could breathe no more.

Aleksei closed his eyes gently and sought to conjure up the faces of Natasha and Katya one last time, and as they entered his mind's eye, he took his final breath and died there on the barren basement floor.

EPILOGUE

'A human being hesitates and bobs back and forth between good and evil all his life. He slips, falls back, clambers up, repents, things begin to darken again. But just so long as the threshold of evil doing is not crossed, the possibility of returning remains, and he himself is still within reach of our hope. But when, through the density of evil actions, the result either of their own extreme degree or of the absoluteness of his power, he suddenly crosses that threshold, he has left humanity behind, and without, perhaps, the possibility of return.'

Aleksandr Solzhenitsyn

ACKNOWLEDGEMENTS

First, there are a number of people I must thank:

My father, Andrew Taussig, for travelling Russia with me, even accompanying me to the Russian Far East, all the way to Magadan.

My wife, Klara Cecmanova, who ensured I never gave up and got the book written and out there.

Justin Marciano, for getting behind yet another book.

Carly Morrell, for her continued support and commitment.

Paul Van Carter, for his literary thoughts, and for naming this book.

Mina Holland, for her critical appraisal and encouragement, from one writer to another.

Ash Stevenson, for his great eye and artistry.

Robert Hastings, for his design and editorial wisdom.

Yuri Goligorsky, for his help with research.

And the following people, for their invaluable thoughts and feelings along the way: my mother, my two sisters, Milan Cecman, Sona Cecmanova, Kal Sandhu, Nick Green, Christine Rose, Norman Rose, Alex Lyons, Danny Hansford, Julien Hammerson, Thomas Delfs, Nicholas Attwater, Mark Bispham, Tom Clark, Rhinal Patel, Niall Conlon, Dave Shear, Howard Davies and Jeff Scott.

Second, I am indebted to the following works and their authors:

Aleksandr Solzhenitsyn, *The Gulag Archipelago*

Aleksandr Solzhenitsyn, *One Day in the Life of Ivan Denisovich*

Varlam Shalamov, *Kolyma Tales*

Anne Applebaum, *Gulag: A History of the Soviet Camps*

Colin Thubron, *In Siberia*

Ryszard Kapuscinski, *Imperium*

Orlando Figes, *A People's Tragedy: The Russian Revolution, 1891–1924*

Martin Amis, *Koba the Dread*

Stephen Handelman, *Comrade Criminal: Russia's New Mafiya*